FULL CIRCLE— REKINDLE, REGRET, REPEAT: A NOVEL

FULL CIRCLE—
REKINDLE,
REGRET, REPEAT:
A NOVEL

ARLETTE ESHRAGHI

This book is a work of fiction. Names, characters, places, and
incidents either are products of the author's imagination or are
used fictitiously. Any resemblance to actual persons, living or
dead, events, or locales is entirely coincidental.

Arlette Eshraghi

Printed in the United States of America

First Printing: Dec 2018

Cover art: Ferdiperdozniy /istockphoto

ISBN 9781790883851

Dedication

To the remarkable people that inspire and to the idealists
that are inspired to make a mark...

Acknowledgments

I thank my husband for his support, my sons for inspiring me, my sister and mother for encouraging me, as well as the family and friends who have enriched my life and continue to do so.

I am truly fortunate and grateful to the family, friends, acquaintances, and strangers that made an impression on me and impacted or influenced the creative or developmental process of this book.

CHAPTER ONE
Tuesday Afternoons (2015)

Natalie's gaze inadvertently focused on the framed wedding photo in front of her, causing her to look away quickly. Bent over, grasping the backrest of the sofa, she enjoyed the feel of Evan from behind. Unquestionably, doggy style was Natalie's preferred position for the utmost sexual pleasure. *I love Tuesday afternoons*, she thought. And as she reveled in sheer ecstasy as Evan rhythmically pounded her, they both came to fruition and collapsed on the couch.

Breathless, they sat back on the sofa. Evan put his arm around Natalie so that her head naturally rested on his chest. She stroked the center of his chest and closed her eyes. Evan twirled the strands of her curly, long hair through his fingers. This was another one of her favorite positions to be in. She could lay there all afternoon. After they made love, they would sit in silence for a few minutes until both regained their bearings. Sometimes they discussed their weeks' events. Other times they chose to remain in a comfortable silence, not feeling the need to speak for the sake of making conversation. Being with Evan just felt natural - emotionally and physically. She had always been self-conscious of her curvy body which due to her short stature made her appear heavier than she was. Evan was five-foot-eleven and somewhat thick but more muscular than flabby. Their bodies complimented each other. She felt petite and feminine when she lay by him.

It was 2:20 pm. Their weekly scheduled "appointment" in Natalie's office would end soon. In ten minutes, Natalie and Evan would carry on with the rest of their day. Natalie made it a habit of scheduling a patient at 3:00 pm to keep her and Evan disciplined about ending at the scheduled time and preventing them from lingering in the haze of their sexual escapades. This time shared between the two never seemed enough. It always left them wanting more.

As Evan reached behind to grab his e-cigarette, he accidentally knocked over the frame. After taking his first drag, his arm reached behind and grabbed the displaced item.

"I remember this day…You looked beautiful." He took another drag and said, "You still are…" and as he exhaled said, "Beautiful. And sexy." He paused as he took another puff and closely examined the photo. "There is one problem with this picture, though." He looked at Natalie with a sly grin. "You chose the wrong guy."

"The fault lies with you," Natalie proclaimed matter-of-factly. "You didn't want a monogamous relationship, Eric did."

"I *wanted* a monogamous relationship."

"After we stopped seeing each other, and I started dating Eric you did." She got up and started gathering her articles of clothing.

"Well at the time, I didn't think I wanted to commit. I guess I took what we had for granted until you stopped coming around. I fucked up."

"That's interesting," Natalie answered, "considering you didn't seem too bothered or lonely by my absence. I had the pleasure of running into you at Jeannine's parties – remember? Showing up with those women that worked for your *producer* friend."

"I had a void. Mindless sex filled that void. No matter how hot those women were, I didn't have the same connection with them that I had with you. Anyways you were with Eric. Why? Were you jealous I was with other women after you stopped seeing me?"

"Jealous!" Natalie exclaimed with a revolted look on her face. "No! I wasn't jealous. I was repulsed! The way you indiscriminately jumped from woman to woman was disgusting! You could have been used as an example of an STD don't in a Safe Sex PSA. It was distasteful on your part. And disrespectful, knowing that I had cared for you. To show up to social events that you knew I would attend and parade your dates du jour under my nose was insensitive. Besides, Jeannine discreetly hinted about what you were up to." Jeannine was Evan's friend, Mike's, girlfriend. In the three short months that Evan and Natalie were seeing each other, the two had formed a bond of camaraderie that continued after Evan and Natalie's relationship fizzled. "Nevertheless, your loss was Eric's gain," Natalie said smugly.

"Yeah, I see how well that's worked out for him. His wife has been sleeping with her former lover for two years."

"You're an asshole, Evan."

"Natalie, I'm sorry. My intention is not to piss you off. When we reconnected two years ago, you expressed your intent to preserve your family even though you were disillusioned by your relationship with Eric. I think it's time you reconsider that decision."

"My kids are still young and impressionable. I must keep my family intact. Do you know how devastated they would be if I divorced their father? Their world would become unstable."

"That's bullshit! Divorce is devastating to kids involved at any age," Evan said sternly. "What is holding you back?"

"Evan, when we reconnected two years ago, I was catatonic from the monotony that was my life. I had just gone back to work and found a meaningful identity other than mother and homemaker. No matter how good my life appeared outwardly, the repetition of the daily grind sucked the life out of me. Eric is a nice guy, but we stopped bringing out the good in each other a long time ago. I was sick of compromising. I resented Eric. He just stopped trying, and everything became uneventful. I wanted excitement in my life. As selfish and shitty as my infidelity is, it made me feel alive. I needed this, and I still do."

"Natalie, I am at that point where marriage is actually appealing. I want a commitment. I'm sick of playing around. Being with lots of different women has become exhausting. I want to be with one woman... with you. We have a great connection. What you and I have goes beyond

4

sex. We dig each other. And we are more compatible than you and Eric. Leave him. You know I would be good for you."

"There is no doubt in my mind that you believe that you would be good for me," she said positioning herself so that she was looking directly into Evan's eyes. "Evan, people have the best intentions when they get together. We are great together now, but what happens five or ten years down the road? Who's to say that if I leave Eric and marry or cohabitate with you, *we* are not eventually going to tire of each other? Or worry about each other's whereabouts on Tuesday afternoons? This works for us. Just because you feel like you have shaken the dirty dog out of your system, doesn't mean I'm going to check out of my current family to start one with you. How do you know you are even capable of being monogamous? You fuck a lot of different women. You are a serial anti-monogamist."

"Yeah, the keyword is FUCK. I *fuck* a lot of women, but I care only for you." Evan was constantly surrounded by women who were not only willing but gorgeous. He was a self-made man. In his early twenties, he realized college was not for him. He dropped out after two years to pursue opportunities others would deem unconventional. It all began in 1994, when Evan and two of his friends, Mike and Josh, met a porno producer in Las Vegas and with the cumulative skills of the three convinced him to allow them to post his movies to be downloaded on the web exclusively. Thus, they founded a successful pornography website. His fortune amassed when they sold the business, and he parlayed his wealth into real estate. From his middle-class upbringing, he had managed to build himself a healthy financial portfolio. Women threw themselves at him for the obvious reasons. He never had to try hard or look far for company. After twenty some years, his lifestyle, while enviable to other men, had grown mundane to him. He realized that his life lacked emotional intimacy. During the last two years, Natalie and Evan had established an emotional bond that was as arousing as their sexual encounters.

Natalie noticed Evan glancing at his watch as the end of their hour was approaching.

"We aren't going to resolve our dispute in the next five minutes. I don't want to end our rendezvous on a bad note," he said redirecting the conversation. He walked over to Natalie's desk and stood behind her where she was staring out the window as she put on her earrings. She patted his arms as he wrapped them around her waist from behind, lowered his voice and whispered, "So you just plan on using me for sex, then?"

Natalie turned around. She couldn't contain her smile no matter how serious she wanted to present herself; she could not wipe the devilish grin of her face. She locked her hands behind his neck and said, "You know this reminds me of an observation my friend Michelle made when she traveled to Argentina one spring break. She was a cross-cultural psychology major. We were in our early twenties then. She was in awe as to how well-preserved and beautiful her aunt and her friends, women twice our age, were. She frequented lots of parties during this trip because she still had lots of family and friends in the country. She marveled at how remarkable these women were *aesthetically*. Her aunt divulged that the secret to their happiness was that most of these women had taken on lovers.

Michelle surmised that the excitement from their affairs resulted in their motivation to maintain their appearances. She was so impacted by her observations during her trip to Argentina, that she was convinced that infidelity had a fountain of youth effect on certain women. She chose aging and sexuality among women of different cultures as the subject of her doctoral dissertation. She found a correlation in her studies; of course, socioeconomic status, sexual permissiveness of one's culture, and spousal compatibility were all factors – but there was truth to her theory. Which is the point I am trying to make…I meant what I said. I do need you. Not like how I need Eric. Eric is stability. You represent excitement. Evan, you make me feel vivacious. I have such a good time with you."

"That is about as ridiculous an argument for infidelity as men who claim their biological function of sperm production encourages them to cheat," Evan said. "Don't bring up that psychology bullshit." He was clearly irritated.

"Don't be like that, Evan," Natalie said, softly. "You know how much I look forward to Tuesday afternoons. Let's not end it on a sour note." She reached for his crotch, stroked his shaft from the outside of his pants and kissed him long and hard. They bid their goodbyes, and Evan left.

Until Tuesday, she dreamily thought to herself.

CHAPTER TWO
Natalie and Evan (1997)

E van and Natalie met at a party eighteen years ago. The attraction between the two was dynamic. And although Natalie left Evan with little energy to seek other women, he wasn't prepared to commit to a long-term relationship. He was beginning to enjoy the rewards of financial success at a time of his youth where mistakes were inevitable. He enjoyed his misogynistic guy's nights out as well as the bevy of women available for sex with no strings attached enough to realize he didn't want to be tied down in a committed relationship. Conversely, he enjoyed Natalie's company immensely. They saw each other a couple of nights a week. No matter how the night began it always ended the same way—mind-blowing sex at Evan's.

Natalie had a casual attitude towards sex, but she felt herself becoming emotionally attached to Evan. Their enjoyment of each other's company was mutual, and although it went beyond their sexual relationship, Evan was evasive. For Natalie, it was a no-brainer. The compatibility and chemistry between the two were superlative, so naturally, the relationship should advance into a commitment.

One night, after a couple of glasses of wine, she garnered the courage to inquire about their status quo. Evan was enthralled by the basketball game on TV.

"Evan, what are we?" she asked.

Evan was taken aback but not completely surprised by the question. He knew the conversation was inevitable. To his bewilderment, it had taken Natalie some time to bring it up. They had been carrying on for three months. In the last week or so, he could tell Natalie was becoming attached emotionally. She knew they weren't sexually exclusive. And although she tried to downplay her disappointment, he could tell she was crushed when they ran into each other at a sushi bar while he was out with another woman. Her distress perturbed him. Evan's intentions were not to hurt Natalie, but he was not ready for a commitment. There was still a vast array of carnal pleasure to be sought. He felt the need to relieve his system of his desire of enjoying different women rather than cultivating a relationship with one. At a different time, Natalie would have been his perfect match. Even though he found great comfort in the intimacy he shared with Natalie; he just wasn't ready.

Oh no, here comes the conversation…and during the game. Keep it together, man. Let her down easily. "We're people," he answered, trying to bring levity to a dreaded topic of conversation.

Natalie wasn't pleased. "No, seriously, what would you label us as?" She spoke sternly yet maintained a level of sweetness so that Evan felt the need to handle the situation as delicately as possible.

Evan took a deep breath. *Here it goes*, he thought. "Well, we are two people having a good time. I like you. I like spending time with you, but if you are looking for a monogamous relationship, I'm not the guy."

Natalie's disappointment was obvious, but she handled it with dignity. "Alright," she said. "So hypothetically speaking, if I were to meet someone and stop seeing you, you'd be ok with it?"

"Well, I can't say I wouldn't miss this, but I can't hold you back from anything. If you find the right guy, go for it. You're a great girl. I'm just not ready to commit. Look, it's not you, it's me."

She repetitively nodded her head as he spoke. As if with each nod she was slowly absorbing his words so that they became more easily digestible. *How cliché*, she thought of his last statement. She didn't want him to know the extent of her disappointment. She gathered her composure, and when she felt secure enough that her voice wouldn't crack, she stoically replied, "Fair enough. I just needed clarification as to where our relationship is headed. You know, as far as expectations go."

"Natalie, the last thing I want to do is hurt you. Let's just live in the moment and enjoy this." He turned off the television and turned on his stereo. Within seconds, Marvin Gaye's "Let's Get It On" streamed through the sound system of the home. Evan stood up and held out his hand. Natalie took his hand, and he gently pulled her to her feet. He drew her in, and as their bodies swayed to the music, he passionately kissed her at great length. Halfway through the song, he lifted her and threw her over his shoulder. He then made his way to the bedroom tossed her on the bed and promptly ravaged her.

Afterward, the two lay in bed silently sharing a cigarette. Evan hoped that he had appeased Natalie and that she would understand his current position on commitment. "I don't want you to be upset, Natalie," he said as he put out the cigarette.

"I'm not. I can't force you into a relationship. I enjoy your company, too and the physical aspect of our relationship. I thought what we shared would have evolved into something more. Commitment just seemed like the next logical step. But I get it...You don't want a commitment now." She began pulling away, but he pulled her back and tightly spooned her. He was built like a linebacker. She liked the feel of him holding her firmly to the point she couldn't break away. She tried pulling away and tapped his arm to signal that she wanted out of his hold. "I've got to go. It's late. I have a class at nine."

"Stay the night, it's almost one," Evan said seductively. "I'll make it worth your while. Anyways, I'm going away in a couple of days. We won't be able to see each other for over a week."

Natalie was of a mind to oblige; she would have loved to spend the whole night with Evan. Considering he would leave for business for ten days, this offer was tempting. And as much as she respected Evan's sincerity and honesty, she refused to give in to his whims when he clearly opposed a commitment. Out of self-respect, she had to decline. Her friend, Michelle, who was not one to sugar coat things would compartmentalize this into a why buy the cow if you can get the milk for free scenario;

whereas Natalie would rather think of their lusty rendezvous as a drug that Evan was addicted to. Maybe he would come around eventually if she withheld herself long enough to make him pine for her.

"No, not tonight. I have to go."

Evan reluctantly let go. He felt a sense of ambivalence regarding the discussion that had transpired that evening. On the one hand, he was genuinely anxious about hurting Natalie. He believed he was fair in not misleading her. At that moment they both realized that the course of their relationship would change. Natalie was no longer satisfied in casual sex status with Evan. She felt she was becoming emotionally attached. She quickly got up to put her clothes back on while Evan sat up, leaned against the headboard, and lit another cigarette. He watched her as she fumbled with her bra hooks.

"Do you need help with that?" he asked.

She smiled impishly and shook her head no. After she was fully dressed, Evan got up to put on his pants. "I'll walk you out."

In the driveway, Evan opened the driver side door, and as Natalie swooped by next to him to enter the car, he stopped her and kissed her softly. She smiled, "Good night," she said.

She drove off feeling a multitude of emotions. Oddly enough, she wasn't angry at Evan. She was upset about the fact that he didn't want to commit, but she was aware of his affection for her. Natalie faced a conundrum. Would she continue to be Evan's friend with benefits? Would she stop seeing him completely? Or would she just fuck him until something better came along? The latter seemed the most favorable option.

CHAPTER THREE
Tipping the Scales (1997)

The next morning Natalie made her way to her 9:00 am English Literature class. Despite the prior night's events, she woke up in a pleasant mood ready to tackle her day. Upon dismissal, she quickly tossed her backpack over her shoulder and rushed out for the fifteen-minute walk to her Art History class. As she walked through the main walkway of the campus, she noticed several guys checking her out. She passed by the giant tree planter in front of the library where the jocks hung out. There were about ten football players that day, and as she passed by, she heard whistles and, catcalls.

Damn, she thought. *I must look really good today. I should wear this dress more often. Did I do something different with my hair?* She couldn't understand why she was getting so much attention. She arrived at the foot of the steep concrete steps that led to the art department. Being a cigarette smoker, she dreaded the ten-minute uphill hike. As she ascended, the whistles increased.

Halfway through her walk, she heard her name. "Natalie! Natalie!" It was Noel, whom she had met in art history class that semester. "The left side of your skirt is caught on your backpack handle. Pull down your skirt."

Natalie's eyes opened wide in shock. She felt the heat radiating from her cheeks. *OH MY GOD! I have been walking through the campus with my left butt cheek exposed for the last ten minutes!*

Natalie was mortified. Her emotions resulting from her encounter with Evan the prior night, coupled with her involuntary exhibitionism that morning was overwhelming. She decided to end her school day early and headed home eager to be engulfed by the solitude that awaited her in the confines of her room.

To her delight, she walked into an empty house. *Ahhh...Morning solitude*, she thought to herself. She walked over to the kitchen, grabbed a cup of coffee, and made her way to the backyard. She loved mornings in the backyard of her family's home. The pool motor whirring, the bees buzzing above the apple seed cover on the hillside, the birds chirping, the faint smell of gardenias, and the fresh morning air were the smells and sounds she had become familiar with over the last twenty years. Whether she played as a child with her sister outdoors, took walks around the neighborhood with her grandmother, or enjoyed gatherings or the pool with her family and friends, those sounds and smells were ever present. Sitting there that warm, spring morning gave her a sense of comfort. At that moment, she felt truly appreciative for the sense of love and security her family had provided her with and realized she didn't need Evan to validate her worth. And as she basked in the morning

15

sun inebriated by warm, fuzzy feelings, she forgot her current woes and fell into a peaceful slumber.

For the next couple of weeks, Natalie kept herself busy with school, as well as her social life. Upon Evan's return, she rejected his requests to meet with her, using her impending final exams as an excuse.

"Is everything ok, Natalie?" Evan asked apprehensively. "This is the third time you are too busy to meet with me. I was hoping you would have stopped by the night I returned from my trip. I've been back for a week, and I still haven't seen you."

Natalie shuddered at the thought of him away on business in Miami. The *producer* had rented a beachfront mansion in Miami to film a new series of adult films. Evan and Josh had joined him to arrange content for their website. Jeannine had presented Mike with an ultimatum. Thus he refrained from attending the Miami trip. How many girls had Evan been with in those ten days? During the last three weeks, her stomach was aflutter as she agonized over thoughts of Evan in the company of these porn stars.

Initially, when Evan had told Natalie of this business venture, she had questioned him about his guilt in exploiting women. He steadfastly maintained that neither he nor the production company he was in business with exploited the women, as they were professional adult stars who enjoyed what they were doing and were appropriately compensated as such. He did concede that although women are exploited in the industry, he only did business with "responsible" and "reputable" adult film companies; statements that Natalie found to be ridiculously oxymoronic. The conversation, and Evan's inability to grasp his role in oppressing these women troubled Natalie. Did he know the circumstances in which these women subjected themselves to such levels of degradation whether voluntarily or not? Did he really believe that these women enjoyed degrading themselves as they did? Having had access to a financial windfall at such a young age, Evan couldn't quite comprehend the power he wielded, particularly with women willing to do anything for money. Natalie never considered herself a radical feminist, yet she saw Evan's lack of a sense of social responsibility and apathy towards these women as a lack of respect towards women in general. It was infuriating and off-putting, and yet, she still wasn't sure if she wanted to break ties with him.

"Everything is fine, Evan," Natalie answered reassuringly. "I have exams coming up this week, so I need to study. I meant to come by, but I've been swamped with studying for finals." She resolved to withhold herself from him intentionally until she could sift through her feelings and articulate her expectations of their future. Hopefully, he would realize what was at stake here and yield to her goal of a commitment. She had succeeded in remaining aloof until she couldn't contain herself any longer.

"I hope that you were responsible in Miami. If you spent ten days fornicating with porn stars, I would be more comfortable if you took an HIV test before we saw each other again." As soon as the words came out, she wanted to kick herself. For the last week, she was tipping the scales with Evan. For every time she rejected him, she felt an increase of power while Evan felt weighed down by insecurity. At first, rebuffing Evan's invitations proved to be a most difficult task. She delved into the depths of her psyche to muster up every bit of self-restraint until she herself believed that her preoccupation with school kept her from Evan. All efforts seemed fruitless now in that moment of weakness, where she had uttered those words and ascertained her feelings of jealousy.

"Miami was business. I conducted myself professionally," Evan replied in a cynical tone. Did he realize Natalie was playing a game? "Not that I owe you an explanation, but I didn't touch any of the actresses. I did go out with other women, but I have always maintained that I practice safe sex."

"I didn't mean to snap," Natalie retorted.

Unbeknownst to Natalie, while he was away, Evan had missed Natalie terribly. At first, he deduced that he had become accustomed to her visits, and thus seemed off due to the lack of routine. Time apart had made him realize how fond he had become of her. He often found himself longing for her presence, so much so that he was warming up to the idea of a commitment. He contemplated flying her out to Miami, then negated the idea given the venue and the nature of his business. He decided that when he returned, he would take Natalie away for the weekend; maybe to Palm Springs or Santa Barbara, where they could discuss the evolution of their relationship as well as spend the better part of their days engaged in hot, sweaty sex. To his dismay, he never got the chance to propose a weekend get-away. Natalie had not been as receptive as he hoped when he returned from Miami.

"So, come over for a little break. I can help you de-stress."

Resist him; you can do this, she thought to herself. *Withhold just a while longer.* "I'd love to, Evan," she took a deep breath, "but I can't." She caught herself smiling maniacally. "How about next week? After finals?"

"If you can go another week without seeing me," he said cunningly, hoping to persuade Natalie otherwise.

"Oh, I can," Natalie said confidently.

Evan felt the sting of rejection. And just like that, the scale tipped in Natalie's favor.

CHAPTER FOUR
Opportunities (1997)

Natalie and her two best friends, Monica and Michelle, attended a party celebrating the end of the semester at their mutual friend, Rick's, home. After a week of finals, everyone was ready to blow off steam. Natalie did not want to miss out on the festivities. Rick, whose parents were always away on the weekends had the perfect home to entertain – outdoor kitchen, pool, spa, theatre room, and a game room complete with a pool table and 80's arcade video games. Thus, Rick's family home had come to be known as "the party house." Although Natalie hadn't seen Evan for almost four weeks, she chose not to bring him and had planned to meet him afterward at his place.

The atmosphere was very upbeat from the moment the girls walked in. The giant foyer had become a makeshift dance floor. Crowds of people were dancing, while the DJ spun records from a booth perched on the stairway landing. The game room was full of billiards and arcade enthusiasts. The girls situated themselves outside at the largest of the four patio tables in the backyard reminiscent of a poolside resort. Shortly afterward, Rick's girlfriend, Karen, along with a crew consisting of three of her girlfriends and two guy friends joined them. Natalie was acquainted with all but one of Karen's friends, Eric. She hadn't seen him around at Pierce College. It turned out he only had one weekly class at Pierce even though he had already transferred to CSUN, the same university that Natalie would transfer to in the fall. Once the proper introductions had been made, Karen's friends each found a seat around the table. Eric sat across from Natalie, where he frequently made eye contact with her. He was attractive and funny, so she welcomed the attention. The entire table of eight was engaged in conversation. They were playing a game Natalie had made up called *One-Up*. One player would choose a topic that could pertain to anything based on one's personal experience. The players would then compare their own experience and attempt to one-up the other players using their own experiences relative to the chosen topic. After listening to everyone's answers, they would choose amongst themselves who one-upped everyone else. That evening the game had evolved into a drinking game. So, the participants would have to take a shot if their answers were "one-upped." Natalie abstained from the drinking portion of the game. She had allowed herself one alcoholic beverage, as she was driving that night.

Natalie began the game. She had asked the players to name the most exotic location they had visited. She was followed by Michelle, who asked about the deadliest experience they had encountered. Karen was up next.

"What is the most embarrassing thing that has happened to you?" she asked and looked around the table. Three of Karen's friends gave mediocre answers.

When it was Natalie's turn to respond, she shouted, "Ok, I think I've got this one! Embarrassing occurrences happen to me all the time, but this happened last month, and it was pretty bad!" She proceeded to tell the group about the day she left her English class and was headed to Art History when she had suddenly become the target of incessant attention, under the impression that she must have looked irresistible that day, only to discover that she had been walking with her butt-cheek exposed to all passerby.

"Hey, I was there! I saw that!" cried Eric. "That was bad! Everyone was staring, and she was oblivious. I don't think anyone can top that. Natalie, you got that one." They all giggled as the group agreed. After a couple of more rounds, the group dispersed to eat the buffet spread in the dining room. After dinner, Natalie headed towards the end of the backyard and enjoyed the view of the valley lights. As she pulled out a cigarette, held it between her lips and rummaged through her purse for a lighter, Eric walked up and ignited his lighter. She tilted and lowered her head to place the tip of her cigarette against the flame.

"Thanks," she said with a smile, grateful that she didn't have to dig through her purse any longer, content to be enjoying her cigarette.

"My pleasure," he said as he lit his cigarette. "Do you mind if I join you?"

"Please, be my guest," Natalie said.

"It was fun hanging out tonight...Hey, I think you should patent and market your game before someone else does. You know Karen is a business major. She's cunning. She might try to steal your idea and one-up you," he said as he smiled. Eric was handsome. His beautiful, green, almond-shaped eyes were so expressive; they revealed a gentleness about him.

"How do you know Karen?"

"We grew up together. Our parents are family friends. She's like a sister to me." he said, emphasizing the lack of existence of any romantic inclinations towards Karen. "Hey, I was wondering if I could take you out sometime. I mean I've already seen your butt-cheek and all, so, the least I could do is take you to a nice dinner. It wouldn't have been the order I would have chosen. I would have opted to take you out first and then see your butt-cheek. I'm old fashioned that way…" He said as he flashed that mesmerizing smile again, "No, but all kidding aside, I'd love to spend some time with you."

"I'd like that," Natalie said as she extinguished her cigarette. She glanced over at her watch. It was 11:45 pm. "Oh shoot! I lost all track of time! I got to go. Eric, it was nice meeting you. Karen has my number. I look forward to hearing from you." And with that, Natalie hastily left the party. Evan didn't live too far away; she would be at his place in less than ten minutes.

Evan had dozed off waiting for Natalie. When he opened the door to greet her, he was slightly disheveled. "I thought you said 11:30? It's almost midnight."

"Why do you look so scruffy? Do you have another woman in here?" Natalie asked trying to deflect any responsibility from being late.

"Yeah, I've got three ladies in here. When you didn't show up, I figured you stood me up." He played along with her silly accusation. He closed the door behind her and seized her. He lifted her as she fastened her legs around him. Within seconds his tongue was in her mouth darting in great depth as if he was attempting to draw from her life force. He leaned her up against the wall, her legs wrapped around his waist tightly and alternated between licking and nibbling her neck. He carried her over to the pool table and sat her up against the edge. Evan zealously kissed her, drew back, and spread her legs open. He began kissing and licking her upper thighs, then gently inserted his finger inside her, not surprised by how wet she was. She leaned back, while he explored her with his tongue, and she moaned with delight. When Evan was sure she had come, he stood and pulled Natalie back up against the edge of the pool table. He was so hard, he slipped on a condom and eagerly proceeded to penetrate her. As soon as he was inside her, he began stroking her metrically. She felt her insides melt. She couldn't get enough of him.

"You feel so fuck-ing good," Natalie breathlessly whispered, annunciating each syllable with emphasis.

"Yeah, you like that?" Evan asked rhetorically. "I missed this," he said as he continued to pummel her. "I missed you."

"Me too," she sighed. As he pounded her harder and harder, the two climaxed in unison and fell back onto the pool table.

Evan carried Natalie to the bedroom for rounds two and three. Afterward, she undressed and made her way to the shower in the adjoining bathroom. Within minutes Evan joined her. Natalie let the hot shower pour over her, as Evan wrapped his arms around her waist from behind.

"I'm glad you came over tonight. I was beginning to think you weren't going to show up," Evan admitted as he began soaping Natalie's back.

"Yeah, I'm happy I was able to make it tonight, too."

Moron, it's your fault I've been staying away, she thought.

Evan got out of the shower and quickly dried off. Exhausted, he pulled the covers off his bed and climbed under the sheets. When Natalie emerged from her shower, Evan patted the bedside to his left and motioned for Natalie to join him. He nuzzled her affectionately, tenderly kissing her every so often until he drifted into a deep and peaceful sleep.

Natalie was sexually energized, but emotionally she had to detach from Evan. In the last few weeks, using the power of persuasion, she had convinced herself that she would no longer anticipate a commitment from him. Instead, she would have to sever her attachment. As a defense mechanism to protect her feelings, she rationalized that Evan wasn't boyfriend or husband material. She imagined a future with him, where the stigma associated with his business associations would complicate their personal life. She acknowledged the fact that her time with Evan was nothing less than exciting, but he wasn't a legitimate suitor one could "take home to mom." She couldn't imagine explaining the source of his wealth to her family and friends. It was common knowledge that some people repugnantly referred to Evan as a "pornographer." If their relationship evolved, her reputation could quite possibly be tarnished because of his involvement in pornography.

Natalie hastily but quietly got dressed. She took caution not to disturb his sleep and stealthily snuck out of Evan's home.

CHAPTER FIVE
Natalie and Eric (1997)

The next morning Natalie was awakened at the crack of dawn by her parents and sister bidding her goodbye as they prepared for their departure to the airport. They would be traveling to New Jersey for a family wedding and would spend the next two weeks on the East Coast. Natalie would have to skip this trip, as she was unable to take two weeks off from work. After they left, she dove back into bed and went to sleep. She woke up at 10:30 am to a series of faint beeps indicating she received a voicemail on her cell phone. She glanced at the missed calls menu to discover she had missed a call from a number she didn't recognize. Checking her voicemail would require way more energy than she wished to exert that moment. *It can wait,* she thought.

When Natalie emerged from her room, she headed directly to the kitchen and made herself a pot of coffee. She prepared a cup exactly to her liking with three heaping tablespoons of powder creamer and two teaspoons of sugar.

Cupping the large mug with both hands, she cautiously headed out to the patio. "What a beautiful morning." Natalie nestled into an oversized patio chair and sipped her coffee. "Mmmmm. Just right," she said sipping the hot liquid. She felt like Goldie Locks, perfectly satisfied regarding her palate and comfort. She retrieved the message from her voicemail. It was from Eric. He assured her he wasn't a psycho calling her the morning after he met her, but that he had enjoyed her company so much the night before, that he wished to take her out that day.

Natalie thought it would be a good idea to explore her options. She realized she would have to start dating other men to get over Evan. She returned Eric's call. The two arranged to go to the beach that day.

Eric picked Natalie up a couple of hours later. It was a perfect day in Malibu—86 degrees and not a cloud in the sky. The two hauled a blanket, two chairs, a small cooler, and a picnic basket to their desired spot. Eric sprawled a heavy beach blanket on the sand, followed by a smaller tablecloth off-centered to the upper right. He began to unload a picnic basket. The sun was shining. As if on cue, a perfectly-timed, occasional, airy breeze blew, cooling Natalie right before the blaze from the sun could cause any discomfort.

"I stopped by Whole Foods before I picked you up," he said as he unloaded the basket containing a variety of salads—chicken, cabbage, pasta, and fruit, as well as a flatbread pizza. He proceeded to lift the lid of the cooler, discreetly opened a bottle of sparkling white wine and poured it into two plastic wine goblets.

"Eric, I'm impressed," Natalie said, as she paused to clink glasses before she took a sip of her wine.

"Bon appetite!" Eric said. He looked on as Natalie began to spoon the various salads on to her plate. "To Carol!" Eric toasted raising his glass.

"Who is Carol?" asked Natalie, although she couldn't care less, as she was too busy enjoying the spread before her.

"This chef I dated. She had graduated from a prestigious culinary school. About two months ago, she was chosen to be an apprentice at a trendy restaurant in Manhattan, so she moved there."

"Were you bummed that she left?"

"No, not really. We are still friends. I mean Carol is a great girl, and we had a good time, but from the start, we were both aware that nothing serious would come out of our relationship. There was no love lost on either side when she had to leave. She had been waiting two years for that apprenticeship, so anyone that came along was a temporary companion for her until her dream was realized. We both served a purpose in each other's lives. I think I gave her a sense of stability for the moment. And she taught me how to cook." Natalie found Eric's practicality to be refreshing. He was pragmatic and real. "What about you? Are you seeing anyone?"

"I am seeing this one guy…we aren't exclusive, but I am at that stage where I realize that we aren't on the same page, and maybe we are better off as friends."

"I can't say I'm not happy to hear that," Eric said as he flashed a smile.

For the rest of the day, the two were engrossed in deep conversation. It seemed the hundreds of people who had come to enjoy the beach on that glorious day were non-existent. Their attention was focused solely on each other as they each gave fully detailed accounts of their lives and got to know one another.

Around 5 pm the breeze picked-up so much that Natalie couldn't get a sentence out without her teeth chattering. Eric suggested they leave the beach and head over to Third Street Promenade in Santa Monica. They walked around and shopped for a while, then headed over to a little Italian restaurant for dinner. After dinner, they began to walk toward the parking lot, stopping to enjoy the street performers who caught their attention along the way.

When they made it back home to the valley, Natalie thanked Eric as he pulled into her driveway. Eric, in turn, thanked her, then leaned over and kissed her softly. An electric shock pulsated through Natalie's body. Eric was an excellent kisser. If he was as good of a lay, she scored herself a winner.

"I'll call you," he said as Natalie jumped out of the car. He waited until she had made it into the house then drove off.

For the next two weeks, Natalie and Eric spent most of their free time together. Natalie had avoided two calls from Evan that first week. By the end of the second week, she realized she would have to break things off with Evan.

*****

When Evan called her on Friday morning, he did not know what to expect. He had been back from Miami for six weeks and seen Natalie only once two weeks ago. Natalie's aloofness, as well as the abundance of other women at his disposal, had hindered him from inviting her away for the weekend to discuss the possibility of a commitment.

"Natalie, hi! It's Evan. Why haven't you returned any of my calls?" He waited for a response.

"Hi, Evan. I have been busy. Since you didn't leave a message, I figured it wasn't important." Her voice lacked its usual effervescence, "I've meant to call. Listen, Evan, I want to let you know I've had a great time with you. I have come to appreciate your honesty, but I don't want to see you anymore—not sexually—anyway. I've started seeing this guy. We aren't intimate yet, but if we do become intimate, I don't care to have multiple lovers. I don't want to complicate things, so I—"

Before she could finish her thought, she was interrupted by Evan. "Well, that puts a damper on my plans," he said with a sad chuckle. "I was calling you to invite you to Palm Springs next weekend. I hoped we could spend the weekend together and discuss the possibility of a commitment. Ever since Miami, I have warmed up to having a girlfriend."

"So, let me get this straight," Natalie said calmly. "Since Miami, you have thought about taking our relationship to the next level?"

"Exactly!" Evan interjected.

"And it took you six weeks to bring this up— conveniently after I have disclosed that I am involved with another guy?"

"Well, I didn't intend on it taking so long to discuss the matter. It just sort of happened that way."

"You did not want a commitment and even encouraged me to find someone else, and I did. Now you have the audacity to want to take me away for the weekend?

Absolutely not." Natalie was irked. "Look, I have to go to work. I will talk to you later, but I am not going to Palm Springs with you next weekend."

The next night Natalie was invited to Jeannine's twenty-first birthday party. When Natalie told Jeannine she was seeing someone, Jeannine encouraged her to bring him and anyone else she wanted to bring along but warned her that Evan was sure to be there. Natalie and Eric had made plans to go out to dinner with Monica and her boyfriend, Jack, that same night. She figured they would stop by the party after dinner.

It was 9:45 pm when Natalie, accompanied by Monica, Jack, and Eric walked into Jeannine's backyard where the party was held. Jeannine had created a very modern and sleek club-like atmosphere. A Plexiglas platform atop the pool served as a dance floor. Along the periphery of the pool were cocktail tables with floor length white tablecloths and geometric illuminated vases displaying long horsetail branches in the center surrounded by cream orchids at the mid-point, weighed down by clear glass pebbles. Guests perched on Lucite barstools appeared to be floating around the cocktail tables. Industrial bubble machines strategically hidden behind planters blew enormous bubbles creating a sense of whimsy.

Natalie looked stunning in a black halter jumpsuit with a plunging neckline accentuated by a long, gold chain around her neck, a thin gold belt, and a sexy pair of strappy gold heels. Her hair was blown out straight and feathered ala Farrah Fawcett style circa the early '80s. Eric, Monica, Jack, and Natalie found an unoccupied table. The men made their way to the bar. Natalie excused herself for a moment to use the restroom. For although Natalie's system of preventing herself from becoming inebriated (guzzling down a bottle of water after each alcoholic beverage consumed) was effective, nature called at least once an hour. She had already consumed two glasses of wine and two glasses of water at dinner and thus had a full bladder.

When she was done with her business, she checked herself in the mirror. She knew she looked irresistible. As she switched the light off and opened the door to walk out, she was stunned as she was pushed back into the bathroom. It took a second to regain her posture when she realized it was Evan forcing himself and her back into the bathroom, locking the door behind him.

"Evan! What the fuck!" Natalie shrieked. She knew deep down Evan could never hurt her. Maybe it was that sinister look of his she had initially found so sexually appealing, or the fact that he was high off cocaine and a tad belligerent, but for the first time Natalie was afraid of Evan.

"Natalie, you look gorgeous," he said as he moved in closer and put his right hand on her waist. He held the back of her head with his left hand and drew in for a kiss.

Natalie pushed back, "Evan, I'm sorry. We are not doing that anymore. I thought I made myself clear yesterday."

Evan avoided making eye contact. He looked down at the floor and took a deep breath as he tried to find the right words to express himself. When he finally found them, he looked up and said, "Nat, I made a mistake. I don't want you to see other men. I'm not going to see other women. I am ready for a commitment."

"Evan, the fact that you wouldn't commit until I found someone else tells me you are doing it for the wrong reasons. You are being forced into a situation you don't want to be in…and I am not going to force you into anything. Please Evan, just let me go about my business. I met a nice guy, and I want to see where it's going to go." Natalie feeling confident now that her safety was never compromised moved closer towards Evan, gently placed her hand on his cheek, and said, "Evan, you are going to be fine. You have plenty of girlfriends to help you forget me." She smiled and planted a kiss on his cheek and walked out.

Natalie couldn't help but feel uneasy for the remainder of the evening at the party. Every time she noticed Evan, his gaze was intensely fixated upon her—while she danced, when she laughed at a joke Monica told, and after Eric passionately kissed her before they lit a cigarette in the far corner of the backyard. When Natalie finally realized she could no longer tolerate the unwanted attention from Evan, she told Eric she wanted to leave. Eric suggested they stop by his place before he took her home. She whole-heartedly agreed. She was ready to take her relationship with Eric to the next level.

It didn't take long before Eric and Natalie were rolling around Eric's bed ardently kissing in a frenzied state. Natalie stood up and untied her jumpsuit at the neck, maintaining constant eye contact with Eric. The jersey material easily slid off Natalie's body adorned only in a pair of black lace panties, her gold necklace, and strappy heels. She leaned over, undid Eric's belt and pulled off his pants. With her panties still on she mounted Eric and rubbed up against his crotch, as he laid back on the bed in a trance. He cupped her breasts, lifting his neck to lick and suck her nipples. His erect penis was ready to be engulfed by her.

"I want to ride your cock," she said as she groaned in ecstasy. Within seconds, Eric had sheathed his penis with protection. Natalie pulled the crotch of her panties to the side and slowly guided Eric's penis inside her. When he was deep inside of her, she intensely grinded onto him, as he stroked back with great ferocity.

Natalie bent over and kissed Eric as she straddled him. After she had climaxed, he rolled on top of Natalie while he was still inside of her. He threw her leg over his shoulder and pounded her until the two of them came in synchrony, moaning and groaning in pleasure.

Winded, the two lie back under the sheets, looking up at the ceiling.

"That was great," Eric said as he tried to catch his breath.

"Yes, it was," Natalie responded.

Eric turned on his left side to face Natalie. He fondled her breast with his right hand and tenderly kissed her.

"Eric?" Natalie asked.

"Yes, Natalie?" Eric attentively retorted.

"What would you label us as?"

Eric gazed into Natalie's eyes as he assertively replied, "Exclusive."

CHAPTER SIX
The Nuptials (2001)

F our years later, Natalie and Eric were to be married, in the company of 250 of their dearest family, relatives, and friends. They chose the Westlake Village Inn as the venue. Natalie, her sister— Sandra, and Monica were the first to arrive at the inn the day before the wedding. Throughout the day, the rest of the wedding party, the immediate families, and out of town guests, would join them. Eric would not be there until 6:30 that evening. After the ladies checked in to the suite, they perused the spa's massage menu. Fortunately, they were able to book treatments before they were to greet the bulk of guests arriving that day. As they prepared to head to the spa to enjoy the facilities before their services, Natalie was called to the reception room by the events coordinator to iron out some details for the rehearsal dinner scheduled for that evening.

"You girls go on. I will catch up. It shouldn't take long," Natalie directed Monica and Sandra. Natalie grabbed her bag and headed towards the reception room. To her dismay, Natalie was taxed with the task of choosing the table locations for the groups of guests attending the rehearsal dinner. Spending the last six months planning her wedding and the accompanying social events, she had become all too familiar with the ease at which family and friends would find offense for the most trivial infractions. These slights included but were not limited to the manner in which an invitation was addressed, excluding non-essential relations of guests, selecting the table one was placed at, as well as the location of the table in proximity to the head tables, excluding of distant relations and friends from the more intimate events pertaining and leading to the forthcoming nuptials, etc. For the last six months, Natalie navigated these issues as delicately as possible, to avoid any intentional offenses. Except for a few hiccups, she managed to do so with flying colors. Often, she would jest that planning her wedding was akin to being groomed for the position of the U.S. Secretary of State. After painstakingly appointing the suitable tables each group of guests on the table list would occupy, Natalie was on her way to the spa.

Just a few yards away from the pathway leading to the spa entrance, Natalie stopped in her tracks when she heard someone from behind whistling to the tune of *Here Comes the Bride*. She looked back to see which one of her guests was attempting to seek her attention. To her surprise, it was not a guest, but Evan who stood directly across from her now as her body had pivoted 180 degrees.

"Evan?" she asked, bewildered, and confused. "What are you doing here?" Natalie had not invited Evan. However, his friendship with Jeannine and Mike provided him access to information about Natalie's life. He was slightly disconcerted when the subject of Eric's and Natalie's engagement was made public. For although he had never sought to contact Natalie after the news that she and Eric had established themselves as a couple had found its way amongst social circles that overlapped with Evan's, he had secretly always believed that Natalie would eventually find her way back to him. And when she did, he would gladly leave behind the scores of women available to him to commit to the one woman he knew would make for his perfect companion in life. As the current course of events was unfolding, such would not be the case.

"Natalie, hi. I'm not here to crash your wedding or anything like that," Evan said sincerely. "Since Mike and Jeannine are attending your wedding, Mike decided to make a weekend out of it. He asked that I join them at the hotel, so we can get a round of golf Saturday before the wedding, and then again Sunday morning."

Natalie blushed at how juvenile she must have sounded after Evan offered his explanation. After all, she did not own the hotel, nor could she dictate who came and went, as it was a public venue.

"Of course, Evan. I wasn't insinuating that you were conspiring to sabotage my wedding! I'm just surprised to see you." Natalie said, gracefully saving face for what she now believed was an inaccurate presumption she had made moments earlier.

"You look great!" Evan said, changing the subject, recovering from their initial uncomfortable exchange. Unbeknownst to Natalie, Evan had a faint glimmer of hope that he could sway her to forgo her wedding to Eric, realizing all along that it was Evan she should have been marrying. "How are you? Are you happy? Are you sure you have made the right choice? Marriage is a life-long commitment."

"Of course, I am sure, Evan! What a dreadful thing to say to me the day before my wedding." Natalie attempted to regain her composure, certain now that Evan was deliberately trying to breach her mind with doubt. As irked as she was now, confident that he had approached her with ill intentions, deep in her subconscious, she still harbored enough positive feelings for him so that her knees weakened, and her heart fluttered.

"I'm sorry, Natalie. I don't mean to upset you at a time like this." Evan said gently. "I think you are a great girl— one of a kind—and you deserve the best. I hope that Eric can provide you with that. I don't mean to disrespect you or Eric."

Natalie's stance softened. "Thank you, Evan," she wanted to believe he was sincere. "You know I have to admit, sometimes I do reflect upon the times we spent together with great fondness. I think it's safe to say that when I do look back at the times we shared, I can't help but crack an involuntary smile. I can see myself doing that when I'm an old lady, thinking back to our sexual escapades," she said giggling. Immediately realizing that she had probably overstepped appropriate boundaries, and was encouraging Evan, she quickly retorted, "I must get to an appointment. It was nice to see you."

"Good luck, Natalie, I do wish you the best." His chest pounded, as Natalie walked away.

For the rest of the weekend, Natalie suppressed the uneasy feelings brought upon by her encounter with Evan.

Natalie and Eric's wedding weekend carried on without a hitch.

A month later that sense of uneasiness resurfaced when Natalie received a small album comprised of candid pictures from her wedding. Her friend had snapped photos—one of them as the wedding party congregated near the golf course for the professional pictures. Natalie could make out a bystander in the distance. To anyone else, the man in the background was a golfer waiting between strokes observing the wedding party. To Natalie the identity of the golfer was evident, while he was waiting for Mike to complete his stroke, Evan was gazing wistfully in the direction of the bride.

CHAPTER SEVEN
Love and Marriage (2013)

Natalie tossed and turned in agitation, as the combined sounds of Eric's deep breathing and occasional abrupt snores hindered her from sleeping. She stared at him with repugnance, as he lay there with his mouth agape. At that moment, she could not tolerate the sight of him. She felt a deep urge to take her pillow, place it atop his face, detrude with all her might, and suffocate him. Realizing the thought brought her an actual sense of joy, she guiltily shook the image from her head. Instead, she shoved Eric and in a loud whisper exclaimed, "Reposition your head! You're snoring so damn loud. I can't sleep!"

Eric startled, stirred for a moment, then collapsed back into a deep slumber. Overcome with regrets for what she believed was a poor choice in mate selection, *what did I ever see in him*, she thought. Early on in their relationship, Eric had done and said all the right things. He was educated, was establishing himself in his career, made a good living, and was kind and faithful. Finding security in their relationship brought forth a complaisance that enhanced Eric's predominantly lazy nature. Natalie's contempt compounded over the years, as Eric stopped trying to make any occasion special. Instead, they became as uneventful as possible. He failed to buy her presents, reasoning that Natalie was hard to please and had access to buy anything she wanted, as she had the household finances at her full disposal. He never took the time to select thoughtful cards, or bring her flowers. Her birthdays became unhappy events due to his lack of planning and last-minute inquiries on how to spend them. Christmas Day brought a sense of joylessness as he left Natalie without a gift under the tree. Mother's Days passed without trinkets of acknowledgment, as her sons' ages and her husband's lack of consideration, precluded them from purchasing gifts.

Slowly but surely, their marriage had become a union of disillusion in which both partners steadfastly drifted further apart. Their sexual encounters became less frequent until Natalie realized but didn't seem to mind that they would sometimes go two months without sex. The lack of maintaining a true partnership with Eric weighed heavily on Natalie. She was more than vocal concerning her displeasures, but Eric continued with his rigid dismissiveness. And so, when Natalie found solace in the arms (and beyond that specific part of the anatomy) of another man, she did not feel a sense of guilt, rationalizing to herself that her actions were justified due to Eric's lack of actions and simply stated, that *he deserved it.*

Encumbered by insomnia, Natalie introspectively pondered whether fourteen years ago she had misled herself to believe that marrying Eric was the right decision. All their friends had paired up with their significant others and were planning weddings at around the same time she and Eric were engaged. Was she following suit to conform to those in her circles? Alerted to the warning signs before they were married, had she just ignored them? Eric was somewhat anti-social and preferred staying home rather than socializing. His interests—camping, hiking and the outdoors—were not aligned with hers. She was well aware that people didn't change unless they wanted to. For that reason, she had broken up with Eric once for a few months. He had asked her to give their relationship another chance and promised that he would change to make things between them better. They were engaged shortly after that. Eventually, she realized Eric, like most people, was set in his ways and was not one to compromise unless it suited his own needs. She wondered what would have become of her life had they not reconciled.

During her years as a stay at home mom, in anger, she would proclaim to her mother that when she was financially independent, she would divorce Eric. Her mother whom Natalie believed had a more unsophisticated view on modern day marriages would immediately express her disapproval. "No marriage is easy," she would say. "He is a good provider. He doesn't gamble or cheat or drink. He is a good father. You will regret it if you divorce him. I know several people from your generation who have regretted divorcing their spouses. Think of your children's happiness."

"I will think of my own happiness first and foremost!" Natalie would angrily retort, dismissing her mother's counsel as provincial ramblings.

Although she had attained the ability to provide for herself if necessary, she was aware that she would have to downgrade her lifestyle, if she elected to uncouple. Financially, for now, it made the best sense to stay married, for Natalie as well as the boys. If their parents were to divorce and split their finances, the boys would have less, as most of the funds would be appropriated to running two separate households. The real estate market in Los Angeles had manifested such that rent was comparable to a mortgage. Uprooting her children from the home they loved so dearly after their parents divorced would not serve their best interest; nor would canceling their extra-curricular activities, or depriving them of their vacations.

Emotionally, the boys would lose a sense of security if their parents were to split. Showered with an overabundance of love, affection, and attention from their parents and extended family, both had developed a high level of empathy. Sometimes Natalie saw this as a disadvantage, for although they were sensitive and loving, she did not want her boys to suffer from feeling too much. They were equally attached to both their parents. The absence of one of them from their everyday lives would impact them negatively. As long as Natalie and Eric maintained civility, remaining married for the time being was most prudent.

There was a time Natalie loved Eric deeply, when she yearned to spend most of her free time with him, and where experiences weren't as profound and meaningful in his absence. Now that time seemed so distant and those feelings foreign. She welcomed and looked forward to time spent apart.

Natalie questioned the fate of her nuptial state and wondered why the universe had aligned her destiny as such. She convinced herself that she wasn't a bad person and that the universe wasn't playing a cruel joke on her. In her insomniac state, she rationalized that some higher power had brought Natalie and Eric together to procreate. Either one or both of her children were intended to make a significant impact in the world. Would Aidan become president one day? Could little Alan grow up to find the cure for cancer?

"That's it! My children are destined for greatness," she said as she looked over at Eric still in a state of deep sleep. "That is the only logical explanation," and as she sighed a deep sigh of relief, she was finally able to quiet her mind and drift into sleep...until Eric loudly farted.

CHAPTER EIGHT
Reinvention

As repetitive as her everyday life had become, Natalie unequivocally looked forward to Tuesdays. For the last two years, Tuesday afternoons signified an awakening so tumultuous that its mere extinction seemed intolerable. It was a matter she did not like to dwell on for too long. For it was her Tuesday rendezvous that brought her back to life from her routine existence.

The last couple of years had brought Natalie great satisfaction, as she reinvented herself from homemaker to professional. Natalie had a good life as defined by her world's interpretation of such. That she had found a sense of self-actualization through her career was evident. Although she was successful and happy, life had a way of rearing its ugly monotonous head. As dictated by human nature, monotony became boring.

Before that, the events of the decade had transformed a once vivacious, alluring, sassy woman into an overweight, unsatisfied, disillusioned grouch. As much as she loved being a wife and mother, she had lost her sense of self. Staying home to raise children had derailed her career. Overcome by thoughts of how valueless her life had become, she went back to school to earn an MS in Marriage and Family Therapy. After completion of her supervised field experience and passage of her state board exams, she established a small private practice.

Natalie had always been approachable. This quality and the way she put people at ease gave way to a stable staple of clients. Her own impressive earning potential unintentionally overcame her original intent on supplementing her husband's decent income. For the first time in a long time, Natalie felt she was the mistress of her universe. This regained sense of purpose, self-awareness, and independence was the fire that fueled Natalie's ability to enhance and subsequently, achieve her potential. Natalie's life had become a series of positive chain reactions, gaining exponential momentum with each success.

The happiness she found within reflected on the exterior, as well. No longer depressed, she shed the twenty of the thirty pounds she had gained in the last ten plus years. Her sense of self-confidence was captivating. The right amount of humble, coupled with the right amount of cockiness was a very sexy quality.

Before Natalie's reinvention, her life had become stale. In her teens and twenties, men noticed her. She lost her virginity at the age of eighteen. However, having developed earlier than most girls her age, by the age of fourteen, she was aware that she was perceived as a sexual being. It wasn't until she was seventeen that she recognized the true powers of her sexuality, a power she enjoyed wielding even when she was a tease.

She was on vacation with her family in Cancun. Most of the women and girls at the resort, like Natalie and her sister, were infatuated by the Australian activities' director, Simon. So, when he would go around soliciting the guests for various scheduled resort activities, Natalie would happily participate. She spent the week shamelessly, but innocently flirting with Simon. On the last night of their trip, Natalie and her sister were hanging out at the outdoor lounge overlooking the sea. Shortly after that, Natalie's sister excused herself and went back to the hotel room. Simon noticed Natalie was alone, so he asked if he could join her. Natalie accepted with delight. For the next hour, Natalie and Simon engaged in a conversation about real estate. Natalie had a part-time job as an assistant to a real estate agent. She absorbed every aspect of her job, and thus possessed a plethora of knowledge relative to the current housing market in Los Angeles. Simon was planning to move to Los Angeles within the next couple of years and found the conversation insightful. He was impressed, entertained, and enamored. For a moment, he forgot the fact that she was underage and longingly gazed into her big, brown eyes.

"I'd like nothing more than to take you down to the beach right this minute and root you," he confessed in a manner that was simultaneously sly and coy.

"Root?" Natalie asked.

"That's Australian slang for…uh…sex." He couldn't bring himself to say the word "fuck." After all, she was a child! What the hell was he thinking?

"Age is relative," Natalie seductively replied. "I'm ripe for the picking. Or shall I say rooting?" She was shocked at her directness, and instantaneously felt her sun-tanned face flush.

"It wouldn't be right," Simon replied shaking his head in dismay blushing uncomfortably. A lesser man would have jumped at the offer, but Simon had a conscience. Natalie was relieved that he had thwarted her advance because she knew she wasn't quite ready to have sex just yet.

For the next ten minutes, their conversation reverted to subject matter more suitable between a thirty-year-old man and a girl of seventeen. When Natalie got up to bid Simon goodbye, he stood up, hugged her, and tenderly planted a kiss on her cheek. Natalie's head tilted upwards, as Simon firmly placed his hands on her shoulders, and looked her square in the eyes. "Take care of yourself. Be good," he said imparting her with the realization that they had averted a brief interlude of pleasure that would have permanent, adverse consequences for both. She nodded attentively to indicate acknowledgment of his implication. While she walked back to her hotel room, a sense of exhilaration overcame her as she replayed the night's events in her head and began to grasp the potential of the power of her sexuality.

Natalie was sexy and confident, confident in the sense that she was comfortable in her skin, not necessarily assertive. It was commonplace to incite attention from men, young and old, in any setting. Although this attention was unsolicited and sexist, she reveled in the thought that men found her desirable. It never occurred to her how ingrained and relevant these occurrences had become to her psyche until the attention stopped. After childbirth, she had gained weight. She had let herself not necessarily go, but be. Lounge pants and tank tops replaced her sexy outfits—and yet, she didn't even exercise consistently! In her youth, she wouldn't be caught dead leaving the confines of her home unless she was done up and dressed up. In her thirties, the sexy siren she once was had vanished into oblivion.

Being a mother and wife had become Natalie's reality. Although she loved her children and was grateful for her life, she felt incomplete. Thoughts of her perceived useless existence and mortality plagued her. *If I die tomorrow, my life would be void of any significant accomplishments*, she constantly thought to herself, until she had a chance encounter with her long-lost friend, Jeannine—an encounter that set her upon a trajectory to establish herself as a successful career woman.

CHAPTER NINE
The Halloween Party (2007)

One October afternoon, Natalie had paid a visit to a local, Halloween store. Her two-and-a-half-year-old son, who was obsessed with the Nickelodeon children's show, Yo Gabba Gabba, had insisted on a Brobee costume. Natalie pushed her younger son, Alan, in the stroller, while Aidan ran up the aisle looking for a costume of his beloved character.

"Brobee!" Aidan squealed with delight as he began pulling a bag off the rack accidentally knocking down a whole peg of bagged costumes that spilled over in the already narrow aisle.

"Careful, Aidan!" Natalie scolded, crouching down to pick up the mess her son had created. "Let mommy pick out the correct size." Natalie was on her hands and knees, gathering the bags of costumes to hang back on the shelf, when a woman passed by the aisle, did a double take and called out to her.

"Natalie? Is that you? Hi! How are you? It's Jeannine!" The two had remained friends after Evan and Natalie had stopped seeing each other, but their lives went in different directions, and they eventually lost contact.

"Of course, I know who you are! Hi, Jeannine! How have you been? What are you up to? You look great!" Natalie exclaimed, as she stood up, trying to find the correct greeting for a friend she hadn't seen in seven years, even though her thoughts had verbalized into a series of garbled questions and exclamations.

"I've been great, thanks! Busy with life, balancing family and career, while carving out time for myself." By the look of it, one could only guess Jeannine had plenty of time for herself. Physically she was polished and radiant and in great shape. She looked chic, in an effortless manner; in a pair of jeans, a button-down billowy blouse, and embellished, flat sandals accessorized to the nines. "My practice is flourishing. Mike is doing fine. I have a seven-year-old daughter and a four-year-old son. Life is good! I can't complain." Jeannine detailed the status of her life enthusiastically.

Yeah, you'd be a totally ungrateful asshole if you did, thought Natalie.

Jeannine had become a successful dermatologist. Her husband, Mike, who had initially gone into business with Evan had become a successful real estate developer. The two had manifested into one of those power couples who led the quintessential perfect life—the type of couple ordinary people love to loathe if the two were ass-holes, but as it happened Jeannine and Mike were decent and centered. So, one couldn't resist but to be happy for their well-deserved success. And as genuinely glad as Natalie was to hear of Jeannine's standing, it left her feeling less than and embarrassed by her own lack of professional success. To make matters worse, next to Jeannine, Natalie felt extremely self-conscious. Her face was free of make-up, her frizzy hair in a messy bun piled on top of her head, all the while sporting a frumpy look in black yoga pants and a black fitted V-neck t-shirt.

"How has life been treating you?" Jeannine asked cheerfully. "Oh, and these two adorable munchkins must be yours!" She said as she blazed a beautiful smile towards Natalie's two boys.

"Yes, these two are mine. Alan is six-months-old, and Aidan is two-and-a-half years old. They are a handful, but they are wonderful!" Natalie said proudly. For even though she felt like a loser when it came to professional achievement, her children were a source of gratification, as proof that she had done something right. "I'm busy with being a mom and homemaker these days. I don't have much time for myself. I quit my job four months after I became pregnant with Aidan. I was kind of fed up with the whole corporate thing. Eric and I wanted to start a family, and we figured my job was not conducive to raising a family with all the travel involved—nor did my salary warrant having me stay at work to hire a full-time decent nanny. So I got pregnant, quit my job, and became essentially unemployable. I've been a stay at home mom for the last two-plus years." Jeannine nodded understandably, as the juggling of motherhood and career—whether it be a work-life balance, finding a suitable career while accomplishing the duties of a mother, or the lack of a career as a stay at home mom—was an all too common subject amongst women of their generation.

"Listen! Mike and I are having a Halloween party this Saturday night. Costumes are mandatory! I would love it if you and Eric were able to come!" Without the exact words, Jeannine had already conveyed in the way she spoke that she would not take "no" for an answer.

"Eric is in Philadelphia on business. He won't be back until Halloween, Monday afternoon." Natalie said sheepishly, hoping that Jeannine wouldn't prod her. The prospect of having to prepare for a night out in the company of Jeannine and Mike and their peers, who were highly probable to be as equally accomplished as they were, at this point of her life was too daunting to grasp.

"Well, come without him then! Bring a guest or two. It will be fun, and it will be nice to get away from the kids for an evening. You do have someone to watch the kids, don't you?"

"Let me see what I can do," Natalie replied. Her response was open-ended, so she could always use the lack of childcare as an excuse if she needed to. "I'll see if I can leave the kids at my mother's."

"Great! What's your cell number? You text me your email address, and I will send you the Evite." After the exchange of information, Jeannine continued with their conversation for a few more minutes until Alan began to fuss. Natalie, realizing it was time to get the children home and fed, bid Jeannine good-bye, and the two parted ways.

Natalie was reluctant to attend Jeannine's party, but a sense of inquisitiveness had overcome her. She was curious if Evan and Mike had remained friends, and if he would be present at the party. Every so often she allowed her mind to become occupied with thoughts of Evan. What had become of him? Was he married or single? Did he have kids? Of all her past lovers, he was the only one she wondered about. She occasionally thought of him with fondness and curiosity. At times, she yearned to feel him again, as she did in those three succinct but indelible months. Time could not eradicate the imprint he had left behind. For although ten years had passed since she had been with him when memories of him penetrated her thoughts, she felt she had left behind a little fragment of herself—a scant ember for which only he could fan the flame. Did he ever think of her and reminisce about their time as fondly as she did?

Ohhhh! Of course, he didn't! What the hell was she thinking? These thoughts had to cease! They went well beyond healthy fantasies. A married mother of two preoccupied with thoughts of a former lover was extremely pathetic. *I've got to get a hobby, or better yet a job!* Natalie thought to herself, repulsed by her desperation and obsession. She decided then she would not attend Jeannine's party.

That Saturday, the day of the party, Natalie was enjoying a lazy day watching *The Way We Were* on TCM. She grew up watching classic movies from the 1950s and 1960s—a pastime she enjoyed with her grandmother. It was jarring that a movie from the '70s was now considered a "classic." Had time really crept by so expeditiously? As the movie ended and the credits rolled, Natalie wiped away tears from her eyes. She was never one for romance, but she truly loved this movie. Barbara Streisand and Robert Redford gave such gut-wrenching and poignant performances that the viewer could not help but feel invested in their love. An intense love complicated by opposing ideologies, so that the two lovers eventually part ways. Then at the end, during a chance encounter,r they realize just how impractical their love has always been.

Arlette Eshraghi

During the movie, Jeannine had texted Natalie several times. When her texts went unanswered, Jeannine resorted to calling Natalie to ensure she would attend the event. Natalie hesitated, but feeling intimidated couldn't manage to decline Jeannine's invitation. She finally agreed to attend.

What would she wear now that the party was five hours away? As she reached for the remote to turn off the television, the answer came to her on the television screen. She saw a scene for the next feature film, a Carmen Miranda movie, and decided that she would fashion a costume after her. After a quick trip to the craft store, Natalie was home hot gun gluing pieces of fake fruit until she had a perfect fruit headpiece. Although in her movies Carmen Miranda donned midriff-baring tops and ruffled skirts, Natalie thought it best to cover her stomach. She coupled the headpiece with an off-the-shoulder, flowy-skirted, ethnic dress she had picked up years ago in Puerto Vallarta. The costume she chose was a reflection of who she was. She had a sense of humor and could laugh at herself, but she was cute.

Natalie had invited Monica to accompany her that evening. Monica's carefree attitude always ensured those in her company a good time. Monica looked fabulous in a three-foot-wide blonde afro, spandex jumpsuit, and white patent leather boots. With childcare and a plus-one secured for the night, Natalie did her last once-over in the mirror and headed out the door. Natalie and Monica arrived at the party an hour after it had started. They made their way through the walkway to Jeannine's door. The grass on either side of the pathway was decorated to look like an eerie cemetery complete with fog and sound effects. The

Halloween décor inside was even more impressive, as it resembled the scenery from the Haunted House attraction at Disneyland. Mirrors, that revealed spirits floating next to the onlooker, lined the foyer, as one gazed at his reflection. Holograms of ghosts shot through the home. Dancing ghosts were projected in the dining room, while a ghost tea party was underway in the living room. *Wow!* Natalie was impressed. Was there anything Jeannine didn't do perfectly? Having a more enriched understanding of design herself, due to a recent complete home renovation, Natalie could visualize how stunning Jeannine's home was minus all the Halloween trimmings.

The stunning aesthetics of the home so enthralled Natalie, she was oblivious to the hundred or so guests. When she was done taking it all in, Natalie began to feel awkward as she noticed her surroundings. Almost all the women at this party were dressed in sexy costume versions of your typical Halloween costumes. It seemed like these women used Halloween as an excuse to prance around in lingerie branded as a costume publicly. There were sexy versions of your vast array of Disney characters, police officers, jailbirds, vampires, nurses and even sexy minions! What was more disturbing was that they all looked fit and fabulous. Natalie couldn't pull one of those costumes off in public.

"I don't mean to sound like a hater, but do you get a sense that these women are using Halloween as an excuse to express exhibitionist fantasies?" Natalie asked Monica.

"Yeah, seriously," Monica retorted.

Just then Jeannine, dressed as a very seductive Cleopatra, spotted Natalie, and rushed over escorted by Mike, dressed as Marc Anthony.

"I'm so glad you made it! Mike, you remember Natalie. And Monica, right?" She asked looking over at Monica and shaking her hand. "I remember you from those girls' nights out!"

"Yes, hello," Monica answered cheerfully. "How have you been? Your home is gorgeous!"

As Jeannine and Monica exchanged pleasantries, Mike leaned over and gave Natalie a peck on the cheek.

"How have you been, Natalie? I haven't seen you since your wedding! How is Eric? Jeannine tells me you have two boys."

Natalie and Mike were engaged in a brief conversation when Jeannine excused both of them to greet more guests. During that first hour, Jeannine kept coming back to introduce her friends to Natalie. Just as Natalie expected, all of Jeannine's friends were perfect—most of whom seemed like superwomen that not only juggled professional careers and motherhood but looked extraordinary, as well. With every introduction, Natalie was reminded of her shortcomings and felt more and more inadequate.

Natalie and Monica spent the next hour enjoying drinks on the deck with views that overlooked the valley. They were laughing and chatting while they observed and mocked the guests. As juvenile as it was to make fun of strangers, it was slightly therapeutic as it made Natalie feel less inferior to the beautiful people surrounding her.

"Oh my. Look at Alice over there," Monica said discreetly pointing to an obnoxiously drunk and loud woman dressed as Alice in Wonderland. "Wow! Her behavior is embarrassing. Poor Alice probably doesn't know her ass from the rabbit hole in the ground." The two laughed hysterically.

"Check out the slave girl Princess Leia," Natalie said pausing to recall why Princess Leia looked so familiar. "Hey! I remember that bitch from some of Jeannine's parties. At the last one we attended, she was bumming cigarettes off Eric and spent almost the entire night flirting with him. It was pissing me off so much I asked Eric if he wanted to take the car and go home with her, and I could take a taxi home."

"I know her! She is a lawyer. Our offices are in the same building. I run into a paralegal from her office named Nancy when I take my smoke breaks. Nancy says she is overly ambitious and self-important—one of those types that must be a bitch to stress she has some authoritative power over others. She thinks her shit doesn't stink," Monica said in disdain. "Look at her, a high-powered ball-busting attorney by day, but at night she embraces a submissive role."

Natalie's giggles turned to gurgled choking coughs, as her wine went down her windpipe when she was suddenly taken aback by the identity of Princess Leia's escort. When Darth Vader removed his mask to smoke a cigarette, Natalie's heart skipped a beat then plummeted down to the pits of her stomach. This was the first time in seven years she had seen Evan. He hadn't changed a bit. He was as sexy as ever.

"Oh my God! Monica, Princess Leia's date is Evan! You remember that guy I saw before Eric?"

Monica inconspicuously looked toward Evan, as she pretended to turn to the side mid-conversation to cough, so that she may get a better view.

"Oh yeah. I remember him."

"We have got to get out of here! I don't want him to see me looking like this... ridiculous and fat." Natalie said in despair. Over the years, she had imagined running into Evan by chance—never did she think it would happen while she was dressed as a silly, pudgy, Carmen Miranda—nor while he was accompanied by his gorgeous girlfriend who happened to be a lawyer. Natalie and Monica snuck out of the party undetected. As soon as the valet brought her car, Natalie quickly got into the driver's seat and headed home.

"I'll text Jeannine tomorrow morning, thanking her for her hospitality. I will apologize for not getting a chance to properly say goodbye and tell her I felt nauseous because I had a couple of drinks on an empty stomach and had to leave before I got sick."

"Why are you so distressed? And why do you care if Evan were to see you?" Monica asked inquisitively.

"Monica, of all the men from my past, Evan is the only one I am curious about. You know, it bothered me when I used to run into him after we broke it off when he was always out with skanky girls...but seeing him with that woman, who is a lawyer, and thin, and beautiful, irked me on a whole new level. It's like I got married, had kids, and became drab and fat; and he looks more distinguished. I would hate for him to see me in such a frumpy state."

"Oh. I see," said Monica sympathetically. The two had been best friends since they were ten. Monica knew all of Natalie's secrets, her hopes, and dreams, her fears, as well as her skeletons in the closet. She was aware of Natalie's resentment and boredom with Eric, in their current situation. Who was she to judge Natalie? If fantasizing about an old flame brought her a little bit of happiness, so be it. She had her insight to offer regarding fantasies, though. "You know, sometimes those fantasies are better left as such—in your thoughts. Remember when Jack and I broke off our engagement for two months? Before we reconciled, I hooked up with Gary, that good-looking guy who was in my accounting class the last year of college. Well, I ran into him years later while Jack and I were broken up. He was an insurance agent whose accounts were in my region. We met up for a business meeting, then ended up having sex. He was an awful kisser, and he was horrible in bed! I didn't get the business, and I realized that he wasn't the legend my fantasies had made him out to be. He wasn't even circumcised, ugh gross!"

"Yeah, but I know Evan is great in bed," said Natalie, "and he's circumcised."

"Well, you might not have the same connection you did over ten years ago!" Monica exclaimed, "Just be careful what you wish for. That fantasy fodder could end up being a major downer if acted upon."

Natalie dropped Monica off and headed back to her house. After a hot shower, Natalie got in bed. Her body was exhausted, but her mind juggled a thousand thoughts. *How could she have allowed herself to give up a career to become a stay at home mom? How far would she have gotten if she never quit? Would she stay with Eric if she was financially independent? Are Evan and that woman together? How do those bitches manage to stay so fucking skinny?* She could not quiet her mind so that she could get to sleep. It was 11:00 pm in Los Angeles, which meant it was 2:00 am in Philadelphia. Natalie sat up and reached over for the phone. She dialed feverishly and waited for

Eric to answer. After the fourth ring, Natalie heard Eric's breathing before he said hello.

"Eric, it's me," Natalie said indifferently to the fact that she had inconsiderately woken Eric from a deep sleep at 2:00 am.

"Are the boys all right?"

"Yes, everyone is ok. You know how I keep going back and forth about going back to school? Well, I decided I'm going back to get my masters in Marriage and Family Therapy."

"That's great, honey. I'm all for you getting back into the workforce and all, but can I go back to sleep now? We can talk about it when I get back. "

"Yeah. Good night."

"Good night," Eric said as he yawned, then hung up.

Natalie got up to fill a glass of water from the bathroom tap. She remembered a Peter Drucker quote a friend had posted on Facebook a few days ago that had made an impression and repeated it aloud as she looked at her reflection in the mirror, "The best way to predict the future is to create it." *This will be my mantra*, she thought.

Natalie got into bed. She pulled the covers to her chin and stared at the ceiling. "I will have a meaningful purpose in life."

CHAPTER TEN
R & R, Reconnect and Rekindle (2013)

N atalie was innately more observant than the average person. Though her disposition was characteristic of one that would be categorized as social—easily engaging in conversation, ability to mingle with strangers, adaptability to various social situations—her preference was to be an observer, rather than a participant. Often, social events became observational studies opportunities for Natalie. After finding a suitable location set at an outermost periphery, with a lack of ease of mobility, a convenient excuse for her lack of movement during the event, Natalie would inconspicuously people gaze. Fascinated by the behaviors and actions, cultural nuances, and rituals of friends, acquaintances, and strangers, Natalie could spend hours people-watching.

Arlette Eshraghi

A common denominator that frequently caught Natalie's attention was how uneasy and strained people were, even in these social situations where the purpose of the outing was to have a good time. Recognizing that everyday stressors were becoming more prevalent and more difficult to manage, Natalie developed an interest in stress and anxiety reduction techniques. She decided to incorporate meditation and breathing techniques with her therapy sessions. Natalie registered for an upcoming continuing education workshop on the topic. The earliest was a three- day course in three weeks in Palm Desert. The fact that the course was held at the JW Marriott, her hotel of choice when patronizing the Palm Springs/Palm Desert vicinity, was construed by her to be an auspicious sign indicating that she should attend the workshop. Not only would she benefit professionally, but she could spend some quality time at the spa. As a spa junkie, The Spa at the J.W. Marriott Palm Desert was one of her favorites. Natalie hoped her friend, Laura, who was also a therapist would join her. As luck would have it, Laura wouldn't be able to attend, due to a scheduling conflict.

Feeling overly-motivated and fearful of losing momentum in her newly piqued interest, she decided to go to Palm Desert on her own, rather than wait for a more opportune time for her colleague to join her. She found a renewed sense of excitement in her career and did not want any delays in practicing what she believed would be an enhanced type of therapy for her clients.

While Natalie did enjoy the company of people, she also appreciated solitude. She believed that while it was important to maintain relationships with others, it was pertinent for one to be at ease with one's self. Doing things alone promoted a level of independence and self-reliance that led to a more evolved, self-actualized person. Natalie was highly critical of friends who adopted a herd mentality. Some friends refused to attend events without a friend or spouse. Others, couldn't fathom a movie, going to the gym, or dining by themselves. The reluctance of these friends to venture out on their own seemed juvenile to Natalie, and thus she began to distance herself from those she perceived to be less evolved due to a lack of self-reliance.

Natalie looked forward to some time on her own—a little R & R—rest and relaxation. She arranged for Eric to work from home and take care of the boys in her absence. Both Eric's and Natalie's mothers were close by to help if necessary. The two alternated the responsibility of picking up the boys from school and watching them for a couple of hours until Natalie came home from work. Having Eric work from home, available to pick the boys up from school, gave their mothers a little break, too.

It was a warm, Monday morning in March, the day Natalie drove out to Palm Desert for the workshop. She had said her goodbyes to the boys the night before, trying to overdose on enough of their kisses and cuddles to keep her satiated for the next couple of days. She embarked on her journey at 5:30 am; early enough to allow for the impacted traffic common to Los Angeles freeways. Registration was at 9:00, and the first workshop would begin at 10:00 am.

What would regularly be a two and a half-hour drive to Palm Desert was extended by an hour due to the morning traffic rush. Natalie was too busy finding beauty and gratification in enjoying the moment that gorgeous, spring morning to allow the traffic to perturb her. Since her interest in anxiety and stress reduction, she was attempting to practice what she would soon be preaching. She had no control over the traffic situation; she would have to accept it and move on. Instead she would focus on the positive aspect of the traffic jam—eventually, this road would take her to the workshop that would teach her techniques that would allow her to be a better therapist. Shortly after 9:00 am, she pulled into the entrance of the hotel. Having arrived too early to check in to her room, she had the bellhop check in her luggage. She made her way to the JW Pavilion ballroom, where the workshop was hosted. After registration, she walked into the ballroom and found an unoccupied row of seats, of which she took the first seat.

"Excuse me?" a woman's voice said close by, again, "Excuse me?"

Natalie looked around until she realized the voice belonged to a woman sitting in the row behind her beckoning for her attention.

"Yes?" Natalie asked.

"Do you have a partner? For the workshops, I mean? You know we are supposed to pair up. If you are here alone, would you like to partner up with me?"

Natalie was perplexed by the woman's initial inquiry. When the woman finally stopped talking, Natalie took a moment to process the questions and told her she would gladly be her partner. The woman took this as a cue to gather her belongings, leave her seat, and situate herself beside Natalie.

"Hi. I am Ellen," she said, as she settled into the seat beside Natalie.

"Natalie. It's nice to meet you."

"I'm sorry if came on too strong just now. Last time I was at a workshop, I didn't know anybody, so they paired me up with a real weirdo," Ellen explained, "an hour into the workshop I left. You look like a normal enough person, so I thought I'd ask you to be my partner. I'd rather take control of my fate than leave it in the hands of others."

"Well if it prevents me from being paired up with a 'weirdo,' I'm glad you asked me," Natalie said chuckling, now that she fully understood the situation.

Shortly after that, the seminar began with a series of lectures that lasted two hours, followed by a ninety-minute intermission. Natalie and Ellen decided to meet for lunch at a casual restaurant in the hotel after the two of them checked in to their rooms. Ellen was a psychologist, who also specialized in transcendental meditation. She had left a position as a social worker at St. Joseph's Hospital four years ago to practice therapy in Pasadena. She was divorced and didn't have any children of her own. She had a stepson from her ex-husband. Though she did not have any ties to her ex-husband, she was still in contact with her stepson, having entered his life at a time where he was young enough to appreciate a mother figure in his life. The two were close, even in the absence of any biological ties.

After lunch, the ladies paired up during the workshop exercises. At precisely 3:30 pm, the workshop came to an end for the day. Natalie left feeling invigorated and excited about the new techniques she was learning and was enthusiastic to try them on her clients. Constantly reinventing herself was leading to positive changes that only lead to upward mobility.

She felt ecstatic as she rushed back to her room for a quick change before her spa appointment. Ritualistically, she used the eucalyptus steam room, then quickly showered before her treatment, making a point to wash and condition her hair. She loved getting massaged while her hair was squeaky clean and damp. Somehow it seemed to heighten the invigoration of her senses. As the masseuse kneaded and prodded her body, she felt all her tensions melt away. Her muscles felt like gelatin; her body felt like it would meld into the table. When her hour was up, Natalie reluctantly robed and emerged from the private massage room, where the massage therapist waited for her outside the door. His words seemed garbled as he handed her a plastic cup of water, infused with a hint of cucumber and orange, and reminded her of the importance to adequately hydrate

At 5:45, the Palm Desert sun still blazed warmly into the evening. Natalie decided to lay out to get some color before showering and getting ready to meet Ellen at 8:00 pm for dinner at Mikado. Fully relaxed, basking in the warmth of the filtered sun, she lay on a chaise observing a group of men dressed in golfing attire pass by on their way to the golf course. In that instant, she recalled the wedding photo sent to her by a guest in which the wedding party had congregated for a photo close to the golf course where Evan was gazing at her.

I wonder what Evan is doing at this very moment, she thought. It had been six years since she saw Evan at Jeannine's Halloween party, yet her curiosity regarding Evan continued to ebb and flow over the years. She couldn't understand the unrelenting inquisitiveness, yet she could. It was as simple as the confession she had made to him the weekend of her wedding. Whenever she thought of the time they spent together, she felt a sense of joy and couldn't help but to crack an involuntarily smile, just as she was doing that instant. Their brief interlude brought her happiness, tucked away in her subconscious, the memories served as a stimulant each time they resurfaced.

At Mikado, Natalie and Ellen enjoyed sushi and sake.

"If you don't mind me asking, why did you get divorced?" Natalie asked.

"Well it's a long and complicated story, so I will try to give you a condensed version," Ellen replied. "John and I had been married for six years. We were married a month after we met, so you could say it was a whirlwind romance. He coached his son's soccer team, and I was the team mom. I befriended this woman whose son happened to be on the same team. Within a few months, we were inseparable. We even vacationed together. One December, we went skiing in Mammoth. I am deathly afraid of skiing, and Annie's husband sustained an injury the second day, which meant the both of us stayed behind while everyone else went skiing." Ellen paused as she took a sip of her sake and carefully refilled the tiny porcelain cup. "Frank was an investment banker, a real uptight, cocksure guy. I suggested I train him in some meditation techniques to help take the edge off. By the second day of our meditation sessions, I thought he was really getting into it when he was really getting into me. We both got carried away, and he kissed me. I didn't dissuade him. I got caught in the excitement of the moment even though I was fully aware of the betrayal I was committing against my husband and friend. Frank's daughter who forgot her goggles at the cabin walked in on us while we were both naked from the waist up kissing and dry humping each other. Needless to say, that trip ended rather abruptly, as did my friendship

Arlette Eshraghi

with Annie and my marriage to John. Annie and Frank tried to make a go of their marriage but ultimately failed and divorced a year later. Annie and John are now happily married, blended family and all."

"Wow, so John didn't even try to make things work out or forgive you?"

"No. The one time I was unfaithful—not even to fruition—was enough for him. He left me and never looked back," Ellen said matter-of-factly. "I have maintained a relationship with his son because I was a mother figure to his son for so long. Not that I am trying to absolve myself of any wrongdoing, but even though it broke my heart, I realized that I wasn't happy with John if I was receptive to the advances of another man, especially a brute like Frank."

"I'm sorry I brought this up," Natalie said, realizing that the mood had suddenly become heavy.

"It's fine," Ellen graciously replied, "How about you? You said you have been married for twelve years?"

"Yes, married for twelve, but together for sixteen. I find myself questioning our relationship at times. I can't say that he enamors me, but is anyone enamored by their spouse after sixteen years together?" Natalie asked rhetorically. "Over the last sixteen years, I have considered leaving him, but what's the alternative? Find someone else to become bored with? Given the circumstances, my two young children, I think it's best if I wait it out. If it were to get intolerable, I would leave. For now, it works."

After dinner, the two shared a gondola ride in the man-made lake surrounding the property back to the hotel lobby along with others whom they recognized from the workshop. Ellen and the others planned to go to the hotel bar for a nightcap. Natalie was too exhausted to hang out. She abruptly ran towards an open elevator as its doors were shutting and managed to get the doors to re-open when she pressed the up button.

"Five please," she said to the only occupant of the elevator, a man standing in front of the elevator panel, distracted as he multi-tasked, making sure the handle of his luggage was balanced properly against his hip, searching for his key card tucked in the key folder.

"Five it is," he said. As he looked up his eyes widened in astonishment while his polite grin altered into a smile that stretched from ear to ear. "Natalie?"

"Evan!" Natalie exclaimed in bewilderment, unable to contain her excitement.

"What are you doing here?" they simultaneously asked each other.

"I'm here for a continuing education workshop, meditation techniques, and you?"

"I'm here to relax and golf for a few days. I just got in. How long will you be here?"

Just then, the elevator doors opened, "I'm here for another day and a half. This is my floor," she said pointing to the hallway as the doors opened and she walked out. "I'll see you around… I guess? It was nice seeing you."

"Yeah, I'd love to catch up," Evan quickly replied, as the doors closed behind her.

Walking through the hallway to her hotel room, Natalie was stunned by a sense of unfulfillment. *How anti-climactic,* she thought. All these years, she had yearned to see Evan, and when she finally did, it was for a brief moment to exchange superficial pleasantries. She didn't have the opportunity to inquire about the details of his life, and just like that, the two were off to their respective hotel rooms.

Once inside her room, her chest began to pound with anticipation. Whereas less than ten minutes ago she was overcome with exhaustion and desired nothing more than to go to sleep, a jolt of energy now swept through her, due to her chance encounter with Evan. She couldn't stop thinking about him.

Beset by extreme restlessness and insomnia, Natalie replayed the exhilarating, yet short-lived meeting that had transpired an hour earlier in the hotel elevator. The physiological responses resulting from the excitement continued to resonate through her entire being. Curiosity regarding everything Evan permeated her thoughts. She could hear his voice, smell his scent, and feel his presence in the abstract. Natalie still found Evan sexually appealing. Knowing that he was in the vicinity but not tangibly present was unbearable. Desirous feelings of a sexual nature which had become dormant and foreign to her suddenly re-emerged, prompting Natalie to recall the sexual prowess she possessed and relished in the past. She yearned for nothing more that moment than to be with him.

She attempted to get Evan out of her head—desperate to get a minimum of six-hours sleep—not an optimum amount to promote a healthful night's rest, but enough to get her to function throughout the next day. It was too late to take a sleeping pill, so she would have to resort to other measures to fall asleep. Her first attempt was of self-manipulation—a good orgasm always put her to sleep, but the further she got into "it," the more she imagined Evan, further prompting her curiosity about him. She then turned on the television, hoping that it would lull her to slumber.

Still, to no avail, she turned off the T.V. a half-hour later and reached for her Kindle. She would read herself to sleep. Sometime around 2:00 am, she finally dozed off.

At 6:12, Natalie groggily opened one eye and looked at the alarm clock. She had another eight minutes before the alarm was scheduled to go off. She turned off the alarm and sat up. She stretched her arms out, then twisted her back at the waist until she heard a series of cracks. As she trudged off to the bathroom, she was taken aback when she saw her puffy-faced and baggy-eyed reflection in the mirror.

Of all the mornings to look like a wreck! Why today, when the prospect of running into Evan was near certain?

Her hair, which she had blown out perfectly yesterday evening and had a shelf life of three days before the next blow out, was disheveled and prematurely wavy because she had restlessly tossed and turned her head on the pillow the night before. A simple body shower wouldn't do this morning. Natalie would have to pull out the big guns. A fresh hair wash and blow out, coupled with cosmetics inclusive of primer and concealer applied with the dexterous precision of a surgeon was necessary if she hoped to look alluring.

Natalie hastily stripped and got in the shower, as she had no time to waste if she were to make it to the workshop on time. Almost immediately, the warm water therapeutically washed away her exhaustion. The fresh scent of her ultra-moisturizing rosemary and lavender shampoo and conditioner revived her.

What a glorious day, Natalie thought to herself, as she prepared for her day. Happily, she examined her fresh blow out which was completed five minutes before her budgeted time of forty-five minutes. She exercised the utmost caution, wavering between the fine line of balancing the extra cosmetic products utilized while still maintaining a more natural rather than an overly done-up look. Upon completion of her hair and makeup, Natalie put on a pair of yellow ankle pants, a navy-blue blouse, and a white, fitted jacket. She completed the look with a pair of navy espadrilles.

Fresh as a daisy, she thought, fluffing the ends of her hair as she gave herself a last once-over in the full-length mirror perched in the hallway. Natalie was so proud of her work, if she could pat herself on the back, she would.

Downstairs at the entrance of the ballroom used for the workshop was a table of baked goods and coffee. Natalie prepared herself a cup of coffee to her liking and grabbed a blueberry muffin. Just as she was about to enter the double doorway, a familiar voice greeted her,

"Good morning, stranger." It was Evan, obviously lingering around the ballroom in an attempt to intercept Natalie before the start of the workshop.

"Good morning!" She retorted, bright-eyed and bushy tailed.

"We never got a chance to talk yesterday. Are you here with your family?" He asked deftly, convincing Natalie he might have been thinking of her all night long as she had been of him. Who knows? He might have been plagued with insomnia as well, although he looked too good. She knew exactly where the remainder of this conversation was headed. Now if she could just maneuver without seeming too overzealous, it would be an accomplishment.

"No, I'm here solo."

"Well, that's great. I can gracefully bow out of dinner with my golfing companions, and we can have dinner and catch up. That is if you would like to." Although the ball was in Natalie's court regarding accepting his invitation, he spoke with such an air of confidence he was certain that dinner and whatever came with it was a done deal.

"That would be lovely," she replied in her most demure manner. "The workshop goes through 3:00 pm. I was planning on lounging at the pool for a couple of hours after that."

"How is 7:00 pm?"

"That works for me."

"Great! Meet me in the main hotel bar at 7:00. We can have some drinks before dinner."

"OK. See you then," Natalie said coolly, as she walked off and entered the workshop precisely at 8:55 am. *We are going to have sex. And he knows it.* The words were unspoken, but the chemistry was too apparent to disregard. It was palpable to both that while they made plans to dine together, their true motives were to quench their mutual carnal appetite for one another. With each step, her heart was beating faster and faster. She had maintained her composure in his presence, but once she was away from him, the adrenaline rushed through her instantaneously.

Once inside, she managed to locate Ellen who was saving her a seat in the third row.

"Are you ok?" Ellen asked. "You look a little flushed."

"I'm fine," Natalie said. "I just ran into an old friend from my college days."

"A fling?" Ellen prodded curiously.

"Oh God no! Just a good friend. Fun to hang out with, but definitely not boyfriend material. We were buddies."

Natalie lied through her teeth, unwilling to divulge any hint of a past romance. If she decided to go through with what she was certain would happen tonight, she would have to adopt a more guarded attitude. Her indiscretion would be a secret that she would take to her grave.

"A group of us from the workshop that went to the bar last night are having dinner tonight? Will you join us?" Ellen asked.

"Oh, I'd loved to, but Evan and I are going to dine together and catch up on old times."

"OK. If plans change, we will be meeting at the Rockwood Grill at 7:30, then heading over to Costas."

"The club?" Natalie mused as Ellen nodded yes. "Oh, no. I hated clubs in my twenties. There is no chance in hell you will find me at a club in my late thirties. I will probably be in bed by ten." *With Evan, fucking his brains out.* Natalie blushed, as she thought to herself.

"Are you sure you are ok? You are as red as a tomato. Maybe you should take your jacket off."

"I'm fine," Natalie brushed Ellen's comment off. "I was rushing to make it to the workshop on time. I couldn't sleep last night. I'm just a tad ruffled. I just need a minute to decompress."

Natalie attempted to do her best to sustain her attention throughout the rest of the day. She did not intend on short-changing herself from the purpose of her trip. She successfully practiced some of the relaxation techniques she had learned the prior day to maintain a sense of calm and focus. The trip had been fruitful after all. She truly was enthusiastic to try these methods on her patients—albeit not as excited to be with Evan, sexually.

At 3:00 pm the workshop let out. After a quick change, Natalie checked in at the spa. She had scheduled a body scrub for later that day specifically to gain access to the more secluded and less crowded spa pool. She found a suitable location where she draped her towel on a chaise.

Although she was eagerly awaiting her dinner date with Evan, surprisingly she was in a state of complete relaxation as she lounged at the pool, soaking in the rays of the afternoon sun, until she sat up to reapply sunscreen on her arms and décolletage. She spotted four men in golf gear crossing the lawn. The last of the four was Evan. He almost immediately recognized her, as if he were equipped with Natalie detection radar. He flashed a gentle smile and discreetly waved. She inconspicuously waved back as he continued to walk by and disappeared around the corner. The communication between the two was near telepathic, as demonstrated earlier that morning. He didn't have to say a word—that smile and wave conveyed it all. *I can't wait to see you tonight.*

Natalie walked in the hotel bar at 7:08 pm. She glanced around to find Evan seated at a bar table, scotch in hand, relaxed and poised. He stood up when he saw her approaching the table.

"Natalie, you look lovely," he said as he kissed her softly on the cheek lingering a few moments enjoying a whiff of her signature scent, Coco Chanel. Natalie dressed in a teal blue sundress splashed with yellow and red flowers. Oddly enough she had purchased it during her last trip to Palm Springs. She wasn't too fond of the fabric, but the cut and color were extremely flattering for her. She had paired it with a yellow cardigan and yellow wedge sandals. He pulled out her chair and waited for her to position herself securely before he pushed it closer to the table. He took his place across from her then shifted his chair closer to her right.

"Thank you, Evan," she said, "I must say, I was extremely delighted to run into you."

"So was I," he said enthusiastically. "So…tell me what you have been up to for the last decade. Still married to Eric? Mike and Jeannine had mentioned you have two kids, right, boys?"

She nodded, "Yes, still married to Eric. I have two boys. Aidan is eight, and Alan is six. They are adorable," she continued as she pulled up pictures on her mobile phone.

"They're beautiful. The little one looks exactly like you," As politely as Evan replied, Natalie could detect a sense of resentment in his tone, in a manner eluding that someone else had snatched the life that was intended for him.

"I'm a practicing therapist. I have been for two years now." Natalie changed the subject.

"The blind leading the blind?" Evan teased "Or in your case, the crazed leading the crazed?"

"I'm not crazy!" Natalie spunkily protested.

"No, just passionate," he said, as he scooted his chair closer to hers.

Nice rebound, she thought to herself.

Just then, the waiter came by and asked for her order.

"Malibu and Diet Coke, please," she said enthusiastically.

"I'll have another Glenlivet 18, neat. Thanks, man."

"You got it. I'll be back with your drinks."

"What are you up to these days, Evan? Are you married? Any kids?"

"No, not married. No kids. I was briefly engaged to a lawyer, but she was too high maintenance for me. We broke up six months after our engagement, luckily before she completed and paid for most of the wedding planning."

So, Princess Leia he was with at Jeannine's Halloween party was his fiancé.

"High maintenance?" Natalie asked. "This coming from a man sporting a Patek Philippe Nautilus diamond-trim, white gold watch, Tom Ford sunglasses, and Gucci loafers?" *You wouldn't catch Eric dressed like that.* His style, selected by Natalie, was classic and understated, unlike Evan's, which was too ostentatious for Natalie's liking.

"What's wrong with my loafers?" Evan pondered aloud as he moved his foot to the side from under the table and examined his footwear.

"Thankfully, nothing because they aren't monogrammed, but what woman wants to be with a man who is better accessorized than she is?"

"Oh, her being high maintenance wasn't due to the material stuff. That doesn't faze me. I enjoy buying expensive shit for women. It was more of her state of being. She was never at ease. She had constant mood swings. I never knew what to expect from her. I think she might have been bi-polar. And she was a total narcissist. I'm just grateful I got out before it was too late. She got pregnant before we broke up. Initially, the thought of having a kid excited me. Then when I realized it would tie me to her forever, I started having serious panic attacks. You could imagine the sense of relief I felt when she miscarried six weeks into her pregnancy. It just solidified my belief that we weren't meant to be and gave me a clean out. Less than two months later, we broke up."

As if on cue, the waiter interrupted the two, "Malibu and Diet Coke for the lady, and Glenlivet 18, *neat* for the gentleman."

"Thank you," Evan said.

"Is there anything else I can get you?"

"No, we are good for now, thanks." Evan dismissed the waiter.

"Wow, to think, you, the perpetual bachelor, was almost married."

"That's an inaccurate and unfair moniker. I'm not a bachelor because I want to be. I just let the right one get away." He looked down at the liquid in his glass in his hand and swished it, attempting to suppress himself from revealing too much. "I think about you sometimes, Nat."

Natalie was flush from a combination of the alcohol on a near empty stomach and the subject matter. She was speechless.

"So, are you happy with Eric?" he asked.

"Yes and no. Marriage is hard. We have our ups and downs like all couples." She wasn't about to turn this into an Eric bashing session, but she would convey her dissatisfaction as mildly as possible. "What I wanted in my twenties is different from what I wanted in my thirties and is changing as I approach my forties. We have our good times and our bad times. I feel like things are stagnant, but who wouldn't feel that way after sixteen, almost seventeen years together?"

"I'm almost certain you wouldn't feel that way with me. Life would have been one big party."

"That would get old, too," Natalie said snippily.

"So, is it common for you to have dinner with other men to keep things from getting too *stagnant*?" Evan mocked.

"Only on days that end with the letter 'y,' but don't you worry, there's plenty of Natalie to go around," she replied flirtatiously.

"You are such a goofball," Evan said shaking his head then gazing directly into her eyes, "but a very sexy and charming one…Are you hungry?"

"Famished," *in more ways than one*, she blushed.

"Why are you blushing?" Evan inquired.

"Am I?" Natalie played it off. "It must be the alcohol making me feel warm."

"Well, I hope you don't mind, but I took it upon myself to ask the concierge to arrange for dinner in my room. I don't want to seem too presumptuous, but I preferred to be solely in your company, rather than a crowded restaurant. The concierge should be done prepping by now. Shall we?"

"That sounds perfect," Natalie replied. She downed what remained of her drink and got up. Evan directed her to the exit. When he put his arm around her waist, Natalie rested her head against his shoulder, as they walked to the elevator.

"Natalie," Evan said as the doors closed behind them.

"Evan," Natalie interrupted before he could finish. She turned to him, looked in his eyes and gently pressed her lips onto his. Within seconds, his hands cupped her rear and drew her body into to his. He fervently kissed her. When the elevator made it to the seventh floor, Evan reluctantly pulled away as the elevator doors opened. He waited as Natalie exited the elevator.

"This way…" he motioned to her. As they walked down the hallway to his suite, he pulled his wallet out of his pocket and drew out the key card.

Immediately upon entering the hotel room, Evan and Natalie ignored the dinner set for them on the dining table. They couldn't keep their hands off each other. Once again, he grabbed Natalie and began to kiss her passionately. Barely taking a moment to catch his breath, he kissed her with the intensity of one that had waited for this moment for seventeen years.

Natalie's heart beat rapidly. Her body quivered in anticipation as it had in the past in response to being explored by a new lover. Evan gently pulled down the spaghetti straps holding up her dress. The fabric draped down to her waist. His pleasure at the sight of her in her strapless bra was evident. So, she was truly perplexed when he inconspicuously pulled out a blue pill from his shirt pocket and popped it into his mouth. Natalie, being the consummate observer that she was by nature, immediately caught Evan in the act.

"What's wrong? Don't you find me attractive enough? Why do you need Viagra to have sex with me?" Natalie asked self-consciously.

Evan laughed. "The problem is you're too attractive. Since I ran into you last night, I couldn't stop thinking about you. I relieved myself once last night and twice today," he said sheepishly. "The last thing I want to do is underperform."

Her ego, content with his explanation, allowed her to carry on. She interlocked her hands behind Evan's neck as he continued to kiss her. The two glided into the room intertwined in their embrace until Natalie found herself leaning up against the dresser for support. She basked in delight while Evan planted nimble kisses on her cleavage then her bare breasts after he unhooked her bra, then made his way back to her lips. Natalie unbuckled his belt and unzipped his pants. She tugged down at his briefs until the restricting garment no longer restrained his erect penis. She guided his penis until she felt him deep inside. Her whole body shuddered at the sheer pleasure of the feel of Evan's manhood.

Overcome by a sense of intense exhilarated delirium, Natalie was ever present in that exact moment, oblivious to any sense of wrongdoing. With every thrust, Evan inched deeper and deeper. Natalie lost all inhibitions in a heightened sense of euphoria. He turned her around and proceeded to thrust slowly at first, then faster and deeper until it felt like they were melding into one. While she clutched the dresser for support, she glimpsed at the sight of them in the mirror. The man behind her was not her husband. Morally, she knew her actions were unquestionably reprehensible. Yet, she did not seem to care. For, at that moment, as they both climaxed, their indecency seemed acceptable.

Evan turned her back around, so she was facing him again and began to kiss her. He shook off his pants, one foot then the other while he still kissed her. When she pulled away briefly to catch her breath, he seized the opportunity to step back, throw her over his shoulder and playfully toss her on the bed. He was still rock hard. He positioned himself on top of her as they continued their sexual interlude for the next hour or so…until both were panting with over-exhaustion under the cool, crisp sheets.

They lay in silence in complete ecstasy for a couple of minutes. Evan sat up and lit a cigarette. He dropped one arm across Natalie's body.

"I thought I would run into you at Jeannine's and Mike's Halloween party that year you attended. What happened to you? Mike and Jeannine said you were there, but I never got a chance to see you." He puffed away at his cigarette, then after he exhaled, he added, "I was with my fiancé then, but I was curious to see you."

"I hid when I saw you; then I hightailed it out of there as fast as I could," Natalie replied sheepishly.

Evan began to chuckle from his gut wholeheartedly. He extinguished his cigarette in a near empty water bottle then turned to his side facing Natalie.

"Why would you hide from me?"

"I didn't want you to see me. I had just given birth six months earlier, and I looked like a cow. The fact that your date looked like a Victoria's Secret model didn't help."

Evan didn't say a word. He just leaned in and kissed her gently. The no bullshit ease at which she could come clean to Evan was appealing. She felt a sense of freedom with him she was unable to feel with anyone else but Eric. And as it happened of late, she was becoming distanced from and resentful of Eric. Was it possible to be in love with two men at the same time? Or love one as a partner in life and be in total lust with another?

He reluctantly pulled away, then got out of bed. The sight of him in his nakedness, penis still erect, walking towards the closet made her yearn for him even more.

"This isn't going to be a situation like one of those six-hour erection disclaimer warnings you hear about in the pharmaceutical commercials is it?" She asked; taking pleasure in the sight of him.

"If it is, we're going to have to go at it for another couple of hours, and if that doesn't work, you're going to have to take me to the hospital," he said as he handed Natalie one of two bathrobes he held. He slipped into the second robe and made his way to the table, "I'm starving. Let's eat!"

CHAPTER ELEVEN
Steam and Mirrors (2013)

Throughout the rest of the workshop and the entire drive back, Natalie could not cease to recall the events of the prior evening. Erotic scenes of her and Evan replayed in her mind, continuously. As a reflex, she would sporadically shake her head while tightly shutting her eyes trying to eradicate the reoccurring scenes from her mind.

"What is wrong with you? You are acting like one of my patients that suffers from Turret's?" Ellen asked her.

"Migraine," Natalie replied with an agonizing look on her face. Lying was becoming easier by the minute.

She was unable to focus at the workshop that Wednesday morning, and was more than overjoyed when the session ended at 11:15 am, an hour before schedule. After declining lunch with Ellen, and exchanging email addresses and phone numbers, Natalie hastily excused herself for the sake of getting back home early enough before her "migraine" escalated.

She felt uneasy around Ellen knowing that she had almost discovered Natalie's illicit rendezvous with Evan. As Natalie made her way back to her hotel room at 1:30 am, she had heard Ellen's voice when she emerged from the elevator along with some of the other workshop attendees that she had gone out with seconds after Natalie's elevator had made it to their floor. Thankfully, Natalie had run into the corridor towards the ice and vending machine galley and hid for a few minutes until she was certain they were all gone.

Evan had pleaded with her to stay the night, Natalie refused. She couldn't risk the chance of seeing anyone in the morning during her walk of shame back to her hotel room. Coincidentally, in her attempt to avoid any run-ins, she had almost been discovered by Ellen.

"When can I see you again?" Evan had asked as she threw her clothes back on in a rush to leave his room before he could pull her back to the bed for what seemed to be his insatiable sexual appetite. After hours of uninhibited sex with Evan, Natalie was too sore to go at it again. She was certain she would develop a bladder infection.

"You can't see me again. I'm married, and I have a family to go home to," Natalie replied, realizing then that she might not have thought through the whole sexual escapade with Evan thing, oblivious to the consequences of misleading him. "Look, what we just had was amazing. I mean you might have single-handedly, or by the use of your penis to be specific, brought me back to life from my mundane existence, but I can't do this again. At least not for a long time…a very, very long time. I have no regrets about what transpired between us. I loved every minute of it and would do it again in a heartbeat, but I can't…I must live with the guilt of knowing I have been unfaithful to my husband… I need time to process this," Natalie stammered.

Evan was speechless for a moment but managed to mutter, "How can you be so cold, after what just happened, Natalie?"

"I'm not trying to be cold or hurtful, Evan. Think of this as my *Bridges of Madison County* moment, like when Meryl Streep's character had a brief love affair with Clint Eastwood's character while her husband was away one weekend. She relished the memories of the experience but carried-on with her routine life with her husband. It's a complicated situation. I have a family to think of."

"This isn't a movie. You weren't thinking about your family when you came several times!"

"No. That would be counterintuitive, given the circumstances," Natalie retorted innocently. "I'm sorry, Evan. It was never my intention to mislead you."

"You can't just come into my life for one night then disappear after the intense experience we just shared. It's heartless."

"I'm not heartless, Evan… I'm married," Natalie said as she gave him a quick peck on the cheek and hastily walked out the door, leaving Evan in a near catatonic state of shock because of her aloof attitude.

As she neared her home, Natalie was haunted by the thought that Evan might forgo discretion and do something rash. He wouldn't confront Eric with the truth? Would he? No, she was paranoid. Or was she? She had a lot more to lose than he did. She would lose her husband and the security of her family life. This affair could briefly tarnish his reputation and brand him a home-wrecker, but she would be vilified far worse, as a whore—*forever*. Furthermore, his reputation would eventually recover as it had when he became a reputable businessman, whereas years earlier he was considered a "pornographer." Society was much more forgiving to scandalous or adulterous men than it was to women.

Natalie felt an anxiety attack coming on as she pulled into her garage. Why couldn't Evan make this easy for her? Why couldn't he just make a clean break? *Breathe,* she thought as she gathered her things and walked into her home.

"Mommy!" her children exclaimed as she walked into the kitchen.

"Hello, my loves!" she exclaimed, as she embraced her children, gaining the strength from their warmth and unconditional love to help her carry on as though all was normal for the next couple of hours.

"Hi, honey. How was your trip?" Eric asked congenially.

"Productive, but exhausting," Natalie said as she hugged him more like a friend than a lover.

"I picked up a roasted chicken and broccoli salad for dinner. Let's eat!"

Uncannily, Eric's last two spoken words triggered a flashback of the night before when a famished Evan had suggested they eat using the same words and tonality. If easily prompted memories of her indiscretion were to deluge her conscious mind continuously, this event was going to be far more difficult to suppress than Natalie had imagined.

Throughout dinner, Natalie feigned to listen to the boys' adventures with their dad attentively. No matter how hard she tried to focus, her mind drifted off to the night before. Natalie watched a cartoon with the boys after their showers, then instructed them to go to bed promising to come up and tuck each one in a few minutes. She checked in on Eric, who was predictably in his office on his computer.

"I'm going to shower and go to bed. Good night."

"Good night. I'll be up in an hour or so," Eric mumbled; too absorbed by the Reddit thread, he was reading to bother to make any eye contact.

Alone in her bedroom, she appreciated the solitude. It was times like this that Natalie was thankful that she and Eric didn't have a habit of going to bed at the same time as some married couples she knew did. She couldn't understand why some couples had to do everything together, even sleeping and getting up in the morning. Instead, she loved having their bedroom to herself for as long as Eric was occupied in his office, entirely comprehending why some couples opted for separate bedrooms. Her bedroom was her sanctuary; contemporary, yet warm. The dark wood floors and furniture coupled with bedding, curtains and area rugs in soothing tones of greys and white was reminiscent of a Zen spa. The master slider opened to a balcony that overlooked a lush tree and gave one a feeling that the room was suspended within the foliage of the tree. That view was the first thing she saw when she opened her eyes in the morning, and the last thing she saw when she shut her eyes at night. She gained a sense of calm from the serenity of the imagery of that landscape, and this was where she spent most of her downtime at home.

She didn't appreciate Eric's untidiness or the fact that he would barge in and demand she turn off the television so that he could go to sleep. Natalie felt most at ease in her sanctuary, perched on the settee positioned at the foot of her bed. Tonight, the serene atmosphere of her bedroom was not enough to calm her.

Natalie didn't like to rely on prescription medications to soothe her anxiety, but the occasion called for a Valium. She ran the shower so that the water would get nice and hot. As she undressed, she blankly stared at herself in the bathroom mirror until her reflection distorted and was barely visible by the steam that fogged up the mirror. At that moment, she made an allegorical connection between the steamy mirror and her affair. The hot water represented their lust for one another. The steam was the sexual interaction between the two. She thought of how her infidelity had fogged up her mind. She now had a distorted sense of self, like her distorted image in the mirror. Who was she? She didn't even recognize herself. How could she have allowed herself to suffer such a lapse in good judgment? She rationalized to herself that her actions that night with Evan, although morally deplorable, in those hours were nothing short of acceptable.

She was frustrated by herself—not because she felt a sense of overwhelming guilt over her betrayal of the sanctity of her family and marriage, but because she lusted for Evan. When he broached the idea of another meeting, she immediately rebuffed his proposal. She couldn't bring herself to initiate another indiscretion. Her voracious desire for Evan was comparable to the hunger of a carnivorous animal that had tasted meat after a long period of depravity. How would she expunge Evan out of her system now? How could she deprive herself of him after she literally and figuratively got a taste of his "meat?"

CHAPTER TWELVE
Patience (and Patients) Are a Virtue (2013)

N atalie attempted to bury all memories of the lustful encounter with Evan deep in her subconscious by occupying her mind with unrelated thoughts. Although she carried on with her daily routine at home, albeit perfunctorily upon her return from Palm Springs, at least during business hours, she managed to subdue her thoughts long enough to focus on her clients. A socially busy weekend with friends and family further impeded Natalie's mind from dwelling on "Evangate."

Exactly a week after her indiscretion, on Tuesday morning Natalie perused her appointment schedule. She noticed a new client referenced only by his initials J.W. scheduled in the afternoon. Those initials reminded her of J.W. Marriott, which in turn incited thoughts of Evan. She stopped herself; she had to focus.

Natalie shared a remote receptionist, Diane, with three other therapists. Having noticed that information was missing from the new patient's profile, Natalie telephoned Diane to inquire.

"Oh, your new patient was paranoid about confidentiality, hence his reluctance to leave his name. And he does not want to go through insurance. He opted to pay cash for his visits instead. He insisted on scheduling re-occurring appointments for the open 1:30 pm Tuesday slots, but I told him you would have to meet with him first to determine you were a good fit. He said he had a feeling you would be, that a friend highly recommended you."

"OK, thanks, Diane, I just wanted to make sure I had all the information," *which happened to be no information.*

As Natalie hung up, she was a little disappointed in the prospect of a new patient on Tuesday's at 1:30. That slot had been vacant for the last three months. She had become accustomed to using that slot right after lunch to catch up on client reports. The extra income from a regular patient would be useful. She wished that she had had the foresight to block that hour indefinitely, but alas her timing was off.

Until she met her new patient, she would not know for certain that he would take over the time slot. It didn't make any sense to fret over it now. She heard the door in the meeting room adjoining her private office crack open. It was 10:00 am, she proceeded to the meeting room and greeted her first patient of the day.

Natalie locked the meeting room door after her 12:00 pm client walked out. She had a half hour to spare before her next appointment, the new patient scheduled at 1:30. She hadn't had time to grab leftovers or make a sandwich that morning. Nor would she have enough time to run to the café to pick something up and eat it before her appointment. She walked to her office, reached in her desk drawer, and found a stash of protein bars. She grabbed one, unwrapped it, and nibbled at it. Since her return, she had lost six pounds. During stressful situations, Natalie lost the urge to indulge in one of her favorite passions—food. Instead, she ate only for sustenance. She didn't have much of an appetite. She ate just enough to prevent her from getting hunger-induced head and stomach aches, and thus had a significantly reduced caloric intake. Once she resumed her normal diet, those six pounds would find their way back to her.

She signed on to her laptop and opened the browser. She had twenty minutes before the appointment, so she decided to do some internet research on Evan. She googled his first and last name. The search produced a list of properties he owned. When she clicked on the images tab, pictures of Evan at various charity events popped up—some formal and others casual. He was either adorned in a tuxedo or golf gear, but every single picture had a common accessory—a beautiful and younger woman at his side.

"He's still a man-whore," Natalie thought aloud, "but a very appealing one." His sense of fashion was still flashy. He had lost weight and was slimmer than he was seventeen years ago. His physique reflected a more health conscious, or at least body conscious, version of Evan than the one she knew. He had just the right amount of muscle tone. He was still thick, but taut. There was no trace of softness on his body.

Ahhh...his body, she thought. How many hours did she spend enjoying the feel of that body only a mere week ago? Natalie wished she could teleport back to that night in his hotel room and relive those hours. She contemplated contacting him; maybe they could have one more night together—so she could get him completely out of her system. It was possible that she needed one more rendezvous for the sake of closure before she could write Evan off for good and consequently regain a sense of normalcy in her life.

Her gut (though flabby in appearance) was a strong one, intuitively. More often than not, her instincts were spot on, and so she heeded her senses of resisting contacting Evan. Deep down, she knew this chapter with Evan in her life was not over. When they would reconnect again, she was uncertain of, but she definitely believed that it was inevitable. Her role was to be patient and wait for him to reinstate communication enabling the opportunity for another rendezvous. She could not and would not initiate contact with him.

After glancing at the time, she got up to unlock the meeting room door and returned to her desk. Shortly after that, she heard the door open. Her new potential client was punctual. She quickly deleted her browsing history and exited the browser. She opened the door that separated the office from the meeting room.

"Good afternoon, J.W.?" Natalie greeted her patient as she opened the door to the meeting room. His back was facing while he scrutinized the reading materials on the magazine shelves.

"Good afternoon, Natalie," Evan replied as he turned to face her.

"Evan, I have a patient coming in now. You have to leave! Showing up at my office unannounced is extremely unprofessional."

"J.W.? The cash patient obsessed with confidentiality?"

"You're J.W.?" Natalie asked.

"I had to find an inconspicuous way to see you. I thought making an appointment under J.W. Marriott would be too obvious, and you would cancel. I can't stop thinking about you. I know you said you weren't interested in seeing me again at least for a long time, but hear me out," Evan said. "You can't deny the chemistry between us. I think it's safe to assume you lack that with Eric. Are you willing to give that up entirely?"

"I'm glad you came, Evan," Natalie said as she locked the main office door and motioned for Evan to follow her to her private office. "I needed some time to process and reflect about what occurred between us. All these years I have been curious about you. Perhaps I thought if we had one final fling, I might attain closure? Instead, I have opened Pandora's Box. I never anticipated that I would form an immediate reattachment to you, but I did. I have been thinking about you—replaying what happened last Tuesday in my mind over and over - wishing I could go back to that night—at least one more time. I'm open to another sexual encounter with you, but I need to be totally honest with you. I am not going to leave my husband for you or anyone else. Let's be clear about that. If you could accept that, then maybe I could meet you occasionally. And you must be extremely discrete. No one—and I mean NO ONE can know about this, especially Mike. Married people tell each other everything. I guarantee that Mike has shared with Jeanine most of what you have told him in confidence. She cannot know about us. No one can. If word got out about this, it would be the end of my marriage, and I can guarantee you that if that happened, you and I would never get together. I'm serious. I have a lot more to lose than you do. I have to be certain that I can trust you."

"I can respect that. You *can* trust me. I won't say anything about our relationship to anyone. I just want to spend time with you, Nat. I've never really gotten over you."

"For some ambiguous reason, I have been very curious about you over the years. I can't imagine why? You clearly didn't know you had a good thing when you did."

"Trust me. I have paid for that mistake. I regret losing you, Natalie. I sometimes wonder how different life would have been if you and I had gotten together and had a family. I feel cheated out of that aspect of my life."

"Well, you have only yourself to blame, Evan. Timing is everything when it comes to opportunities. That applies to life as well as business."

"I guess I banked on the hope that you and Eric wouldn't last. I was disappointed when you got married. I thought we would eventually end up together."

"Well, we didn't, and we won't," Natalie said haughtily. "Our relationship will be based solely on sex. You can't expect any more than that from me. While I am quite fond of you, my family is my main priority."

"That's fine, Natalie," Evan said, exhausted by her quantifying disregard for his feelings as well as the hypocrisy of it all, "now come over and kiss me, please."

Evan held both of Natalie's arms at the wrists and pulled her over to him as he backed up to the couch. He sat down. Natalie stripped down to her bra and panties.

"Please try your best not to mess up my hair and make-up," she asked sweetly.

Natalie sat on top of him in a straddling position. They began to kiss each other. She had forgotten how erotic kissing could be. Eric and Natalie never kissed each other anymore—not passionately at least.

As they kissed, Natalie felt Evan get harder and harder. The feel of Evan was sheer perfection. She couldn't be more content for the next half hour. Disappointment overcame her when she glanced at the clock and realized the end of their hour encroached upon them.

As Evan redressed, he looked over at Natalie who was basking in the afterglow of their lovemaking and said, "That was very therapeutic. You know I have never been open to therapy, but this kind of therapy I can do." He seemed at ease with Natalie today. Not only did he successfully convince her to meet with him, but she engaged in another sexual encounter. He didn't want to intimidate her from subsequent meetings, but he wanted to establish concrete plans for their next encounter. "So…when can I see you again? I won't do anything to jeopardize your marriage. What we have between us is too intense to walk away from. We need to ride this out for a while."

"Like I said, if you could approach this with the utmost discretion, and the absence of any expectations from me, I would be willing to see you again, regularly," Natalie added, hoping that he would agree because what he failed to realize was that Natalie wanted this as much, if not more, than he did. "Evan, how would you like to take over the regular Tuesday 1:30 pm slot? We can have an hour to ourselves every week, free from interruptions. Your visits wouldn't arouse any suspicion because it would seem like you were a regularly scheduled client."

"That is a clever plan!" he retorted grinning from ear to ear. "Natalie, how much do you charge your clients per hour?"

"$150 an hour. Why do you ask?"

"I have to pay you per session."

Natalie mortified, protested immediately, "That would be prostitution! And that is illegal!"

"Natalie, the devil is in the details. We can't overlook anything. You need to create a fake client report for J.W. every week, and you need to receive compensation for therapy sessions. What is your office manager going to think when you don't get paid for reoccurring sessions?"

"I didn't think this through thoroughly," Natalie said acquiescing to his insistence on making payments. "I don't feel comfortable keeping your money, though. I guess I can donate all your fees to the National Alliance on Mental Illness. That's the only way I would agree to take your money."

"That's fine with me," he said, "I'll see you next week." He kissed her good-bye and left.

Natalie, elated, got dressed and freshened up to receive her next client. Her day carried on. After organizing her notes for her last patient report, she decided that it would be a good time to create a report for J.W. *This should be easy*, she thought, as she began typing away at her laptop:

Mr. W is a forty-two-year-old, single male who is seeking therapy for his commitment phobia and his inability to emotionally connect with the opposite sex. He actively seeks the company of women solely for sexual gratification, often engaging in misogynistic behavior with little or no regard for the consequences of said behaviors…

CHAPTER THIRTEEN
Culture Clash (2015)

"The kids are staying over at my mom's tonight," Eric said as he walked in on Natalie while she emerged from the shower. "Let's have dinner at the Brazilian place, then come back home and spend some time together." He smiled wickedly indicating that sex was on the agenda for the evening.

"Sounds like a plan," Natalie said faking a cheerful disposition. Ever since she had begun her affair with Evan, she complied with her husband's requests for sex more often. A combination of the slightest feelings of guilt and a strategy to keep Eric distracted so that he would not suspect his wife of infidelity, increased the frequency of their sexual encounters. For Natalie, sex with Eric became more effortless. Once again, she felt competent and confident in the power her sexuality wielded.

Eric enjoyed Natalie's renewed interest in sex. Oddly enough their relationship was benefitting from her infidelity—a distorted argument she used to justify her unfaithfulness to herself. She hadn't felt this good about herself in years. She was ashamed to admit it, but was this extramarital affair improving her relationship with her husband by forcing her to be a more doting and caring wife to ward off any suspicions of another man? The vitriol she had felt towards her husband years earlier had been suppressed and subdued by her weekly trysts with Evan.

Her relationship with Eric had two extremes. When she was feeling resentful, she was angry at him for not being her version of the ideal partner. The fact that she blatantly told him what she wanted and his dismissiveness regarding her wishes would infuriate her. To the detriment of their relationship as the years progressed, Eric's complacency and lack of acknowledgment for any special occasion overshadowed his will for any gratuitous and sweet gestures towards his wife. She reprimanded him when he sent her $200 flowers and asked instead that he stop at Trader Joe's and pick up an orchid or a bouquet that was a fraction of the price. Her stance against these purchases was justified by that fact that it was too easy to go to an online florist, click on an arrangement and proceed to provide shipping and billing details. For a man like Eric, who never participated in household shopping, it would be an inconvenience and a step out of his comfort zone, thus a gesture of a mild sacrifice for his wife—a sign that he was attempting to make his wife happy. In the absence of his willingness to try, Natalie would lash out.

On the other extreme, when things between the two were amiable, and Natalie felt her husband was venturing out of his comfort zone to appease her, she felt grateful to him. These were the times that the guilt would set in and gnaw at her. Gradually, she recalled why she had developed feelings for Eric in the first place. She began to feel the missing sense of like for him, but she couldn't ignore her deep affection for Evan. She had internalized the belief that her infidelity had absolutely nothing to do with loving her husband anymore or any less—only that she was capable of loving two different men in two different ways. One love instilled a sense of comfort through security and familiarity, while the other cultivated her erotic side and her awareness in her existence as a sexual being. Perhaps her participation in an extramarital affair wasn't as reprehensible as she thought. Could Evan have a right in perpetuity to her vagina since he had conquered it before Eric? Evan and Natalie had shared a bond inclusive of a sexual relationship before Eric was in the picture. For inexplicable reasons, she had an unsevered curiosity and attachment to Evan even after all these years. Could this be the psychological rationalization that permitted her to be intimate with a man other than her husband with only the slightest tinge of remorse?

"You look good," Eric said. As Natalie, rubbed lotion all over her body. "How about a quickie before we go?" His hands began groping at Natalie's body.

"Will you stop!" Natalie demanded. "I don't want to get messy before we go out."

"I can't help it. You just look really good right now."

Would Eric remember that comment Natalie had made in jest a few years back and put two and two together? *If I start looking good and taking care of myself, chances are I'm fucking someone else*—a twisted joke that had now become a reality. Years earlier, Natalie felt the life sucked out of her. Being a stay at home mom had not made a kind impression on her. Her internal thoughts reflected on the outside as manifested by her physical appearance. Although she found an identity and started projecting a vastly improved appearance, it wasn't until her affair with Evan started that she radiated from within. She was having her cake and eating it, too.

"I've been disciplined about exercising and eating better," she replied instead.

Eric would never forgive her indiscretions if he were ever to find out. She was haunted by fear at times, by what it would do to her family if anyone discovered her secret. In the last two years, her upstanding appointment with Evan although a welcomed occurrence was also a great source of anxiety and guilt-inducing, self-deprecating introspection. *I am a whore and an asshole,* she would tell herself. *But I can't help myself. I'm going through a selfish phase.*

She tried to cease her affair once, a couple of months after it had begun for fear of being discovered by her mother-in-law.

"There is something different about you, Natalie," she said in her thick Farsi accent, looking at her with what seemed to Natalie with a hint of suspicion, as Natalie showed her dresses she had picked up from a shopping excursion. She had noticed that Natalie not only started dressing differently but behaving differently as well.

Natalie didn't know if she was paranoid, or if her mother-in-law sensed something, being a victim of an adulterous husband herself. The two had divorced when Eric and Natalie had just met. His father had fallen in love with a woman who worked at his company and was five years older than Eric. Almost twenty years later, Natalie upon numerous instances detected a psycho-sexual chemistry between her divorced in-laws she found fascinating. Was it possible Nilu recognized these adulterous signs in Natalie?

"I can't let my husband's mother outshine me, can I. Nilu Joon.," Natalie retorted coyly, using the Farsi term of endearment, joon, to address her.

Nilu was a beauty in her own right. In her mid-sixties, she put women half her age and younger to shame. A self-professed tease, for years she claimed she lacked interest in sex. A claim Natalie found bewildering and contradictory, as Nilu always projected a very, sexually-charged appearance and demeanor. Eric's father was her first love. Keon fell madly in love with Nilu. The two got married in their early twenties. In the near two decades, Natalie had been a presence in the family, she witnessed the love-hate relationship between the two. Although they had divorced almost twenty years ago, it seemed their torch for one another was never truly distinguished.

A couple of years before Natalie's and Eric's marriage, Keon had married the woman who broke up his marriage. Nilu, who got the short end of the stick regarding finances at the end of the divorce, once confessed to Natalie that had she known her financial circumstances would have a dismal future, she would have turned a blind eye to her husband's philandering ways to ensure financial security. Natalie sincerely wished Nilu would find a companion truly worthy of the woman she was.

Natalie was enamored by her. Nilu and Natalie had a very tight bond. They were very open with one another. Their relationship resembled that of best friends rather than that of mother-in-law and daughter-in-law.

"With all due respect, Nilu Joon, your ex-husband was selfish. You need a real man — a true companion in your life, who appreciates your assets and values them without feeling threatened. And I think some great sex would do you good," Natalie had candidly told her.

"I am a sixty-five-year-old grandmother. It's not proper in my culture for me to be dating or having sex with strange men."

"I am not suggesting you have sex with strangers. Just be open to the idea of meeting men. Why do you dress the way you do then claim you have no interest in sex? Obviously, you are aware that you are a sexual being. You're not kidding anyone. It's obvious you love the attention you get from men."

"It's not proper for a daughter to talk to her mother like this, Natalie," Nilu would attempt to formalize their conversation when it suited her purpose. She often referred to Natalie as her daughter. She didn't like the term *daughter-in-law*. She had never had a daughter, and thus Natalie filled that void in her life. Natalie was not only betraying Eric but his mother as well. She was a hypocrite — years of bad-mouthing Keon for being an adulterous pig, now resonated with her as she came to terms with her infidelity. She was the adulterous pig now.

Not only would her infidelity disappoint Nilu, but her own family, as well. Her father whom she adored more than anything in the world, had passed away five years ago. Her father was spared the tarnishing of his daughter's image, but her mother would probably hyperventilate. Although Natalie was born in the United States, her father and mother came from Greece but were both of Armenian descent. Given that ethnocentrism is a naturally prevalent characteristic of the Armenian culture (further fueled by a need to increase their population because of the Armenian genocide), Natalie was ostracized by many when she dated, then married a Persian man. For years, right before her marriage, Natalie's mother frowned upon her relationship for the sole reason that Eric was an "odar." A term used by Armenians to identify a non-Armenian. The word could have a neutral or negative connotation, but when Ani used it to describe Eric, its tone was of the latter implication. Ani was too preoccupied with what others within the Armenian-American community would say or think—an element that infuriated Natalie and was the factor for most of Natalie's resentment towards her mother. She reminded Natalie of how she was "disgracing her family."

Although her relationship was fodder for gossip, Natalie was unyielding to the banter of imbeciles motivated by ignorance. Eventually, Ani was embarrassed for her role in actively attempting to destroy her daughter's relationship in its early phase. She realized the world was changing, and what was important was that Eric was a faithful husband and devoted father. Little did she know that her daughter who spent years defending her relationship with her then boyfriend was whoring around with another man now.

From Natalie's perspective, the Persian culture was far more sexually permissive and tolerant. The women were more sexually evolved, almost trained to cultivate the powers of their sexuality, as evident in how women from Nilu's and Ani's generation preserved themselves. The Persian women were sexy and youthful, whereas the

Armenian women appeared more matronly and less well-maintained.

Sexual promiscuity in Armenian women, though it existed, was frowned upon. The preservation of one's virginity for their future husband was a common practice even in Natalie's generation, a population that reached sexual maturity twenty to thirty years after the emergence of the sexual revolution, but still held on to the prim values of their culture.

Natalie was sheltered for most of her life attending an Armenian private school. However, her parents, who had migrated to the states in the early '60s and met in the states, didn't shield her from "odars." She held a job as a teenager and socialized with non-Armenians. Her parents' open-mindedness was essential when it was time to assimilate in a non-Armenian environment. While most girls her age were struggling to meld aspects of their Armenian and American selves, Natalie was able to integrate seamlessly.

Ani had survived the scandal of her daughter marrying an "odar," but she would not endure the disgrace of her daughter's involvement in an extra-marital affair. She would curl up and die. The severity of the situation was lost on Natalie for a brief moment when she relished in the discomfort Ani would experience. Not that she did not love her mother, but she still held a bit of a grudge for the unhappiness she caused in her life during times that should have been marked only with joy. The repercussions of Natalie's actions if ever exposed would have a disruptive ripple effect that would affect her immediate and extended family. And still those fears subsided enough for Natalie to continue her affair with Evan as it reached its two-year mark.

Natalie never imagined that the affair would carry on for as long as it had. When she initially began her adulterous relationship with Evan, she assumed that the passion between the two would fizzle within a couple of months; the two would tire of each other and eventually part ways. To her surprise, the opposite occurred. For although they had consistently seen each other once a week for the last two years, with a few missed "appointments" here and there due to illness, holidays, vacations or unavoidable business, the passion shared between Natalie and Evan didn't decline, yet, deepened. Their weekly hour-long rendezvous coupled with the forbidden aspect of the circumstances gave them just the adequate interaction time to fuel their propensity for one another.

After months of agonizing over her betrayal against Eric, she conceded to the fact that she would continue to seek excitement with Evan by living out this double life—overcompensating for her guilt by being an obliging wife when it came to Eric's desires. For two years, she had managed to keep these two lives from intersecting, until that night she and Eric had dinner at the Brazilian restaurant.

Natalie and Eric walked into the eatery at around 7:45 pm. Paulo, the waiter who for years waited on them, yet still didn't know their names, warmly greeted them and directed them to a table. Eric ordered a bottle of wine and a starter. The two engaged in conversation about their day.

"There's an opening for a director position at work. I have formally applied for it and have four interviews with the head honchos scheduled for next week," he said proudly.

"Eric, that's wonderful," Natalie supportively retorted. "Are there many people interviewing for the same position?"

"Well, there are some formalities involved with publicly posting the position and interviewing candidates, but logistically, they would have to promote from within because the director needs to have a vast knowledge of the current day to day operations immediately. Otherwise, it will set our schedules behind."

"I hope this works out for you…What are…"

Eric interrupted, "Professionally and financially, this would elevate me to a higher level."

"That would be fantastic!" Natalie chimed. Before Natalie's affair, the prospect of Eric's salary increases always aroused Natalie. For others, aphrodisiacs came in the form of food, drinks, or drugs. For Natalie, Eric's income increases served as an amatory. "You would be a lot sexier if you made more money," she would often tease him. Her obsession with Evan however, negatively affected her desire for her husband, and Eric's increases earnings no longer aroused her.

As Paolo poured the wine, Natalie glanced at her phone. She had placed it on silent and noticed she had three missed calls and a voicemail. All three missed calls were from the same number.

"Excuse me, Eric. I'm going to wash my hands." She didn't want to check her voicemail in front of Eric. She restricted the use of their phones at the table whether at home or a restaurant, so she didn't want to seem like a hypocrite by breaking one of her own rules. Overcome by an unsettling feeling as well as a sense of urgency to check the message, she headed to the restroom.

"Hello, this message is for Natalie Amini. This is Janice from the Tarzana Hospital. I'm calling on behalf of Evan Zarian. First, let me say that the situation is under control. Mr. Zarian had chest pains earlier this evening and was brought in by ambulance but is now free of pain and is in stable condition. The doctors are running additional tests. His emergency contact is out of town, and he asked that I contact you. You can reach one of the nurses here at…" Natalie transcribed the number left in the message.

At that moment, Natalie could not assess how to handle the situation appropriately. She was in a combined state of shock and concern. How would she excuse herself from dinner to go to the hospital to see Evan? She walked back to the table.

"Eric, I am so sorry, but I have a client emergency, and I need to handle it." Before she could say she would go to her office, she stopped herself. Everywhere she went, she was sure to run into someone she knew. She had run into acquaintances at the hospital before, so she had to tell Eric exactly where she was going. If necessary, she would have to play the therapist role. What would people think if they were to see her in the ER with a strange man? "I have to run over to Tarzana hospital. You want to take the car, and I can take an Uber?"

"No, no. You take the car. I will take the Uber. Is everything ok? You have never had to meet a patient at the hospital."

"Yes, everything is fine. But I must handle this now. I'm sorry."

Eric motioned Paolo over and asked that he bring them the check because they had to leave due to an emergency.

"You go on. I will see you back at home," he said. His mild-manner and empathy made her betrayal more difficult to bear.

"I'm sorry. I will make it up to you," Natalie said as she walked out of the restaurant in haste.

CHAPTER FOURTEEN
Bedside Manner (2015)

Evan lay in the ER bed attached to monitors and medical equipment. For the first time in his life, he was terrified. The cocksure manner he faced all aspects of his life with had been replaced by fear—fear of death, and worse, of dying alone. His feelings of invincibility had been stripped away in the last three hours, and each beep from the monitor was a reminder of his mortality.

Insecurity and indecisiveness which were foreign concepts to Evan were becoming familiar as he grappled with regret for having the hospital contact Natalie. Would she be angry at him for this presumptuous act? He had panicked in his moment of weakness. He didn't know who else to call. His family that consisted of his parents and his two siblings lived in Newport Beach. Years earlier when Evan had started to amass a fortune through his website business, Evan had bought his parents a home a couple of blocks away from the beach. The whole family had moved to Orange County. Evan's base was in Los Angeles, but he frequented his parent's home where he had a room dedicated solely to him. He couldn't have called them until he was sure that he was ok. He didn't want to put them through the agony of worrying about his health while attempting to drive up to Los Angeles – a ninety-minute trip which increased to a three-hour drive because of Friday evening traffic.

Would Natalie even show up? How would she manage to get away from her family? She was always concerned with protecting what was important to her, mostly at Evan's expense, repetitively reminding him that it was she who had the most to lose if they were found out. Evan often pondered about Natalie's argument. Discounting his feelings while stressing the sacrifice she made risking her family life was one-sided. It infuriated Evan that Natalie failed to take into consideration the sacrifice he was making in continuing his relationship with her. By doing so, he neglected to seek a committed relationship that could eventually blossom into a family of his own. It wasn't Natalie who had to go home to an empty house, or who had to sleep alone at night.

Four hours ago, when he sat at home alone watching TV and began gasping for air as his chest started to tighten, the first thought that came to mind was of Natalie, and how he was going to die alone with the possibility of being undiscovered for days. He was able to dial 911 because his cell phone which he usually left at the kitchen counter, incidentally happened to be next to him on the couch.

As he lay in the hospital bed, regret came over him for the direction his life had taken. Years of an unhealthy lifestyle inclusive of partying, drinking, and occasional cocaine use had finally caught up to him. He couldn't die at the age of forty-four. This was not the legacy he wanted to leave behind. He loved Natalie and wanted to start a life with her. He would take care of her and be prepared to do whatever was necessary to make any concessions to achieve as smooth of an adjustment for her children and Eric as possible. Sooner rather than later, he would confront Natalie with an ultimatum.

In the emergency room, Natalie identified herself as a friend of the patient. The nurse took her back to the exam room.

When she pulled back the curtain, she immediately noticed the sense of relief that overcame Evan.

"Evan, are you ok?"

"Natalie, thanks for coming. I didn't know who else to call. I'm sorry. I guess I panicked. Mike and Jeannine are the closest people I consider family, in L.A., and they are on vacation…"

"Evan, it's fine," Natalie interrupted, sensing that he was uncomfortable and unaccustomed to communicating his feelings. He had exposed his vulnerability at times when he expressed his feelings for her, but this was a different vulnerability—one where his sense of powerlessness was evident. Natalie put her hand on top of his hand and gave it a reassuring squeeze indicating she wasn't upset by his decision to contact her.

Before Natalie could continue, the ER doctor walked in.

"Mr. Zarian, your test results are here. Is this your significant other? Shall I proceed with the results, or would you prefer she leave the room?" The doctor asked looking at Natalie, with an air of caution before he proceeded with the outcome of the results.

"She is a friend. She can hear what you have to say."

"It seems as though you have early symptoms of cardiomyopathy. Your left ventricle is slightly enlarged. You had indicated daily nicotine and occasional cocaine use, which is the probable cause. However, I believe the effects can be reversible if you abstain from nicotine and narcotics. You seem otherwise healthy," the doctor declared, judgmentally. "We would like to keep you overnight for observations, to rule out the need for medications."

"Thank you, doctor," Evan replied slightly reassured.

"Sit tight, and we will make those arrangements for you," he said as he scurried out.

"I hope this is a wake-up call and you stop smoking and using cocaine altogether," Natalie said curtly.

"It is, and I will," Evan retorted. "I have meant to quit cigarettes, and as far as cocaine use, I only imbibe two to three times a month for the last twenty years. I didn't realize it would be that detrimental."

"Two to three times a month over twenty years is too much. Get your shit together!"

"No more cigarettes and coke, I promise," he said reassuringly. "Thank you for coming. I was about to lose my shit there for a minute."

"It's all right. I get it. I had to leave Eric at a restaurant when I got your message."

"Again, I'm sorry. I just panicked. You were the first person I thought of. It wasn't my intent to cause any suspicion."

"Don't worry about it. I'm just relieved you are fine," Natalie said, "I hate to leave you, but I think I better head home now. Text me your room number once they check you into a room. I will call and check up on you tomorrow morning. If they discharge you tomorrow, and I can slip away for a couple of hours, I will gladly drive you home." She looked over at the curtain to ensure that the two sides overlapped and did not have a visible gap so that they had complete privacy. She went over by him and kissed him softly on the lips.

"Promise me you will take care of yourself, Evan. I don't want to lose you," she said softly; her eyes were glistening as she fought back the tears.

As she began to pull away, Evan pulled her back in, so their foreheads were touching. A gesture that communicated his gratitude, admiration, and the hope that the duration of her visit would be lengthier. Yet, Natalie pulled away.

"Feel better; I have to go." Natalie drew one side of the curtain open. Her eyes widened in shock. For although a nurses' station separated the corridors, Natalie had a clear view of the room directly across Evan's. Across the way, she recognized Keon's wife, Roya, beside their fourteen-year-old daughter, Yasmine, as she lay on a gurney while a nurse attempted to evaluate her. Roya was visibly distressed and engrossed in her daughter's well-being so that she did not see Natalie. Natalie quickly drew the curtain closed.

"Shit! Shit! Shit!" She screamed in a whisper. "Fuck! Shit!" She closed her eyes and covered her temples and forehead with her hand indicating that she was extremely distressed.

She leaned over towards Evan and continued to whisper-scream, "Eric's dad's wife and his sister are in the room across the way! I can't get out until the curtain is completely closed!"

"Natalie, relax. There will be an opportunity for you to leave. Just chill," Evan was slightly agitated. "I can't believe you are stressing me out under these circumstances."

"Oh my God, Evan, I am sorry for being so selfish! I just freaked out when I saw her. I'm so sorry. You relax. I'm going to hang out with you for a while longer…until the coast is clear."

For the next several minutes, they sat quietly. Evan closed his eyes and pretended to nap while Natalie perused her emails on her smartphone. At that moment, she felt uneasy and embarrassed by her outburst. She had thoughtlessly troubled Evan, disregarding his fragile state to evade discovery. For the first time in two years, the silence between the two was uncomfortable. She sensed Evan's embitterment and wished she could expunge the episode from his memory.

"Evan? I really am sorry. Please forgive me for being insensitive."

He opened his eyes and cracked a smile, "I can't be angry at you, Nat. I adore you." He couldn't bring himself to utter the words, *I love you*, even though he was bursting at the seams with intense adulation towards her. He often wondered if Natalie realized the depth at which he was in love with her. Evan believed Natalie's attachment to him was emotional as well as physical. How would he be received when he presented her with an ultimatum? He was unsure as to whether Natalie would reciprocate his love. Natalie had made her position clear from the beginning. She would not abandon her family for him. Yet, for two years, he had hoped that her stance would soften. It wasn't her lack of feelings for him that prohibited her from leaving her husband, it was the guilt of destroying her family, even though she was committing the ultimate betrayal.

Natalie grabbed Evan's hand with both hands and held it up to her chest. "I adore you, too."

Just then she was startled by the sound of a nurse pulling back the curtain. She let go of his hand and turned to see a striking woman in scrubs approach Evan.

"Mr. Zarian, I'm Alexa. I will be your nurse for the rest of the evening. I'm taking over for Julie until we get you settled into one of the rooms upstairs. Is there anything I can get you to make you feel more comfortable?"

Evan could not contain his pleasure. Beautiful women always lifted his spirits, "Call me Evan, please," he said beaming. "Could I possibly get another pillow?"

"Of course," she said in a perky manner, "I'll be right back."

Natalie was slightly jealous of the fact that Alexa and Evan were a tad too flirtatious with one another. To add insult to injury, as Alexa propped the pillow behind Evan's head, she pressed her abundant bosom right up his face. Alexa was drop dead gorgeous. She had beautiful wavy medium brown bouncy hair and hazel eyes that gave her an exotic look. She stood 5 feet 5 inches tall and had a toned body. She looked fabulous even while sporting a pair of scrubs.

"Is that comfortable?" Alexa asked Evan seductively.

"Yes, thank you," Evan replied.

Alexa turned around, gave Natalie an innocent smile and walked out.

"If she was an inch closer, you could have motor-boated her," Natalie said in disdain.

"It's not my fault my nurse is flirting with me. Don't be jealous, Natalie. I'm not the one who has a spouse to go home to."

"It is your fault that you are encouraging her." Natalie peeked across the way to Yasmine's room. The curtain was completely closed, "And stop throwing it in my face that I'm married. You knew exactly what you were getting into when you got into this. I made my intentions clear from the get-go. Anyway, now that Florence Nightingale is here, you don't need me anymore. Good night!" And with that, Natalie stormed out of his ER room.

She walked down the corridor in haste, right before she opened the door to the Emergency Waiting Room someone from the other side opened them, and there she stood face to face with her father in law, Keon.

"Natalie, hello. What are you doing here?" He asked surprised to see Natalie at the ER. "Are Eric and the kids ok?"

Natalie's disdain for Keon tainted her judgment and clarity. She was always prepared to blame him or highlight his negative attributes and behaviors. She blatantly refused to see any good in him. Thus, she inaccurately interpreted his questioning as offensive. Whereas his questions stemmed from a natural concern of unexpectedly running into his daughter-in-law at the ER and logically inquiring about the well-being of his son and grandsons.

"Yes, Keon. They are fine. I am here for work, for a patient of mine. I can't discuss it any further…you know confidentiality laws and all," she replied curtly. Hopefully, he hadn't seen her with Evan. "And what brings you to the ER? I hope it's not serious."

She couldn't care less if he dropped dead before her, she was only going through the motions as civilized social conduct mandated her to do so. Societal etiquette norms often conflicted her. On the one hand, she wanted to behave like a civilized member of society. Yet, she was growing increasingly less tolerant of conforming to social protocol, particularly when it pertained to exchanging insincere pleasantries with people she disliked. Her preference was to cut all ties with these types of people, rather than to make nice. Eric and Natalie didn't see eye to eye when it came to their family's involvement with his father. Natalie didn't care to have herself or her children maintain a relationship with Keon, while Eric believed in the opposite. For even though Keon was a shitty father to Eric, it was the only father he had.

"Yasmine might have fractured her ankle during ballet practice. She is devastated. She had one of the leads in a recital coming up next month. She will miss it along with an opportunity to get evaluated and chosen for a summer ballet program run by a prominent ballet instructor that cultivates young, talented ballet dancers with the potential to become professional dancers," he said waiting for a gesture or words of sympathy.

Natalie was in awe as to how Keon had adapted to the role of a doting father with his second family. His lack of full-time paternal responsibility and devotion to his children from his first marriage dissipated concurrently with the dissolution of his marriage. Although he was still around, his presence as a father was flighty and inconsistent. While he was preoccupied with other facets of his life, he had the luxury of suspending his sense of responsibility for his children, disappearing for weeks, sometimes even months at a time. When it suited his needs, he played the role of the involved father. As minimal as his dedication to his first three children had become after his divorce, it became increasingly non-existent after his marriage to Roya and the subsequent births of their two children, Yasmine, fourteen, and Arman, ten.

While most men his age, were comfortably accepting their roles as grandfathers, Keon was still siring children, the core cause of Natalie's disdain for him. That Keon had married a woman he was unfaithful with during his first marriage and close in age to his eldest son, although frowned upon by his first family, could be overlooked. However, the fact that he continued to have children with his second wife after becoming a grandfather was distasteful. The whole thing had a Jerry Springer-ish feel to it that Natalie found embarrassing. Natalie would have no part of it.

Natalie's resentment towards Keon compounded because he lacked an interest in bonding with her children and intensified after the loss of her father. Her father could not tolerate a day where he was unable to see his grandchildren. These extremities in the relationships between her children and their two grandfathers further fueled her apathy for Keon. And while he agreed that his father should be more invested in his grandkids, he also argued that Keon was the only father he had, and she should be more accepting of him.

Regardless of all her negative feelings towards Keon, Natalie put forth an Oscar-winning performance, "I am so sorry about Yasmine's injury. I hope it isn't serious," Natalie placed her hand on Keon's shoulder. "Please give my best to Roya and the kids, I hope it works out for Yasmine." She planted a kiss on Keon's cheek and backed away. She smiled politely, and when he nodded in acknowledgment, she pushed open the door to the waiting room.

As Natalie turned away, she noticed Alexa staring at her with suspicion as she recorded the vitals of a patient just twenty feet from the entrance to the evaluation corridor. How much of her conversation with Keon had Alexa heard? Did she overhear her say that she was there for a patient? Thankfully, she was almost certain that Keon or anyone else in his family didn't see her in Evan's room. Natalie had spent more time at the emergency room than she had anticipated.

As Natalie pulled into the driveway of her home, she was alerted to a text message on her phone.

Room 114, the text read — nothing else. It was obvious that Evan was displeased that Natalie had just stormed out. As Evan and Alexa flirted, Natalie had become so overcome by envy and preoccupied with protecting her ego, that she disregarded Evan's medical emergency and just abandoned him. Although they were not part of Natalie's core characteristics, her narcissistic tendencies precluded her from admitting fault. Thus, she decided against apologizing to Evan, surmising that his flirtation was the root of their disagreement, oblivious of her insensitivity in the situation.

Feel better. She texted back, content that the minimum communication would suffice. She wouldn't console Evan or extend a second offer to take him home upon his release from the hospital. And with that, she headed inside her home to conjure up a story for Eric.

CHAPTER FIFTEEN
The Sleepover (2015)

The next morning Eric had fortuitously decided on a last-minute weekend outing, to take the boys to the tidal pools in Rancho Palos Verdes, then head over to Laguna Beach to visit his relatives. He decided that they would spend the night there and return Sunday afternoon. Natalie had graciously bowed out of the outing insisting that she had some work to catch up on. She felt guilty for not joining her family for what she was sure would be a memorable weekend, yet she believed the uneasiness brought upon by Evan's medical situation would burden her to the extent that she wouldn't be able to relax and enjoy the weekend away. She couldn't go away for the weekend without knowledge of Evan's well-being.

As soon as her family vacated the home, Natalie showered and headed over to the hospital. It was 10:30 when she walked into Evan's room, where a nurse was reviewing Evan's discharge instructions.

"Natalie," Evan said surprised to see her.

"I came by to give you a ride home in case they discharged you," she said.

"I just texted a friend to pick me up, but I will text him that I no longer need a ride."

"He's ready to go. He just needs a few minutes until the orderly is called to take him down with a wheelchair," the nurse replied.

"I don't need a wheelchair," Evan retorted politely.

"I understand, but it's hospital policy," the nurse said, clearly irritated as she walked out of his room.

"It seems some of the nurses here can resist your charms.," Natalie said arrogantly, "I take it all is well since you the doctor discharged you?"

"Yes. I will not die today, at least not of cardiovascular disease," he said coldly.

"Good," Natalie said, "I'm pleased to hear that."

On the way home, they drove in silence both simmering in their own juices; waiting for the other to bring up the discussion regarding their disagreement. Finally, Evan began to scold Natalie for her inappropriate behavior the night before.

"Natalie, I don't understand you. You won't leave your husband, yet you expect me to be fully committed to you to the point that you punish me for innocently flirting with some random woman."

"I don't expect you to be committed to me. I am fully aware of the fact that we are not monogamous, but I don't expect you to flaunt your flirtations with other women under my nose!"

"On the contrary, the conditions that you have placed on our relationship is a constant reminder of your husband.

You are a total hypocrite," he said angrily. "You are constantly flaunting your marriage under my nose!"

"What do you expect? Should I let Eric in on our affair? Should I ask him for his blessing to fuck another man on the side?" Natalie retaliated.

"No, but I want you to consider leaving him to give our relationship a shot seriously. And you are wrong. I am monogamous to you, *emotionally* for the most part. Not physically. But what do you expect? That I forgo any chance of finding someone I click with and having a family of my own in the event you decide to stay with Eric?" There was a long pause, and before Natalie could speak Evan continued, "Look, what happened last night shook me to my core. I thought I was going to die in my home. And the worst part of it was that I thought I would die alone. You were the only person I hoped to see at that very moment… I love you, Natalie."

Natalie was no longer remiss, "I'm sorry, Evan. I never really considered our relationship from your point of view. I don't want to hurt you. I love you, too…but I still have a family."

Natalie could sense Evan's softened stance growing into frustration when she reminded him of her family. Her intention was not to infuriate him but to appeal to his sense of logic.

"Evan, please be patient with me. I do love you; it's just that I have an obligation to my family. I promise that I will seriously consider leaving Eric, give me some more time. And if you do meet someone you'd consider having a serious relationship with, promise me that you would give me fair warning. I would hate to lose you abruptly. I can't imagine not spending Tuesday afternoons with you."

"Do you ever consider anyone else's feelings but your own, Natalie?"

Natalie couldn't argue with Evan any longer. He had some valid points, and he reiterated what she often thought to herself—that she was a selfish asshole.

"I don't want to upset you. Let's get you home."

For the next five minutes, Evan navigated as Natalie drove through the hills of Tarzana. He directed her to go up a private driveway to a beautifully landscaped exterior leading to a modern home.

"Why don't you park in the carport? Your family is not home, so..."

"No, I better head back home and catch up on some work," she couldn't face him.

"I'd like it if you stayed a while," he said as he caressed her cheek until her eyes met his gaze.

"I'd like that, "she said as he leaned in and gently kissed her.

Evan and Natalie made their way to the front door when he realized he didn't have a chance to grab his keys the night before. He had instructed his neighbor who had come to Evan's after he noticed the ambulance go up the driveway to lock his house and leave through the garage, as the paramedics were preparing to take him to the hospital.

"I have to gain access through the garage keypad. I don't have my house keys. You stay here. I will let you in from the front door." Less than a minute later, Evan unlocked the front door. His modern home was exquisite but very masculine. The presence of a woman's aesthetic would add warmth, yet she was still very impressed.

"Your home is beautiful, Evan."

"Just think, if you leave Eric it could be your home, too," he said facetiously. "I'm going to jump in the shower and get this hospital grime off me. Why don't you order some Thai food off that menu and make yourself at home?"

Natalie reviewed the menu and placed an order. She made herself comfortable on the sofa in the den adjacent to the kitchen and attempted to work the remote control. After several unsuccessful attempts, she lost interest in the television and sauntered to Evan's room. She walked over to the patio door to admire the view from his bedroom, which was stunning. The sound of running water from the shower stopped, and within a few minutes, Evan emerged from the bathroom.

He was unusually cheerful, content to be in his domain with the woman he loved. His body wrapped only in a towel from the waist down glistened with moisture. He pulled out a pair of underwear from a drawer and headed into his enviable walk-in closet.

Just then, the doorbell rang.

"That was fast," he said, "Could you get that, Nat? It must be the Thai food. Grab some cash from my wallet," he said as he pointed to a distressed, leather Ferragamo wallet on the dresser. "Give him a good tip. I always order from this place."

Natalie grabbed Evan's wallet and headed to the front door. Her smile distorted as her lips pursed in disdain in reaction to the uninvited guest that stood before her. The guest's face immediately became flushed as she had not anticipated being greeted by anyone other than Evan.

"Nurse Alexa?" Natalie asked, "What are you doing here?"

Flustered, Alexa defensively answered, "Evan forgot his sunglasses in the ER, so I came by to drop them off."

"Why wouldn't you have someone from the hospital call him and tell him to come pick them up?" Natalie asked suspiciously.

"I noticed they were expensive, so I held on to them and decided to drop them off personally."

"How did you know where Evan lives?" Natalie asked haughtily.

"I looked it up on the computer," Alexa replied sheepishly.

"That is extremely unprofessional," Natalie began to preach. "How dare you look up confidential patient information…"

"You want to discuss professionalism?" Alexa interrupted. "I heard you tell that man that you were at the hospital to see a patient," Alexa sanctimoniously retorted, "If Evan is your patient, I'd say you have crossed the lines of professionalism as well."

"Look, I don't know what you thought you heard, but Evan and I are good friends. He even disclosed that to the doctor when I came in last night. Since you are so adept at looking up information that doesn't concern you, you might want to check his ER report for that. Furthermore, if you don't leave this minute, and forget you ever crossed paths with Evan, I will file a report with the hospital against you for an invasion of privacy. I don't know who you think you are, but..."

Again, she was interrupted by Alexa, "You'd have a hard time proving it."

"Oh yeah, you see those cameras up there?" Natalie said pointing to the security cameras perched strategically outside the home. Although the cameras had given her an unsettling feeling because they provided concrete evidence of her visit to Evan's home when she noticed them upon her arrival, they now provided her with ammunition against this presumptuous bitch that stood before her.

"Keep your boyfriend on a leash! He shouldn't send mixed signals," she said as she threw Evan's sunglasses at Natalie and hastily walked to her car.

"Mind your own fucking business, hussy!" Natalie yelled, as Alexa flipped her off and drove away.

"Who were you yelling at?" Evan asked as he walked over to the door while he pulled a t-shirt over his head, "Not the Thai delivery service, I hope!"

"Looks like you have a stalker situation with your nurse friend," Natalie said as she handed over his sunglasses, "She dropped these off for you. Said they were expensive, so she preferred to bring them to you personally. She looked up your address in the hospital computer." Evan laughed as he took the sunglasses. "It's not funny, Evan. She was snooping around while I had a conversation with Eric's dad. She heard me tell him I was seeing a patient." She turned to face him.

What had transpired between the two after Natalie's departure that would prompt Alexa to drop by Evan's home unannounced?

"What would you have done if I wasn't here? Let her in and fuck her?"

"No. I think it would weird me out if Alexa showed up at my house," he explained as he drew Natalie to him. His hands were clasped together behind her waist as he pulled her closer and gazed into her eyes, "I'm glad you are here.

There is no one I would prefer to be with at this very moment than you." They kissed softly, but passionately. When he stopped for breath, he exhaled deeply and touched his forehead to hers, "I love you, Natalie. I meant what I said. I want you to leave Eric."

Before Natalie could grace him with a response, the doorbell chimed. *Ahh, saved by the bell,* she thought.

"That must be the Thai food," he said, "Do you have my wallet?"

Natalie walked over to the counter and picked up his wallet, "Here you are."

Shortly after that, Evan returned and placed two bags atop the kitchen island. He approached Natalie and began to kiss her again. As he kissed her, he slowly backed her towards the den, then the hallway and then to his bedroom, until he gently pushed her on the bed. He stood at the side of the bed and pulled his t-shirt off. She admired his upper body while she ran her hand down his chest. When she reached his waist, she pulled him by his belt onto the bed. He was on top of her now. She felt protected and safe, blanketed by his body. He stared into her eyes.

"I let you get away the first time, but now that you are in my life again, I won't let you get away. It feels like you belong here."

Natalie held Evan tight, as the two kissed. For the next hour, they made love, gently and tenderly. Evan had collapsed on top of Natalie. His head lay on her chest as she softly stroked his hair, intoxicated by her scent, her touch, and the feel of her skin against his.

"I love you, Natalie," he said. As her fingertips grazed his head and shoulders, electric impulses radiated throughout his body, pulsating from his head to his toes. If he died then and there, he would be content.

"I love every second of every minute of every hour I spend with you," Natalie responded. "Sometimes I wish I could freeze time and spend days with you. You make me feel alive. I look forward to the week because I know come Tuesday, I will see you again. Without our Tuesdays, my life would be aimless."

He reluctantly pulled away from Natalie and rolled off the bed. He slipped on his jeans.

"I'll be back."

Natalie smiled. She clasped her hands around the edge of the bed sheet and pulled it up to her décolletage. She stretched and sighed. Euphoric by this glimpse into this potential idealistic life with Evan, she felt elated. Could she leave Eric for Evan? She would seriously have to consider this matter; judiciously weighing the pros and cons before making a final decision. Was it worth sacrificing her happiness for the sanctity of her family? Was the essence of Evan's appeal contingent on the forbidden aspect of the relationship, or a deeply rooted bond shared between the two? That was the part she struggled with.

Natalie had never been a romantic. She preferred lust to romance. This absence of romantic inclinations enabled her to develop what she perceived to be a practical interpretation of marriage. People are emotionally and physically attracted to each other. They connect on both levels and may choose to marry. Eventually, the excitement fades, giving way to the development of different types of attachment bonds. If Evan and Natalie were to get together, they would eventually come across the same problems couples deal with daily. The novelty of their relationship would wear off; the sense of mystery would disappear. Ultimately, passion would be sacrificed for partnership. Why couldn't he understand that their relationship was better this way, that he was able to fulfill desires that her husband could not? Two years into their affair, her yearning for Evan was as intense as ever.

Evan returned holding a tray with plates, silverware and the cartons of Thai food. He placed the tray on a coffee table in the sitting area of his bedroom. Natalie sat up and began to tuck the sheet behind her. She got up, wrapped and adjusted the sheet further, and made her way to the bedroom sitting area, where Evan now sat and served healthy portions of the Thai specialties on his plate. Natalie dipped a spring roll in the apricot sauce and took a nibble.

"I wish you could stay tonight," Evan said as he took a bite of chicken satay. He had proposed getaways for the two on several occasions, but Natalie had never been receptive for fear of getting caught. This visit was the first time in two years that Natalie had been to his home.

"Actually…Eric and the boys will not be returning until tomorrow afternoon," Natalie replied coyly, "I guess I could stay." She assessed the threat of being discovered and surmised it was low-risk. "I'll text Eric that I am out with friends and won't be home until late in case he tries to get a hold of me."

"For real? I was making a hypothetical statement." Evan hadn't expected Natalie to oblige, so he was truly astounded when she complied with his request. He realized his answer might imply dissatisfaction with her response, so he quickly added, "I would like it if you stayed, though," exalted by the prospect of Natalie being an overnight guest. "What do you want to do first?"

"For starters, I would love to take a bath," Natalie said.

"Ok, you go ahead, while I clear up these dishes. Do you mind if I join you in a bit?"

"Not at all. I'd love it, in fact," Natalie said as she bounced off the couch. Halfway to the bathroom, she turned back. Draped in a bed sheet strategically exposing enough skin to leave Evan wanting more, she brushed away a lock of her sexily tousled hair from her face, and seductively asked, "Do you have an unopened toothbrush by chance?"

"Yes, top drawer on the right next to the sink closest to the door," Evan laughed, as what he thought would be a sexual proposition was an exaggerated request for a toothbrush. "Fresh towels are in the cupboard on the top shelf."

Natalie scooped up the sheet and made her way into the bathroom. She gathered her hair on the top of her head and secured it with a rubber band. She found the drawer that contained several unopened packs of toothbrushes. Either Evan was serious about oral hygiene, or unexpected, overnight guests frequented his home. The latter was the more plausible explanation for the abundance of packaged, unopened toothbrushes stored in his bathroom drawer. She brushed her teeth as she waited for the tub to fill. She poured some liquid body soap in the bath for bubbles. When she was satisfied with the water level, she climbed into the giant tub. Her eyelids closed, as she reclined to a comfortable position. She couldn't recall the last time she felt this relaxed.

Ten minutes later, Evan joined her. He climbed into the tub behind her and placed his arms around her waist. She leaned back against his chest. It didn't take long for her to feel his erection. He slowly inched his hands up to her breasts and cupped them, while he kissed the back of her neck. As his hands moved down her torso, to her thighs then back up again he began to fondle her. Natalie's arm reached behind so that her hand clasped his head while they kissed.

Past sexual experiences had marred Natalie's affinity for aquatic copulation. She found having sex in the water to be a cumbersome task, yet entertained Evan's attempts to penetrate her in the tub. After losing the rhythm of his strokes due to buoyancy for the third time, he became frustrated.

"Get up," he commanded as he stood up after Natalie got up. He wrapped a nearby towel around Natalie and grabbed another for himself. He stepped out of the tub and held his hand out to help Natalie out. "Let's move to the bed."

Surrendering to Evan was never difficult. The more unrestricted and uninhibited they were, the more intensely they connected. An hour later, both lay on their backs in total fatigue, panting, drenched in perspiration—the aftermath of their rigorous carnal festivities.

"You're not going to have a heart attack on me, are you?" Natalie asked initially jesting yet contemplating the possibility of such an occurrence as a result of his visit to the emergency room the prior night.

"You are just as out of breath as I am," Evan retorted, "it wouldn't be a bad way to go." He adjusted the pillows against the headboard and leaned into them. Natalie scooted up beside him. Evan turned the television on and scrolled through the channel guide.

"Oohh, *Fatal Attraction* is on. Let's watch that! I haven't seen it in like twenty years."

"Ok..." Evan replied unenthusiastically. "It might give me some ideas. Do your kids have a rabbit?"

"No, hamsters. And I wouldn't mind if you boiled them," Natalie said. "They are vicious little shits."

They spent the rest of the afternoon in bed watching the movie. As the credits rolled, Evan leaned over and opened his nightstand drawer. He popped a Viagra in his mouth and chased it down with a swig of water.

"I don't think you should be taking a Viagra after last night," Natalie protested.

"It's fine," he said. "It would be a wasted opportunity if I didn't. It's not even 7:00 yet. We have all night."

Natalie was uneasy about his decision, but she consented to his choice in consideration for his insatiable appetite for her. After all, this was the first and only time in two years that the two would spend together overnight.

The two had been engaged in another round of intercourse for about twenty minutes when Natalie nudged Evan that she wanted to get on top. Evan held on to her as he artfully rolled to his side then on his back and propped her on top, without pulling out. Natalie adjusted herself slightly and began to ride Evan; slowly at first then more intensely grinding deeper. It seemed that the two were in such a deep, metaphysical trance that Natalie was barely able to comprehend anything beyond her current state of blissful being. So, when Evan began to groan in discomfort, Natalie was initially oblivious to the fact that he needed medical attention. She became aware thirty seconds later when his upper body contorted then stiffened to a rigid position, which in turn caused her to disengage from their physical "connection." As he clutched his chest, his facial expressions, which moments earlier revealed a state of ecstatic pleasure, transformed into a distressed grimace.

"Evan! What's happening?" Natalie frantically asked as she dismounted Evan.

"I think I'm having a heart attack," Evan replied.

"Oh my God! Oh my God!" Natalie exclaimed, almost immediately exhibiting her inability to perform under duress.

"Natalie, I need you to calm down and call 911." Natalie pulled herself together as best she could when she realized the irony of the situation, where Evan, the victim in this state of emergency, was attempting to calm her down.

Natalie grabbed the phone and dialed 911. She paced back and forth as she waited for an operator.

"This is 911 what's your emergency."

"My boyfriend. He is having a heart attack." She grabbed Evan's ID from his wallet and relayed his address.

"Is he conscious?"

"Yes."

"Ok, keep an eye on him, and make sure he is awake and breathing while I take your info."

"Where is he?"

"He's in his bed. I think he had a heart attack while we were having sex," Natalie admitted guiltily.

"Is he on drugs?"

"He took a Viagra...Evan, stay with me!" Natalie exclaimed as Evan appeared to be losing consciousness.

"He is unconscious!" Natalie managed to blurt out as she tried suppressing her crying from becoming hysterical sobs.

"I need you to check if he is breathing. You need to calm down and follow my instructions. Maintaining calm is of utmost importance right now. It could make all the difference in the situation you are in." Natalie managed to calm down and listen to the directions provided by the 911 operator.

The invasive questions and first aid instructions continued until the sounds of sirens advanced, and there was a pounding at the door. Natalie hadn't realized that in all the commotion, she had neglected to get herself dressed. She was still naked, but she couldn't waste time letting the paramedics in the home. She quickly grabbed a bath towel and wrapped it around her, as she scurried to the front door and led the paramedics to Evan.

Natalie couldn't remember the last time she had felt so mortified. There she stood, wrapped in a bath towel, in a room of a half a dozen fully clothed, uniformed men, deluging her with questions. The whole scenario precluded Natalie from focusing; she was scatter-brained.

Sensing her humiliation, one of the older firefighters who appeared to be the highest ranking of the unit approached Natalie and gently said, "I understand this situation might be a little uncomfortable, but time is of the essence. The sooner we can get some answers to some pertinent questions, the sooner you will be able to get dressed."

Natalie complied with the Captain's request. After several minutes, she was finally relieved from her obligation to report the evening's activities to the paramedics. She grabbed her clothes and proceeded to the bathroom. Her heart raced. She couldn't leave Evan alone; she would have to accompany him to the hospital. After she dressed, the gravity of the situation began taking its hold, realizing that Evan could die. Her knees felt wobbly, and her stomach began to churn. She felt the heat radiating her cheeks. Moments later, she was projectile vomiting into the toilet. She brushed her teeth and went back out to the bedroom. The paramedics were hovering around Evan. He was stable but still unconscious.

The captain approached her once again. She dreaded what she was about to tell him. Before he could speak, she interrupted.

"Captain, there is no right way to go about this, so I am just going to come out and say it," she whispered, "I am a married woman. This man is not my husband. I was hoping to keep my name out of any reports for the sake of discretion. While I understand the gravity of the situation, if this were made public and my husband was to find out, it would definitely tear my family apart."

The captain's eyes widened in surprise, but he attempted to maintain a level of professionalism, "I understand, and we will do our best to conceal your identity. I can't make any promises, though," he responded attempting to obscure the judgmental tone in his voice.

He walked away and whispered something to another paramedic. She didn't need a scarlet letter to identify her as an adulterer; the scarlet flush of embarrassment in her cheeks was enough.

As the paramedics were moving Evan onto a gurney, Natalie quickly did a check of Evan's home, room by room, looking for unlocked doors and windows. By the time the home was secured, the paramedics wheeled Evan's gurney to the ambulance. She was instructed to meet them at the hospital.

Although the likelihood of encountering an acquaintance was highly probable, the thought had evaded her conscience for the time being. She eventually made her way to the ER. When she checked in at the ER, the nurse, denied Natalie entry.

"I'm afraid visitors for Mr. Zarian are restricted for the moment. The doctor will provide you with an update as soon as he can."

Natalie found a seat in the ER, and completely zoned out as she waited. The sounds from the TV, the conversations of the others in the waiting room all sounded like jumbled white noise. All the activity around her appeared as though it were occurring at light speed, apart from her activity, which seemed exaggeratedly sluggish. She felt detached. Had the distress caused her to hallucinate?

She had been sitting silently for over an hour when the doctor opened the ER waiting room door and called out,

"For patient Evan Zarian?"

"Yes, that would be me!" She said as she hurriedly gathered her purse and jacket and walked over.

"Come with me, please," he motioned for her to go through a quiet hallway and in private room.

"Where is Evan?"

"Please have a seat."

"What is going on?" Natalie asked impatiently.

"I'm afraid Mr. Zarian didn't make it. I'm very sorry. We tried everything we could. He died as a result of myocardial ischemia." The doctor continued to speak, but

Natalie couldn't comprehend what he was saying. The announcement blindsided her, and she felt as though the doctor sucker-punched her. She stood up in a daze and walked to the door.

Through the glass square in the door, Natalie could see law enforcement officers out in the corridor speaking to Alexa. Her heart began to palpitate as she realized that Alexa was attempting to implicate Natalie in Evan's death.

"The EMTs stated that the two were involved in an extra-marital affair. You need to question her. It's quite possible that she hesitated to contact emergency units for fear of being discovered. Mr. Zarian could have survived if she acted more expeditiously. Her negligence might be the cause of his death."

Natalie could not believe what she was witnessing. Surely, that nefarious woman wasn't incriminating her!?!

As she opened the door, Alexa looked her way, pointed, and said, "There she is. She is negligent! She needs to be questioned."

The officers walked towards Natalie and attempted to guide her back to the private room.

She pushed back and yelled, "Don't you dare touch me! What is the meaning of this?"

"Ma'am, we have a couple of questions for you. The deceased had a heart attack while the two of you were engaging in consensual sex?"

"Yes," Natalie responded in an irritated but low voice.

"And did this sexual intercourse involve any unconventional or risky activities?"

"NO! Absolutely, not!"

"You respond as if our questioning slights you. Your manner implies that we are insulting your moral character and that the audacity of us questioning your innocence is preposterous. Yet, you are guilty of adultery. If you are an adulterer, then you are not of the upstanding character that you are purporting to make yourself out to be. Unless you want us to throw your ass in jail, then I would suggest you cooperate!"

With the exception of the hospital staff busy with emergency duties that very moment, the entire corridor of staff, patients, and visitors attentively watched the scene between the two police officers and Natalie.

"You can't talk to me like that!" Natalie demanded, "I have rights!"

"Your husband has the right to have a spouse who isn't a whore!" Yelled one of the bystanders.

"You killed your lover! You probably waited around before calling 911," chimed Alexa.

Just then the crowd forming around Natalie was being parted. Someone was trying to make their way to Natalie.

It was Keon, "I knew you were hiding something yesterday! Fancy that! The pot calls the kettle black!"

"Whore!"

"Murderer!"

"Hypocrite!"

Insult after insult was hurled at Natalie by the bystanders—all of whom were total strangers—EMTs, nurses, doctors, and visitors, except for Keon. She was at the receiving end of a witch hunt. And as the crowd cinched around her closer and closer, Natalie began to hyperventilate and gasp for air.

"Natalie! Wake up!" Natalie, startled by the sound of gunshots from the TV, opened her eyes to see Glen Close's character mortally wounded slide down the bathroom wall leaving a trail of blood splatter against the white tiles. "You fell asleep during the movie. I didn't want to wake you up, but it seemed like you had a bad dream," Evan said.

Evan! He is alive and well! It was just an unpleasant dream!

"It was horrible," Natalie said, "which reminds me…" She rolled over Evan and jumped out of bed. She pulled open the nightstand drawer and rummaged around for bottles but couldn't find any.

"What are you doing? What are you looking for?" Evan asked with increasing suspicion.

Natalie ignored him and stormed into the bathroom. Evan followed her. She pushed open the medicine cabinet and found a bottle of Viagra. She proceeded to the toilet and dumped the entire contents of the bottle in the bowl.

"Natalie, what the hell are you doing?" He asked angrily.

"Evan, you died. In my dream, you took Viagra, we had sex, and you died! And everyone accused me of being a murderous whore!"

"Natalie, it was just a dream," Evan said attempting to conceal his laughter, "Relax. I'm fine."

"Well, it felt real! And I don't want to take any chances!" Natalie exclaimed. After disposing of the pills in the toilet, Natalie returned to bed.

"Natalie, I get that you are freaked out by what has happened to me, but I am fine."

He coaxed Natalie back in his arms, and as her head rested on Evan's chest, she heard the thumping of his heartbeat. The swooshing sound was comforting to

Natalie; it gave her an inexplicable sense of reassurance that his heart was in proper working order.

"Just promise me that you will stay away from Viagra, for a while, until your doctor clears it," Natalie requested.

"I can do that," Evan said, "Promise me you will seriously consider leaving Eric already. I think you are extremely unfair to him, and us."

"I can do that," Natalie managed to mutter, uncertain herself if her pledge held any merit.

The next couple of hours felt as though time had been suspended for Natalie and Evan. The two enjoyed conversing with one another without any time limitations. The little time allotted to spend together each week kept their discussions interesting and meaningful, with both eager to share some aspect of their everyday lives to maintain a connection with one another. Today was a different story. They had all the time in the world.

For Natalie, the evening felt as though she had walked through a doorway to life in a parallel universe that was as natural to her as her life with Eric was. She had a place in Evan's world. She couldn't deny how normal it felt despite the deception and duplicity. The roles she assumed separately with Eric and Evan somehow contented the needs that were otherwise unfulfilled in each of the opposing roles of the dutiful wife and the desirous lover.

Although Natalie had been an optimist for most of her life, her thoughts and dreams were balanced by her equally pragmatic approach to life. She believed that the possibilities in life were endless and abundant—provided one put himself on a path rather than relying on direction or input from external influences to instigate or motivate. The dichotomous nature of her character at sometimes presented her with an existential crisis. *Who was she, really?* She often thought. Was she an idealist or a realist? Could she be both without contradicting herself? She struggled with these extreme differences in her personality.

Her attempts to suppress her anxiety and guilt to conceal her other life were short-lived. The negative thoughts would often resurface from the unconscious, stirring up uneasiness from within, manifesting itself into physiological symptoms of a sense of suffocation and tightness in the chest. It was obvious to Natalie that the stress of her affair was affecting her health, slowly eroding her mental well-being as well as the physical. For as long as she experienced the elation from the highs of being with Evan, she conversely experienced the despair of her betrayal to Eric—a reality that heavily weighed down on her.

These constant remorseful thoughts and rationalizations influenced her decisions. She often believed that any negative experience that came her way was well-deserved karmic retribution. The bliss she found through her extra-marital affair could not go unchecked. She would pay the price. The universe would correct itself. The same delightful occurrence that caused her heart to skip a beat in excitement also triggered the tightness and pain in her chest resulting from the stress of her burden.

Guided by this thought process, an overwhelming sense of uneasiness crept over Natalie. Whereas minutes earlier she felt relaxed, her mind now began to wander. She contemplated reversing her decision to stay the night. Her fill of pleasure was satiated. She would now repent as the guilt resulting from the aftermath of her actions overcame her.

"Evan, I truly enjoyed spending all day with you, but I think it's best I get back home. If Eric or one of the kids were to try to get a hold of me, and I couldn't answer…"

"I get it, Natalie. It's ok. Just think about what I said," Evan retorted. In his heart, he was certain that Natalie was close to leaving Eric; certain that the angst that overcame her at the mention of Eric was a result of her waning patience resulting from the dual roles that were demanded of her because of her hapless marriage and how it interfered and imposed on their interludes. He was unaware that Natalie's anxiety was a result of her angst over her deception to her family and the fear of being discovered.

As Natalie drove back home, she wondered if she had made the right decision by refusing Evan's invitation to stay overnight. Before the guilt-induced stress overcame her, she couldn't deny that her time spent with Evan was nothing less than pleasant. She realized that she didn't even think of her family while she enjoyed the day in Evan's company. For a brief moment, she detached from her identity as wife and mother. She was able to reside at the moment only as Evan's lover. As she began to second-guess her decision whether her sudden departure was justified, all doubts disappeared when she pulled into her driveway only to find Eric's car parked in its spot in the garage. Eric and the boys had returned home contrary to their original plans. As the garage door opened causing the light inside to illuminate the dark driveway. Natalie literally and figuratively, *saw the light*.

Temporary detachment wasn't the solution; change was.

CHAPTER SIXTEEN
Signs (2015)

I f Natalie was to find inner-peace and free herself of the cumbersome feelings of guilt to carry on with a clear conscience; she would have to choose between her husband and lover. Deferring her obligation to decide between her two lives was no longer an option. She had to stop being unfair to Evan and Eric. She had to choose while she was still able to maintain a sense of control.

If she decided to leave Eric now while no one knew of her indiscretion, she could eventually introduce Evan as a post-separation suitor. She would probably have the upper hand in the matter of custody of her children. While she believed Eric loved his children, she thought he could be neglectful when they were left in his charge, neglectful not in an abusive way, but one in which he was guided by his too lax attitude to keep to schedules pertaining to the children's feeding, sleeping, and chores. Often, when Natalie returned home from a brief out of town departure, she found the rhythm of her household clock out of balance. Eric's reluctance to adhere to the rules where the children were concerned was unacceptable to Natalie. If it were known that she was an adulteress, perhaps a judge wouldn't find Eric's irresponsible behavior as reprehensible.

Natalie's point was demonstrated when she came home to discover Eric and the kids passed out on the couch, TV blaring, dressed in the same clothes that they had left in that morning. It was obvious that the kids hadn't showered. Hence, her decision to leave them on the couch rather than move them to their beds. Two days earlier, she had replaced all bed linens with fresh ones, as she had done every Thursday morning before the housekeeper came to clean the house during her recurrently scheduled Thursday morning appointment for as long as she lived at her home. If the kids went to bed, without showering, and in their play clothes, they would soil the sheets with "street germs." A term Natalie coined to describe anything that came into contact with anything outside the home. Natalie would have to change the sheets before schedule. Eric's disregard for Natalie's house rules and the additional, *unscheduled* work it would cause infuriated Natalie

Fucking slob, she thought to herself. It was difficult to respect Eric when she harbored so much resentment towards him. It was as if he purposely went out of his way to exasperate her temper. She didn't comprehend why it was difficult for him to comply with her requests to maintain order in the household. It would make his life so much easier to have a wife that didn't fantasize about swinging a baseball bat to his head at least a couple of times a week. Did he expect her to take care of everything while his only task was to go to work? Or did he think that he would absolve himself of responsibility by being neglectful? Either way, the result was the same for Natalie. Eric's behavior made him out to be a total douchebag who neglected his duties and overburdened his wife with household work and business.

These were the times when Natalie believed she could bring herself to leave Eric, particularly when he exhibited this type of carelessness. Eric was intelligent enough to realize that his behavior was unacceptable; it baffled Natalie. Awareness was the most powerful motivation in one's attempt to change or avoid behaviors. Eric was aware, yet he continued to behave in a manner that infuriated her and compounded the resentment she felt towards him.

Regardless of her feelings for Eric, Natalie had made the right choice in returning home. Had she shown up in the morning, she would have had to add a layer of deception. In the morning, she learned that the boys did not want to spend the night at Eric's cousin's home. Ten-year-old Aidan was eager to return home to his Sony Playstation where he would meet his friends, in real time, in the virtual world known as Minecraft. Alan preferred to go home because he missed his mother and his hamsters. It was reassuring to know that she was missed by her youngest child, even if her son shared the same sentiment for his pet rodents.

Eric and the boys had woken up to find they had spent the entire night in the family room, each one of them sprawled out on various parts of the sectional. Natalie had not woken them up so that they would sleep in their beds, but she was considerate enough to place a blanket on all three of them. This way she wouldn't have to spend the morning changing and laundering three sets of bed sheets. Washing three blankets and wiping down the couch was a more palatable task for a Sunday morning.

"Why didn't you wake us up when you got home?" Eric asked as he brought Natalie a cup of coffee, the next morning.

"You all looked so peaceful, I didn't want to disturb your sleep," she said trying to take the higher road by not scolding him for the state she found them in; but she could not resist. He knew she disapproved of the boys sleeping in their beds before they showered. "Also, you didn't have the boys shower; they were covered in street germs. If I woke you up, you would all have to shower before going into bed."

"The boys were tired," he protested, "What kind of a mother forces her kids to shower while they are half asleep? Are you going to flip out if you find wire hangers in their closets, next?"

Natalie didn't appreciate the reference to Mommie Dearest. The audacity to immediately label Natalie as a compulsive control freak was not well received. Eric's total disregard for his contribution to the conflict, as well as the absence of the realization that all this could have been avoided if he just followed the established house rules, caused Natalie to lash out.

"Then bring them back home promptly so that they aren't too tired to shower," Natalie retaliated. "Follow the SIMPLE rules of the house! Rules are necessary to maintain order."

"Or what?!" Eric yelled rhetorically, "The chaos of street germs will be unleashed in your house?" He said, mocking her for her slight obsession with cleanliness.

"Yes," Natalie replied calmly. "This is how I want to run my home. Free of street germs."

"It's our home, and not only are you subjecting everyone else to your obsessive-compulsive behavior, but you are asking us to accept it and enable you."

"What's the alternative?" Natalie asked as she hurriedly got out of bed and wrapped her robe around her. "Should we keep the rest of the home as you keep your office? Like a pig sty?" The condition of Eric's office was incongruent to the pristine condition of the rest of the house. When first-time visitors asked Natalie for a tour of her home, she always by-passed Eric's office, telling her guests that the state of Eric's office was not representative of the rest of her home.

Eric had decided years ago, that the cleaning lady would not have access to his office. He assumed the role of cleaning up his office every couple of months. Natalie went into his office only when necessary. The room resembled that of a college student's living room rather than the office of a respectable businessman in his forties. She never hid vocalizing her repulsion when she did enter his domain, so he preferred that she stay out.

"You are crazy," he retorted calmly. His cool and composed demeanor further incensed Natalie. She picked up a heavy candle and hurled it across the room where Eric stood. Eric darted out of its trajectory just in time. The candle hit the wall so hard; it left behind a crescent-shaped indent at the point of impact. Eric examined the damage and shook his head.

"That could have done some serious damage if it hit me. I think you should stop obsessing over germs and focus on your temper. It could be much more harmful to you in the long run." And with that, he walked out of the room.

****

A few days later, Natalie and Eric were still reeling from their argument. They had spent most of the week avoiding each other, resorting to minimal civil contact in the presence of the children. That Tuesday, Evan and Natalie were unable to meet due to parent-teacher conferences at the kids' school. Although disappointed, Natalie was slightly relieved to evade Evan's attempts to persuade her to accept his ultimatum. She was confused by the mental and emotional back and forth of trying to decide upon and reconcile her feelings about leaving Eric. She rationalized that the argument between herself and Eric served as a reminder that their relationship was dysfunctional. The two continued to have less in common and grew further apart. Was this a sign that she should leave? Or was she unwilling to let go of the ill-will resulting from their last confrontation to convince herself to leave, disabling her from making a truly objective verdict; tainting her decision from the impartiality she sought in choosing the correct path? The clarity she sought became more convoluted as she examined her conundrum from various aspects and viewpoints. True to form, she was complicating the issue by overthinking things through.

On Friday, Natalie had dinner plans with Ellen. After that eventful workshop where she had reconnected with Evan, Ellen and Natalie had maintained regular contact.

Once a month, the two would meet up for dinner. Six months into their friendship, at a dinner party at Ellen's, the two realized that they shared a common fiend, Melanie. Natalie and Melanie had met in junior high school when Melanie started her freshman year at Natalie's school. They had become good friends, and maintained their friendship through adulthood, seeing each other and their families regularly. The ladies served as each other's bridesmaids at their respective weddings. They had a presence in each other's lives during weddings, showers, births and other milestones.

Ellen and Melanie had met each other through work, twelve years ago at St. Joseph's Hospital in Burbank. Melanie was a nurse, and Ellen was a social worker. Although Ellen had left her position at the hospital four years ago, the two had maintained their friendship. Once the ladies realized they were all acquainted, Melanie joined their monthly dinners.

The ladies had decided to meet at a central location so that that none of the three would have to drive too far. They decided on a restaurant in Sherman Oaks. Natalie arrived five minutes late to find, Melanie and Ellen in a huddle sharing what appeared to be a wicked exchange, as evident by Melanie's facial expression—eyes opening wider, mouth agape, upper body stiffening and pulling back in shock and awe.

"Hello, darling!" Ellen exclaimed as she embraced Natalie. "It's been too long!"

"Ellen, you look great!" Natalie said.

"I just got back from the Turks and Caicos, Natalie. Didn't I mention I was going this month when we last met for dinner?"

"Oh, that's right! You did!" acknowledging Ellen's question, then diverting her gaze towards Melanie, "Hi, Mel," she said as she blew her an air kiss, "how are you?"

"I'm good, thanks… Ellen has been entertaining me with stories about her naughty adventures in the Turks and Caicos."

"Oh, pray do tell," Natalie said as she leaned in closer to Ellen.

"Let's just say, that for the first time I had a massage with a happy ending…" Ellen retorted, giggling slyly.

"Wait, did you plan it that way?" Natalie asked.

"No, it was a legitimate massage at the hotel's spa that ended up with me having one of the best sexual experiences of my life."

"Did you initiate it?" Followed by another question after Ellen shook her head, no. "How did he know that you would be receptive to his advances?" Natalie asked with genuine curiosity.

"I was curious about that, too. So, I asked the masseur. He said it wasn't uncommon for women to expect sex from their masseurs at that spa. An indication of the massage recipient's expectations is gauged by the way the woman's body responds when the masseuse's hands inch up the recipient's upper inner legs. Some women tense up; others lean into it. My body's response was the latter. So, he moved to the next step, massaging the back of my legs while his fingers "accidentally" brushed up against my lower buttock. Again, I leaned into it, so he went for it. I had myself a boy toy for the next couple of days. It was liberating and empowering to pay for sex," Ellen said.

"That is crazy!" Natalie said.

"I know, right?!" Melanie chimed. "So, is that a real thing? The way these guys gauge the situation?"

"Apparently, it is," Ellen retorted as she took a sip from her wine glass.

Natalie attempted to hide her shock from Ellen so that she did not seem judgmental. Yes, she was free to do whatever or whomever she wanted because she was single, but Ellen was a catch. She didn't need to pay for sex. Wasn't she worried about disease, or being bamboozled by professional conmen that preyed on rich (in their standards) foreign women seeking a good time in their country?

"Well, ladies. I finished my drink. Unfortunately, I can't stay for dinner. I have to go home and prep for the twins' birthday party," Melanie said standing up and adjusting her skirt discreetly. "Are you sure you can't make it tomorrow, Nat? Even Ellen will be there."

"You know it's not by choice that I'm missing their party. It's Eric's company picnic. I'm so sorry…Oh, darn. I forgot the twins' gifts at home. I will stop by sometime this week or next week to drop them off. I hope your party is wonderful."

After Melanie's departure, Ellen and Natalie shared an uncomfortable silence while they both inspected the menu. Natalie feigned indecisiveness and went back and forth with the menu pages to further avoid conversation. The silence broke when the waiter came to inquire about their order. After he left, Ellen started a superficial conversation.

"So how is everything with you, Natalie? Anything exciting happening? Are there any workshops you are thinking of attending this year?"

"Nothing interesting to report really. Same shit different day. As far as workshops, no…nothing speaks to me right now." Ellen nodded with a displeased look on her face – like she was expecting more from Natalie's response. And as if on cue, Evan accompanied by a striking woman passed by their table. He didn't see Natalie because she sat with her back turned, but Ellen got a good look and recognized him. Natalie immediately recognized him but attempted to conceal her shock.

After he and his date sat at their table, Ellen asked, "Isn't that the *friend* you ran into at Palm Springs?" Overly-emphasizing the word "friend" immediately caused Natalie to tense up.

"Who? Where?" She felt disoriented by this blindside but attempted to maintain her composure as best she could.

"Over there…by the window."

"Oh yeah, that's him," Natalie answered hoping that the shade of her face would not expose how flustered she felt.

"Why don't you go say, hello?" Ellen asked encouragingly.

"No, I don't think that is a good idea. He looks like he is on a date, and I wouldn't want to intrude," Natalie said, trying to play it cool.

"You know, about three weeks ago, Melanie and I were at a St. Joseph's charity golf event, when Melanie spotted this guy and said you dated him a long time ago. The guy looked familiar; I couldn't quite place why he looked so familiar. It drove me crazy for a couple of hours until I remembered he was the guy we ran into in Palm Springs." She took an exaggerated pause as she sipped her drink and continued, "I wasn't going to say anything, but your hypercritical attitude regarding my Turks and Caicos story really struck a nerve. So, I'm going to come out and say it. I have long suspected that something had happened between you and your 'old, platonic friend.' You were acting very strange after your dinner. I even saw you going back to your room in the wee hours…"

So, Ellen had seen her as she hid in the ice and vending machine galley that night. *Deny, deny, deny. Lie, lie, lie,* Natalie chanted to herself.

"I don't know what you are talking about, or insinuating, but I am offended by your baseless accusation…furthermore…"

"Cut the bullshit, Natalie. I am offended that you undermined my ability as a therapist to detect lying. I briefly questioned the validity of my ability to assess situations based on the BS you fed me. I thought we were sharing and connecting, and I believed you wouldn't have any reason to be deceitful. But maybe I was wrong. And still, I didn't question or judge you."

Just because Ellen had shared her sordid indiscretions back then and now, Natalie wasn't about to disclose her infidelity for the sake of connecting with a friend she perceived was engaging in self-destructive behavior. She didn't owe Ellen anything. Her stance on her infidelity was deny and lie. If Ellen wanted to embrace and publicize her sexcapades, that was her business. Natalie would not entertain Ellen's need for acceptance by identifying with Natalie as a fellow deviant.

"Look, I did leave my room in the middle of the night. I felt nauseous and wanted to get something from the vending machine. I heard people approaching, I looked like shit, so I hid in the galley…As for me being judgmental about your adventures in Turks and Caicos, I can assure you with certainty that I am not judging you. I was just shocked because I do not see you as someone who needs to pay for sex. You are gorgeous, sexy and confident."

Natalie believed she was convincing enough and assumed that this explanation would begin to put their derailed dinner back on track. Unfortunately, the opposite occurred.

"You sit there silently, yet you don't realize how loud you are. It's obvious you think you are morally superior, but you are not. If you take that stick out of your self-centered ass, you might take the time to process what I told you earlier. I know I don't have to pay for sex. The experience was empowering to me. You chose to paint it in a negative light. Is that because you are deflecting?"

"NO! And I don't have to sit around and listen to this shit either! She grabbed her wallet out of her purse, tossed three twenty-dollar bills on the table. "I don't know where this hostility is coming from, but it is undeserved." Natalie retorted as Ellen remained silent.

Natalie stood up. When she threw her napkin on the table, she caught a glimpse of Evan and his companion. As she stormed out of the restaurant, she realized that the sight of the two of them disturbed her far more than her unpleasant exchange with Ellen.

During the drive home, Natalie realized that her friendship with Ellen was over. She could never forgive Ellen for what she said at that dinner. Withholding a secret didn't make her a bad friend. And while she didn't approve of Ellen's risky behavior, she would not voice her opinions about her gigolos but would rather keep her thoughts to herself. Ellen was a grown woman who knew right from wrong. It wasn't her place to advise Ellen on how to live her life. It was probable that Ellen herself subconsciously disapproved of her behavior and projected the disapproval on to Natalie. How could Ellen condemn her for concealing a private matter? She couldn't share every detail of her life. She was a firm believer in guarding some of her secrets, once shared, the probability of exposure was highly likely. It was human nature—people liked to talk.

Her experiences had proven that eventually, even the best-intentioned friends betrayed her confidence. Her mind started to go into panic mode. Although she dismissed Ellen's suspicion, she wasn't certain whether Ellen was convinced. Who else had Ellen told about her suspicions regarding Natalie's infidelity? Had she discussed it with Melanie? If such were the case, she had to plan damage control options. She wasn't sure whether she should discuss what transpired during dinner with Melanie, or if she should wait before Melanie brought it up first. It would be possible that Melanie would misconstrue her avoidance of the topic as proof that Natalie was guilty of what Ellen was accusing her of. Natalie was disappointed in Ellen's behavior.

What a bitch! She thought to herself. *The audacity that she believes I should disclose the intimate details of my life to her is ludicrous!*

Natalie was struggling with the additional weight of seeing Evan out with another woman. Although she was aware that he saw other women, the thought of it, let alone witnessing it was still unsettling. The reasoning for her instinctual reaction to refrain from accepting Evan's ultimatum was becoming clear. For all his declarations of love and promises of fidelity for Natalie, Evan was incapable of being completely monogamous. Even though he believed what he told Natalie, his actions and words seemed meaningless now. Her marital status and unavailability reinforced the unrelenting attraction towards Natalie. The forbidden fruit was always sweeter, for some. He was a man who measured his worth and achievements based on conquests, both in business as well as his personal life. He was a successful man, unable to reconcile loss in any aspect of his life. His conquest of Natalie was partial—it always had been. His resolution for a favorable outcome regarding the situation with Natalie was a self-serving attempt to satiate his ego and his quest to win.

If Natalie did accept his ultimatum, it would only be a matter of time before he tired of her. Even if he set up home with Natalie, she could see him straying eventually. The women he went out with were at least a decade younger than she was. A detail that bothered her immensely, for youth was something she could not compete with, as she could never recapture it. Natalie no longer had gravity or nature on her side. She believed she was prematurely pre-menopausal. The realization that her body was changing was more startling than the first time she noticed cellulite on the back of her thighs, or when she realized she had to wear shapewear because simply sucking her tummy in didn't hide her mid-section pouch anymore, and even worse than when she found her first gray pubic hair. Comprehending the idea that eventually her body would no longer be capable of reproduction even though she didn't want more children was still difficult to accept. If one considered sexual attraction based on primitive physiology and psychology, she was no longer in her prime and was becoming undesirable, like an old farm animal being put out to pasture. A younger woman could give Evan children. If she left Eric to be with Evan, and down the road, Evan was to cheat on her with younger women; the devastation would set her on a downward spiral.

Evan continued to court other women less than a week after his proclamation of love for and his desire to only be with Natalie. For this reason alone, she could not take him seriously. If he felt as he said, how could he see other women so soon after he presented her with an ultimatum? If he couldn't remain monogamous for a week, it was inconceivable that he could manage it for the rest of their lives.

On Sunday, Natalie felt she should reach out to Melanie for breakfast or coffee. She could use the excuse of meeting for the sake of giving Melanie her kids' birthday gifts while assessing whether Ellen had disclosed her suspicions about Natalie being unfaithful. She dialed Melanie's home phone number.

"Hello, Arthur? Hi! It's Natalie. How are you?"

"Oh, hi, Natalie. I'm good thanks. How are you?" Melanie's husband replied. Arthur was a gregarious, yet distasteful fellow who lacked boundaries. He had a penchant for making people feel uncomfortable through his inappropriate jokes – which from his perspective were never ill-intentioned. His lack of awareness and his inability to refrain from carrying his jokes too far at the expense of others made him less likable.

"Thanks, Arthur. I'm doing fine. Is Melanie available?" She wasn't in the mood for his shit. She just wanted to talk to Melanie.

"No, she's at a Pilates class. She left about ten minutes ago. Why weren't you here yesterday, for the twins' birthday party?"

"We had to go to a social event for Eric's work."

"Ohhhh," Arthur said in an exaggerated manner, "and here I thought you ran off to Palm Springs for the weekend…"

Natalie's cheeks immediately flushed with heat. Had she been in Arthur's presence, her guilt would have been as clear as day. It took every ounce of self-restraint she could muster to abstain from telling Arthur to go fuck himself.

"No, I was in town," Natalie retorted curtly.

"Hanging out with old friends?"

"Noooo….," Natalie replied annoyed, attempting to maintain her composure, and end the conversation as soon as possible, "Arthur, I'll try Melanie on her mobile phone. Thanks, bye."

Arthur had crossed a line he should have never crossed. At that moment, Natalie realized her friendship with Melanie and Arthur would change forever. Either Ellen had shared her suspicion with both Melanie and Arthur, and god knows who else; or she had disclosed it to Melanie, and Melanie had shared it with her husband. And now, Arthur was taunting her that he was aware of her sordid secret—a distasteful act she found completely reprehensible. Whichever was the case, Arthur should have kept his mouth shut, or Melanie should have had the good sense to keep this secret from her obnoxious husband. A secret both he and she were aware could destroy Natalie's family, if ever revealed.

The damage caused by Ellen's and Arthur's actions was irrevocable. In the course of one weekend, Natalie had lost two friends, three if she counted Arthur. Natalie found herself in an unpleasant predicament. Her double life had finally caught up with her. Too ruffled by Ellen's confrontation and Arthur's innuendo, Natalie, overcome by paranoia, feared that someone would discover her affair, and thus she canceled Evan's approaching Tuesday appointment for the second week in a row.

Natalie could no longer evade or postpone the inevitable. She had to make a decision.

CHAPTER SEVENTEEN
Won't Forgive, Can't Forget (2015)

Melanie had attempted to contact Natalie on three occasions early that week. Natalie was too angry to speak to Melanie. She ignored her calls. She would never know the context in which Arthur was enlightened about Ellen's suspicions regarding Natalie and Evan. She detested Arthur for his tactlessness. What was he trying to accomplish by making such a comment? Was he attempting to exert some psychological power over her? To have someone she thought of as a decent guy insert himself in these circumstances was inappropriate.

Regardless that Natalie might have engaged in infidelity, Arthur should not have been made aware of the suspicions. Ellen didn't know for certain that it was the truth. And if she shared her suspicions with him, he should have had the good sense to keep his senseless comments to himself.

Natalie's chest tightened as she replayed the conversation in her head days after it had occurred. She feared that Ellen, Arthur, and Melanie would disseminate this gossip to their various circles, where it would then spread like wildfire, eventually making its way to Eric. The physiological responses to these thoughts became worse, as she felt her heart race with fear. She had to defuse the situation before it spiraled out of control.

Natalie prided herself on being sensible throughout her life. She fucked up along the way, a whole lot. Nothing about her relationship with Evan had been sensible. It was reckless; the extreme opposite of the image of herself she wanted to portray.

Now that the fear of being discovered was becoming more of a possibility, Natalie could no longer linger between the two separate personas she had created. As exciting as a new life with Evan seemed, she was certain that he would eventually become uninterested in her. Thoughts of being older than the women he kept company with before her, would always plague her. Those thoughts would erode her self-confidence, eventually giving way to her insecurities which would, in turn, make her less attractive. Evan wouldn't hesitate about replacing her with a younger and prettier substitute. Eric was the safe bet. Continuing her relationship with Evan would not be practical.

Natalie's mobile phone vibrated on her desk. It was Melanie. She would eventually have to speak to Melanie. She couldn't avoid her forever. Now was as good a time as any.

"Hello," Natalie answered with a distantness often utilized in her professional conversations with her clients.

One could never guess that Melanie was a dear friend of Natalie's from the way she greeted her.

"Hi, Nat!" Melanie exclaimed in an overly enthusiastic manner that immediately revealed she was overcompensating. Her guilt over wronging Natalie was more than evident.

"Are you free in the next couple of days for lunch or dinner? Melanie asked sheepishly.

"Oh, Mel, I would love to have lunch or dinner, but the next couple of days and weeks will be a little hectic. Can I call you to schedule something for a later date? I have a client coming in, and I have to review some notes."

"Of course! Not a problem. Let me know what works for you," Melanie conceded, "have a good week. I'll talk to you soon."

"Thanks, Mel. I'll call you." Click. Natalie hung up.

Fucking amateur, Natalie thought. At that moment, Natalie's feelings of love and the fondness of emotional bonds that developed through sharing milestones and important experiences in their lives dissipated. Her feelings for both Arthur and Melanie were replaced with repugnance and indignation.

Natalie would slowly remove them from her life. She would have to play nice until she nonchalantly distanced herself from the two. If she confronted Melanie, she would alienate her and could be subject to a smear campaign by Ellen and Melanie. Even if Ellen was to blame, and Melanie hadn't told Arthur, Natalie's revulsion for Arthur would remain constant. She couldn't sustain a friendship with Melanie void of a connection to Arthur. The loss of Melanie's friendship was collateral damage.

Arlette Eshraghi

Natalie's right temple throbbed—it felt like the right side of her head would explode. The additional layer of worry resulting from her infidelity was cause for great stress. She had to do her best to contain it. She would end things with Evan and put her marriage back on track. This is how she would proceed. It was the prudent thing to do.

CHAPTER EIGHTEEN
Conflicting Schedules (2015)

Natalie had convinced herself that she would have to follow through with her decision. She would tell Evan that their affair would come to an end, but not before one last fling. She had it all planned. She would clear her Tuesday appointments, take the day off, and suggest they meet at Evan's all day long where they would have one final sexcapade so satisfying that the memories would have to sustain her throughout the rest of her life.

She dialed Evan's mobile number. It rang several times before she heard his voice on the other end.

"To what do I owe this surprise?" Natalie caught him off guard. He hadn't seen Natalie for three weeks. The only time Natalie would call Evan was for canceling their standing rendezvous in case of a conflicting event or an illness. He wondered why she had contacted him on Friday. "Is everything alright, Natalie?"

"Hi, Evan. Yes. All is well," she retorted calmly, "I was hoping we could spend all of Tuesday together, at your place. If you are open, I can clear my appointments for that day and," Evan interrupted Natalie before she could finish her thought.

"Oh, Natalie. I would love to, but I have a doctor's appointment that day. I was going to cancel this Tuesday. I'm sorry. How about the following week?" Evan replied.

"That's a bummer," Natalie thought for a moment then asked, "Couldn't you postpone your appointment?"

"This has been on the books for a long time. It was the first available. I had to take it or wait another two weeks." Evan turned down Natalie's request. He wasn't completely truthful, but the facts would remain undisclosed for the time being. He would reveal the truth to Natalie eventually.

Natalie was disappointed. She didn't take to rejection very well, particularly in this instance because Evan was doing the rebuffing. Overcome by her insecurities and envy, she revealed, "I saw you out with another woman last week. I was out having dinner with some friends, and you happened to walk by our table. You didn't even notice I was there."

Evan knew exactly what Natalie was talking about. The only woman he had taken to dinner was a business associate. Ever since his visit to the hospital, he had not seen any other women but Natalie. He hadn't seen much of Natalie either; she had canceled two consecutive Tuesday afternoons. He was now canceling the subsequent Tuesday visit. Nearly three weeks void of any physical contact between the two had left them both agitated and restless.

"That was a job interview. I haven't been with any women but you since the ER visit, Natalie." Her complaint miffed him. "That woman was the designer for a prominent builder. Their relationship was also personal. She wasn't getting what she wanted out of him, so she made a clean break professionally and personally. I know her professionally. I ran into her. She was visibly upset, due to personal reasons. I asked her if she needed help, and she told me about her predicament about having to leave her job. Running into her was serendipitous. The timing couldn't have been better. I needed a designer, and she needed a job. That night at the restaurant, I was interviewing her to do the design work for an eight-unit apartment building I acquired to convert into condos."

While Evan's response was truthful, he conveniently elected to omit the drama he had been subjected to by his business colleague from the moment he had run into her in the parking lot of the medical building

"I thought you were on a date," Natalie said.

"No. I wasn't," Evan replied. "You are always making these incorrect assumptions about me which usually lead to false accusations. It's aggravating."

"Sorry, I just thought it was odd that you would ask me to leave Eric because you want us to be fully committed to each other, then take someone out a few days later. Under those circumstances, your proclamations of love and devotion lose credibility... And I'm very jealous. I know I have a husband, but it makes me jealous when I think of you with other women," Natalie confessed.

Evan refused to state the obvious; that he didn't owe her any explanations. They weren't monogamous, and she was married. He wasn't in the mood to quarrel with Natalie.

"Let's postpone to the following Tuesday, Natalie. I can't cancel my doctor's appointment."

"Sounds good," Natalie said agreeably. "Evan, I miss you terribly. Have a wonderful week."

"You, too, Natalie. See you next week."

*****

The prospect of Natalie leaving Eric seemed more tangible now. Why else would she want to spend a whole day with him? Natalie probably wanted some quality time with Evan because once she left Eric, the two would have to avoid each other for a while to avoid any suspicion of being involved during Natalie's marriage—including his therapy sessions. After a couple of months, when Natalie was "ready to date" the two could resume seeing each other with one key difference—their relationship could be public. Of course, they would have to arrange to meet a few times within those couple of months, maybe at his place or at a hotel. He didn't like the idea of losing all contact with Natalie for such an extended amount of time.

Natalie and Evan would have the life they were meant to have. Hopefully, he could convince her to have one more child. She often told him that she and Eric had wanted to have three children but decided against it because the cost of living was so expensive. The more children she had, the sparser the resources allocated per child would become. By the time she felt that there was more flexibility in her income to entertain the thought of a third child, she felt she was too old. She was forty, prone to high blood sugar levels during pregnancy, and had high blood pressure. Due to these issues, she feared pregnancy complications for herself and developmental issues for her potential baby. She came to peace with not having a third child. It wasn't difficult to come to terms with it. She had been blessed with two beautiful, healthy boys.

Would she agree to a third child if she knew Evan wanted a *biological* child of his own? She knew Evan had undergone a vasectomy. He had told her from the start of their affair of the procedure he had years earlier. He explained how preoccupied he was with protecting his fortune from women intending on getting pregnant to make paternity claims. Would she be swayed to change her position on having another child given the extent to which Evan had taken measures to make this possible?

Since the time they reconnected, he realized how much he valued his relationship with Natalie, and that weekly meetings focusing on casual sex had left him with an emotional void only Natalie could fill. He began to pressure Natalie to leave Eric, intent on having a monogamous relationship with her, and eventually to her consenting to have his child. So confident was he in himself that he would succeed in persuading her, he secretly reversed his vasectomy. Concealing it from Natalie was easy. He canceled two consecutive Tuesday afternoon meetings until he perfectly healed, then resumed his "regular" activities.

On Tuesday Natalie proposed they spend all day together, he had a follow-up visit with his urologist. The prior week, Evan had left a sample to have his semen tested for the presence of sperm. Being that his urologist was extremely sought after, the earliest his receptionist could schedule him to see the doctor to discuss his results was twelve days after he dropped off a sample. It took months after a vasectomy reversal for sperm to reappear in the ejaculate. If a reversal was successful, it could take six to twelve months to impregnate a woman. The presence of sperm three months after his procedure was promising, but only after retesting it at his upcoming six-month post-op appointment would he know if his sperm count had normalized and he would be able to father a child.

He couldn't imagine having a baby with anyone other than Natalie. He could imagine spoiling her to no end if she became pregnant—catering to her every whim and desire. He was determined to be a good partner to Natalie and a good father to their child. He would be accepting of Natalie's children with Eric and be the best possible step-father. Surely, Natalie and Eric would have joint custody, but he would guess that Natalie would assume majority custody, which meant that the boys would be with them more than with Eric. That scenario would be most practical considering Eric's work schedule. Evan could buy a bigger home with a pool and basketball court, so the boys would have their own space when they were in the custody of their mother. He would help raise them while respecting his boundaries as a stepfather—never attempting to replace their birth father, yet still having a rewarding and fulfilling relationship with the two boys.

Such would be the direction that Evan's life would take. He always managed to get what he wanted. He would have Natalie to himself, too. He believed that they were perfectly compatible, and no one else would make him a suitable partner as she would. For so long, Evan had believed he had missed his chance to be with Natalie, that ship had sailed nearly twenty years ago, but perhaps he was wrong. There could be no other explanation for Natalie's request to spend a full day with him; she was ready to leave Eric. Natalie was coming home to Evan.

CHAPTER NINETEEN
Ava (2015)

Ava couldn't believe she was going through with her crazy plan. How could she have conjured such a plot? She credited her scheming to all those prime-time soap operas she watched as a child, in the absence of adult supervision. Being exposed to such theatrical manipulation since the impressionable age of eight somewhat influenced her emotional development and gave her a thirst for the overly-dramatic. She was clever, cunning, and could be deceptive to suit her needs.

At the age of thirty, Ava was far more confident than her peers. She knew what she wanted and was determined to have anything she desired. She was a diva. Her affinity for the superficial had allowed her to develop a highly specialized design aesthetic and thus thrived as an upscale residential designer. At the age of twenty-four, she had secured a job as a design specialist for RMLH, Richard Morgan Luxury Homes.

Arlette Eshraghi

RMLH was run by Richard Morgan, a prominent second-generation builder who had started working as a teen at his father's residential development firm, Morgan & Sons, in the '70s. The Morgans made a fortune building tract homes and gated communities throughout California. In 2001, Richard branched off into a subsidiary specializing in luxury home development and grossly compounded his fortune during the real estate boom. Ava joined his team in 2009, when most people involved in real estate and all aspects of that industry, were feeling the repercussions of the housing bubble burst. Such was not the case at RMLH, where they catered to an elite clientele base with an abundance of wealth. Clients whose financial portfolios though negatively impacted still had the good fortune of being unaffected by the housing crisis—the kind of people that were out of touch with most Americans. This was a quality Richard Morgan admired as a youth, strengthened during the summer when at the behest of his father he worked on job sites performing hard manual labor, he aspired to attain a level of wealth unimaginable to many. He recognized and appreciated his father's will to instill a strong work ethic in him. It served its purpose in developing Richard into a hands-on, shrewd, and successful businessman.

By 2012, Ava was promoted to Director of Design Planning & Implementation. She managed scores of designers. Ava was ambitious and hard-working. What would have been recognized as traits of leadership and assertiveness in a man and highly commended had labeled Ava as a ruthless bitch. Ava recognized the value of utilizing her assets to benefit and maximize her potential to succeed. She had captured Richard Morgan's attention

178

in both the boardroom and the bedroom. Although she used her sexuality and feminine charm to advance when necessary, the promotion at RMLH was a well-deserved achievement.

Richard was still married to his wife of twenty-seven years, Kate, who happened to be his high school sweetheart when the lines of professionalism in his business relationship with Ava began to blur. Working long days and nights in and out of town afforded them the opportunity to develop a flirtation that eventually encompassed a relationship of a sexual nature.

For two years, Ava assumed the role of the homewrecker, as Richard finagled his way out of his marriage. Immediately after their initial tryst, overcome by guilt and embarrassment, Ava had given Richard her resignation. He had rejected her resignation and dismissed it as a mere gesture; not fully convinced that she would hastily relinquish her title and salary over their encounter. He confided in her that he was intrigued by her and was willing to explore where their relationship was headed—with the intent that he would keep their professional relationship totally separate. The two carried on an affair, abandoning all discretion and the intent to keep their personal and professional lives "separate." They were often the subject of gossip at RLMH.

Ava was apathetic to the hurt she caused Richard's wife, Kate, for two reasons. One, marriages came to an end. Theirs was not the first failed marriage, nor would it be the last one for that matter. Richard and Kate's marriage had run its course. Richard was no longer in love with Kate. He shouldn't have been condemned to spend the rest of his life in a hapless marriage. Secondly, Kate had always had an indifference and sense of superiority in her limited interactions towards Ava, before the affair. Kate, being the wife of the CEO, was insulated from any retaliation by the staff who were often subject to her judgmental arrogance. She had targeted Ava with her smugness several times, and thus Ava could not help but feel a sense of schadenfreude when Richard left Kate.

During the last two years, Ava patiently accepted the conditions Richard had placed on their relationship. Trusting that the circumstances she complied with so unquestioningly were for the sole purpose of benefitting his divorce judgment, and not because Richard was having doubts about committing to Ava. He had promised Ava that once his divorce finalized, she would move in with him and that they would then discuss her desire to have a baby.

Ava had never had a desire to become a mother. Void of any maternal instincts, her life was not lacking in the absence of dependent, helpless beings whose well-being and survival she would be responsible for. While visiting friends who had embarked on the journey of motherhood, her disinterest towards their newborns was perceived as offensive. Although she lavished these friends with the latest and greatest gifts for their newborn infants, her inability to sincerely acknowledge and make a connection with these babies was cause for the end of many of her friendships. Ava was perceived to be callous—a trait she had picked up while adapting to her male-dominated industry. Design work could be categorized as "feminine," but continuously dealing with developers that happened to be predominantly male, had caused her to form a harsh exterior over the years.

Ava always looked ahead. She was calculating. Her desire to have a baby had nothing to do with her connection to Richard. Instead, it would serve as an insurance policy. Her child's paternity would guarantee her a continuous comfortable life, in the plausible event Richard tired of her. The role of mistress and subsequently the live-in girlfriend of Richard Morgan had bestowed many privileges upon Ava. The loss of such privileges would be insufferable. Relinquishing her lavish lifestyle would be devastating. She had to look out for her future, no matter how *callous* her reasoning was at present. Certainly, she would eventually warm up to the idea of having a child.

Richard had made good on his promise to cohabitate with Ava. After the divorce, Richard asked Ava to move into his new main residence in Malibu. The property was breathtaking. It sat atop a bluff overlooking PCH. This was the project that had earned Ava the title of director. Richard had bought the property at a steal, as a foreclosure in need of serious rehab. After completing all the structural repairs to restore the integrity of the building and its foundation, the design phase of the project was delegated to Ava. Although the property itself was spectacular, Ava's vision transformed it into a grander level of magnificence

Richard reversed his initial decision to sell the house when he decided he would leave Kate. He had recognized how invaluable of a property it was, and thus decided to establish it as his primary residence. He rejected one unsolicited offer after the other for the home. Ava was beyond the moon when he surprised her with the news that they would reside in the masterpiece she had designed.

When she was tasked with the design of the home, she often daydreamed that she was designing it for herself, realizing how impossible the realization of that dream was considering that selling the property would be the wisest choice for Richard, to recover from the loss of liquid assets after his divorce from Kate. Having Richard decide that they would make this property their home without her input was cause for great happiness. Her life couldn't be more perfect, except for the fact that Richard had made her sign legal documents relinquishing any rights to the home. He explained that his lawyers insisted on taking these drastic measures solely to protect the business. Ava wasn't convinced.

When Ava began pressing for a baby, Richard could not conceal his reluctance, "I have two adult children. My son is settling into his career; my daughter is graduating from law school. I'm done with babies. I am fifty years old. I know lots of men over fifty that father children, I don't want it for myself. I've been there and done that. I prefer to live this phase of my life free of babies unless they happen to be my grandchildren. Luckily, I know my children well enough to say with certainty that won't be happening any time soon. I no longer have to be responsible for other beings, it's a very liberating feeling."

"*You* have children, Richard. *I* don't," Ava would retort icily.

"I thought you didn't want children, Ava. You were always repulsed whenever one of your friends announced a pregnancy. You would complain about the obligatory visits to congratulate your friends when they became mothers. What changed suddenly?" Richard asked suspiciously, wondering if Ava truly wanted a baby. He didn't believe she wanted a child for the right reasons.

"Something changed after I turned thirty. I have a fulfilling career and relationship, but something is missing. I want a baby. I want to experience motherhood. I want to be able to love someone unconditionally."

Richard was certain she lacked maternal instincts. He was intelligent enough to recognize that a baby would ensure Ava a life of comfort if they parted ways. He wanted Ava to be a continued presence in his life. He couldn't blame her. Although Ava was a successful woman, she had grown dependent on a lifestyle that could be attained by only a slight percentage of the population. As successful as she was, it was doubtful she could achieve the level of wealth necessary to maintain the luxuries she had become accustomed to. Although he had asked her to move in, he did not feel an urgency to remarry so soon after his divorce was finalized. Perhaps in the future, he would be willing to make Ava the second Mrs. Richard Morgan—except, he wouldn't present it as such. Down the road, the thought of marriage provided she would sign a prenuptial agreement was a likely possibility. Though, it was highly unlikely, impossible, even that he would reconsider another go at fatherhood. He attempted to appease Ava by offering a compromise.

"Why don't we table the baby talk for now? In six months, if you still want a baby, then we will try for one."

"So, in six months if I come to you and say, 'I want a baby,' we will actively try?" Ava asked for clarification.

"Absolutely. Think of it as a grace period," Richard continued pitching his proposal, "One condition though, and it's non-negotiable. I will not subject my sperm to any testing or submit any samples. If you must see a specialist to asses your fertility that is fine, but I ask that you wait six months. We will not have a baby through IVF or artificial insemination. If we try to get pregnant the old-fashioned way and it works, great. At fifty years old, I will not actively pursue impregnating you. The act of it though, I will rigorously engage in…" Richard said with an impish smile and a wink, attempting to soften his stern requisites. "I'm going to prove to you that a baby would cramp our style. We are free to go out, travel, and pursue leisurely interests. A baby would deter us from the freedom to do whatever we desired. I don't want to the burden of raising another dependent for the next twenty years. If you still disagree with me in six months, then I will be open to having another child."

Ava was wary of Richard's proposal. He didn't succumb to the will of others, particularly when they contradicted his wants, and not without fierce opposition. She agreed to his proposal but decided she would underhandedly redefine the terms to give herself an advantage. After all, she needed the leverage to protect her interests. Richard was enamored by her now, but would he replace her eventually? Men like Richard lacked substance. A better man would have kept his marriage intact, sparing his family the humiliation while keeping his indiscretions completely discrete. Richard was too self-absorbed to make the sensible choice. His loyalty was wavering. She could not fully trust him considering he betrayed his wife to be with her.

While Richard attempted to dissuade her desire for a baby, the wheels in her head were turning. She had already conjured a plot even though she falsely agreed to wait six months. She would seek the help of her neighbor, Tina, who happened to be a nurse practitioner for a highly sought-after fertility specialist. Tina owed her a favor. After Tina divorced her plastic surgeon husband, she wanted to renovate the entire interior of the home to eradicate any memory of her husband, Dave, who had left her for another woman. Ava determined that Tina would have to spend a fortune on her home improvement project. She couldn't bring herself to charge her neighbor the exorbitant design fees she charged for the limited freelance projects she occasionally accepted. Besides, she would receive kickbacks from the contractors and vendors in the form of a small percentage of the cost of labor, design materials and furnishings for the project. Perhaps it was a sense of guilt, as she herself had been complicit in the demise of someone's marriage; and thus, wanted to participate in a pay it forward type of act of kindness for a woman scorned by another homewrecker.

Before Tina became aware of her husband's infidelity, Ava dished the sordid details of her affair with Richard, during her weekly dinners with Tina. Tina had found the stories to be fascinating and was often intrigued by them. After she learned of Dave's affair, Tina developed an intolerance for all infidelity—whether it involved her relationship or not. Ava sensed a bit of resentment from Tina and stopped talking about her relationship with Richard altogether until his divorce finalized, and they were officially recognized as a couple. She felt compelled to help Tina free of charge, provided Tina would give her an idea of her vision, and Ava would have carte blanche to transform her home's interior. Tina happily agreed as she couldn't be any more disinterested in the actual design work. She only cared for the finished product, which did not disappoint and made her fall in love with her home all over again.

The day after Richard and Ava had the baby conversation, Ava invited Tina over for the last supper, at her home, a company-owned residence in the Pacific Palisades she occupied rent-free as one of the many perks of her job. She had called the Cape Cod style 2500 square foot residence "home" for the last two years. It was one of the more modest properties she designed, but one of her favorite projects. The interior was designed in a freshly modern transitional Hampton's style beach-chic theme. She had been quite comfortable in that house. It was cozy but sophisticated. She was preparing to vacate the home. Most of the packing was completed. She would be ready to move to Richard's new residence by the end of the week.

Tina rang the doorbell promptly at 7:00 pm. Ava opened the door and greeted her guest, "Hello, Tina, dear. I'm so glad you could make it on such short notice," she said as she gave Tina a quick hug and welcomed her into the home. "This will be our last weekly dinner date as neighbors. I hadn't anticipated it would be so soon, but I will be moving out at the end of this week."

"Oh, Ava! I know, I can't believe you are moving out so abruptly. I'm going to miss you. We will have to meet up once a month for lunch or dinner to catch up," Tina said unable to conceal her disappointment at losing Ava as a neighbor.

"I will miss you, too. I couldn't have asked for a better neighbor. Come, let's have some prosciutto and cheese with our cocktails. Dinner will be ready in twenty minutes," Ava responded, as she led Tina to the outdoor/indoor living room. They each took a seat in the deep cushioned chairs arranged on either side of the cocktail table, where an artfully arranged charcuterie platter and a bottle of chilled wine awaited them.

The two chatted for a while. Ava listened intently, as Tina vented about her ex-husband and his girlfriend. She was still extremely bitter, even though she liked to pretend that she had moved on. Ava offered support and encouraged Tina to stay positive. During dinner, Ava attempted to unveil her plan.

"Tina, I hate to put you in this kind of a position, but I am truly in a bind, and I need your help."

Tina was dumbstruck. She quickly chewed her maple-glazed Brussel sprouts. What kind of a "bind" could Ava possibly be in? Ava was a decade younger but was way on top of her game. She had all her ducks in order. Regardless, Tina felt indebted to Ava for all her gratis design work.

"What is it, Ava? What do you need?"

"I want to have a baby. Richard doesn't," she began, attempting to garner some pity. "He agreed to a baby if I wait and still want to have one six months from now, provided it happens naturally—without IVF or artificial insemination...I know I won't change my mind; so, when the time comes, I want to give myself the upper hand to maximize the chances of getting pregnant as soon as possible."

"What is it exactly that you want me to do?" Tina asked hesitantly.

"Will you be able to provide me with Clomid? That way, when we start trying, I'm hopefully ovulating?" Ava asked nervously.

"Do you have fertility problems? Have you tried getting pregnant before?" Tina probed.

"Yes," Ava lied, "my last relationship, three years ago, my fiancé and I tried to get pregnant, but we couldn't. It's why our relationship ended. I don't want to have to go through the frustration of waiting an additional year after Richard's imposed six month waiting period. I can see your doctor in six months for fertility testing, but Richard can't know about any of this. I have promised to wait six months."

"I can't just bring you fertility drugs without jeopardizing my job. If you come to the office, I can fake an exam and sign off on a round of fertility medication. If you are serious about getting help, I suggest you see the doctor after this 'six month waiting period. It's a good idea to ask Richard to submit his ejaculate for testing, too. It's usually the first step and the least invasive in determining the cause of infertility."

"Oh no, Richard refuses to submit any semen samples. He said if we get pregnant naturally, 'fine.' He will not agree to any outside assistance. So, I need to be prepared to get pregnant as soon as the six months are up," Ava explained.

"Ava, you know that there is a chance that you can become pregnant with multiples? If you are fertile and take these drugs the number of multiples can increase. These drugs are not a joke. You will become irritable and may develop depression or Ovarian hyperstimulation syndrome..."

"Or gas with oily discharge, frequent bowel movements, an urgent need to take them?" Ava chimed in imitating the bizarre disclaimers listed by the narrator in pharmaceutical commercials, giggling as she spoke. Tina was not amused. She had to shift gears. "Please, Tina. Just help me out. I want a baby," Ava pleaded, shedding a few crocodile tears in a performance worthy of an Oscar.

Tina didn't feel comfortable about complying with Ava's request, but she felt beholden to Ava since she had redesigned her home. She realized then that she should have never ignored the unsettling feeling that overcame her the moment that Ava had offered to do the work free of charge. Accepting that magnitude of work, gratuitously, was never gratis. For eighteen months, a cloud of indebtedness hung over Tina, as she wished for a way to settle the score. Now was her chance, but the unethical aspect of providing Ava with fertility drugs she might not need was disconcerting. On the other hand, she could do this one favor and absolve herself of this burden of obligation.

"Ok," Tina agreed meekly, "I will do this one favor." As soon as she spoke the words, the same uneasiness she felt when Ava offered to design her home for free overcame her.. Again she ignored the feeling.

Nine Months Later...

"Why did I get myself involved in this mess?" Tina asked herself aloud as she took a long, exaggerated puff from a cigarette. She unlocked her mobile phone in her third attempt in two minutes to contact Ava. It went straight to voicemail. What had begun as supplying Ava with fertility drugs had now escalated into analyzing Richard's semen sample without his knowledge or consent. Tina was unable to resist Ava's manipulation, for fear that she could complain about Tina to the nursing board. She couldn't wait to do this one last favor and be rid of her for good. Tina had misjudged Ava. Ava didn't care about her. She was determined to find a means to an end, even if it meant jeopardizing Tina's career and nursing license. She had unwillingly allowed herself to be dragged into a situation she did not want to be a part of. Never again would she accept a favor or participate in unethical practices that could cause her to lose her license. She just had to get through this last imposition.

Tina had to return to work soon. She could stall another ten minutes, to intercept Ava in the parking lot to stop her from bringing Richard's sample to the office for testing. Shannon, the technician at the lab in the suite next door had agreed to test the semen sample Ava would bring in, without the consent of the male it belonged to in exchange for $500 in cash. Shannon would come in an hour before everyone Thursday mornings to leave an hour early to take her son to his little league practice, so she was alone in the lab during lunch hour, while everyone would leave the office. This Thursday was different. The lab director was in the office running a calibration check on one of the blood chemical analyzers. If Ava brought in a sample, she would have to be accompanied by a man pretending that the sample belonged to him to give his written and signed consent to test the sperm. After the lab director left for lunch, Shannon could test and analyze the sample.

*****

Ava's heart hadn't stopped beating since the moment she put her plan in motion less than an hour ago. After two days of feigning illness to refuse Richard's sexual advances, she had planned a quickie in the office to collect a sample of his semen secretly. Ava had blocked off an hour of Richard's day in his appointment scheduling software to ensure that they would be uninterrupted. She had specified the appointment as a "Private Meeting" because the smart office technology would automatically set the electric shades in his office to roll down when his calendar specified a private meeting.

From the moment she entered his office, there was no time to waste, "Richard, I want you this very moment," she demanded as she walked over to him, sat on his lap and began to kiss him.

Richard didn't have the opportunity to respond. By the time he processed what was happening, Ava was already on her knees pulling his erect penis out of the fly. She had hoped she had choreographed it perfectly. Although she didn't like to, she resorted to giving Richard a blow job to ensure he was completely distracted. After working his penis with her mouth for what seemed like forever, Richard reclined back into his chair closing his eyes in ecstasy. Ava discreetly pulled out a special specimen collecting condom from her pocket.

"Why are you using a condom?" Richard asked. "Aren't we trying to get you pregnant?"

"I don't want things to get messy. I have a meeting, and I don't have time to go home to change. We can use a condom this time."

She slipped it on Richard's penis and stood over him in a straddling position, as she pulled the office chair upright. She tormented him, as she guided his penis in up and down only half way. She did this over and over until Richard could no longer endure the teasing. He held onto her and pressed her inwards. She rode him with intensity, like her life—or in this case—her lifestyle depended on it. Ava was too nervous to come, so she faked an orgasm as Richard came. Ava immediately stood up, kissed Richard and simultaneously pulled the condom off, careful not to spill the ejaculate.

"I will get rid of this. I need a minute to freshen up," she said walking to the private bathroom in Richard's office. She locked the door behind her, opened the cabinet under the sink and reached for the specimen bottle she had hidden there a few days ago. Her hands were shaking as she poured the semen from the condom to the specimen bottle. She fastened the lid, threw the condom in the trash and hid the specimen bottle in the sink cabinet. She cleaned up and walked out of the bathroom.

When she emerged, Richard got up from his desk and headed towards the bathroom. As he washed his hands, he called out to Ava, "Do you want to grab a quick lunch in an hour?"

"I can't," Ava said in a disappointed voice, "I have to meet a freelance client during lunch." She grabbed a mint from the candy dish on the coffee table. "I will be back. I'm going to grab my purse from my office so that I can fix my face in your bathroom."

Upon Ava's return, Richard had resumed his position at his desk and recommenced reviewing proposals for new projects. The electric shades had been drawn up, and his office was now in full view. He was completely oblivious to what Ava had done. She walked back to the private bathroom in his office and closed the door behind her. She quickly reapplied her lipstick and refreshed her powder and blush. She opened the cabinet carefully and reached behind the stacks of toilet paper for the specimen bottle. She made sure the lid was fastened securely and placed the bottle in her purse. She bid Richard farewell and made her way to the elevators. As she started her ignition and pulled out of the office parking lot, she finally let out a deep breath of relief.

Stay calm, Ava. The most difficult part is over.. Just get this sample over to the lab, and you are good, she thought to herself.

She turned into the medical center parking lot, scanning the perimeter for Tina. She had a half hour before the ejaculate in the specimen bottle would lose its testing viability. She noticed Tina nervously approaching the car.

"Hi Tina," she said happily. "Thanks again for…"

"Don't thank me just yet, Ava. I tried calling you on your cell phone, but you didn't answer. My friend in the lab isn't alone. The director stayed behind."

"Well, what does that have to do with me?" Ava asked. She turned off the ignition button and got out of the car.

"You didn't think about the legalities of sperm analysis, did you?" Tina replied; irritated by the fact that she and a colleague were taking a risk that could jeopardize their careers, while Ava remained clueless and careless. "You need to bring a man in with you to pretend the sample is his and have him sign a Semen Analysis Consent Form, as well as a Semen Analysis Communication Consent Form. The paperwork will disappear after she gives you the results, so you don't need to use your actual names. It's just a formality since the lab director is in the office. If you come back for the results and he happens to be in the office, she can go through the motion of verifying that she can share the information with you because of the communication consent form."

"Where am I going to find someone to pretend to be my partner and could meet me immediately?" Ava asked panicked, "I have less than a half hour to turn this sample in." Ava was clearly stressed. She couldn't manage another attempt to steal Richard's sperm without risking a heart attack. It was too chancy.

"I have to go back to work," Tina said, "If you think of anyone who can get here ASAP, then text me. I will meet you outside of the suite and let Shannon know you are coming."

Ava's hope had completely diminished. Deflated, she leaned against her car and tried to think of a solution to this conundrum. Who could she entrust with this in the eleventh hour? She racked her brain for a plausible candidate but couldn't think of anyone. There was no one else she could share this secret with. Testing Richard's sperm behind his back was a violation on so many levels. Ava convinced herself that she was taking the right course in her quest to get pregnant. They had tried unsuccessfully for three months, while she took fertility drugs on the sly for six of those months, and with Richard's knowledge for the last three. She didn't want to continue with the fertility drugs if the issue was Richard's inability to impregnate her. That would be the end. He had stipulated that he wouldn't cooperate with fertility treatments if they couldn't get pregnant naturally.

Ava couldn't help herself. In a moment of despair, she lost her calm and began to sob in the parking lot. It was over; she had lost. If Richard left her, she would be powerless without a child to establish paternal obligations to ensure her a continued life of luxury. If she had a child, and he left her, Richard wouldn't care to be involved in the day to day life of the child, but his ego wouldn't allow his offspring to live a life without privilege. Perhaps she could find a sperm donor that looked like Richard and pretend the child was his? *OK, now you sound borderline crazy,* she thought to herself, as she quietly whimpered while she dug in her purse to locate tissues.

"Are you ok, miss?" A bystander asked as he approached his vehicle which was parked next to Ava's, "Do you need help?"

"No, no thank you. I am fine…" Ava said, wiping her nose with an overly crinkled tissue. She looked up and asked, "Evan, is that you?"

"Yes?" Evan said unable to recognize the woman hiding behind the oversized sunglasses.

Ava pulled up her shades to reveal her identity, as well as a pair of red, puffy eyes.

"Ava! Are you ok? What's wrong?" Evan asked. The two were acquainted professionally; they had met five years earlier at a business event. Evan admired Ava's work, as well as her ability to advance at RMLH. He had heard through the grapevine that Richard and Ava were having an affair, and he had subsequently left his wife, but knowing the kind of businessman Richard Morgan was, he was certain that Ava's advancement was solely contingent on her job performance. Richard didn't reward employees with titles unless they were deserving of them. Evan and Ava would run into each other a couple of times a year at industry events and had a mutual respect and admiration for one another—strictly on a professional basis.

"Oh, Evan. I'm in a bit of a bind. I don't have time to explain, but if you can do me a favor, I would truly appreciate it. And I would be more than happy to explain everything afterward. What I'm about to tell you will sound strange, but please go with it. As I said, I will explain everything later. Right now, I must turn in my boyfriend's semen sample for analysis; I need you to pretend it's yours and sign the consent forms. After I receive the results, the nurse will destroy the forms, so you don't need to use your real name."

"What is this all about, Ava?" asked Evan, suddenly apprehensive to assist her.

"Please, Evan. Just help me. I will explain later. I'm trying to get pregnant, and Richard is too stubborn and manly to submit semen samples. We have been trying to get pregnant but have been unsuccessful. I don't want to go through the whole infertility ordeal if the problem is with him. I just want a child..." she said as her voice quivered and tears pooled in her eyes.

"Ahh, understood. You can elaborate later," Evan said sympathetically. Her last words said it all. He understood her pain, as he was struggling with his desire to become a father eventually. Coincidentally, he had just submitted a semen sample to his urologist with hopes that he was producing viable sperm six months after his vasectomy reversal.

Evan protectively put his arm around Ava and guided her towards the entrance of the medical building.

"Thank you, Evan," Ava whispered as she quietly sniffled. *I should have become an actress,* she thought to herself.

All did not go as smoothly as planned at the lab. Tina walked them to the lab and introduced Ava to Shannon. The lab director was still in the office when Ava and Evan walked in. After submitting their samples and signing the forms, Ava and Evan watched the lab director discuss Ava's file. They couldn't hear the conversation because of the glass partition separating the receptionist's desk from the waiting room. A few minutes later, Shannon informed them that because they didn't have a file at the lab, Evan would have to return with Ava for the results, a common practice for patients referred by the fertility specialist next door.

Evan was sympathetic to Ava's eagerness to have children, so he agreed to meet her the following day to continue to pose as the source of the sperm sample. In all his years, this was probably one of the craziest things he had agreed to do. *Oh well,* he thought, *it will make for a funny story to retell one day.* Ava was embarrassed for the imposition, but she was desperate to rule out Richard as the cause of their infertility, so she could move forward with more intense fertility treatments if necessary. She believed that running into Evan was serendipitous; the fact that she was able to circumnavigate through the obstacle she was presented with in the parking lot only reinforced her resolve to ensure a quick pregnancy, even if she went behind Richard's back to attain her goal. She was meant to get pregnant with Richard's baby.

Ava's self-assertiveness had was restored. She should have never doubted herself, she thought. It was only a matter of time before she would be bonded to Richard Morgan and the decadent lifestyle that accompanied being a part of his world. As cunning and smart as Ava thought she was, she forgot one thing—the fact that she was dealing with someone who had a twenty-year head start at being cunning, and as a result, she overlooked the fact that Richard was always a step or two or twenty ahead of her...

CHAPTER TWENTY
Richard Morgan (2015)

R ichard's attempt to take legal measures to ensure he would have the most favorable financial outcome possible for his divorce was not only futile but a testament to his entitled and delusional character. Richard and Kate were on equal footing when they married in 1990, thus the absence of a prenuptial agreement. As a lawyer working in her father's firm, Kate netted a higher income in the first three years of their marriage. In 1993, when Richard's father deemed his son finally worthy of a higher position and responsibilities at Morgan & Sons, his financial status was significantly elevated. While he believed that he should set up Kate sufficiently enough that she would be able to maintain the lifestyle she had grown accustomed to over the last twenty-five years, he did not believe she deserved half of his net worth. Kate disagreed. She believed she had every right to half his net worth, not only because it was California law, but because she was the driving force behind his success.

Arlette Eshraghi

For the last twenty-five years, she had fostered a home environment where his success was inevitable. She had perfected the role of supportive wife to a tee, abandoning the advancement of her career for the first seven years after the birth of her children for the sake of her family, just as her mother had done before her. She was a beautiful, doting wife and mother, an impeccable and gracious hostess, and a charitable and invaluable community member. In the absence of a financial need, she took on pro-bono cases her father brought her, where she represented socioeconomically disadvantaged women to sustain her need to continue to keep mentally active. To the outside world, she was demure, but outspoken when necessary. To her husband, she was a force to be reckoned with—powerful, influential, and unyielding.

Kate was aware of the requirements that accompanied the role of the wife of a wealthy, commanding, and significant man. She was mindful of the existence of the threat of being discarded for a younger woman. Men like Richard often carried out indiscretions behind their wives' backs, unbeknownst that their wives chose to feign ignorance rather than disrupt their status quo. Most stayed with their wives and kept mistresses; for others, the need to recapture their youth by coupling with significantly younger women was too dominating to evade. Richard's desire to abandon common sense prevailed, he sought a divorce from Kate. She would not relent to his self-serving valuation of what he deemed she deserved. She was aware of her value and self-worth. She would accept her consequent indoctrination into the first wives club with the sense of determination and ownership she assumed with all roles of her life—she would unequivocally succeed in this new chapter, prepared to defend and endure a battle for what she deserved and then some.

Kate had upheld the promise she made to herself, both in her acceptance of letting go of Richard as well as her unwavering resolve during the divorce proceedings. She had retained complete ownership of their main residence. Of the twenty-seven properties owned by RMLH, twenty-four were considered community property. Richard and Kate would split the properties. Each one would take twelve properties to avoid co-ownership. She agreed to receive a lump sum settlement rather than monthly alimony. The fact that she never had to worry about finances during marriage remained unaffected. Her lifestyle was upheld to the levels it had pre-divorce. She had a network of supportive friends and family. Kate would be fine.

Kate was aware that she would become prey to men who targeted wealthy, older, divorced women with hopes of leeching off their fortune. Little would they know that Kate's love for her wealth would supersede all else. Unlike other divorced women her age, Kate no longer had romantic notions, nor was she a cougar. At fifty-two years of age, she was impeccably preserved—vital and beautiful and often received attention from men even her junior by decades who believed she was younger than she was. She was still a catch. Her preference, had she never married Richard, would have been for an older partner, as Richard who happened to be the same age looked as perfectly well maintained as she did. An older man would have appreciated her more as she aged. If she were to meet a well-suited companion, she would be open to the possibility of a relationship, provided he was older and wealthier than she was. For now, she would embrace her current single status and explore the endless possibilities of her new-found independence with an open mind and an open heart.

Richard wasn't surprised by the outcome of his divorce judgment. If he were to marry again, he would be well protected by a prenuptial agreement the second time around. However, Richard currently didn't want to be married. Would things be different if his father hadn't influenced him? For starters, Richard alone, without the interference of his father would be responsible for his mate selection. It was his father's request that he settle down at the age of twenty-five. Collin Morgan reminded Richard that Kate, a most suitable match, had been with him since they were seventeen, and might decide to leave him if he didn't further solidify their commitment through marriage. If Richard had his way, he probably wouldn't have settled for another ten years. He canoodled with many women behind Kate's back when she was away at law school, and he still hadn't exasperated his playboy ways when he proposed to her at her graduation party from Stanford Law School.

Richard had been mostly faithful to Kate, aside from the occasional one- night stands with strippers or high-priced escorts when entertaining business clients. It wasn't until his affair with Ava that Richard became attached to another woman and wanted to leave Kate. The prospect of upgrading to a younger wife was appealing two years ago. Now that Richard's divorce was final, his feelings regarding marriage were drastically changing.

His eldest child, Richard Jr., or R.J. as everyone called him had received his MBA while he was employed at RMLH and was promoted to Junior Vice President of Research and Development. His daughter, Emily, followed in her mother's footsteps and was completing her last year at Stanford Law School. His children would become productive members of society. They no longer relied on him, nor their mother. They were establishing their own lives, autonomous from the family unit they were a part of for over two decades. Richard accepted this reality as a bittersweet crossroads. Bitter, because his children were now adults. In the blink of an eye, these two babies had transformed into self-sufficient, capable adults. And though it brought him to terms with his mortality, he also realized that the sweet side of this was that he was unrestricted, as he had fulfilled his responsibility of raising dependent children. He was now permitted to be spontaneous and carefree.

Beyond fulfilling the basic needs for survival, Richard had become self-actualized. All aspects of his life greatly satisfied him. He was prepared to enjoy the rest of his life by relinquishing the reigns of RMLH to RJ. Two years ago, Richard had set forth a seven-year plan to groom his son for his succession as CEO. At the end of that term, Richard would remove himself completely from the day to day operations, to serve loosely as a retired advisor.

Although he had to part with half of their net worth after his divorce, Richard was content, as he was still a very wealthy man. Even though the ink on his divorce decree was still drying, at times he second-guessed his decision to leave Kate. It was possible that he had made a grave mistake by leaving Kate for Ava. He realized this before his divorce was finalized but was certain that Kate would never forgive him—especially because he aired their dirty laundry so publicly. Kate was proud; forgiving Richard would make her look foolish. Not to take away from his relationship with Ava, she was youthful and fun, but she wasn't Kate. They broke the mold when they created Kate. She was one of a kind.

Kate would have appreciated their new-found freedom from the responsibility of their children if they were still together. She would have turned that sentimental event into a cause for celebration, rather than lamenting about fleeting time. Kate always made the best out of any situation. She found the bright side of unfortunate events, always focusing on the positive. She would be devastated if Richard and Ava were to have a baby. Would she look for a positive twist on the situation in that circumstance? Richard refused to further embarrass and disrespect Kate by fathering Ava's baby.

Ava, however, refused to concede to Richard's reluctance to have children. Her disinterest in becoming a mother fueled part of Richard's attraction for her. Since she had divulged that she now wanted to experience motherhood, it was becoming more difficult to appreciate Ava or to see her as a potential life partner. Before his divorce, he was certain that Ava was on the same page as he was. He was willing to marry her if she agreed to sign a prenuptial agreement to safeguard his wealth from another costly divorce. Of course, he would be amiable to give her a decent sum of money, if they were to divorce at his will, but he would never expose himself to losing half his wealth ever again.

Richard's instincts were almost always accurate. Ava's sudden desire to conceive a baby aroused his suspicions regarding her motive for wanting a baby. If, and only if he believed that Ava whole-heartedly desired a baby, he would objectively consider the matter and possibly move forward with having one child. Because Ava had expressed such revulsion at the thought of motherhood, and she consistently maintained that she would never have a child, he believed her intent was not pure. He sensed that Ava's desire to have a baby with him was propelled by her desire to stay connected to him, or rather his wealth if they broke up. Although he had been referred to as a silver fox on numerous occasions, he was aware that it was his power and wealth that attracted younger women to him. He accepted the superficial aspect of his casual affairs, and while he believed that he connected with Ava emotionally as well, he didn't think Ava would have expressed any interest in him had he been a fifty-something low-level employee.

As Ava grew more intent on having a baby, Richard became more intent on dissuading her. He did not intend on starting all over now that his two children had become independent adults. He was fond of Ava enough to keep her around, minus a baby. He felt a level of comfort in being with her. Richard had originally admired Ava's perseverance when she began her employment at RMLH. She would complete the task at hand, with the determination to conquer any hindrance. Ava was determined to get her way, and she almost always succeeded.

Richard had seriously considered his situation with Ava, the moment she began hinting for a baby long before his divorce was final. He had determined definitively, that Ava's sole desire to have a child with him was the financial security that the baby's paternal lineage would guarantee her. Without a shadow of a doubt, Richard was decisively certain that he did not want to become a father again.

He unsuccessfully tried to convince Ava to reconsider a baby and reminded her that her sudden urge to become a mother was incongruent to the plans they had tentatively hoped to realize after he told Ava he was leaving Kate. The two were eager to take a long sabbatical from RMLH to embark on a journey to travel. The whole trip would be unplanned. They would start with one country and end up wherever they wished to go, whenever they wished to leave. Richard would have three of his vice presidents run the company, while he remotely checked in throughout his indefinite vacation. It would be a long-deserved break. If Ava were to get pregnant, this new carefree lifestyle he sought would indeterminately be postponed.

Richard surmised that he could not—in good conscience—father another child. He had three very valid reasons. The first, being that he wouldn't further embarrass Kate. While he realized his relationship with Ava could be seen as a cliché, he wouldn't subject himself to an irreversible act that he believed was downright foolish— seeing that he had adult children, and was already a half a century old, he was well beyond his siring years. Second, Ava's intentions were convoluted and solely based on financial gain. Lastly, a baby would interfere with his future for a dependent free life. Except for a baby posing as an encumbrance to his lifestyle, he was unable to disclose these reasons to Ava without offending her, so he chose to conceal them. He believed Ava would not change her mind, even though she had agreed to a six-month moratorium. Knowing her, she was probably plotting her pregnancy even though she agreed to wait. Richard had to do what he did best. He would have to take matters into his own hands to ensure that he would solely control the situation. A baby was entirely out of the question!

CHAPTER TWENTY-ONE
The Results (2015)

"Thank you for helping me out, Evan. I really appreciate all you have done for me these last two days," Ava said as the two walked to the entrance of the medical building, "I'm sure you wanted to tell me to go to hell when I asked you to meet at 5:30 instead of noon. I'm so sorry. I had a meeting that went into overtime. Thanks for being so flexible."

"Yeah, no problem, Ava. I didn't have anything scheduled then, so it all worked out," Evan replied, wondering what the hell he had gotten himself into, realizing that he had failed to consider the legal implications of what he was doing. The less he knew, the better.

They walked into the lab and noticed Shannon immediately look up as the door chimed.

"Oh, hello. You are here to pick up your results, right? I just need your partner to sign some forms. Tina said the doctor is waiting for you next door," Shannon preemptively stated nervously before the receptionist could greet Ava and Evan.

She slid the partition window open and had Evan sign a couple of forms. She handed Ava the file. As soon as the two walked out, Tina was waiting for them in the hallway, just outside her office suite.

"Let's go to the parking lot," she commanded as she motioned them to the stairway.

The three rushed down to the parking lot. Evan's phone began to ring.

"I have to take this. Excuse me, Ava. I'm no longer needed anyway," he said politely, relieved to excuse himself as the fake source of the semen sample that was tested by the lab. He stepped away and took the call.

"Where did you park?" Tina asked. "The farther we get from the office windows, the better," Tina said as she lit a cigarette.

"So, what are the results of Richard's semen quality analysis?" Ava eagerly asked as they walked towards the far end of the parking lot, where she and Evan had parked their cars.

"Ava, his semen is azoospermic," Ava stared at Tina blankly, so she continued, "which means his semen does not contain any sperm. The most common type of obstructive azoospermia is a result of a vasectomy. Is it possible he has had a vasectomy and hasn't told you?"

Ava was flabbergasted. She was stunned by the diagnosis and thus was rendered speechless for a moment.

"It's not unusual for men to have a vasectomy without the knowledge of their partners," Tina said clinically. "It has happened on several occasions at the urologist's office next door. Do you think Richard would have misled you?"

"It's possible," Ava said faintly, "Right after he asked me to wait six months to resume baby talks, he didn't want to have sex for a couple of weeks. He said the stress of the divorce was getting to him."

"Within six months after a vasectomy, a man's semen becomes azoospermic. So maybe he got a vasectomy behind your back and asked you to wait for six months before you started trying, knowing full well that you wouldn't get pregnant. You did say he didn't want any more kids. Maybe he acted proactively to ensure that he got his way?" Tina said, trying to do her best to ease this discovery, "No offense, Ava, but you can be very persuasive and relentless. It's possible he didn't want to argue about it." Tina was uncomfortable with the whole conversation. She just wanted to be done with this unethical drama and lose complete contact with Ava. "Please remember to be extremely discrete about this. Shannon and I stand to lose a lot if you reveal what we did. You can't tell Richard that you know he is azoospermic. I can't even say with certainty that he has had a vasectomy, but again, it happens all the time. Men get vasectomies behind their partners' backs… Look, I'm sorry to bring this up now, but Shannon is expecting me to deliver her cash at the end of the day, which is in fifteen minutes."

"Oh, of course," Ava muttered as she rummaged through her purse and handed Tina an envelope filled with cash, "here you are. You have my word that I will be extremely discreet about the lab test…and Tina, thanks for your help."

It was the first time Tina had witnessed this deflated side of Ava. Though she had recently begun to dislike her, she couldn't help but pity her. For months, she had been pumping herself with fertility medication trying to be careless particularly when she ovulated, hoping for an "accidental" pregnancy when it was just an exercise in futility all along.

"Look, for what it's worth, at least you know he is the one that is infertile, you can still be a mother. Maybe a sperm donor?" Tina's attempts to soothe her were failing. Little did Tina know that Ava only wanted to become pregnant if it was Richard's baby. "Take care. I have to go back to work. We'll get together soon, for dinner," she lied. She felt it was necessary to feign interest in their friendship a little while longer, so she would be certain that Ava would uphold her end of the bargain, and keep her mouth shut about Tina's involvement in analyzing Richard's semen.

Ava stood motionless in the parking lot, attempting to process the information she had discovered. She was almost certain that he had a vasectomy behind her back. There were too many coincidences that supported this idea. For starters, Richard had always been extremely paranoid and careful about birth control, even when Ava insisted that she was on birth control at the start of their affair when she really was. He was adamant about using condoms and pulling out. In fact, he was so controlling, he followed Ava's cycle and avoided intercourse when she was ovulating. He would not leave anything to chance to risk an unwanted pregnancy—as long as he was able to control it. This paranoia stopped a month before the end of the six-month waiting period. He must have known then that he was shooting blanks, at times, avoiding the use of condoms as well as withdrawal before ejaculating altogether; feigning that Ava had made him abandon all impulse control so that he wasn't fast enough to withdraw, falsely stating that if she got pregnant by chance, he would accept it.

When the six-month waiting period had come to an end, and Ava told Richard she had not changed her mind about a baby and was determined to have one, he uncharacteristically conceded and agreed to try to impregnate her. His behavior was strange, considering that only six months earlier, he had obstinately objected to another child, and pledged to convince Ava otherwise. However, during those six months, he never attempted to persuade her to forget the notion of becoming a mother.

Ava also recalled an incident shortly after they had agreed to wait right before they had started living together, where Richard was at home resting wearing loose athletic shorts with an ice pack on his pubic region. Richard had claimed that he had pulled his groin while playing tennis earlier that morning. When Ava offered to "massage" him, he rejected her advances that night and abstained from sex for two weeks, claiming the injury caused pain for that long.

Hindsight is 20/20; Ava thought to herself as she recalled specific quirks and instances that conclusively validated her theory.

"A behind the back vasectomy," she said aloud in disbelief, shaking her head.

She was shocked at how heartless Richard could be with someone he purportedly claimed to be very fond of. He never used the word *love*. Richard Morgan didn't *love*. He was incapable of feeling the emotion. People pleased and gratified him, or they didn't, and he disposed of them.

This is how he measured his affinity towards others. How could he unconscionably agree to father her child when he knew all along that he was sterile? He had a total disregard for her emotional and physical well-being, while she pumped herself full of fertility medications that completely threw her hormones out of whack!

Ava leaned against the driver's side door of her Audi A7, another job perk—a company leased vehicle. If she left RMLH and Richard now without securing another job, would she be able to afford this car and a nice home? Where could she find a comparable position? Where would she live until she sorted everything out? She couldn't believe it! That son of a bitch had outsmarted her! She was insulted by his actions and the fact that he secretly had a vasectomy. The most plausible explanation was that he was aware of Ava's motive to get pregnant, even though she had never uttered a word about it to anyone. He read people well. Ava was attracted to him; she cared for him, but more so he realized she appreciated the material incentives associated with his life.

Grappling with the realization that she did not have control of the situation was a hard pill to swallow. Richard had seized the reigns. His deceit was a complete turnoff, yet she was unable to recognize if her irritation originated from his dishonesty, or because she couldn't have his baby—her golden ticket to lifelong financial security. As she played out scenarios of leaving Richard in her head, her breath became progressively labored until she was hyperventilating.

"Relax," Evan said, "slow down your breathing. Purse your lips and breathe." He was approaching his car parked next to Ava's just in time to come to her aid.

After a few minutes, Ava regained a sense of calm, "Evan, I think I have to leave RMLH, and Richard, too…" she said shaking her head in an impassive state. She was still in complete shock over discovering Richard's betrayal.

Evan was unaware of what had just transpired, but it was apparent that the results of the test visibly perturbed Ava.

"Ava, let's get out of this parking lot and get a bite to eat. You look like you could use a friend right about now."

Ava nodded her head in agreement. Evan gently escorted her to the passenger seat of his car. Ava watched him pull out his phone and text while he walked towards the back of the car, then to the driver's seat.

"My car…" she slightly protested.

"Don't worry; I have a friend who works down the street. I texted him. I asked him to have his assistant give him a ride over here. He will drive your car back and park it at his office. We can pick it up later. Let me have your key…"

Ava was relieved that Evan had preemptively taken charge of the situation. The single thought preoccupying her mind at that moment was the logistics of leaving her job and Richard. Handling other details, no matter how mundane, like her car, would have resulted in a mental breakdown. Ten minutes later, she noticed a car pull up behind Evan's in the side-view mirror. She couldn't hear the exchange between Evan and his friend. Within a few moments, the friend drove away in Ava's car. Evan got into his car and started the ignition.

"My friend will park your car at my house. That way, we don't have to worry about getting back to a closed parking lot after hours," Evan said, "You can tell me all about what's happening over some drinks and dinner."

"Thanks, Evan. I don't know what I would have done if I hadn't run into you," Ava said, "Fortunately for me, you were around. What were you here for anyway, if you don't mind me asking?"

Had he known what had upset Ava minutes ago, Evan would not have answered honestly, "Follow up tests for a vasectomy reversal I had six months ago…" The irony was not lost on Ava.

CHAPTER TWENTY-TWO
A Friend in Need (2015)

"So, let me get this straight," Evan said pausing to take a sip from his glass of scotch, "you are convinced that he had a vasectomy behind your back approximately nine months ago? And you have been trying to get pregnant for three months? And he is aware that you have been taking fertility medication for these three months?"

"Exactly," Ava nodded, leaving out the part where she was taking fertility medications behind Richard's back for the full nine months. Disclosing this detail to Evan was irrelevant in painting herself as the victim of Richard's deception. It was possible that Evan could assist her in transitioning to a new career, so revealing her sly, yet failed attempt to outsmart Richard would not necessarily benefit her in this case. "He has betrayed my trust. I'm disgusted that he would stand by while I was taking all these fertility medications to get pregnant when it was impossible all along!"

"Yeah, but how could you be so sure he had a vasectomy?"

"There were too many occurrences that coincided with the aftercare of a vasectomy, and how his paranoia about me getting pregnant suddenly disappeared before the six-month waiting period. The details are too uncanny to ignore. I am certain he has had a vasectomy..." Ava took a long pause while she daintily placed a forkful of scallop in her mouth, and slowly chewed before continuing, "I can't work with him any longer, I can't live with him, and I can't stay with him. I can't," she said with determination.

"Well, if you are serious about leaving RMLH, I need a designer for a current project. I'm converting an eight-unit apartment into an eight-unit condo. I don't know what kind of compensation you receive at RMLH, but I'm certain I won't be able to offer you comparable income and benefits. I can offer you a handsome commission for this project, and any other subsequent projects that come along. I can't guarantee that you will have steady work for the full year since my business does not operate on the same scale as RMLH does, but you can see I have done well for myself, and I am constantly taking on projects with a break for a month here and there. If you are interested in working with me as an independent contractor, I will gladly hire you." Evan didn't mind paying a premium to contract Ava for the design phase of his projects. He was aware that her design direction would translate into increased profits. It would be a mutually beneficial business relationship.

Before RMLH, Ava's career plan was to work for an established design firm, gain some experience, and eventually start her firm. Within three years, she realized that her position was too lucrative to abandon for self-employment. With Richard's blessings, she accepted a few free-lance jobs from clients who had the potential to benefit her in the future, as long as these projects did not interfere with RMLH business. Ava's client's selection always favored the wealthy and influential. Her decision to forgo self-employment and selectively take on side projects was one she made with ease after she asked herself one rhetorical question. Why would she consider the headaches of self-employment when she was comfortably situated at the firm receiving handsome compensation in exchange for doing what she loved as well as building a network of powerful contacts? She had the best of both worlds.

Considering Richard's recent actions, Ava had cause to leave the confines of RMLH and venture out on her own. Having a steady flow of projects from Evan as well as her savings would allow her the financial flexibility to build a steady clientele base to start her own firm eventually. Her serendipitous encounter with Evan was becoming exponentially advantageous throughout the last two days. She would accept his proposal and arrange to leave RMLH.

"Sounds like an amazing opportunity, Evan. When can I start?"

Evan hadn't anticipated her immediate acceptance and was initially uncertain of his response, "You can start in two weeks. I will send you a proposal for the project in the next few days. If you accept it, I can take you to the job site, not this Tuesday, but the following Tuesday morning," he answered as he perused his phone calendar. "Oh no, sorry not Tuesday!" he immediately corrected himself, "I have a prior engagement. I can do Thursday at ten." Evan would meet with his urologist to discuss the results of his semen analysis. Having to wait a week and a half to see his doctor to receive the results of his six-month post vasectomy reversal semen analysis was nerve-racking, to say the least. He was eager to find out if he could father a child—Natalie's specifically.

"That works for me," Ava said agreeably. This sense of sudden relief brought on by Evan's job proposal allowed her to enjoy the rest of her meal fully. Everything was going to be all right. With her career situation sorted out, her next step was to focus on dealing with her relationship with Richard. She would leave him for certain. Packing her things and moving out immediately would be the wisest choice, in case Richard tried to persuade her to stay.

"What are you going to tell Richard? You can't tell him about the semen analysis test, so what are you going to say?"

"Somehow, I'm going to get him to confess. I need to hear it from him, even though I am convinced he has had a vasectomy," Ava responded. "Evan, I'm asking because you mentioned it in the car, you really had a vasectomy reversal?"

"Yes, I did, six months ago," he replied trying to answer as concisely as possible, a vain attempt to keep Ava's curiosity from peaking. She extended her neck and leaned her body forward while her eyes widened inquisitively, indicating that she wanted him to elaborate because she wasn't satisfied with his response. When he continued to refrain from expounding, she rolled her hand to gesture for him to keep on. Hesitantly he continued, "There's this woman from my past. I let her get away, and she is back in my life…for good now, I think…so the idea of settling

219

down and having a family with her appeals to me," Evan attempted to explain his relationship with Natalie as condensed and nonspecific as he could. He wouldn't disclose any details that could reveal he was involved with a married woman.

"What made you decide you wanted children now, after taking such a drastic measure to avoid it?"

Evan wasn't about to tell her that his original intent was to prevent gold-diggers from making paternity claims in the event of an unplanned pregnancy.

"I've grown attached to this woman, from my past, and I want her in my life. Aside from the obvious hope to share exciting ventures, I mostly want to experience the conventional with her. That includes a kid. I want to integrate her into my life—wholly."

"That's endearing, Evan. I hope it works out for you."

"I hope so, too," Evan retorted, "And I hope things work out for you as well.

"Thanks, they will eventually," Ava replied certain that all would end well in due time, "If you will excuse me, I'm going to head over to the ladies' room," Ava said as she wiped her mouth with her napkin, then placed it next to her plate, "be back in a minute." She pushed her chair back and stood up.

"Of course." Evan watched Ava disappear into a corridor.

Evan was pleased to contract Ava to work on his project. However, the events that had unfolded throughout the last twenty-four plus hours had left him feeling somewhat discombobulated. He couldn't quite identify what it was, exactly, but something about the exchanges between Ava and himself made him feel off kilter. After pondering about it for a few minutes, he attributed the source of his uneasiness to two factors. He had aided Ava in an unethical act and was unaware if he could truly trust her to keep from disclosing his involvement in the incident. If people found out about the favor he obliged Ava, he would be mortified. His participation in this fraudulent act would taint his reputation as a businessman. The possibility of Richard discovering Evan's role in assisting Ava at the lab further perturbed Evan.

Regardless of his knowledge or ignorance concerning Evan's role, Richard would not appreciate having an invaluable company asset poached by a rival developer—even one whose operations were on a much smaller scale. The likelihood that Evan's development firm would be the subject of retaliation from Richard Morgan for contracting Ava's design services immediately after her departure from RMLH was probable. Richard Morgan had enough clout to blacklist Evan from contractors, real estate agents, building inspectors, and other services useful in their industry. Richard could cripple Evan's projects simply by making requests over a few phone calls.

Evan felt his heart pulsating, and his forehead beading with sweat. He would ask Ava to temporarily refrain from disclosing their business relationship to keep Richard in the dark. Evan was successful, but he was realistic enough to differentiate that the level of success Richard had achieved made him an extremely influential man. Evan eagerly waited for Ava to return to the table so that he could discuss the matter.

"Ava, I need to ask you for a favor."

"Sure, anything, Evan. I feel like I owe you…" Ava said.

"I have never done business with Richard personally, but I know others who have. He is powerful and influential, and I would hate for him to target my business because of our business agreement, and so…"

"You don't want me to do the project anymore?" Ava interrupted before Evan could finish. Her tone had a sense of despair and desperation one would feel after a short and premature sense of relief from finding a resolution to a problem only to realize the problem had immediately resurfaced because the resolution was implausible, and thus would not be carried out.

"No! No! It's not that. Of course, I want you to do the design work for my project…I was hoping you could keep it confidential until Richard has gotten over losing his Director of whatever your title is or was…"

"Design Planning & Implementation," Ava replied with a sense of relief, "of course I can be completely discreet when working on your project, so Richard doesn't know who is employing me. Or I could tell him that this was a consultation project I had agreed to before leaving RLMH. That might be better, considering Richard's connections. He could easily find out who is writing me checks. All he needs to do is ask one of his bank friends to look up my account."

"That might be a better option. I can also write you a predated check to corroborate the timeframe."

"Perfect," Ava said with a restored sense of relief now that she was aware that Evan wasn't backing out of the project he had offered her.

"Great! I look forward to collaborating with you on this project," Evan said agreeably. "Should we head out? I will drive you back to your car?"

"Yes, please," Ava said realizing that she would have to go through with the inevitable. "I will be packing my things and leaving tonight. In the morning, I will head over to the office to resign from my position and tell him I'm leaving him."

"Have you thought about the reason you are going to give him for leaving?" Evan inquired, "Remember, you can't tell him you suspect or know that he has had a vasectomy."

"Oh, I won't reveal that, but I am hoping that he will. I will have to manipulate the conversation to have him confess to that, and I do have an idea. As for a reason as to why I am leaving, I'm going to tell him it's not working because I want a baby and he isn't being 100% supportive by refusing to be involved with a fertility specialist."

"Ok, looks like you have thought this out…and you planned it all out in the two hours we were at the restaurant while we were having a conversation," Evan stated impressed by her quick thinking and worried by her deceitfulness, simultaneously.

"I'm great at multi-tasking," Ava replied, "what can I say?"

Multitasking at being quick thinking and deceitful, he thought. *I need to be wary of her.*

Shortly after, Evan drove them back to his place, Ava got in her car, started the engine and lowered the window. Evan waited in the driveway, and the two began to chat. She reiterated how appreciative she was for all that Evan had done for her and for being so supportive. They bid their goodbyes.

"See you later," Evan said. By *later* Evan referred to their appointment a day short of two weeks when he would show Ava the project they were to collaborate on. Little did he know how soon *later* would be…

CHAPTER TWENTY-THREE
The Resignation (2015)

Richard wouldn't be home until much later that night, as he was entertaining business clients. It would be easy to gather her belongings and leave before his arrival. She only had her clothes, jewelry and toiletries to pack. Her furniture had been placed in storage nine months ago when she moved in with Richard. Fortunately, she still had the moving boxes she used for her clothes stored in the garage. After packing everything, she would drop her boxes off at the storage facility and check in to a hotel. She planned to return to the office in the morning to resign from RMLH, as well as to leave Richard. Richard always made it a point to stop by the office every Saturday morning at 7:00 am, for an hour or so, before he went to play a round of golf, or to the marina to sail. Ava didn't want to make a scene in front of the other employees, so resigning on a Saturday would be preferable.

Ava packed quickly and efficiently, managing to pack up her belongings in less than two hours. She had stopped at the office building underground parking lot to drop off the company leased Audi and pick up her eight your old BMW X5 before she returned home that night. She was grateful she had kept it, even though the corporation gave her a company car as a benefit. She didn't like driving the RMLH pick-up trucks when she needed an SUV for various aspects of the project. She felt they were too big, and she was steering a boat, so she elected to use her old car. She used it a couple of times a month. As she was packing boxes in the back seat of her car, the headlights of an approaching car in the driveway blinded her. Richard had returned much earlier than she had anticipated. He parked his car in the garage and walked out to the driveway.

"What the hell are you doing at this hour?" He asked in a condescending tone. "It's…." he paused to look at his watch and moved to the left where he squinted and held his wrist under one of the lights positioned above the garage, "10:37…You should be inside. Take care of these boxes in the morning…What are those boxes anyway? One of your moonlighting projects?" Although he was supportive of the consulting projects she accepted, he enjoyed hassling her over them because he believed she didn't need the additional work, "You could use one of the company pick-up trucks…instead of shoving these boxes in your car," Richard continuously commented and questioned, without giving Ava an opportunity to respond. It didn't surprise Ava that he managed to come off as arrogant even when he was trying to be helpful by offering to lend her an RMLH truck. He became less talkative once he glanced in the open trunk to discover Ava's set of designer luggage for which he had paid $30,000 at a charity auction they attended, shortly before they moved in together.

"Richard…" Ava began before she was interrupted.

"Where are you off to, Ava?" Richard asked, confused by what he had come home to.

"Richard, I'm sorry. I wasn't expecting you home this early; I was hoping to leave before you got home. I was going to come into the office in the morning to explain…" despite practicing potential conversations with Richard in her head during the entire course of packing, confronting Richard, in reality, was more difficult than she anticipated.

"What's going on here, darling?" Richard's displeasure was apparent in the way he addressed her. She sensed it the moment he called her "darling" in that icy, disconnected voice; he had detached from her emotionally. Further disconcerting was that the decision to detach had been made the instant he uttered the word. It had taken him a split second to determine the fate of their relationship.

Ava attempted to suppress her tears. Even though she wanted to leave him, the fact that he could disengage so effortlessly and hastily, hurt her feelings and bruised her ego. She understood that she had been discarded with minimum consideration.

The moon shone brightly in the driveway, illuminating Richard's features in great detail. He looked particularly handsome that evening. He couldn't conceal the contemptuous smirk fast enough to evade Ava's attention. His micro-expressions revealed his true emotions. Learning that she planned to leave that night without an explanation, replaced the fondness he felt towards her with disdain. With every passing moment, Richard grew more distant in his impatient stance and harsh gaze.

227

"Richard," Ava finally spoke. "I was going to show up to the office to resign from RMLH tomorrow and to let you know that I am leaving you. The baby situation is stressing me out. It's non-negotiable, I want a baby."

"And we had been trying to get you pregnant for the last three months..." Richard interjected. It was too late for Ava, she had crossed the threshold to the point of no return, but for the sake of argument, he brought up this point.

"And I have been taking fertility meds for the last three months, and I'm not getting pregnant. You refuse to have your semen analyzed; you don't want me to get pregnant through artificial insemination or IVF."

"Right, because if we got pregnant naturally, I'd be ok with it," he was already referring to their attempts to have a baby in the past tense. He was over her and the situation.

"And what if the problem lies with you...Here I am, pumping my body with these medications when there is a possibility that the reason I'm not pregnant is due to the poor quality and low sperm count of your semen!" Ava had calculated that insinuating that he might be sterile, would not be well received by an egomaniac like Richard. It might prompt him to go out of his way to prove the opposite, to restore the virile image he liked to project by admitting that he was indeed fruitful and that he had undergone a vasectomy to prevent him from fathering any more children.

Richard fell into Ava's trap, "My semen was never of poor quality. I told you from the beginning I didn't want any more kids. I just took control of the situation to ensure it would never happen."

Ava's astounded expression followed by several nods of acknowledgment clarified that she understood that he had undergone a vasectomy, "At the expense of my physical and emotional well-being? Giving me false hope when you knew all along that I wouldn't get pregnant?" Ava argued.

"I thought you would come to your senses, eventually. We could have had a good life together. Besides, I don't think you are the maternal type, let's be honest, having my child would serve as an insurance policy. You aren't the first gal to want to play that game." Richard haughtily retorted.

Unable to contain her anger, Ava raised her right hand to slap Richard. Standing across her, he caught her wrist mid-air and held it tightly, while he smiled slyly.

"Goodbye, Richard," Ava said, as she pulled her wrist out of his grip. Richard backed away. She picked up the last box, shoved it in the passenger side back seat of the car, and slammed the door.

As Ava walked over to the driver's side, Richard walked back towards the garage. She climbed into the driver's seat and leaned over to pull the door closed, but kept it ajar when she heard Richard's voice. He had turned around right before he was to enter the garage and called out to her.

"Ava, I expect to see you in the office tomorrow morning at 7 am sharp. I tee off at 9 am, so that will give us an hour to meet. I think it's best the exchange happens on a Saturday, out of sight of the other staff. You will be spared an audience and their speculation, while we discuss the terms of your resignation," he stated nonchalantly.

Without waiting for a response, he walked into the garage and clicked on the garage door button.

Ava watched the garage door slide down until it was completely shut. She was flabbergasted. Did she mean so little to Richard? Things had not gone according to how she predicted they would turn out, but Ava was sure that Richard would put up some resistance when she confronted him, yet he had written her off the moment he discovered she was leaving. He didn't protest her decision or ask her to reconsider. At the very least, manipulating him into revealing that he had a vasectomy gave her a sense of closure. She knew for certain that he had deceived her into thinking they were trying to have a baby. She would never have to wonder.

Although she initiated the break-up, Ava felt like Richard had dumped her. Knowing Richard and his preference for prompt resolutions, the words exchanged between the two were the last they would speak regarding their relationship. He was over it. The subject of their break-up would be one that Richard would no longer broach. Tomorrow mornings conversation would solely pertain to business. Richard would finalize the details of Ava's resignation so that her departure from the company and the transitioning of the new director would be as seamless as possible. As much as she would love to believe that her exodus from RMLH would temporarily cripple operations in the Design Planning & Implementation Department, she knew such would not be the case. True, she excelled at her job, running the department efficiently and profitably, implementing exquisite and unique design elements for projects, but the reality was that she was expendable. There were a couple of designers at the firm suited to replace her. Within months, either candidate could proficiently head the department.

Overcome by both physical and mental exhaustion, Ava lacked the motivation and energy needed to transport her belongings to the storage space late at night. The storage facility was close to the office, and though she had a drive-up unit that offered twenty-four-hour access, it was probably best not to go by herself, late at night. She should have waited until the morning to leave, but her anger had gotten the best of her. She had hoped Richard would have attempted to dissuade her from leaving, by making a grand gesture of generosity like gifting her one of the RMLH homes, as proof of his devotion to her and his remorse for having a vasectomy behind her back. Though she would not be bound to Richard by having his baby, she would have a sense of security and the peace of mind that she owned a valuable piece of property, which could serve as a nest egg for her if he ever dumped her. She was unable to manipulate the situation to suit her need. Verbalizing her grievances would surely create a disagreement between the two, but after calming down, Ava was certain that Richard would realize his fault and attempt to appease her. Yet, when she told him she was leaving, he hadn't put up the slightest bit of resistance.

That night, during their confrontation, Richard had a drastic change of heart for Ava. It was like a switch had gone off in his head, and his feelings of adulation towards her had transformed into disdain, instantaneously. Ava had never seen this side of Richard, neither personally, nor in business. Even though Richard hadn't verbalized it, it became clear as day that at that moment he had seen her as ungrateful, and thus immediately shut her out. She had made an irrevocable and unforgivable error. He would never let her back in.

Ava drove to the office. She would park her packed car in the subterranean parking lot and spend the night at the office. With a duffle bag hanging over her shoulder, and a vanity case in hand, she walked towards the double doors leading to the foyer of the RMLH offices. The weekday night security guard, Salvatore, who looked to be mesmerized by a Netflix series he was watching on the computer, jolted by this unexpected visit, was now fully alert.

"Hello, Miss Ava," he said startled, "can I help you with those bags?"

"No thank you, Sal. I have some pressing work to take care of. I will be working through the wee hours of the night and early morning, so I brought a change of clothes," she said nervously. Her key cards still afforded her clearance and entry into the RMLH building; thankfully, Richard would wait until the morning to notify security of Ava's status as a non-employee to limit then eventually restrict access to the RMLH offices. Thus, she was spared the humiliation of being restricted of access to her office that night.

Her fingers clumsily dropped the key card before she inserted it into the elevator card slot, a security measure to track and regulate access to the building after hours. When she finally managed to slide the card in, the elevator door opened. She entered the elevator and again inserted the card in the slot on the inside of the elevator. This time, she held the card with both hands and guided it in. When the panel lit up, she pressed the button to her office floor. She nervously smiled at Salvatore as the doors shut close.

As soon as she got to her office, Ava released her sweaty grip from the handles of her duffel bag and vanity dropping them on the floor and placed her purse on the coffee table. She sat on the couch and laid down on her side, her body sluggishly moving and adjusting to find a comfortable position. Her arm felt heavy, as she reached for her purse and dug for her phone. She instructed Siri to set her alarm for 5:30 a.m., then passed out in a deep sleep.

At precisely 5:30 a.m., she awoke to the shrill, piercing beeps of her phone alarm. Stretching out to relieve her stiff neck and sore body, she let out a grumbling sound. She grabbed her duffel bag and vanity case. Dragging her feet against the floor like a zombie, she headed to the women's locker room of the office gym for a quick shower. In the locker room, she placed her bag on a bench and unzipped it. She rummaged through the bag and pulled out a pair of black cigarette pants, a black tunic, and a scarf splashed with a grey, turquoise, and black print. She would complete the look with a pair of black wedge side-zip booties.

By 6:30 a.m., Ava was dressed and ready. She gathered her belongings to take back to her car. At the foyer, she greeted Salvatore,

"Morning, Sal. I'm heading over to the Starbucks across the street, can I bring you anything?" There was an unfamiliar dullness to her usually lively voice. Her eyes didn't sparkle when she smiled that morning.

"No thank you, Miss Ava. My shift is coming to an end in fifteen minutes. Have a good day and enjoy your weekend."

"Thanks, Sal. You, too." This would probably be their last conversation. She lingered for a while, smiling at him, trying to find the right choice of words, so that when he found out about her departure, he could look back to that morning and understand the source of her bittersweet demeanor. All she could come up with was, "Goodbye, Sal."

After grabbing a cup of coffee, Ava returned to the RMLH office building. The weekend day security officer greeted her in a manner that made it obvious that he was expecting her, "Miss Ava, good morning. Mr. Morgan is waiting for you in his office. He asked that you head over there immediately."

"Thank you, George. I'm on my way," she replied. *Douchebag,* she thought to herself. She wouldn't miss seeing him again. He was a total imbecile and a pervert. George had been at RMLH for two years. Ava had never warmed up to him, sensing something was off about the guy from the get-go. Discovering his termination from the TSA after an incriminating internal investigation stemming from numerous complaints stating that he excessively singled out attractive women for pat downs proved that her initial gut feelings about the guy were spot on and rightfully justified.

"Good morning, Richard," Ava said as she walked into his office. She could only see the back of his head, as Richard's chair was facing the window. He had been gazing out in the distance in a meditative stance when he was alerted to her presence.

"Hello, Ava," Richard replied. He turned his chair around and scooted closer to the desk, "please have a seat," he said as he motioned to the two chairs in front of his desk, "I believe I have drafted a fair resignation agreement. You can take a few minutes to read it before you sign it.

Basically, RMLH asks that you sign a non-disclosure form baring you from discussing our projects with others, including competitors. We ask that you delete our design software from all your private electronic devices, as the software is the intellectual property of RMLH. Please do not replicate RMLH designs for future projects. Rather than have a security guard escort you to your office to watch you gather your belongings, or to submit your laptop, mobile phone and key cards to human resources, I will wait here until you gather your belongings in your office and turn over your equipment to me. You can hold onto your phone for a few days until you get a new mobile phone, but you will not be able to transfer business contacts to your new phone. You can drive the Audi for the remainder of the lease if you want to take over the lease. If you agree with the terms and sign the agreement, you get a six-month severance check. In doing so, you also abdicate any rights to pursue litigation against RMLH for any grievances that occurred during your employment."

The agreement seemed fair enough. She realized that being asked to give up her right to litigation was Richard's attempt to absolve himself of any sexual harassment lawsuit. He realized that Ava had the option to reject the agreement to play the sexual harassment card. While he was confident that he would win the case, considering Ava moved in with him and continued to work at RMLH after their initial sexual encounter, if he refused an out of court settlement and proceeded with a court case, the experience would be a loss of time and money.

Ava realized that signing the agreement would be the most amicable and mutually beneficial way to end her business relationship at RMLH. After reading the last sentence of the draft, Ava looked up and said,

"Do you have a pen? I can return my mobile phone today, as well as the Audi." In addition to keeping her old car, Ava had never canceled her personal mobile phone. She had simply forwarded her calls to her business mobile, so she could receive personal calls without carrying around two phones. As for her business contacts, she had saved them to her personal Gmail account, but she would not poach RMLH clients. If she needed to reach out to previous clients, she could. Or if they wanted her services, they would be able to seek her out and find her.

Richard, gratified and slightly surprised by her abrupt acquiescence, smiled and handed her a pen. After signing the draft, Ava stood up and placed her bag on the desk. She hovered above it, as she searched through the contents of her purse. She pulled out her key cards, the keyless remotes, and her mobile phone and placed them on the desk. Anticipating that she would have to relinquish her mobile phone, she had backed-up the necessary files and reset her phone to factory settings, while waiting for her coffee.

"I need about a half hour to clear out my belongings from my office."

"That's fine. Let me know when you finish cleaning out your office," he said turning to his monitor to his right.

Ava walked to her office in haste. Twenty-four hours ago, she never thought she would be undergoing such a drastic life change. She had misjudged her influence over Richard and was already regretting her actions. She didn't recognize the man she just met with. He was reserved and cold during their interaction. She stopped at the supply room to grab a few boxes. She didn't have much to pack, as she followed a minimalist philosophy about possessions and clutter, except for her shoes and clothing. When she was done gathering her belongings, she returned to Richard's office.

"I am ready, Richard," Ava said after parking a cart with three boxes outside his office door, trying her best to appear aloof and unfazed, even though she was homeless, with the possibility of being jobless, once she completed Evan's project. Though she was offered and accepted to work on Evan's project, she really didn't know if he would continue to offer her projects upon completion of the eight-unit conversion. She noticed Richard press a button on the intercom panel at his desk.

"This is for you," he said, holding out an envelope, of which she presumed was her severance. She stared at the envelope, uncertain if she should open it. "Six months' pay," he clarified. "Thank you for keeping this as civilized as possible." From his stance and his grin, it was obvious he was enjoying every minute of Ava's discomfort. That he had stripped Ava of her prestigious title and position at RMLH and left her momentarily homeless obviously pleased him. She knew he thought of her as ungrateful— after everything he had bestowed upon her, so he would show her that he could take all of it away. Richard's position in life afforded him a sense of control. While others of similar status felt a sense of heaviness and discomfort in influencing situations pertaining to others' livelihood, Richard relished it. Wielding that kind of power fed his ego. Often likening himself to a benevolent despot, he believed himself to be harsh yet fair, while others viewed him as an egotistical asshole. He knew that

Ava wouldn't be destitute. She would find a gratifying job elsewhere, but she would be inconvenienced and humiliated—and most importantly she would be punished for being unappreciative.

Ava wouldn't thank him. She pursed her lips, in a sour and silent acknowledgment and put the envelope in her purse. Without a card key, she assumed that he would escort her to the elevator, but to her disappointment, she saw George standing at the door when she turned around.

"Can I push the cart down to the parking lot for you, Miss Ava?" he asked politely, but his smug smirk revealed his dislike for her.

"No!" Ava snapped, "I'm quite capable of pushing a cart myself." She stormed out of the office. George followed behind her. When they got to the elevator, he took his time pulling out his key card to place it in the slot and press the button. Like Richard, he enjoyed exercising control over others—even in this limited capacity of having access to the building while Ava did not. Since the beginning of his employment, he had sensed Ava's scorn for him. Years of brownnosing Ava because of her position in the company and her status as Richard Morgan's girlfriend had been fruitless, as his flattery was reciprocated with contempt. The rejection had festered and brewed into abhorrence and was now manifesting into satisfaction, as he witnessed Ava suffer through this humiliation.

When they finally made it to the lobby door leading to the parking lot, Ava turned around and stated, "I can take it from here, George. That will do. You can go back to the desk."

"That cart is RMLH property. I can't leave you unattended…."

Ava held up her hand before he could finish and said, "Get a fucking life!" She hastily carted the boxes to her car and quickly loaded them behind the passenger seat in the back. The trunk and the seats were already full of her belongings. She turned around and shoved the cart towards George but was mindful not to hit him with it, "There's your damn cart!"

It wasn't until after Ava had left the office parking lot, drove to the storage facility, and was unloading boxes into her storage space that the gravity of the situation struck her. While her financial standing was secure given her six-month severance, as well as her robust savings, she would have to find employment with comparable compensation to maintain a desirable lifestyle. Most disconcerting was the fact that she was homeless. Her spirits lifted once she realized that temporary housing would not be an issue. She would reach out to her network of developers and ask to rent something short term as a favor. She couldn't commit to a living situation until she sorted out her employment status. Would she rent or buy? Was it time to invest in her future and buy a property rather than rent one? Attempting to answer these questions was futile until she resolved her employment situation. Hopefully, all would go well with Evan's project so that he would rehire her for subsequent projects while building a client base for her own design firm. She could then decide if and where she would rent or buy. For now, she would take residence at a hotel. The Luxe in Brentwood would make for a nice temporary residence in a desirable centralized location. Ava would overcome this temporary setback; she would piece together these fragmented parts of her life and prevail. She would look back at this impediment to discover Richard Morgan was a mere stepping stone. Ava was determined.

CHAPTER TWENTY-FOUR
The Grand Finale (2015)

That morning was like any other beautiful, May, southern California morning. Natalie awoke to a sensation of chills from a fresh breeze blowing through her open balcony door. Sunlight filtered through the leaves of the tree outside her window creating a warm glow. The sound of birds chirping echoed in the peace of the morning. With the stimulation of each sense, Natalie arose from her peaceful slumber to a state of consciousness. Excitement overcame her entire being when she realized it was Tuesday. Spending the entire day with Evan was something she had been looking forward to for the last two weeks, but that day was also bittersweet. She would have to end her relationship with Evan. It had become too risky. Leaving Eric for Evan might have initially seemed more appealing, but she believed in time various circumstances would eventually lead them to be unhappy with one another. Eric was the safe choice.

Manically she rushed through her morning routine and was relieved when Eric announced to the boys that it was time to head to school. She kissed and embraced each child and bid them farewell.

"Have a great day at school, boys. I love you!" she said giddily handing them their lunch boxes. Unable to contain her excitement, she couldn't stop smiling.

"What's so amusing?" her eight-year-old, Alan, asked suspiciously.

"Nothing…I'm just so proud of the little men you two are becoming," she rebounded, suddenly aware that she should try not to appear so overzealous to see them leave. She ruffled the hair on the top of his head and gave him another kiss.

"Amusing is one of my spelling and vocabulary words this week," Alan said as he shoved the last apple slice from his breakfast into his mouth. He was no longer suspicious or offended.

She smiled at him and said, "Morning interactions with you are always *amusing.* Now off you go."

She watched him as he threw his backpack over his shoulder and walked out the door. She felt a pull at her heartstrings. Aidan and Alan were a great source of pride to her and her most cherished accomplishments. She loved them more than anything. They were well-adjusted, sweet, conscientious, and loving. The trivial exchange that transpired between her and her child reminded Natalie of how important it was to follow through with her decision today. She couldn't disrupt their lives. The reckless behavior had to stop.

Forty-five minutes later, Natalie found herself at Evan's door. "I'll be right there," Evan's voice echoed through the intercom, startling her after she rang the door chime. She ironed out her skirt with her hands before the door opened to reveal Evan with a towel wrapped around his waist, beaming ear to ear, "Sorry, I was running a tad late this morning...I just jumped out of the shower."

"No worries," Natalie said as she glided inside, almost floating on air, high on happiness and the anticipation of the pleasure she was about to receive. He reached behind her and shut the door. She couldn't take her eyes off Evan.

Within moments, she threw herself at him, her legs wrapped around his waist, her hands clinging to his shoulders. She stared intently into his eyes, then tenderly kissed him on the lips. His lips tasted like minty mouthwash with a hint of aftershave. He parted her lips with his tongue and began ardently kissing her, while she rubbed her lower body against his, feeling his manhood harden with each stroke.

She pulled her lips away from his and nibbled on his right ear before she breathlessly whispered into it, "I missed you so much, Evan."

"I missed you, too, Nat," he retorted, as he lifted her slightly to get a better grip of her to carry her off to the bedroom, where he gently placed her down.

It didn't take long for Evan to strip Natalie. She stood in the middle of his bedroom, their gazes interlocked for the duration. He lifted her arms and pulled her blouse off. He then unbuttoned and unzipped her skirt and watched the article of clothing fall to her feet. He held her hand as she stepped out of the skirt and kicked it to the side. Wrapping his arms behind her back, he unhooked her bra. Sliding his hands to her breasts, he then lifted the cups up and off her breasts—taking her breasts into his hands and then his mouth. He backed away and pulled his towel off. The sight of her standing in his bedroom in nothing but a pair of black panties made his cock throb painfully. He slid behind her, wrapping her in his arms again. He patted his penis against her silky panties, stroking her from the outside. When her panties scrunched to the side, and his penis brushed against her, he could feel her wetness. Her crotch pulsated, eagerly awaiting to be conquered by Evan. Evan backed up and sat down on his bed at the foot of the bed. Natalie turned around and faced him. She pulled her panties down over her hips until they slid off her legs and feet. She walked over to Evan and straddled him, gliding up and down his penis. As he pulled her inwards to penetrate her deeper, she felt radiating heat with each stroke. Natalie pushed Evan down so that he was no longer sitting up but lying back. Aggressively, she held each one of his wrists down on the bed for support and clasped her thighs on each side of his hips. She began grinding into him intensely. With her eyes closed, she concentrated on the rhythm of her strokes, emitting variable grunts illustrative of the pleasure and the intensity of each movement, as if in a state of trance attained by a sense of sexual pleasure on a most primal and animalistic level.

Evan was beside himself. In the absence of any carnal contact with Natalie for three weeks, followed by a fiery start to their day of sexual escapades, he felt as though he could explode. *How was it possible that sex with Natalie only got better, even after two years?* He couldn't take it lying on his back anymore. He felt an impending urge to overpower and ravish her that moment, so he tossed her on the bed and climbed behind her. As he pounded her doggy style, she looked back at him seductively. He tugged at her hair with one hand and held onto one of her hips with the other, guiding the pace of his strokes to make their interaction as mutually pleasurable as possible. The two moaned and groaned in ecstasy until they came simultaneously. He lay on top of her for a minute, both breathing heavily. Evan rolled to Natalie's side and pulled Natalie on her side. Their naked, sweaty bodies clinging to each other, their legs intertwined, as they kissed passionately. Natalie derived immense pleasure from this type of post-orgasmic skin to skin contact with Evan— physically, mentally, and emotionally. While in this vulnerable state of nakedness her clothes weren't the only thing shed. She had also discarded her inhibitions, letting herself go without any restraint. It was in this exposed state though that she realized she wielded the most sexual prowess over Evan.

"Natalie," Evan said softly, "that was amazing."

"Mmmmm," Natalie purred and stretched, "it was, Evan. I feel rejuvenated…"

How would she be able to give this up? She couldn't, but Evan had given her an ultimatum. And their affair was at risk of being discovered, so she had to. She wouldn't bring that up now and risk ruining this day with Evan.

The two laid on their backs in silence for minutes, their breaths finally slowing to a normal pace. Natalie felt a chill, goose bumps formed on her skin as the air conditioning vent blew cool air over the bed. She reached for the bed sheet and pulled it over them backing up into Evan until the two were spooning. Their naked bodies once again came into contact. Evan put his arm over Natalie and fondled her breasts. She scooted back and felt him harden again.

The two continued to engage in sultry and unbridled sex, intoxicated by their all-consuming, insatiable desire for one another. Shortly past noon, Evan got out of bed and slid open the patio door.

"Come on," he said to Natalie, "Let's take a quick dip in the pool until our lunch arrives."

Natalie jumped out of bed and followed Evan outside.

"Can anyone see us out here?" she asked, worriedly surveying the backyard for a privacy breach. Although Evan had 180-degree views from his backyard, the perimeter was outlined with strategically placed shrubs, plants, trees, and modern wood fencing to ensure total privacy.

"Not unless they were flying overhead. It's absolutely private." Evan responded, then jumped into the crystal-clear infinity pool that butted at the outermost periphery of his yard.

Natalie jumped in after him. The water was warm enough to jump in without causing a shock, but at the same time cool enough so that it was refreshing. Natalie swam a couple of laps back and forth the length of the pool, then joined Evan who was resting his chin on his arms flanking the edge of the pool, beholding the breathtaking valley view.

"It's peaceful up here, isn't it?" he asked

"It is," Natalie agreed. This was only the second time she had been to Evan's home. The first time was three weeks ago after he was discharged from the hospital. Just like the previous visit, she felt a life with Evan suited her. Being with him did feel like second nature, but she still had her reservations. She had considered all aspects of her relationship and had conceded that her best course of action was to end their affair.

"So, when are you going to move in?" Evan asked slyly looking over at Natalie and grinning. His grin turned into a confused grimace once he saw Natalie's facial expression—a look of burden that could only be relieved by a grave confession contradictory to the expectations of the recipient of the revelation. In that one look, he felt a pang of pain—not for the potential of losing the woman he loved, but for recognizing the agony, the decision caused her. At that moment, that look communicated the emotional and mental struggle that had overwhelmed Natalie for the last two years. He understood that she cared for him deeply, possibly even more than she cared for Eric, but her underlying responsibility to her family could not be neglected or overlooked. He suddenly got it, and he didn't want to burden or fault Natalie for failing to leave her family to be with him. He bore culpability for this predicament, realizing he should have fought harder to convince Natalie to be with him before she got married. It finally clicked. Sadly, theirs was a love plagued by inopportune timing.

"About that, Evan…" Natalie struggled with her words, "I'm sorry, I understand where you are coming from, and I don't have any right to expect that you wait around for me and give-up your chance to have your own family…"

"It's ok, Natalie," Evan interrupted, "I get it. I know this has been a difficult decision for you."

"Well, let me finish, Evan. Again, I want to reiterate that if it were just me, I would have left Eric a long time ago. But the fact is, I am responsible for these two little humans, and I just want to give them stability and comfort.

You make me happy, and I love you, but I have to be accountable for my children," Natalie managed to divulge her thoughts. She didn't feel it necessary to disclose that she had serious doubts about Evan's fidelity if she were to leave Eric. She did find it necessary to tell her about Ellen's accusations, Arthur's suspicions, and her sudden disdain for Melanie, as well as her fear of their affair being exposed. "For now, we will have to end this. Who knows what the future holds?" Evan quietly listened until it was clear that she was waiting for a response.

"I have a confession to make," Evan said calmly, "I truly believed that you were coming here for some celebratory sex fest to let me know you were leaving Eric. I guess I believed what I wanted to believe. I've felt for some time now, that we would eventually end up together, and we could have a family of our own. About six months ago, I decided that I had to take some action. That's when I began to pressure you to leave Eric. I believed you would, eventually… I had a vasectomy reversal. I thought once you discovered the effort I made to make these goals realizations, you would change your mind, and everything would fall into place."

"Evan, I've told you I wouldn't have any more kids," Natalie started but was interrupted before she could continue.

"You said what you had to say, now let me…" Evan stated, "It's pointless to discuss having a baby with you, now that you have decided to stay with Eric. I also realize that I should find a partner; continuing to see you would only hinder that. I don't want to grow old and die alone. I meant what I said; I still want a family. Maybe then I will completely understand your reluctance to leave Eric. I mean I get it, I understand what you are saying, but it's hard to accept. Casting me aside for Eric and your children is easy to comprehend, but difficult to digest. After today, we can no longer continue to see each other—not even after your friend's suspicions subside."

"You do realize that this decision doesn't make me happy, right? It's just that, as adults, we sometimes have to make the right decision even if it isn't the preferable choice—for the common good."

"We aren't writing the Declaration of Independence, Natalie, we are ending an affair. It is what it is," he said disappointedly. He got out of the pool and walked over to the cabana. Less than a minute later he emerged wearing a bathrobe. He handed Natalie a towel and said, "Lunch should be here any minute, why don't you dry off? Let's enjoy the rest of the time we have with each other."

"Ok," Natalie said, "I'll be out in a minute, just set the towel on the lounge chair."

Evan did as she asked, then disappeared inside when he realized that the delivery guy was at the door. Natalie swam a few more laps, then exited the pool. She wrapped the towel around her and took a seat at the patio table. During lunch, they managed to suppress the melancholy and focus on the positive.

They spent the rest of the afternoon enjoying each other's company. After some meaningful conversation, they moved back into the bedroom and spent the rest of the day making love. Evan was on top of Natalie, as she clung to him with her legs wrapped around his mid-section. Each time he thrusted she cinched her legs tighter to ensure she felt all of him inside her. Ecstatically taking him in deeper each time, until she turned her head to the side and saw the time on the alarm clock on the nightstand. When Natalie realized her time with Evan was fleeting, a wave of emotion washed over her, just as they began to climax, Natalie began to cry. The intensity of feelings and emotions were overwhelming. She could not contain her tears or maintain her calm, and yet she didn't care. She felt it compulsory to expose this vulnerability in all its candor, with the intent of letting Evan know how deeply she cared for him, and that the choice to end their affair was something she did not look forward to.

"I love you," she stated emphatically, as tears streamed down her cheeks.

"Shhh, don't cry, Natalie. It's ok," he whispered, "I love you, too." He knew this to be true.

A half hour later, Evan watched Natalie pull out of his driveway. They had agreed to stop seeing each other—cold turkey—a feat that would prove difficult for both, but a necessary measure if Natalie was to preserve her marriage and Evan was to carve out a slice of happiness of his own. Evan took a deep breath, turned around, and headed towards the front door. When he heard a text notification on his phone, he pulled it out of his pocket and checked the incoming text.

Is it safe to come home now? Read the text from Ava.

Yes. Evan replied.

CHAPTER TWENTY-FIVE
The Houseguest (2015)

F ive days earlier, Evan was on his way to meet Ava at the vacant, run-down, eight-unit apartment building she had accepted to do the design work for, untroubled by the heavier than usual traffic. As he patiently navigated through the morning rush hour, his mind drifted off to the conversation he had two days ago with his urologist. His vasectomy reversal was successful. Once Natalie confirmed that she would leave Eric, Evan would inform her about his procedure. Although Natalie had mentioned in several casual conversations that she wouldn't have any more children, he was certain that he would be able to convince her otherwise, at least to agree to have one more child with him.

When Evan pulled into the parking lot of the property, he was happy to see Ava waiting for him. She had gotten there earlier than their scheduled appointment.

"Ava, good morning, it's nice to see you," Evan said, as he emerged from her car.

"Good morning, Evan," Ava said cheerfully, "I can't thank you enough for this opportunity. I'm convinced that I can be an invaluable benefit to your organization," she continued with her exaggerated enthusiasm.

"I think you are right," he said humoring her eagerness. Obviously, she was putting on some act, but Evan didn't understand the reason for it. Her qualifications were unquestionable. Evan could delegate the design work to Ava and comfortably remove himself from that aspect of the project, confident that the results would be nothing short of exceptional. "Ready to see what you have signed up for?" he asked.

"I'm ready," Ava said. She was no longer with RMLH, but she wasn't disheartened, as she realized this transition could have the potential to propel her in a path towards self-employment.

Evan's belief that bringing Ava on this project would only increase the project's value was reinforced after she shared her preliminary design ideas throughout the walk-through. The woman was a true visionary. After the initial tour, she excused herself to take photographs, measurements, and notes, while Evan reviewed structural plans with the contractor and engineer. An hour and a half later, Evan and Ava converged inside a bungalow brought on site and used as an office, where Ava enthusiastically elaborated her plans to transform the units, assuring Evan that she would have initial design plans ready to review within a week. Though Ava's excitement regarding the project was obvious and sincere, Evan sensed that there was some impediment to Ava's satisfaction, like an encumbrance restricting her from fully enjoying this moment.

"Is something not to your liking, Ava?" Evan asked, "it seems like you are holding back."

"Evan, the project is perfect for me. I am pleasantly surprised by the scope, the creative freedom, and the arrangement as a whole;" Ava began explaining. "The truth is, I am in essence…homeless. While I am currently staying at a hotel, I need to find a more permanent residence. Until I can resolve my relocation predicament, I'm going to feel this constant stress to find a home. Though I can guarantee you, that my residential status will in no way interfere with my capacity to professionally fulfill my obligations to the fullest of my capabilities for this project as stated in our contract…"

Evan interrupted her before she could continue.

"Is there any way I can help?" Evan asked innocently, momentarily forgetting how much trouble helping Ava had proven to be a couple of weeks ago. Yet, he couldn't resist, as he felt compelled to offer some sort of assistance.

"Well, considering you are asking…I mean, I would never come out and ask you, but since you have offered to help…" Ava stammered as she tried finding the best way to verbalize her jumbled thoughts –thoughts that came out of her mouth before her brain could fully process them. She took a breath, regrouped by focusing on her thoughts for an extended period, then proceeded, "Evan, I would be indebted to you and so very appreciative if you would allow me to rent one of the units while I worked on the project. I need some time in determining where I will live and whether I will rent or buy, so, if you allowed me to lease a unit short term while I'm working on your project, you would be helping me out tremendously."

Arlette Eshraghi

"Ava, you can't live here. It's a construction site. We will tear down walls; you won't have access to water and power. Obviously, it's dangerous." Evan played into Ava's trap just as she hoped he would, "There's got to be a better solution to this."

"I don't know, Evan. I can't really focus on making a home for myself while I'm undertaking a project like this, and staying at a hotel is getting expensive," Ava said attempting to garner Evan's sympathy. "I mean, could you imagine if you were suddenly displaced from that beautiful home of yours during a considerable project like this? Having to look for a home while devoting all your energy on a project of this scope would be difficult…" And then as if something in Ava's brain clicked, her eyes and mouth simultaneously widened. She covered her mouth with both hands as if attempting to contain some magnificent realization. After a theatrical pause, she removed her hands from her mouth, and said, "Oh my god, Evan! Your house! I mean it's so big, couldn't I rent the cabana in the back temporarily?"

Evan was taken aback. Stunned by this proposal, he couldn't distinguish the exact source of his bewilderment—Ava's idea or how brazen she was in asking him for this favor.

"Ava, I can't rent you the cabana. That wouldn't work out. With all the people you know, I am sure you will be able to find a short-term rental."

"I just haven't had the chance to find something yet. I promise I wouldn't be a bother, if I could rent the cabana temporarily...you wouldn't even notice me."

"Well, like I said, renting the cabana wouldn't work out. I use that space a lot when I entertain. I'll tell you what. You can stay in the house as a guest for a couple of weeks, but you must promise me that you will actively seek out rentals. You can take the guest suite. It has an adjacent sitting room you can use as an office."

"Oh, thank you, Evan. I can't thank you enough. You have been so kind to me. So, I can check out of the hotel tomorrow, and bring my things over around 11:30 in the morning if that's ok?" Evan nodded unenthusiastically. "Thank you!" She exclaimed a second time, as she wrapped her arms around his neck and planted a kiss on his cheek.

"You are welcome, but remember the condition," he said hoping to reiterate that this was a very temporary solution to her problem, "Oh! I do have one more request. You can't be at the house all day Tuesday, from 9 am to 6 pm. I have some business to take care of…an all-day meeting," he lied.

"An all-day business meeting at your home?" Ava cynically questioned.

"It doesn't concern you, and it's very important—so, you will have to be gone, *all* day" he repeated the original sentiment with the implication that his request was serious, and she was not to meddle in his personal affairs.

"Of course," retorted Ava, "I can do that." She sighed a long exhalation of relief, "I truly am grateful to you, Evan. You have come through for me. I won't ever forget your kindness."

"Sure, Ava, just don't make me regret it," he said jovially, concealing his concern about being manipulated by Ava again.

"Ok, my work here is done for today. I will see you tomorrow," Ava cheerily said, gathering her belongings.

Evan was beginning to think that his interactions with Ava were becoming more and more exhausting each time he saw her. He placed his left thumb and middle finger on either side of his temples and closed his eyes, applying pressure in a circular motion in an attempt to relieve himself of the stress he endured during his last exchange with Ava. He was discontented for repeatedly allowing this woman to bamboozle him. Whether it was convincing him to become an accomplice to one of her devious schemes or weaseling herself into becoming his houseguest, he realized he would have to establish strict boundaries with Ava to avoid falling victim to her manipulations. When he second-guessed his decision to work with Ava, he looked on the bright side. At the very least, the stress caused by her dramatic episodes was well worth her artistic ability to transform residences from the humdrum to exquisitely tasteful abodes; for her designs would result in increased profits.

CHAPTER TWENTY-SIX
A Twist of Fate (2015)

Evan awoke to a pounding headache. He felt a throbbing pain shooting through his head like he had just come to after violently being knocked unconscious. Blinded by the bright burst of sunlight cascading in his room, he squinted his eyes as he lifted his wrist closer to glance at his watch. It was 6:18 am. The last thing he remembered from the night before was finding solace in a bottle of whiskey just after Natalie had left his home. They had decided that the best course of action was to end their affair. It was over between the two of them.

Moving the bed sheet lower away from his upper body, he scratched his chest. As he yawned, he stretched his arms above his head. When he dropped his arms on either side, to his right, he felt a soft lump, like the flesh of a woman's body covered by the sheets. Startled by the fact that he was unaware of whom he had shared his bed with, Evan froze.

Flashbacks of the night before began playing in his head. Slowly, he began to piece the events of the prior night. He was pouring himself one drink after the other until the bottle of Gentleman Jack was bone dry. Halfway through the bottle, Ava had come home, distraught about some gossip an ex-co-worker had shared with her. Rumor had it that Richard wanted to reconcile with Kate and was aggressively pursuing her. Kate repeatedly rejected his advances. Evan pretended to listen to her, feigning interest in her story, as he drunkenly attempted to concentrate on the movie playing in the background. It was one of his favorites, *Die Hard*. He recalled Ava joining him on the couch to watch the movie after she grabbed herself an entire bottle of wine. At some point, he remembered they started making out after a quick skinny-dip in the pool, where they eventually made their way to the bed. Snippets of their sexual romps replayed in his head, a smile formed on his lips as he recollected how pleasurable the night had been. *Oh, shit!* He thought to himself. It was Ava who was beside him.

Initially, he was onset by a sense of panic, because of his current state of being. His thoughts became preoccupied with the uncertainty of the direction their relationship would take after this unexpected turn of events. How would their current business and living arrangement evolve after their post-coital interaction? They could move forward from this experience, couldn't they? They were mature adults who found companionship with one another while they were hurting. They could either decide to maintain a sense of professionalism going forward or continue having fun. Evan was uncertain of how a sober Ava would react to waking up in his bed.

Would she think he had taken advantage of her while she was intoxicated? They were both inebriated; she could have easily taken advantage of him. He was anxious to see how this would play out. So, he decided he would follow Ava's lead. He would be comfortable with however Ava wanted to handle this. At the very least, he knew he had enjoyed the prior night because Ava had managed to get him to stop brooding over Natalie.

Evan quietly emerged from the bed, making his way to the kitchen. He reasoned that the initial post-coital exchange between the two would be easier after he had consumed a large dose of caffeine.

****

The aroma of freshly brewed coffee permeated the kitchen and quickly wafted towards the hallway leading to the bedrooms stimulating Ava's sense of smell, and gently nudging her out of her deep, drunken stupor. Ava opened her eyes. It took a moment to orient herself with her surroundings. She too had intense pressure pulsating in her forehead, which muddled her sense of balance, making it a tad more challenging just to sit up in bed, let alone stand up. She was in Evan's bed, she realized. It was never her intention to sexualize her relationship with Evan, but now that she had, she was not disappointed.

While she realized that she lived calculating almost all aspects of her life, she found this unexpected turn of events to be refreshing and a welcomed distraction. She would have to tread with caution, though. She could not risk jeopardizing her business relationship with Evan. Currently, he was her lifeline to establishing herself as a self-employed designer. His business offer had come at a most crucial time, and she had to prioritize that above anything else. Yet, she could not force out thoughts of how much she had enjoyed last night, as decisive as her professional relationship with Evan was.

Once out of bed, she found one of Evan's t-shirts on the counter in the bathroom and pulled it over her head gently, with hopes that minimizing her head movements would stabilize her headache. Sunshine poured into the glass walls of the home, following her from the master bedroom through the glass walls of the house leading to the kitchen. She squinted as she attempted to adjust her eyes to the bright natural light.

"Morning," she was able to murmur as she entered the kitchen and came upon Evan as he just finished pouring coffee into the first of two large mugs. He nodded and smiled in acknowledgment of her greeting, and handed her a mug, while he motioned to the creamer and sweeteners laid out on the island counter. She held the oversized mug in both her hands and slowly sipped the coffee. Evan took his place on a stool beside her, prepared to have a conversation to smooth out any wrinkles regarding their current predicament.

"Look, Evan, I don't want to weird you out or anything. I don't expect anything from you. Last night was fun, but you don't have to worry about me becoming attached to you or anything. I was upset after I heard the gossip about Richard attempting to reconcile with Kate. And from what I gathered from your drunken ramblings, you were devastated about your married lover not leaving her husband for you," Evan's mind began to wander in confusion and fear, hoping that he hadn't blurted out specific details about his affair with Natalie, like her name or meeting weekly at her office under the guise of being one of her clients seeking therapy.

"What did I actually say? My memory is a tad foggy," Evan asked concerned about divulging too many details.

"Not much," Ava said, "you refused to tell me her name, her profession, or where she lives."

"Oh," Evan said nonchalantly, as he let out a sigh of relief in his head; pleased by his insistence of discretion even while in a befuddled state.

"Well, as I was saying," Ava continued as she tried to regroup her thoughts, "I don't see why this should complicate our relationship. There is nothing wrong with what happened between us. It was quite enjoyable. We found comfort in one another for a night, but I am quite certain that we will be able to maintain a normal friendship, even after what has happened." Evan intently listened to Ava as she reassured him that the normalcy between the two would remain unaffected. He sensed that she was not completely honest in her affirmations of resuming their friendship to pre-sex status.

"I'm detecting that you are withholding something," Evan responded.

Ava had selected her words painstakingly with the intent to conceal her budding attraction towards Evan, as she had become aware of it only minutes earlier, after waking up in his bed. Although she had imbibed in a considerable amount of alcohol the previous night, she had seduced Evan mindful of her actions, anticipating that it would lead to intercourse. Initially, she hadn't planned on their relationship changing its course as such; but now that it had, she was pleased. Her reluctance to reveal her feelings without the opportunity to process the sudden onset of affection towards Evan was a protective measure. If their relationship were to develop into something serious, she would have to take precautions to avoid them from categorizing their connection as a rebound. The opportunity of choreographing the progression of their bond at a more appropriate time was non-existent now that they had slept together. Her ability to orchestrate the situation to her liking would not be possible in this case. For the first time in a long time, Ava realized that she could not control every aspect of her life. Her desire to manipulate the origins of this possible new relationship could taint it. Resigning to her feelings at that moment, with the hope that it would lead to an organic evolvement of their relationship, Ava decided to come clean.

"Whether that friendship will kindle something romantic or be inclusive of certain benefits, is debatable." Her face flushed as she felt overexposed after confessing. She would be mortified if Evan didn't reciprocate interest in her.

Evan nearly choked on his coffee after hearing Ava's revelation. It had happened all so fast, that he hadn't had much time to consider it, but he was intrigued by this unexpected twist. It was a welcomed distraction for both. Jumping into a new relationship immediately after the demise of another was a questionable reaction, but they certainly weren't the first couple, nor would they be the last to engage in such behavior. Ava was more than a rebound. Yes, she was dramatic, ambitious, and calculating, but those qualities were necessary for propelling her towards her goals. In some aspects, Ava was perfection; Evan recognized and appreciated this in her, and thus could overlook her undesirable qualities.

"This is good," Evan said, reassuring Ava that they were both on the same page, "we could be good for each other, Ava." Relieved, she smiled at him. He smiled back, and the two proceeded to drink their coffee, content with the outcome of their conversation.

That night, Evan took Ava out to dinner, pleased to discover that they enjoyed each other's company on a personal level, even when sober. And though their drunken state had been the catalyst that ignited their intimacy the prior night, the possibility of a blooming relationship absent that event would have been highly likely with increased interaction between the two.

For the second consecutive morning, Evan woke up with Ava beside him. He stretched his arms out, then rested his hand on Ava's hip and began to shake her gently, as she slept soundly on her side. She lightly stirred and quietly sighed as she tried to awake from her deep slumber. When she emerged from under the sheet she had pulled over her head, she turned so that she lay on her back. She swept away her dark brown tousled locks covering her face.

"Good morning," she said, in a manner so content it would be equivalent to a cat's purr.

"Indeed, it is, and unlike the prior night, I remembered everything that happened last night. This good morning was preceded by a very good night," said Evan.

Ava smiled naughtily, "How about a repeat performance?" She asked as she mounted Evan. The skin to skin contact alone was enough for Evan to become instantaneously hard.

"You won't find me complaining," he said, shifting and thrusting, as he and Ava found a pleasurable groove. She had enjoyed the prior night's activities as much as he had. Ava was sexy. He had never really thought of her in this way, but he always thought she was beautiful. He watched her grind into him. *God, she's hot*, he thought. He could have come right then and there; but he controlled it, not wanting to give Ava the impression that he was a premature ejaculator. He wasn't. It was just that she so aroused him, the possibility of coming too fast was probable. He successfully distracted himself by thinking of work and all the responsibilities that lay ahead, thwarting an ill-timed sexual peaking.

Afterward, the two enjoyed their morning coffee and breakfast on the patio just outside Evan's bedroom. They realized that they had found comfort and happiness in each other's presence. Preoccupation with this sudden onset of feelings for one another smothered the heartache they felt for their previous lovers. Their grief over love lost was short-lived.

"I am going to see some rentals today in Sherman Oaks," Ava said cheerfully as she meticulously spread cream cheese on top of a bagel, then stacked it with lox, tomato, and sliced onions. "I've decided the best option, for now, is to rent a small home."

"Why bother, Ava?" Evan asked. "You might as well stay with me for now. I'm leaning towards selling the place in four months, or maybe not, I was thinking about it but…" he said shaking his head correcting himself. His original plan to sell this home was predicated on the basis that Natalie would leave Eric and move in with him needing more space for her and her kids. Since his plans had not come to, there was no longer a need for a bigger home—for now. He didn't know what the future held for him and Ava. If they became serious and started a family of their own, they would need a bigger home. "Come to think of it, I still might sell it," he professed, "but I would love it if you moved in with me." In four months, he would have a clear picture of the role Ava would play in his life. If it were geared towards marriage and a family, he would find them the perfect home.

"I feel like I would be imposing on you, "Ava protested, "living with each other might also be detrimental to our developing personal relationship. I want to give us a fair chance."

"You have your own room, but you are more than welcome to stay in mine, and you have your own office. We don't have to be in each other's presence twenty-four hours a day. I have some business trips scheduled so that I will be away at least four days each month," Evan said convinced that cohabitation would be a good idea, "you would be helping me out too. I'd have someone staying at the house while I'm gone."

"Well, it seems like you have given this some thought…"

"I haven't actually until now, but it just makes sense, don't you think?"

Ava pondered for a moment, and began to nod her head in agreement, "I guess it does. And if it doesn't work out and you want to get rid of me without hurting my feelings you can go ahead with your plan to sell the house…" Ava mused.

CHAPTER TWENTY-SEVEN
The Adjustment (2015)

For as long as Evan and Natalie had settled upon advancing their one-night stand to a reoccurring, weekly, affair, when the anticipation of its culmination burdened Natalie, she consistently suppressed those ideas, and convinced herself that the affair would last as long as she wanted it to last, self-soothing her psyche into believing that she was in total control of the situation. The despair she had felt over ending her relationship with Evan while she was still very much attached to him was emotionally crippling.

Three weeks had gone by, and her Tuesday 1:30 pm appointment slot had been devoid of him completely. Attempting to exist without that part of her life, had thrown Natalie out of sorts. At work, she functioned in a monotonous and robotic state; mentally disengaging herself from her clients, feigning just enough interest to do the bare minimum required of her professionally, yet fully aware that she was not acting in the best interest of her clients, by short-changing them of her full attention. Her clients had noticed that she had become rather distant and removed. Her sincerely empathetic nature, a characteristic she had been gifted with, and a source of great comfort to her clients had shifted to one of indifference. *I will get over this;* she kept telling herself. *I will not continue to disservice my clients as I have been. I cannot allow this event to impact my career negatively.* She knew she had to snap out of this funk. *Get your shit together, Natalie!* She often reprimanded herself.

At home, she had become impatient, moody, and intolerant. She had very little patience when the boys were mischievous and thus found herself raising her voice more often than appropriate. When they exasperated her nerves, she snapped. Immediately after, she was overcome by a sense of guilt for allowing her feelings regarding her breakup with Evan to affect her interaction with her children. Prone to drastic shifts in her mood, she overcompensated for her anger by overindulging the children's whims during these periods of remorse.

Natalie had grown increasingly resentful of Eric. He was the obstruction that prevented her from maintaining a relationship with Evan. Evading accountability, as well as her inability to take ownership of her actions and feelings, she surmised that Eric was the root cause of her unhappiness. Thus, she blamed him for her dissatisfaction. The relationship between the two became exponentially strained over the last three weeks. Natalie resisted Eric's attempts to connect with her in any aspect. Her careless attitude towards and the lack of respect for her marriage further fractured their bond and began to cause irreparable damage.

Natalie refused to withhold her grievances from Eric, criticizing and insulting him for almost all he did. Their days started and ended with her routinely chastising him.

"Put your damn dishes in the dishwasher!" she would yell early in the morning. Eric had a bad habit of leaving his dinner dishes in the sink when he came home from work later than usual and did not dine with the rest of the family. Natalie did the dinner dishes right after she and the children had dinner. Waking up to a sink full of crusty dishes from the previous night infuriated her immensely, "At the very least, rinse them! I am not your maid!"

On the weekends, Eric liked to go on hikes that lasted for hours. Sometimes he would take the boys on these outings. Often, he would leave alone, early in the morning, without advanced warning, unbeknownst to him that Natalie had plans and was relying on him for childcare.

"You can't go on a hike today. Aidan has a cold. You need to stay home with the kids. I'm meeting some of my friends later today."

"I work all week long and look forward to these outings in nature to decompress. Ask one of our moms to watch the boys," Eric would protest.

"No! My mom has plans. You ask your mom if you want to go. These children are not my sole responsibility. You might be working hard all week, well I work hard all day, every day—and every night, too! I do the groceries, the cooking, the dishes, and the laundry. And I work outside of the home. You need to pull your weight around the house!"

"I never asked you to pull your weight financially when you didn't work. And I do contribute to the household chores!"

"Not at the rate that I do! You are a slob, and I can't stand being married to you." She would scream and storm out.

For the last two years, her marriage had been a sham, as she feigned marital contentment to evade any suspicion from her husband of the possibility of another man in her life. She had convinced herself to maintain a sense of separation in her life where practicality and passion did not intersect but existed in different realms. She went through the motions emotionally and physically with Eric as she pretended to be a good wife. Perturbing to Natalie, was that Eric failed to detect her duplicitous behavior for over two years now. It was possible that he was as detached from her, perpetuating the façade of their dysfunctional union.

Ignoring the truth that she could tolerate being Eric's partner, as long as Evan provided her an escape from her everyday reality, she persuaded herself that preserving her marriage was the right decision. Now that she realized that Evan was a core source of happiness for her, and her relationship with Eric had run its course, she wished that she had told Evan otherwise.

Natalie had pondered over her decision for the last three weeks and had determined that she could now bring herself to leave Eric. She needed to contact Evan. She wanted to tell him that she had made the wrong decision and that she would leave Eric for him. Surely, he would be accepting of Natalie's change of heart? She wondered to herself. He had stated that he would actively pursue a relationship with hopes of having his own family. How far would he have gotten in three weeks? She hoped that a reconciliation with Evan was not too late. She was prepared to do what needed to be done to secure a permanent position in Evan's life— disrupting her family, leaving Eric, and even having another child after the age of forty. She loved him and could not expend any more energy suppressing that love. She would stop fighting it and accept any backlash that accompanied it.

Natalie had less than five minutes to spare before her next client was scheduled to arrive. She desperately needed to speak to Evan. The angst caused by their separation had begun to unravel her sense of sanity. She could finally start looking towards the light at the end of the tunnel. Natalie picked up the phone and dialed Evan's number. Her heartbeat hastened with each progressive ring. By the third ring, she was relieved to hear Evan's voice.

"Hello, Natalie?" he said in a lowered voice.

"Evan, I need to see you, to talk to you. I have made a terrible mistake." She could hear a considerable amount of commotion in the background and was unsure if he heard her.

"Natalie, I'm out of town scoping out a potential business opportunity. I'm at a site now, as we speak. I can barely hear you."

"I need to see you, Evan. We need to talk," she restated louder.

"Yes, I got that. Look, let me call you when I get back," he said, "I will be back in L.A. in two days. We can meet sometime before the weekend." He sounded rushed and distant, "I have to go, Nat. Bye."

"Bye," she said softly, "call me when you get back."

She heard the door in the adjoining room open as she hung up the receiver. She didn't have time to analyze the abruptly culminating conversation, as her client waited in the next room. Natalie pulled herself together and emerged to meet her client.

****

Two thousand five hundred miles away, Evan felt a flutter in the pit of his stomach. Though he was preoccupied with Ava from the moment Natalie dumped him, he had occasionally drifted into lapses of missing her, especially on Tuesdays. His involvement with Ava was still superficial and could easily be severed if Natalie were to be available. Had Natalie come to regret her decision? Was she finally coming around? It was clear as day to him that Natalie's relationship with Eric was far from salvageable. He realized the damage done to their marriage due to the affair was irreparable, deteriorating any hope of recovery week after week as their interludes progressed, and Natalie grew increasingly attached to Evan. She had sought more than excitement elsewhere for two years. Her connection with her husband wasn't going to improve miraculously while she found pleasure with another man. Eric no longer did it for her. It was obvious to him from the beginning. Natalie's denial of the truth allowed her to remain in her stagnant relationship. The guilt resulting from her infidelity clouded her judgment and impeded her ability to make the necessary changes in her life. The reality of her marriage was that it was troubled before her affair. It was possible that ending their affair had made her realize that Evan provided more than sexual gratification for her and that she wanted to be in a relationship with him. Was she finally ready to leave Eric?

Evan had come to the Florida Keys at the request of Mark Padilla, a business associate who resided there. He wanted to unload a property he had purchased five years earlier. Mark had purchased an oceanfront bed and breakfast with hopes of tearing it down and developing a small boutique hotel but had discovered that he had lung cancer shortly after that. His plans came to a halt as he faced an uphill medical battle. The sale of the property—a mutually beneficial transaction would provide Mark with instant cash to live out whatever remained of his life in luxury and comfort while giving Evan a very lucrative investment opportunity.

Evan was extremely enthusiastic about the project, even though he didn't have the liquid cash funds necessary to purchase and renovate the project. He would have to sell his home to make up for the required capital and temporarily move to oversee the project. If Natalie wanted to leave Eric, which seemed plausible based on her phone call, it would allow him to have some distance from Natalie so that she could sort out whatever needed sorting. His mandatory absence would ward off any speculation of a relationship, as they would not be seen with each other until months after she left Eric. The timing was impeccable. He would be back in Los Angeles full time, as both this project and her divorce would likely be finalized around the same time. Natalie and Evan would finally publicize their relationship. Of course, they would keep their affair a secret to make it appear as though they just started dating.

Evan felt a sense of relief. He would finally get what he wanted—or so he thought. Just when it seemed like everything was falling into place, he realized that if Natalie did want to reconnect, he would have to take care of one uncomfortable detail—his budding relationship with Ava. He would have to let her down gently. While she was an exceptional woman, his heart still belonged to Natalie. Surely, she would understand that he couldn't disregard his feelings for the mystery woman that was in his life longer than she had been? If the shoe were on the other foot, and Richard had wanted to get back with Ava, she would have likely given it a chance.

Evan could not walk away from Natalie. He would attempt to meet her before any external forces would cause her to change her mind. Then again, it was possible that her request to meet might be an attempt to persuade him to continue their affair while remaining married to Eric. Overcome by a sense of urgency, he texted Natalie; *I fly back Thursday afternoon. Should I come to your office after your last appointment?*

Forty-five minutes later, Natalie walked back into her private office. She had ten minutes before her next client arrived. She saw the green notification light on her mobile flashing. She picked up the phone to see the text from Evan.

Just after five, that would be perfect, she replied. His request was a cause for relief and elation. *He still cares,* she thought to herself. *It's not too late.*

CHAPTER TWENTY-EIGHT
Impeccable Timing (2015)

At precisely 3:10 pm, Evan's plane landed at LAX. As the pilot made the final announcements, and the signs in the plane indicated that it was safe to unfasten seat belts, Evan quickly pounced out of his seat to open the overhead compartment and grab his carry-on luggage. Though he wanted nothing more than to disembark the plane as fast as possible, he could not resist helping the two senior ladies that occupied the two seats next to his. He pulled out their luggage and allowed them to take a place ahead of him in the line waiting to exit the plane. There was a considerable distance between the ladies and the passengers in line ahead of them, as the two shuffled at a slower pace, and thus delayed his hopes for a quick exit. He immediately got over his frustration over the sluggish mobility of the ladies, as they reminded him of the times he frequently accompanied his grandparents on outings as a teenager. During those outings, he was disheartened by the bittersweet reality that his grandparents were noticeably aging, and that time was fleeting—a fear magnified by the visible decline in their agility. Instead, he decided he would offer to help the two ladies.

"Do you ladies need any help retrieving your luggage?" He offered to accompany them to baggage claim to pull their bags off the carousel and situate them on luggage carts. The ladies were astonished by his gesture and accepted his kind offer. After he placed the last piece of luggage on the cart, they thanked him for his kindness and parted ways.

When he arrived at the parking lot of Natalie's office, he waited in his car, as he was ten minutes early. He texted Natalie to let her know he was downstairs and asked her to text him when her client left.

As he waited in the car to hear back from her, he received a phone call from Ava.

"Hello," he answered.

"Evan, it's Ava," she said immediately after his greeting, "are you back in town? I'm feeling sick. I think I have that stomach bug that is going around. I can't hold anything down. Would you mind getting some ginger ale on your way home?"

"No problem, Ava. I don't know when I will be back home, but I will try my best to get home as soon as possible."

"Thanks, Evan," she said and hung up.

Evan felt the butterflies in his stomach while he waited for the elevator in the sterile lobby of the medical building that housed Natalie's office. Almost a month ago, the affair between Natalie and Evan had ended. His preoccupation with Ava was a welcomed distraction, but she wasn't Natalie. The anticipation of being reunited with

Natalie was a cause for excitement. Forcing her out of her mind was easier to do with Ava around, but when he allowed himself to think of Natalie, he felt a profound sense of yearning and sadness.

When he got to her office, he opened the door to find the door leading to her private office open.

"Natalie?" He called out quietly.

"Evan!" Natalie exclaimed as she rushed over to embrace him. Unsure, whether he would reciprocate the physical warmth with which she greeted him. Evan's initial stance to her embrace was guarded, as his shoulders and upper body became stiff and unwelcoming. Regardless, Natalie threw her arms around his neck, then brought them lower to his upper arms and continued to draw him in closer. His posture suddenly became relaxed, and he scooped her into his arms. They held their embrace tightly, while they professed to one another how much they had missed each other.

When Natalie pulled away to look at Evan as she spoke, their arms remained interlocked.

"Evan, I've had almost four weeks to think about this, andw eigh my options…" she stammered as she spoke, "and I have decided that I will leave Eric if it means that the two of us can be together." She paused, and thoughtfully searched for the right words, "These last month has been very unpleasant for me. I don't want you out of my life." Speaking the words out loud, deep down, she was still unconvinced that this option would be the most favorable course. If she could have her way, she would have continued her affair with Evan while remaining married to Eric, until her children were older. She still feared that Evan was incapable of long-term monogamy, and would tire of her, at the expense of her marriage to Eric. The thought of being the subject of speculative gossip from Melanie and Ellen also weighed down on her. There was no doubt in her mind that Ellen would share her suspicions about Natalie's affair once it was public that she left her husband. Melanie and Arthur might consider discretion. Ellen, who obviously felt empowered by the justification that she had been judged by Natalie, who presented herself sanctimoniously but was a total hypocrite, would have enjoyed destroying Natalie's reputation. Natalie's plan to introduce Evan as a post-separation or divorce relationship would be muddled by salacious chatter within shared circles. Natalie would have to brace herself for the backlash. Though she wished she wouldn't care about gossip pertaining to her circulating in her social circles, her culture's over-importance on societal judgment had been embedded in her psyche since birth. And though she tried not to care, being judged negatively—even by those she didn't give a shit about—still impacted her.

Unfortunately for Natalie, as long as Evan refused to have a relationship with her while she remained married to Eric, she would resent her husband and thus could not stay with him. If only Evan had agreed to continue their prior arrangement, one more suited to Natalie's advantage, she could remain married to Eric. If she ended her relationship with Evan and remained in a marriage with Eric where she resented him, divorce would be imminent. She would have lost Eric and risked Evan's unavailability.

"If this is what you want, Nat, then it makes me very happy." Even pulled her in close and kissed the top of her head. "Have you told Eric, yet?" he asked suspiciously.

Pushing her back so that her face was visible. Being strung along by Natalie for the past two years had taught him to take her declarations and promises at face value—mere words to entice him with the possibility of a future real relationship, while their affair and her marriage continued.

"I'm seeing someone, she had to move out of her home abruptly, and I'm letting her stay at my place, so if you are serious about this, I am going to end things with her and ask her to leave. But I refuse to do that until I have concrete proof from you that you have left Eric." Evan was stern. Natalie was taken aback by the revelation that Evan had already sought the company of another woman so soon after they had ended their affair. The unexpected disclosure was a blow to her ego, even though he had told her of his intentions to move forward the day they had broken up. The realization that she had been replaced so soon was a hard pill to swallow.

"I haven't said anything to him yet," she replied. The pitch of her voice increased when she saw the look of discontent on his face that conveyed that he was fed up of Natalie's indecisive inner-struggle, "I needed to know that you and I were on the same page before I went ahead with it," her voice projected as a plea. "Now I know that I can move forward with this decision. It's Thursday night. Give me until this weekend to tell him. I want to arrange for the kids to stay at one of our parents, in case the banter between us becomes ugly. I don't know what I am going to tell him, but I'm definitely not going to tell him about our affair. Honestly, I don't even think it will affect him that adversely. We have both been complacent. I can't imagine that he is happy considering how I have been feeling about our marriage for the last couple of years. Eric and I had detached from each other long before our affair."

"I think that's perfect. That is what you should tell him, minus anything about our affair. It sounds organic, and not so contrived. I expect you to tell him by Saturday. Text me afterward. I can assume it will be a difficult conversation. We can meet for dinner. That night, I will end things with my *friend*. She will understand. This was kind of an unexpected rebound for both of us; things just progressed fast."

"Ok, it's set then. I am leaving Eric," she exhaled an exaggerated breath, not of relief but to alleviate some of the tension she was feeling, like a pressure cooker releasing steam. Evan pulled her closer, holding her tightly.

"You are doing the right thing, Nat. We are going to be happy together. I promise I'm going to do anything and everything in my power to make this easy for your boys and Eric. I want things to be civil and respectful. I love you."

Natalie wanted to believe him with every fiber of her being. She knew he meant well, but was he truly capable of a monogamous, long-term relationship?

"I love you, Evan. Just please don't fuck me over, huh?" She regretted uttering those words the moment they came out of her mouth.

Evan was agitated by what she had just blurted out, but he decided on giving Natalie a pass. She had, after all, agreed to leave Eric, but he never wanted to be blamed for the demise of Natalie's marriage. The decision to end her marriage would have to be her choice, one that she would be held accountable for solely.

"I only want you to leave Eric if you are certain that you want to end your marriage. I will not accept blame for assisting you in reaching that conclusion. I don't want you resenting me in the future for this decision. While I want to have a monogamous relationship with you, if you want to remain with your husband, I am fine with that. I will be fine without you. I will not, however, continue to have an affair with you. I think it's fair to say that it would be unfair to me."

Natalie wondered if Evan was attempting to convince her to follow through with her decision to leave Eric by using reverse psychology. The more he told her to stay with Eric unless she was certain she wanted to end her marriage, and the declaration that he would be fine without her if she chose to stay married, the more compelled she was to leave Eric. His indifference towards her attracted her to him. Oddly enough, as aware as she was of his attempt to mind fuck her, it was still effective in bringing forth her insecurities and prompting her to feel like Evan was pulling the strings of the relationship, which seemed to spark some anger within her.

"Evan, I take full responsibility for the decision to leave Eric. Is that what you want to hear? What I want you to understand is that I am leaving my family for you. I want you to realize how impactful this decision is, not just for me but to my children and Eric, and our families. This change will have a ripple effect, on many levels. I will be ostracized and talked shit about, but I will do it as long as I know that you can be monogamous."

Evan could see that Natalie's response was driven by fear and uncertainty. If he was to win her over successfully, then he had to offer her a sense of reassurance. It seemed that all their conversations of late escalated into intense arguments between the two. He did not intend on them starting their life together in such contempt and mistrust.

"Natalie, I need you to learn to trust me. If you and I are together, I don't need anyone else. Please believe me. I understand that the relationship between us has placed your family life in jeopardy, and if I were able to separate my emotions from our physical relationship, I would continue with our affair. The reality is that I can't. I want to be with you. And if you can't make that sacrifice, I understand. If you do move forward with it, I'm aware that you might be facing some turbulent times for what you are about to do, but I will be there with you."

Natalie felt reassured and realized that it was the stressful situation that was putting a strain between them. Once she had informed Eric that she would leave him, things would get easier.

"I'm sorry, Evan…I don't want you to think I don't trust you. I guess my insecurities are getting the best of me. I will let Eric know I am leaving him this weekend. I will be in touch."

"Natalie, don't worry. Everything is going to be ok. We are going to be happy." He pulled her in and kissed her passionately. A sense of calm suddenly overcame her, and for the first time, she believed that she was making the right decision for herself. She wanted to be with Evan.

****

On the way home, Evan felt a sense of uneasiness overcome him. While he was happy that Natalie had finally agreed to leave Eric, his impending conversation with Ava and its after-effects weighed down on him. He, like Natalie, wanted to be over with that aspect of notifying their significant others about the end of their relationships. He could not fully enjoy the victory of winning over Natalie, while the certainty of a negative encounter with Ava loomed in his head. He was only beginning to get to know Ava and was unsure of how she would react to getting dumped by him. He was a tad intimidated by her, as her temperament was unpredictable or rather predictably unscrupulous, as had been demonstrated by her devious scheme to get pregnant with Richard's baby. Evan didn't know if she would be sympathetic or vengeful. After all, he had confided in Ava that he had deep feelings for a woman before their tryst. Would she understand that he had reunited with the mystery woman he loved? Or would she feel slighted and discarded? It wouldn't be difficult for Ava to discover who this woman was once Evan and Natalie became public. If she wanted to hurt Evan and Natalie, she could inform people that the two were engaged in an affair long before Natalie left her husband.

The relationship between Ava and him had started as a relationship of convenience and was so recent; Ava couldn't possibly be attached to him. She couldn't be vindictive towards him considering he had helped Ava when she needed a job and a home. As he pulled into the driveway of his home, he felt tightness in his chest while his heartbeat escalated, and his breathing became labored. He recognized he was having another panic attack. His eye caught the large succulent that lined the end of the walkway to the front door. The landscape light below it illuminated the plant so that its texture and colors were visible even in the darkness of night. He focused on the plant and its details and began to breathe rhythmically to slow down his heartbeat and relax his body's psychosomatic response to his eventual interaction with Ava. His muscles relaxed when he realized that he had two days to think about how he would approach Ava regarding breaking off their romantic entanglement.

Evan opened the front door to complete darkness, except for the faint light radiating from one of the rooms along the hallway leading to the bedrooms.

"Ava, I have your ginger ale. I got you some Saltines, too."

"Evan…" Ava's voice echoed through the house in a manner that conveyed physical weakness and distress. Evan rushed to the hallway and found Ava lying on a towel in the fetal position in the bathroom adjacent to the bedroom Evan had designated for her. "I'm so sick. I can't move. I can't hold anything down."

"Let's move you to your bed. I'll get you a bucket you can use to puke in. At least you will be more comfortable. I'll get some ginger ale, see if you can hold that down."

"No, please. Just leave me here. I don't want to move. My legs are cramping."

"Ava, it sounds like you are dehydrated. I should take you to the emergency room. I have some Zofran; it will stop your nausea. Would you like me to get you one?"

"Yes, to the Zofran, anything that will stop me from puking my guts out. As far as the ER goes, no, I don't want to go to a hospital emergency room, but I did use this urgent care facility a few months ago that is very clean and fast. They close at nine. You can take me there. Help me up, please. I want to put on a sweatshirt and my Uggs."

Evan helped Ava up and to her room. She asked him to grab various articles of clothing, and to assist her in putting them on. She also requested a trash bag in case she felt the urge to vomit in his car.

While stopped at an intersection, Evan glimpsed over at Ava. She looked frail and weak, but the Zofran had temporarily relieved her nausea and vomiting, as she had fallen asleep in the passenger seat. In this vulnerable state, she was very beautiful. He gently swept her hair away from her face and hoped that Ava would be ok, convinced that what ailed her was nothing more than a stomach bug. He found the realization that Ava had grown so comfortable around him rather endearing. At that moment, he decided he would do what he could to help her. He would not abandon her after he ended their romantic relationship. He would find her suitable accommodations and even pay her rent for the first few months. If Natalie hadn't decided to end her marriage with Eric, it was quite possible that Evan and Ava would end up in a long-term relationship. Knowing this, he wanted to be as respectful towards Ava as possible.

To Ava's satisfaction, the urgent care facility was empty. She sat down on a chair in the waiting room as Evan checked her in. When the nurse opened the door and called her name, Ava looked over at Evan so that he would join her in the examination room. She didn't want to be alone, she felt extremely miserable, and she appreciated the way Evan took care of her.

Ava laid on her side on the examination table, relieved to be in a reclined position. Sitting up and walking to the exam room had expended whatever remaining energy she had left.

"What brings you here today, Ava?" the nurse asked her calmly.

"I have been throwing up most of the day. I can't hold anything down. I feel like I am going to vomit my organs out because I don't have anything left to puke. I have a pounding headache, and my legs are cramping. I was over a friend's house a few nights ago, and her child had the stomach bug that has been going around the last month. I assume I must have been exposed to it there."

"Any diarrhea?" the nurse questioned her.

"No," Ava said, blushing as she glanced over at Evan, thankful that she did not have to discuss her bowel movements any further in his presence.

"How about a fever?" the nurse pressed on as she prepared to take Ava's temperature.

"No," said Ava, "not that I was aware of," she said before the nurse inserted the thermometer in her ear.

"Are you on any medication or have you taken anything for nausea?"

"I took a Zofran before I came to urgent care. It seems to have helped with the vomiting. I still feel queasy."

"Any your last period?"

"Almost four weeks ago. I'm scheduled to start my period in three days."

"Are you fairly regular?"

"For the most part. I stopped taking the pill about seven or eight months ago, my ex and I were trying to get pregnant. I've been regular except for the first two months. I was meaning to go see my doctor about getting back on the pill."

"Were you on any fertility medication?" the nurse asked, "and if yes, which ones?"

"Briefly. I didn't want to take them after a few months. I can't even remember the names to be quite honest," she lied as she answered the questions in haste, eager to get home.

"The doctor is going to need a urine sample, sweetie. The bathroom is right down the hallway to the left," she handed Ava a urine specimen collection cup. "You might want to walk her to the bathroom, and wait just outside the door in case she is dizzy or lightheaded," she kindly ordered Evan.

Five minutes later, the two were back in the exam room. Ava reclined only to feel her nausea return, so she turned to her side and closed her eyes. She was tired, and her body was sore from dehydration. All she wanted was to be in her own bed, or rather the bed in Evan's guest room. Her head pounded, and her insides felt like they had turned to mush.

"You ok?" Evan asked as she flexed her feet to stretch out her cramped muscles in her calves.

"A little better than before. That Zofran helped with the nausea. I want to go back home, take a hot shower and go to sleep." Ava declared as she closed her eyes again, "I feel like I will feel a lot better after a good night's sleep."

After a precursory knock, the doctor opened the door without waiting for a response from Ava, "Ms. Shirazi?"

"Yes, that's me," Ava said flatly.

"I will wait outside while the doctor examines you," Evan got up and exited the room.

"Ms. Shirazi," the doctor continued after the door closed behind Evan.

"Please, call me Ava," she interrupted the doctor.

"Ava, your urine results have indicated that you are pregnant. Now, you are sure that your last period was almost four weeks ago?"

"Pregnant! How?! I mean, I was off the pill, but my partner and I have been using condoms. I was supposed to get back on the pill in two weeks. I have a doctor's appointment scheduled..." the first night with Evan – the night of drunken sex! *Shit! Shit Shit!* She thought to herself.

"Ms. Shirazi—Ava, your period... are you sure you had one last month?" the doctor paused as he concentrated on Ava's urinalysis results on the laptop.

"Yes, I'm certain," Ava answered assuredly.

"Your HCG levels are extremely high for this stage of pregnancy, which I believe is the cause of your severe nausea. Based on your symptoms, you don't have the stomach bug that is going around. These elevated HCG levels could also be indicative that you are carrying multiples, but it's not a guarantee. You need to make an appointment with your OBGYN as soon as possible.

Additionally, you are dehydrated, so we are going to have to replenish the loss of fluids intravenously. I'm also going to write you a prescription for Zofran which will hopefully stop the vomiting and allow you to eat and rehydrate. We will start you off with one pill now."

Ava was flabbergasted by this most unexpected news like a brick had smacked her upside her head and her ability to process information was muddled.

"Pregnant? Multiples?" She managed to stammer. "How is that possible?" She was visibly disappointed.

"Well by your own admission, you had stopped taking your birth control pills," the doctor responded, "as for the possibility of multiples, it could be genetic or a result of fertility medications. I see here in the notes that you had been attempting to get pregnant and briefly took fertility meds which obviously increased your chances."

"When can I go home?" Ava asked flatly, realizing she was repulsed by the doctor who stood before her simply for his role as the messenger of this unwelcomed information.

"As I said, we have to get you rehydrated through IV, which will take about half an hour. We need to make sure you aren't dehydrated anymore. You will probably be here for another hour at most. Sit tight; the nurse will be here to administer the IV any minute now." The doctor stood up and walked over to the door. He placed his hand on the doorknob, but before turning the handle, he looked back at Ava, "It's important that you make an appointment with your OBGYN as soon as possible. Would you like your friend to join you in the examination room?"

"Not yet, Doctor. I need a minute to myself."

Ava's mind fast forwarded to the week ahead. She would absolutely make an appointment with her OBGYN immediately, as the good doctor instructed her to do so. Only, she would not seek prenatal care. She planned to schedule an abortion instantly. She wouldn't bother discussing her predicament with Evan, let alone entertain an inkling of a thought to proceed with her pregnancy. Though the two had begun to spend time together and get to know one another, Evan was still very much a stranger to her. Ava's lack of interest in children was enough to convince herself that she lacked a maternal gene.

Her own childhood experiences had influenced her desire to remain childless. After a problematic pregnancy due to placenta previa and an exceedingly difficult labor where she nearly bled to death, Ava's mother, Farah, had undergone severe postpartum depression before the condition was notarized by the mainstream. Neglecting herself, as well as Ava, Farah's mother had feared she would harm herself or the baby. She arranged to have her sent to a therapist in Switzerland who specialized in the depression of women who had recently become mothers. The facility could best be described as a spa retreat inclusive of daily therapy sessions and psychiatric drugs. Ava's mother never quite developed an emotional attachment to Ava while she was a baby. Her experience with her pregnancy and the abyss of hopelessness she felt after the birth of her child precluded her from ever wanting another child, a factor that contributed to the dissolution of her marriage. Before her parents' contentious divorce, Ava was left in the charge of their Guatemalan housekeeper, Elena, who treated Ava as one of her own and gave her the love and attention she so needed yet lacked from both her detached parents. It wasn't uncommon for Ava to spend the night with Elena and her four children in the guest house they called home situated on Ava's parents' property.

At the age of six, Ava's world as she knew it would change drastically. The beautiful home their parents shared in Beverly Hills, with the guest house that she came to know as her haven, was sold during her parents' divorce. Farah and her husband, David, who fought over the exquisite rugs and fabric import business the two had built for over a decade agreed to separate the business into two distinct entities. Farah took over the fabrics business and moved to the east coast. The love and attention a mother provides a child, though absent from her relationship with Ava, manifested into nurturance and passion for her fabrics business. Farah was driven to succeed. Where she failed as a wife and mother, she far surpassed her abilities as a keen businesswoman. Her fabrics company became synonymous with luxury and quality.

As the years progressed, Ava saw less and less of her father. When she was ten, David married Sheila. Though she would visit him during certain holidays throughout the year and a month in the summer, she felt more like a stranger, and less wanted after Sheila gave birth to a daughter. To her stepmother, Ava was more of an encumbrance than a part of their family. In David's presence, Sheila pretended to be accepting of Ava. When he was at work for most of the day, she passive aggressively made Ava feel awkward during her visits. She wouldn't allow Ava to watch her favorite shows insisting that the baby's exposure to media could only be in the form of educational baby developmental DVDs. And though there was more than one television in the house, Ava could only watch TV in the family room. When the baby took a nap, Ava would have to turn off the T.V. and read, so that the television wouldn't disturb the baby, even though they lived in a 4000 square foot home, and the baby's bedroom was upstairs.

Knowing how creative his daughter was, and her love for art, Ava's father had bought her an easel and art supplies, but at Sheila's insistence art supplies could only be used in the garage, where it was either too cold or too hot. Rather than making meals that would appeal to a child, Sheila forced Ava to eat her health conscious, vegetarian fare, refusing to buy sweets, snacks and the sugary cereals consumed by children of Ava's age.

By the time Ava's half-sister was two, Ava stopped visiting her father on the west coast altogether. The visits became too unpleasant. On the day she was scheduled to fly out to Los Angeles, she begged her mother not to send her to California. When her mother insisted that she maintain a relationship with her father, Ava told Farah about Sheila's behavior towards her. Something snapped in Farah that day. She was offended that her ex-husband allowed his wife to treat their daughter so poorly; she became fiercely protective of her daughter.

When Ava didn't show up at LAX as scheduled, and David frantically contacted Sheila inquiring about her whereabouts, Sheila scolded her ex-husband for his complicity in his wife's ill behavior towards their daughter. He blindly insisted that Ava was exaggerating and that Sheila sincerely cared for Ava. Farah assured him that as long as their daughter ferociously protested her visits to California, she would stand by her, seeking legal action if necessary. It took twelve years, but Farah had finally felt a maternal urge or necessity to protect her child. From then on, Farah took an active interest in her daughter. When Ava wasn't in school, she could be found at her mother's business assuming the role of an eager apprentice, observing and absorbing all aspects of the fabric business her mother had cultivated.

Ava had planned to attend Parsons to obtain a BFA in Interior Design, and upon graduating would work at the family business. In their intent to expand the business, Ava would focus on consultations to develop the design services aspect. Farah was confident that her daughter had the eye necessary for design projects. During Ava's third year at Parsons, Farah was diagnosed with stage three breast cancer. Ava was devastated but assured her mother that she would drop out of school to run the business. Farah was adamant that she wouldn't allow Ava to abandon her education. Her only option was to sell the business. When Farah's ex-husband discovered that she was selling the business and a competitor of his was interested in purchasing it, David offered to buy it. Farah told him that she would sell it to him under one condition, for double the price of his initial offer. He accepted.

Fortunately, within a year and a half of her diagnosis, Farah had made a full recovery and was cancer free. Due to the sale of her business, Farah was forced into early retirement at the age of forty-eight. The full realization of her employment status did not fully impact her until her battle with her illness had ended. At the age of fifty, Farah immersed herself in tennis, a life-long hobby, she found time to indulge in even when she was a workaholic. At the country club she belonged to, she met and partnered with John, a divorced, retired judge, for mixed doubles tournaments. Within weeks of becoming tennis partners, the two were inseparable. Their chemistry as tennis partners transcended into real life. He was eight years her senior but didn't show it. He too had retired around the same time she had and spent a significant amount of his days at the club. Among the more seasoned single women at the club, he was recognized as a considerable catch, but he dismissed them as uninteresting clichés incapable of offering him relationships of substance and thus dated some on a superficial level. When he met Farah, almost immediately he recognized that she was proper second wife material. Six months later, the two were married.

From the age of twelve to twenty-two, Ava had her mother all to herself. Having to share her with a strange man after all these years was an encumbrance. As the two newlyweds embraced their new lives, they decided to embark on a journey to travel the world. Farah would spend the next two years traveling. Ava felt slightly abandoned and resented John for occupying all of Farah's time. She refused to place any blame on Farah, and instead placed her on a pedestal. Farah could do no wrong. Ava had managed to suppress the first decade of her life where her mother had neglected her. Farah had become a constant in her life, though considerably late, she had still come through.

In her mid-twenties, Ava reconciled with her father. At their first meeting, in an effort to clear the air and subsequently move forward, the two felt the need to rehash past offenses for which they still held resentment towards each other. David felt Ava judged him harsher than she judged Farah. He accused her of distorting the facts and revising history to make Farah out to be a devoted and loving mother all along when she knew that she was absent from her life for the first twelve years. Ava told David that she was happy to have him back in her life, but that if he wanted to maintain a relationship with her, he was forbidden to speak poorly of Farah; she would not tolerate it. Ava's absence in his life for the last thirteen years had profoundly affected David with a sense of remorseful guilt and had hurled him into bouts of depression. His younger daughter at thirteen was a product of her mother's worst attributes. She had become a shallow, selfish, and spoiled

Arlette Eshraghi

little bitch, unlike her older half-sister who was on the path to success. It pained him when he realized he could not take any credit for the woman that Ava had become. He wished to right the wrong; so, he agreed to withhold any negative comments about Farah to regain his daughter's favor.

David suggested that Ava return to Los Angeles and work in the family business, considering his mother was traveling, and she didn't have family in the east coast. Ava agreed that it would be best to move back to the west coast. At twenty-three, she impressed David with her knowledge of business and her work ethic. She reminded him of a young Farah. It was clear that Farah had devoted the last decade of her life to repairing the relationship with her daughter and understood his daughter's willingness to overlook her mother's initial negligence.

Since Sheila was a presence at the family business, Ava never firmly planted her roots at David's business. She didn't have the energy to battle with her stepmother and was fully aware of California community property laws. She would not spend her talents building her father's business when it was highly likely that she would not inherit any share of the business with Sheila and her daughter in the picture. Ava saw this as a temporary position. A year later, she accepted an offer at RMLH.

These tug of war relationships made Ava feel somewhat damaged and more alone than ever. Her mother's newfound happiness took her away from her, while her father's guilt brought them to reconciliation. Her life was ridden with one dysfunctional experience after another, even in good times.

Her childhood experiences, as well as her past and present relationships with her parents, served as a deterrent from having any positive feelings regarding anything about motherhood. Ava had automatically associated motherhood with negative thoughts. Now that she was faced with a pregnancy, she was forced to confront these feelings. She did not have to follow in the footsteps of her parents, she rationalized. Yet, was she capable of breaking the mold? Or would she fall into the same pattern of dysfunction? The fact that she was questioning her stance on motherhood was perturbing to Ava. Perhaps, discussing the matter with Evan would prove to be beneficial. The two were still unsure of how to define their relationship. She was still getting over Richard. She knew that that ship had sailed and that the prospect of rekindling anything with Richard was nil, but she still had to process and get over that relationship before she could fully commit to Evan. Surely, he was getting over his previous relationship with the mystery woman. And although he had been extremely attentive in helping Ava to get medical assistance, Ava had sensed that Evan was distant in the last two conversations they had.

Ava's thoughts were interrupted by a knock at the door.

"Ok hon, let's get those fluids back in your body," the nurse said, as she pulled in an IV through the door," do you want to use the bathroom first?"

"No, I'm fine," Ava said, turning her head to look away so that the nurse could insert the IV needle without Ava flinching.

When the nurse completed the task, she asked Ava if she needed anything.

"You know my friend that was in here earlier? Would you send him back here? He is in the waiting room."

"No problem, hon. I'll get him for you."

"Thanks," Ava replied appreciatively.

A few minutes later, Evan joined Ava.

"Is everything ok, Ava?" He asked sincerely.

"Not really, Evan. It seems as though I don't have the stomach bug that's been going around. Although I think I would prefer it to my diagnosis," she replied in a depressed tone.

"I hope it's nothing serious." Evan retorted, concerned that Ava might have been diagnosed with some grave illness. He moved closer to the exam table and clasped her hand to offer her comfort, bracing himself for what he was certain would be bad news.

"Oh, it's serious…seriously sobering….and I thought I was certain about the direction I'd be taking to *rid myself of the condition…*" Ava stammered as she tried to explain her condition to Evan delicately, "but then I thought I might discuss it with you and see what you think."

Evan was confused as to why Ava would discuss her personal medical issues with him, as those matters were none of his business. The two were getting to know each other; it was too early for him to consult in decisions regarding her medical plans. It wasn't his intention to string Ava along, but he couldn't break things off with her until she was feeling better. He felt anxious about telling Ava that his mystery woman had decided to give their relationship a chance and that she would have to move out eventually.

Perhaps, she didn't want to discuss personal medical issues and just wanted to tell him that she would be unable to fulfill the business contract for his project—which would be understandable given the circumstances. He would absolve her of any contractual obligations. If necessary, he was prepared to let her stay at his place a while longer. If she needed somewhere to convalesce, he wouldn't evict her.

"I don't think I'm qualified to give you medical advice, Ava. I wouldn't feel comfortable."

"Regardless whether you feel comfortable or not, this involves you," Ava snapped, agitated by Evan's detachment, "so if you could shut your mouth, while I try to explain the situation, I would really appreciate it."

"I'm sorry…" Evan said quizzically, more perplexed now than before, "I will try…"

Ava interrupted before he could finish his thought, "Evan, I'm pregnant."

CHAPTER TWENTY-NINE
Backpedaling (2015)

N atalie groggily opened one eye and looked over at the alarm clock. It was only 4:48 am; too early to start the day, particularly after such a restless night of sleep. She forced both eyes shut and attempted to fall back into a slumber, but it was useless. As she tossed and turned, she rehearsed possible introductions for her divorce proposal to Eric, but they all sounded too contrived. She turned to the opposite side. Eric was in a deep sleep, his mouth agape, breathing heavily, bordering on occasional snores. As she watched Eric, she attempted to muster any positive feelings she had for him, to gauge whether she felt any love towards him, and to assure herself with certainty that leaving him was the best decision. As her mind delved into memories of their experiences, she was painfully conscious of how unhappy she had been these past years, in her stale union. Deep down, she knew she should have never married Eric twelve years ago.

She knew they were a poor match well before they were married. Eric was introverted and loathed being around people. He wasn't interested in maintaining relationships with friends from his youth, and eventually lost contact with all but one. When Natalie offered to host dinners for his friends, he refused. While Natalie appreciated solitude, she also enjoyed the company of friends. As the years progressed, their social interactions with other couples dwindled, until their social circle consisted of two couples. Natalie's resentment towards Eric continued to build, as her world became smaller due to Eric's insistence of living like a hermit. They lived mutually exclusive lives under one roof, each doing their own thing. Natalie was able to maintain a façade to ward off any suspicion from Eric, as long as she had Evan in her life. Without Evan's presence in her life, she could not fathom staying with Eric. She no longer liked or respected him.

In the absence of mutual respect, the willingness to compromise, a fair division of responsibilities (inclusive of the day to day mundane tasks), and a willingness to work towards a common goal, their marriage could not survive. Natalie knew that her marriage was unsalvageable. Her infidelity towards Eric had graduated her to the point of no return. If she came clean, Eric would leave her. In the unlikely event that he forgave her, he would have difficulty trusting her, making it impossible to move forward. If she never came clean and stayed with Eric, she would be ridden with guilt and feel like an imposter.

Natalie had asked her mother to take the kids that Friday night so that she and her husband could have a date night. She had not confided in Ani that she would leave her husband. If she had, her mother would make every attempt to dissuade her, including rescinding her offer to take the children for the evening.

By 5:30 am, Natalie realized that it was unlikely that she would fall asleep. She rationalized that physical exercise rather than lying in bed would benefit her most. She jogged almost every morning. Although she lived in a nice neighborhood, she didn't feel safe walking by herself this early, while it was still dark.

Natalie quietly dressed in workout clothes and went downstairs to the family room where she found an H.I.I.T. workout on demand and followed it to the best of her abilities. Fifty minutes later, she made her way back to her room and jumped in the shower. She and Monica had scheduled a breakfast date at 9:00 am. She didn't have a 9:00 am Friday client, and her 10:00 am client had canceled her appointment that week because she was going out of town with her family since her children were on spring break. This would allow her enough time to discuss her plans to leave Eric if she felt it was appropriate to tell Monica.

Natalie was finishing up her makeup when Eric walked into the bathroom.

"Morning," he grumbled as he made his way to the toilet.

"Morning," she said, "My mom is taking the kids tonight. What time are you coming back home from work?"

"Why do we have plans to be somewhere at a certain time?"

"No, I would just like a chance to get to talk to you," Natalie indifferently replied, then immediately caught herself and followed it with, "I would like an opportunity to run some things by you. And I'd appreciate your full attention, free from interruption." Her voice was warmer when she clarified her intentions. She didn't want to scare him. If he thought she was going to come down on him, then he would stay at work longer and find an excuse to come home later. The discussion had to happen that night, she couldn't delay it any longer, or she would lose her nerve.

"I'll be home at the regular time. What are you making for dinner? Or should we go somewhere to eat?"

"No, we will stay home. I'll think of something to make," she retorted.

"Ok," Eric mumbled as he turned on the shower and waited for the water to warm before he got in.

After dropping the children off at school, Natalie headed to the Lakeside Café in Encino. Just as she walked into the restaurant, Monica texted her that she got an outdoor table.

"Good morning!" Monica said gleefully holding up a champagne flute in a toast, "care to start with a mimosa?"

"I have an appointment with a client in two hours…I don't think I should," Natalie retorted.

"Ohhhh, quit being such a Debbie Downer! One glass won't do you any harm," Monica insisted wiggling her eyebrows like Groucho Marx.

Natalie giggled. Out of all of her friends, she adored Monica the most and was in awe of her *I give zero fucks* attitude. She didn't let things bother her the way Natalie fretted over everything. Where Natalie struggled with mild anxiety and a sense of unease in most situations, Monica was comfortable in her skin wherever she was and wasn't obsessed or concerned with forces that were out of her control. Natalie had always remarked on how she wished she could be more like Monica; realizing that people like Monica enjoyed life more than others.

"You could be more like me if you wanted to," Monica would reply when Natalie brought up the subject, "you just need to learn to be more chill about stuff."

"Well, then I can't," Natalie would retort, "until the day I die, I will be uptight. It's innate. I can't change that aspect about me. Asking me to stop being apprehensive is like asking me to have my hair grow out blue naturally. It's just not possible. You will have to accept me as I am, or lobotomize me."

Natalie sat on the chair opposite Monica, smoothing out her skirt and then scooting the chair closer to the table.

"Can we get one of these for my friend?" she asked the waiter from a distance holding up her glass and pointing to Natalie. He was too far to hear her, but her gesticulations enabled him to understand what she wanted. He smiled and nodded in acknowledgment, disappearing behind an alcove that led to the kitchen.

The two friends exchanged the essential salutations, inquiring about each other's well-being, as well as that of their families and updates about their jobs.

"A mimosa for the lady," the waiter interrupted, "will you be having the bottomless mimosa or just the single glass?"

"Just a glass, thanks," Natalie replied.

"And are you ladies ready to order?" he asked.

"I'm ready," Monica said.

"I need a minute, please."

"Of course, take your time. I will be back," he excused himself as he bowed theatrically and walked back a few steps.

Natalie perused the menu and decided on her usual breakfast dining choice, eggs benedict. After they placed their orders, and the two had the opportunity for some uninterrupted conversation, Natalie decided it was the right time to tell Monica of her plans to leave Eric.

"Monica, I need to tell you something. I'm leaving Eric," Natalie started as she took a small sip of her mimosa, "I just haven't been happy for a long time, and I've come to realize that Eric and I have stopped bringing out the best in each other."

"I can't say I'm surprised, given the conversations we have had, but what about the kids? Are you sure you want to go through with this?" Monica would support her dearest friend if she decided to move forward with divorcing her husband, but she wanted her to look at the situation from all angles and make an informed decision before making such a drastic, life-altering decision.

"I've given it a lot of thought. I'm prepared for the lifestyle change and the financial repercussions. I don't want my kids to grow up in a home where there is an absence of love and respect between their parents. I don't want them to think dysfunction between spouses is acceptable. I think Eric and I could manage to be civil for the sake of raising our kids, but I don't think I could stay with him. We don't share any common interests, and we are so distant from one another."

"Have you tried counseling?" Monica interrupted.

"I don't think Eric would go for that, and realistically, I'm not convinced that either of us would want to make an effort to repair our relationship."

"You realize the prospects of you finding a mate are not very promising, right? At our age, we are often overlooked for younger women. Are you prepared to go through life without a partner?" Monica questioned.

"I am," Natalie said hesitantly. She did not want to divulge the fact that she wouldn't be alone and that her choice of mate was just waiting for her to leave her husband so the two of them could graduate from secret lovers to a couple. She felt guilty for not being completely honest with Monica, but she couldn't bring herself to tell her that she had been unfaithful to her husband for two years. Natalie knew her well enough to know that Monica would disapprove of the situation—not necessarily the act of being unfaithful, but for the continuity of it. Monica would argue that in fairness to her family and her husband, she should have immediately ended the affair after the first indiscretion or that Natalie should have left Eric if she decided she wanted Evan in her life. "I would rather be alone than to be unhappily married to Eric," Natalie said.

The two continued the conversation all through breakfast. Monica presented Natalie with hypothetical scenarios so that if she did proceed with these plans, she was certain that Natalie evaluated and considered all possible outcomes. She wanted the best for her friend, and though she realized marriage was difficult, she wasn't completely convinced that leaving Eric was the right choice or the wrong choice for that matter. Her goal was to make sure that her friend made an informed decision. It was a choice that she could not influence because it had to be Natalie's choice, alone. Once her friend made the decision, her job would be to offer unconditional support.

"Well, as your best friend I want you to know that I will support any decision you make, I just encourage you to think long and hard before making the decision."

Just then, Natalie received a text from Evan: *DO NOT TELL ERIC YOU ARE LEAVING HIM. Can we meet today? Very important that we talk.*

Natalie tried to maintain her composure after receiving such an ominous text. *What the heck? Is Evan having second thoughts?*

"Anyway, it's not definite yet. I'm not 100% sure," Natalie said to Monica, "maybe I won't leave Eric."

CHAPTER THIRTY
In the Event of the Unexpected (2015)

The moment he heard those words, was the moment Evan fell in love with Ava. He became consumed with unbridled delight at the prospect of becoming a father. It was something that he had wanted for a long time, but his longings were suppressed due to Natalie's reluctance to leave Eric and her undetermined position regarding having another child.

Ava's irresistible allure was magnified exponentially now that she had made this revelation. He would not leave her. Their relationship was in the process of flourishing before Natalie had reached out to Evan and changed her mind about leaving Eric. The two were well suited for one another. He could easily resume his relationship with Ava. She was unaware of his original intentions to break things off, and now she would never have to find out. His hopes to have a family of his own would come to fruition. The fact that he would have a beautiful, talented, and sexy wife would be the icing on the cake.

Evan's reaction to her condition was not what Ava had expected, considering she felt that he began to distance himself a couple of days ago. His response slightly shifted her subconsciously forced stance against motherhood. It was the reinforcement that she needed to sway her views to realize that she could become a mother and was capable of loving a child, unconditionally. She did not have to repeat her parents' mistakes.

From the moment Ava uttered the words, Evan's recent remoteness instantaneously transformed into gentleness and warmth, as he enveloped her in his arms and began to kiss her. Although it was unspoken, their fate had been sealed without so much as a conversation regarding their status. Her pregnancy, and what it offered the both of them—companionship, stability, love and the foundations of a partnership—was a gravitational force that drew the two towards each other. Suddenly, they were a couple, and they were going to have a baby.

"I might be pregnant with twins," Ava managed to mutter when she finally broke away for air.

"That's even better," Evan said drawing her closer and kissing her harder.

Upon leaving the hospital, Evan doted on Ava. When they arrived home, she insisted on a bath to get rid of the urgent care germs. Evan insisted on drawing her bath, making sure the water wasn't too hot to raise her temperature. As Ava undressed, she threw her articles of clothing on the floor, then bunched them together using her foot until she had pushed the clothes to the corner in a pile. She slowly climbed into the tub, sliding her body lower as she reclined until all but her neck up was immersed in the warm, soothing, sudsy water.

Evan returned a few minutes later with a mug of hot tea.

"I brought you some tea. I will set it here until it cools a little."

"Thanks, Evan," Ava retorted appreciatively.

"Ava, I'm going to start looking for a new place for us. This house is more suitable for a bachelor rather than a family. Do you have any preferences? Would you like me to find something that is move-in ready?"

"Are you kidding?!?" Ava exclaimed, "I want to personalize our home according to our tastes, not someone else's. I prefer a fixer that needs total rehab."

"If that's what you want, that's what you'll get," Evan responded, as he got into the separate shower, "any preferences regarding the location?" he raised his voice to be heard over the running water of his shower.

"The south valley is fine, anywhere from Woodland Hills to Studio City. I wouldn't mind going as far west as Calabasas if we had to."

"I'll start looking at suitable properties this week."

"Sounds good," Ava said still trying to absorb all that had transpired in the last couple of hours. Strangely, Evan and Ava had made plans to couple, find a new home and have a baby with minimal discussions of their plans, but it felt right. The ease in which they slipped into their new roles was effortless and intuitive.

When Evan woke up the next morning with Ava cradled in his arms, he felt extreme contentment. He never guessed his life would have taken the direction it had less than nine hours ago, but he was pleased that it had.

Oh shit! He thought to himself. *Natalie!* Knowing what he knew today, he hoped that Natalie hadn't told Eric she was leaving him. There was no way that the two could be together now. He wouldn't abandon Ava. If Natalie had left Eric when Evan had given her the ultimatum, Evan and Ava wouldn't have had their sexual encounter, and they wouldn't be in this predicament.

He slowly turned towards the nightstand, grabbed his phone and texted Natalie, *DO NOT TELL ERIC YOU ARE LEAVING HIM. Can we meet today? Very important that we talk.*

*****

Natalie had planned on lingering during her breakfast date with Monica, but after receiving the text, she realized she had to meet up with Evan as soon as possible. She didn't like the tone of his text, and thus felt a sense of urgency in discovering the reason why Evan had sent such a message. It was 9:50 am. She was five minutes away from her office, and she did not have to meet a client until 11:00 am.

"Monica, I'm sorry, something has come up with work. I'm afraid I have to cut breakfast short," Natalie said in an apologetic tone.

"That's ok. I needed to get a manicure anyway. I can do that before my first appointment."

"Thanks for listening to me bitch and whine for the last hour. You go ahead and get your manicure, and I will take care of the check," Natalie urged Monica.

"Ok, hon. Thanks for breakfast. And I want you to know, I'm here for you, Nat. What are friends for? Just think about what you are doing before making your final decision. Love you, pal."

"Love you back, doll," Natalie replied.

The two friends hugged and parted ways. While Natalie waited for the waiter to return with her credit card and receipt, she texted Evan. *I can be in the office at 10:00 in ten minutes. I have a client at 11:00. Can you meet me before my appointment?*

Within a couple of minutes, Evan responded to her text. *I will be there in half an hour.*

Natalie's sense of relief to the sound of the office door opening was short lived. From the moment she saw the expression on Evan's face, she realized the exchange would not be pleasant.

"Evan, what's wrong? Why after all these years of asking me to leave my husband and me finally agreeing to do so, do you send me this text? And on the day I have planned to move forward with telling him?" She demanded to know in a very serious manner.

"Natalie, something has happened that is going to change the course of our lives. I never meant to do this, but I can't be with you now that I know what I know." Evan realized that what he was about to impart to Natalie would be a major blow. He didn't know where to begin, but he realized that the significant factor contributing to the reversal of a future together was timing.

"What the hell are you talking about?" Natalie said, clearly annoyed by Evan's vague yet portentous introduction, "Get to the point!"

Evan took a deep breath as he struggled to explain his current predicament to Natalie.

"When you finally agreed to leave Eric for me, I thought I was finally getting the one thing that I wanted most and had waited for...for a long time. I didn't think anything else could make me happier." Natalie's impatience was evident. She glared at Evan as he continued with his story. "Now bear with me as I have to backtrack to the night you decided to end our relationship. A friend, who happens to be a woman, was over and coincidentally was nursing her own heartache. The two of us had a lot to drink and became excessively inebriated which led to us sleeping with each other. And until you called to ask to see me, we were seeing each other..."

"So now you are dumping me for another woman?" Natalie asked attempting to conceal her anger unsuccessfully, as her voice quivered uncontrollably.

"No, no, hear me out, Natalie. Please, just give me a chance to explain, "I'm not leaving you for another woman. I'm leaving you for the chance of having my own family."

"And you had to wait this long to figure out you wanted your own kid, right after you convince me to leave my husband?"

"She is pregnant..." A sobering dose of reality shocked Natalie's system as Evan continued, "I just found out last night. Up until then, I was ready to leave her once you told me you would leave Eric," Evan spoke with a graveness that conveyed a sense of finality. "Natalie, I'm sorry, there was no way of predicting this, but now that she is pregnant, I want to stick by her side. From the moment she told me she was pregnant, I just knew what I had to do. I wanted to be with her, and it doesn't feel forced. It feels right."

"What if I had already told Eric I was leaving him before you texted me? Have you thought of the mess you could have created for me?"

Evan was in no mood for Natalie's hypothetical scenarios. Ava was pregnant. The situation they were in was real. He had to act considering the parameters of the current circumstances, not in one of a theoretical context.

"What if you had left Eric three weeks earlier when I had given you the ultimatum? I wouldn't have been with another woman, and we would not be in this situation," Evan replied sternly.

"Oh, so it's my fault you got another woman pregnant?" Natalie asked aggravated by Evan's revelation.

"Yeah, kind of… it is…I'm sorry that I can't move forward with our plans, but if you had left Eric sooner, this wouldn't have happened."

"Well, good luck to you then, Evan," Natalie's demeanor softened. It was obvious that Evan had made his decision. He had wanted a family, and he would have one now. She was approaching forty-one and would have been unwilling to have another child for a multitude of reasons—lack of patience, her age, potential fetal developmental problems, Aidan's and Alan's reaction to a divorce followed by a half-sibling, etc. Natalie was aware that she was in a stage of her life where her patience was growing thinner by the hour. Taking care of an infant required a great deal of patience—a commodity which she was short of. She also worried about how Aidan and Alan would adjust to their new life. Introducing a half baby sibling in the mix would add to their ambivalence and insecurities. Finally, she was petrified of the possibility that her eggs were not in a prime state and that she would produce a child with developmental problems. She didn't think she had the strength to endure such a heartbreaking and taxing responsibility. All of this was moot now, as a future with Evan was nonexistent.

"I'm sorry, Natalie. I don't think time has ever been on our side. When I realized that we couldn't be together considering what I had just learned, it dawned on me that the one factor that has always prevented us from being with each other has been timing. It's always been an issue with poor timing."

"True," Natalie responded sadly, "somehow our paths never align. They crisscross here and there, but they never align. Maybe the universe is trying to tell us something. Maybe we are just not meant to be together, Evan," she said it as convincingly as possible, even though she didn't mean it.

"I only wish you happiness, Nat. You are the only woman I have loved…until now I didn't think I could feel that way about anybody else, but it's a possibility with Ava."

Ava, she thought to herself. *How very chic. She sounds skinny.*

"I wish you all the best with Ava," Natalie managed to mutter. Reluctant to endure the dialog, as there was no point to continue—what had to be said and done, had been said and done; Natalie eagerly wanted to end the unpleasant interaction. "I'm sorry I'm going to have to ask you to leave, my client will be here soon."

"Oh, yeah, well excuse me, then. Good luck with everything, Natalie. I'm sorry about this, and I hope you understand why I have to do this."

"I understand. Take care of yourself, Evan, and I hope you are happy. A child will change your world in a very multi-dimensional way. It will alter your perceptions. You will experience a love that is unconditional and unlike any other. You will feel profound love and agony through your child's eyes. It's a beautiful thing, and I am happy that you will get to experience it. Maybe then you will comprehend why I couldn't break up my family; for the sake of my boys."

Evan stepped forward and put his arms around Natalie. He held her for a few moments in an embrace, "Bye, Nat. Take care," he whispered in her ear.

After Evan left the office, Natalie, mesmerized by the flickering patterns on the dark wood floor cast by the sunlight walked over to the window. She looked out to see that the source of the patterns was the leaves of the birch tree swaying in a gentle breeze filtering the light through bare patches. She stood there for a while. Her gaze focused on the tree, as she tried to calm herself and hold back the tears. She would have to suppress her emotions until she could manage to squeeze in a good cry. Her client would arrive shortly. She could not cry in her presence. A few minutes later she spotted Evan's car drive off. And just like that, the moment she dreaded in her thoughts had come to fruition. There would be no more Tuesday afternoons, and there would be no more Evan.

CHAPTER THIRTY-ONE
The Aftermath (2015 -2016)

Having to stomach the reality that Evan would have his happily ever after without her, while her marriage would crumble was a hard pill to swallow for Natalie. Managing circumstances, provided they were under her control, was a mechanism she used from her coping repertoire. She could handle situations if she was in control and didn't feel powerless. Her marriage was a union of dysfunction; it had been for a while. She could fix the situation by either working on her marriage or dissolving it.

The one circumstance out of her control that she could not remedy was her age. It perturbed her that Evan was with a younger, *fertile* woman.

As long as *Ava* could reproduce, she could do the one thing that Natalie was unwilling to do for Evan. Though biologically she was still able to get pregnant, she didn't deem it prudent given she was in her early forties. True, women her age and older had successful pregnancies, but the probability of complications and risks was sufficient to convince her that her "factory" was closed—forever. Having to reconcile the notion that Evan's attraction towards her had diminished because she had become biologically redundant was disheartening to her specifically and a rebuke to women of Natalie's age in general.

While she was powerless in matters regarding Ava's womb, Natalie was still in control of her destiny. Her last interaction with Evan, their breakup, was the catalyst she needed to incite change in her marriage. That night, whereas she had originally planned to leave Eric, she presented him with an ultimatum instead.

"Eric, I am not happy. If you want me to continue to be a part of this marriage, we are going to work towards repairing it and making it functional. Or, I'm going to file for divorce."

Eric was caught off guard but not completely surprised. Over the years, he had sensed Natalie's emotional detachment. The two coexisted and tolerated each other on the surface while contempt and resentment brewed internally. He was aware of her unhappiness and cognizant of his complacency in the demise of their relationship. Eric believed that Natalie complained too much about his shortcomings while remaining unappreciative of his contributions. To avoid conflict, he played his role in maintaining the façade of their marriage. He wasn't a dullard; he could sense her dissatisfaction emotionally and physically, and her attempts to conceal them. He couldn't blame her, because he was engaging in the same behavior — the woman who was once his lover in every aspect of the definition, transformed into his roommate. Interactions became contrived, and sex became a tedious obligation.

Things had changed so drastically from when they had met eighteen years ago. At the beginning of their relationship, he wanted to do better for Natalie, an effortless task considering she was the motivation he needed to strive towards achievement and success. As the years progressed, so did Natalie's nagging, and the realization that his efforts would always be criticized. Slowly but surely, the carping chipped away at his manhood; stripping him of his confidence, and in doing so stopped bringing out the best in him. To Natalie's credit, Eric was equally responsible for the degeneration of their marriage. He stopped caring about making her happy, which prompted her to nag. It was a vicious cycle that was perpetuated by an unwillingness of either party to yield and make the changes necessary to repair their relationship.

Faced with the invitation to opt out of his stagnant marriage, gave Eric a pause for thought. Though the offer would afford him the freedom to act upon the months-long flirtation between him and Candace, a marketing assistant at his place of employment, he felt it necessary to make a final attempt to preserve the union between Natalie and himself, specifically for the sake of their children. Wisdom gave him the clarity to realize that at twenty-six, Candace had less in common with him than his wife and that the thought of being with a woman seventeen years his junior was better in theory than in reality. He didn't doubt though, that the experience would be amazing. Being with a twenty-six-year-old woman, unscathed by the unfairness of age and the unkindness of childbirth, would jolt his system like a set of defibrillators used by paramedics to restore cardiac function. He kept himself from acting out his fantasies with Candace. Though he was certain she would be receptive of any physical advances, those thoughts remained only in his fantasies, by reminding himself that he couldn't afford her. He could not maintain a separate household, provide alimony, and child support while keeping a woman like Candace. There would be financial expectations of Eric that would be difficult to uphold unless he found a new job with higher compensation—a move he was unwilling to make for fear of change, as well as being comfortable where he was. As hot as the prospect of Candace was, he surmised that eventually, she too would become an ungrateful nag. Thus, in the end, it wouldn't be worth it. Had Eric been aware of Natalie's infidelity though, he would have left her in a heartbeat.

"Well, to say that our marriage is in a stagnant state is an accurate description. Change is necessary for either working to improve or choosing to end our marriage. For the sake of the kids, we should make all efforts to keep our family intact...Let's try to make this work," he said half-heartedly, "you tell me what you need from my end. Date nights? Therapy sessions?" The more he spoke, the less convincing he sounded in his desire to maintain his marriage.

"Ok," she replied, "I will arrange for us to see a marriage counselor...And taking the initiative to find ways to reintroduce romance in the mix would benefit us as well. We should both make an effort," her demeanor was equally as uncompelling.

Eric and Natalie eventually decided to put their best feet forward to save their marriage. Each surmised on his own that they could no longer go through the motions of living their everyday lives as a couple, they would have to make a sincere effort to salvage their relationship.

One November afternoon, Natalie received a cancellation call from her next client. Having been up to date on her reports and office work, she decided to check her emails. Afterward, she signed on to Facebook. As she perused the usual posts from her Facebook friends, she grew agitated by the incessant selfies, the numerous solicitations from friends that peddled side businesses, those that continuously posted religious posts, as well as those friends who felt it necessary to air their private matters, radical political views, hypocritical rants about social injustices, and other annoyances through this medium. Every time she signed on to Facebook, she swore that she would deactivate her account after scrolling through a bombardment of what she deemed as nonsense until she stumbled upon a post worthwhile of her attention and would decide to keep her account active for a little longer.

Jeannine had sent Natalie a friend request years ago, of which Natalie had accepted. And though Jeannine's Facebook activity had dwindled to non-existent in the past couple of years, her name would frequently pop-up in posts that she had been tagged in. That day Jeannine's name was tagged in a post titled, *Ava's Baby Shower.* Natalie recognized the beautiful house in the photos. Jeannine had hosted the elaborate affair at her home, with no expenses spared. Natalie clicked on the pictures, careful to avoid inadvertently clicking a reaction to any of the photos.

As she scrolled through the album in the post, Natalie felt a pang of heartache when she discovered that Evan and Ava were expecting triplets. Based on the blush color scheme of the shower, and the lack of male gender specific colors, Natalie surmised that they had girls.

Being a daddy's girl herself, she knew that those three little girls would have Evan wrapped around their little fingers. Though Evan seemed slightly rough on the exterior, he was a very sweet and gentle man. She was certain that he would cater to their every whim and spoil them at every opportunity. Ava, clad in designer clothing and accessories, and adorned with baubles, exemplified how much Evan enjoyed showering women with luxury trinkets and gifts. To Natalie's dismay, seven months into her pregnancy, Ava was a glowing vision of beauty.

Eventually, Natalie made her way to Ava's Facebook page, which was public and lacked any security settings for any of the albums and photos. Through those images, Natalie got a comprehensive glimpse of the life that Evan and Ava shared for the last six months.

Immediately after Evan broke things off with Natalie, Evan and Ava had arranged to have a quaint wedding with fifty of their closest family and friends at a picturesque hotel in Carmel. A month later they bought a structurally sound yet cosmetically decrepit fixer on an acre and a half of flat land in Encino. The two spent the next four months renovating and customizing their dream home, with before and after photos documenting the progress along the way. The last post on her timeline was a picture of the triplet's nursery. The large room was decorated in a Parisian theme and boasted exquisite fabrics, tasteful art, and high-end furniture and lighting. Pink and white striped wallpaper lined the walls. The custom-made white Italian cribs were detailed with pink dupioni silk tufting on the outer panels of the head and footboards. The cribs were equidistantly set apart — each one with a canopy perched against the wall with black & white Damask print drapes that framed the headboards of the cribs and were complemented with matching Damask print bedding. Three Rococo chandeliers in black hand-blown glass hung from the ceiling, while white, Rococo style frames with custom renderings of Parisian life and white, Rococo style mirrors adorned the walls. The room was fit for a princess, or three.

With each click of the mouse, Natalie pieced together facets of the idealistic life Evan and Ava had begun to share. With each click, it became more evident to Natalie that Evan had forgotten her. Witnessing the joy and the anticipation of the possibilities that awaited them as depicted in the photojournalistic progression of the last six months of their lives made Natalie's heart ache. With each click, she felt a pang in her chest. With each click, Evan became further distanced from her reality. She had lost Evan for good.

As uncomfortable as it was for her to look through these photos, she couldn't tear herself away. Natalie obsessively perused the albums on Ava's Facebook page. There were pictures of Evan and Ava with Mike and Jeanine and the same clique of friends at dinner parties, weekend getaways, dinners at trendy hotspots, group vacations, etc. Natalie felt instantaneous resentment towards Ava. She was living the life intended for her. The social circles, the parties, the vacations, and the lifestyle associated with

Evan appealed to Natalie as the perfect life; she rationalized, however, that she would never be a part of that life. And though her experience with Evan had ended only six months ago, the possibility of attaining that life had become inaccessible. It seemed that the experience the two shared was so remote that it had occurred in another lifetime.

A wave of sadness washed over Natalie. She had been given the opportunity to live the life she wanted to lead with the one man who continued to intrigue her but let it slip away. Her overconfidence in the bond that she shared with Evan afforded her a sense of recklessness, causing her to take him for granted. The physical bond had long been broken between the two, and as Ava's pregnancy advanced, any remnants of an emotional bond Evan shared with Natalie was becoming exponentially severed. Evan was now far out of her reach.

Throughout the next couple of months, Natalie tried her best to steer clear of Ava's Facebook page. To her dismay, she was unable to stop her cyberstalking activities. Even her preoccupation with the holidays couldn't completely distract her snooping. She put on a convincing façade of holiday spirit and cheer, hosting Thanksgiving and Christmas Eve to near perfection, going through the motions without being fully present and in the moment.

By New Year's Eve, her tolerance for Eric had become non-existent. His reluctance to ring in the New Year by going out for dinner and live music with a few couples had angered Natalie profusely. Natalie did not want to spend another uneventful holiday at home, so she decided to join Monica and Jack, along with two other couples.

Shortly before 8:00 pm, Monica texted Natalie that she and Jack were outside. They did not dare to come inside to pick-up Natalie, for fear of being caught in the crossfires of another couple's dispute.

"Have fun!" Eric called out as Natalie was putting her coat on while rushing out the door.

Natalie fought an urge to tell Eric to "Go F himself," and instead, completely ignored him. She abhorred the way Eric would try to act like things between the two were fine when she was fuming over the fact that he wasn't accompanying her. Since April, the two were attempting to piece together their marriage, but as the months passed, they were repeatedly reminded that their marriage was irreparable. What Natalie thought would be comparable to gluing back large pieces of a broken vase, was beginning to seem more like gluing back small, fragmented pieces of a broken vase—a nearly impossible task. Even if one managed to piece together all bits of the vase meticulously, it would forever be riddled with fractures.

Though the night started with Natalie in a livid state, she managed to enjoy herself. Monica and Jack made an extra effort to ensure that Natalie had a good time. When slow music began playing while the entire group was on the dance floor, Natalie excused herself from the group and went back to the table. She pulled her phone out of her clutch and was beckoned to Facebook by the notifications alert. Her feed was populated with photos of friends ringing in the New Year. She was immediately drawn to a photo that Jeanine was tagged in. The photo was of five couples, one of which were Evan and Ava. Evan looked irresistible, dressed in a suit without a tie. His dress shirt was unbuttoned at the collar and first button. Ava who was due to give birth in February looked gorgeous in a black wool and silk blend Valentino mini cape dress. Her hair was pulled up in an Audrey Hepburn style updo. It was unfair that a woman that far along in her pregnancy with triplets could look so good. The photo was snapped while the two were mid-laugh, but they both looked picture perfect. The photo could have been used as an ad for a range of upscale products. Evan had his arm around Ava. The two were glowing, their uncontainable happiness emanating from their pores. Their expressions of sheer joy nauseated Natalie.

As the series of slow songs ended, she noticed her friends were making their way back to their table, while the lead singer of the band announced that they were ten minutes away from ringing in the new year. Natalie logged out of her account and shoved her phone back into her clutch.

"Are you having a good time?" Monica asked as she slid into the seat beside her.

"I am having a great time!"

"I'm glad you decided to join us. It would have been a shame if you spent another New Year's Eve on your couch doing nothing."

"I'm glad, too, Monica. I'm ready for a change. This year is going to be different. It's going to be eventful."

Two days later, on the first business day of the new year, Natalie filed a petition to divorce.

CHAPTER THIRTY-TWO
Greener Pastures (2016 -2018)

U pon filing for divorce, Natalie was determined to live a life that made her happy, while trying to be the best version of herself possible. She was prone to periods of self-loathing due to her infidelity and her inability to come clean to Eric. She had to forgive herself for her indiscretions with Evan to move forward, but she had to do it on her own terms. She surmised that she would never disclose her affair, but would have to make it right somehow. Her self-imposed punishment would be to absolve Eric of his responsibility to pay spousal support, and that he would only contribute to monthly child support. She asked that Eric give her spousal support for the next six to eight months, while she took on more clients to become financially independent. Though the two had initially endured a few months of contention after Natalie filed for divorce, the path to the dissolution of their marriage became amicable when they both agreed that their priority would be the well-being of their children.

For financial reasons, they decided they would live together until they sold the house. Eric moved into the game room. It was similar to a large studio, complete with a sitting area and its own bathroom. As much as Natalie ignored her role in the demise of her marriage and whole-heartedly resented Eric for their current situation, she held her end of the bargain to maintain a peaceful and constructive co-parenting relationship. Their divorce would take two years to finalize.

Eric had allowed Natalie to stay in the house for as long as she wanted after he moved out. He offered to let her live there with the kids until she was ready to sell, even if it took years. When his business venture succeeded, he gifted his share of the home to Natalie. Although Natalie loved her home, she felt it best to move to a new house, for the sake of having a fresh start—new life, new career opportunities, and a new home. She decided to stay in the house until she knew what direction her life was headed. Her next residence would rely on the successful expansion of her business.

A year after Natalie initially filed for divorce, Eric moved out. He had reconnected with a childhood buddy, Sean, that he had lost touch with after Aidan's birth. That friend had married his long-time girlfriend, Mia, two months before Natalie and Eric married, and had divorced five years ago. Natalie and Eric were unaware of his divorce, remarriage, and new baby. Natalie continued to send them Christmas cards every year, even though they had lost contact. She made the realization that Sean and his wife were divorced when Mia sent a greeting card picturing just her and her daughter. Natalie told Eric that Sean was either dead or divorced; the latter being the probable explanation for his absence in the greeting card photo. It took another couple of years for them to reconnect, but when they did, it proved to be beneficial for Eric.

Sean had remarried a woman who was eight years younger than he was. Kiana was a divorce attorney, who along with her sister, Ellie, co-owned a successful firm. Eric had met Ellie at a gathering at Sean and Kiana's home. The two had hit it off almost immediately. A few months later, Eric moved in with Ellie, on the west-side. He had always been a valley boy, growing up in Encino, then moving to Woodland Hills after Natalie and he had bought a home. Slowly, but surely Eric was changing.

Early on in their separation, Natalie urged Eric to have a vasectomy. He was forty-three years old, and the probability that he would re-marry was highly likely. Nevertheless, he refused to comply with Natalie's request; he assured her that he wouldn't father any more children. His refusal concerned Natalie. Sean had fathered a new baby with wife number two. Though Eric and Natalie were both shocked but not surprised when they discovered he had fathered a child with his second wife, both had agreed that having to start over at forty-four after having pre-teen children was unimaginable.

Circumstances had changed now. The introduction of a new and younger lover in Eric's life had reinvigorated him. It was the push he needed to take the plunge and start his own business. With the backup of an inheritance his grandfather had left him years ago, which he had refused to touch except for paying for his car in full, and vowed to use only for retirement, Eric had the financial security he needed to survive for the next four years. As long as he produced software solutions for clients, he would get paid. The projects just kept coming. His clients multiplied exponentially, and he became exceedingly successful. Six months after Eric's divorce was finalized, he married Ellie in a quaint ceremony for their nearest and dearest in Saint Lucia, another uncharacteristic move on his part.

Natalie had witnessed the complications involved with divorced fathers procreating with their subsequent wives. The children from the first marriage were neglected, while their half-siblings had the advantage of having their father in their lives daily. It wasn't that these men had suddenly become wonderful fathers at their second go around; it was the fact that the off-spring residing with the current wife reaped all the benefits, whether that involved finances, emotions, or time.

Natalie could not bear to imagine the heartache that her children would feel if their father were to introduce half-siblings in the mix. Eric had told Natalie that he didn't plan to have any more children two years earlier, but she was willing to wager that Ellie would become pregnant in the next year. The change in Eric's confidence was palpable. Spreading his seed would further strengthen his dominance on a primal level. He was a man after all. It was clear that Ellie had been directing their lives more suited to her likings than Eric's, and judging by the way their lives had progressed, a pregnancy would fall in line with their trajectory. At thirty-five years old, Ellie could easily have more than one child. Natalie didn't know what the future held for her children regarding their relationship with their father. If Eric's relationship with his father were indicative of the pattern, then they would not be in an advantageous position.

Given the uncertainty that her children were at risk of being cast aside by their father, who in the last two years had risen to a new level of wealth and married a woman ten years his junior, causing a slight inflation in his ego, Natalie realized she had to overcompensate in his absence. She would create a more financially sound future for her children and expose them to enriching life experiences.

Natalie saw her children off the morning Eric came to pick them up to head to the airport for his wedding getaway. Natalie hid her emotions from Eric. She was not upset that Eric was remarrying, but she couldn't forgive Eric for his sudden motivation to succeed after their separation, as well as the possibility of Alan and Aidan becoming disregarded by their father, in the near future. Natalie felt insulted that Eric lacked the motivation to succeed while they were married but found the drive shortly after he moved in with Ellie.

The power of the prospect of new pussy is a marvelous driving force, she thought to herself, especially to a middle-aged man. So cliché...

She felt contempt and disdain for Eric as he beamed while he took the boys' luggage to the Town Car that awaited them. For a brief second, she wished he would trip down the concrete stairs and fracture his skull. She bid the boys and Eric farewell and watched the car turn off her street.

That morning Natalie went on a hike, fascinated by the concept of motivation and ambition, as well as the drive to succeed. She felt like a failure for her inability to push Eric to become self-employed the latter years of their marriage.

During her hike, she was inspired to put her thoughts in writing. Upon arriving at home, she spent all her free time for the next week glued to her computer.

FOFA: Fail to Overcome, Focus to Achieve became the title of her book. What began as an initial attempt to achieve catharsis by writing her thoughts, astoundingly became a self-help best-seller eight months later. Her motivational self-help book, partially anecdotal, and her newly recognized motivation method, FOFA, opened doors she never imagined—book tours, seminars, guest lectures, and stints as a panelist on news shows.

Her experience in the corporate world, and one of her favorite movies, Office Space, had taught Natalie early on that most people were ass-clowns. They were full of shit, and their success relied simply on how well they could market themselves. For this belief, she could not fully embrace her new-found success. Although she felt grateful, she struggled with her accomplishments at times because it seemed satirical—like a Saturday Night Live skit. She felt like a poser for gaining recognition for simply stating the obvious, marketing it as a self-help book, and being asked to discuss the subject at length—dwelling on the matter for more time than it was worth. It seemed so silly to her, but the public lapped it up. Regardless, she tried to enjoy her fifteen minutes of fame, until she realized that she had a following and could further capitalize on her observations, while actually helping people. Thus, she published her subsequent books. Her first was *Fake It 'Till You Make It: Navigating Up the Corporate Ladder*, which contrary to its title, urged readers to develop the proper skills and work ethics in becoming effective and qualified leaders in the corporate world. The second book, *Break*

Away From the Herd: A Guide Towards Independence, delved into human nature's tendency towards the pack mentality and encouraged readers to develop a sense of independence and self-reliance instead.

To Natalie's surprise, the sale of her books and the appearances had generated a significant income. She had fulfilled her goal of becoming financially secure. Eighteen months after her divorce, Natalie found a new home for her and the boys. Just as she had predicted, Eric and his wife, Ellie had announced Ellie's pregnancy. For the sake of convenience, Eric and Ellie offered to buy Eric's and Natalie's home back from Natalie. Natalie refused to sell it. Instead, she proposed to transfer ownership of the home in trust to her two sons and offered to rent the home to Eric and Ellie. The boys had not stayed with Eric since he had moved out, given that he and Ellie lived in Ellie's two-bedroom condo. Now that Eric and Ellie needed to buy a home, he supposed the transition of shared custody would be smoother if the boys were in familiar territory. Ellie was too exhausted from taking care of a newborn to resist. They needed the larger space, and she didn't want to make things difficult for Eric or his boys. Though Eric tried to maintain a close bond with his sons, the strain of a stepmother and the impending arrival of the new baby were cause enough to vocalize their displeasure with shared custody. Natalie convinced them to spend two weekends a month with their father. Ellie was kind to them, but their fierce loyalty to their mother kept them from completely accepting her. They respected her as their father's wife, but they would not accept her as a mother figure. Natalie outwardly encouraged the boys to be kind to their stepmother, but she secretly enjoyed their intolerance for Ellie.

Although her professional life was thriving, Natalie's personal life was lacking. Right after her separation, Natalie was deflated by the lack of prospects in her dating pool. She had managed to gain an unflattering ten pounds after her affair ended, which brought her to about twenty-pounds over her healthy weight. The discovery that men her age and a decade older were interested in women in their twenties and thirties was a sobering and depressing fact. At the gym where she worked out, she continuously noticed men in her age range ogling the twenty and thirty-year-olds while avoiding her and most of the other women above forty like the plague. To her dismay, she learned that she was popular among the sexagenarians and septuagenarians. Though she had always found older men attractive, the thought of being with a man in his sixties or seventies did not currently appeal to her. Granted she acknowledged that some of these men were very attractive, she was not yet prepared to brave a sixty or seventy-year-old penis. And though she embraced the don't knock it until you try it attitude, her internal dialogue convinced her to put it off for the moment.

Determined to attract a man under sixty, she decided she would have to work on her physical attributes and lose thirty pounds. Natalie hired a trainer and accomplished her goal in seven months. By the time her divorce was finalized, Natalie had transformed from flabby to fit, once again regaining her sense of confidence.

Since her separation and divorce, Natalie casually dated several men for brief periods, proceeding through these encounters with trepidation and suspicion. Of the six men she dated, five were divorcees with families; one was a fifty-something bachelor. She courted one beau at a time, but hastily ended the association if the man wanted more of Natalie than she was willing to give, or at the first hint of any excess baggage. She had yet to meet someone that she felt worthy of a long-term commitment. In the interim, she dated different types of men. Men she knew were not partner material, but she was otherwise curious about, given they were not what she deemed her type. She saw these experiences as learning opportunities, as well as research and fodder for potential new literary projects.

Natalie had gained a new perspective on relationships. Her non-committal attitude was a result of the incidents and men she was exposed to, rather than her lack of a desire to commit. She had reached a point in her life where she preferred to remain without a partner rather than compromise. Ultimately, she surmised that true happiness wasn't contingent upon external forces but should manifest from within. With this realization came the thought that she would not deprive herself the indulgence that brought her joy, nor would she make concessions for the sake of convenience.

CHAPTER THIRTY-THREE
Moving On (2018-2019)

Almost two years since her divorce, Natalie finally felt at ease with her new life. She and the boys had settled into their new home. Her career had taken a twist she never imagined, allowing her to fulfill both the business and creative aspects of her personality while achieving financial success. Now that her time was divided among her private practice, authoring self-help books and consulting, she saw patients on Tuesdays and Thursdays only. She didn't want to abandon her clientele even though she was juggling several projects, so she hired two other therapists who had adapted her style of therapy to join her practice, and care for her clients. Natalie vetted and interviewed all new clients and placed them with the therapist that she believed suited them best for their treatment. If she felt the client would benefit under the care of a different practice, she would refer them to other colleagues.

A year ago, she was scheduled to interview a potential new client. Her demanding schedule did not allow her the opportunity to review files until a few minutes before the appointment. That Tuesday morning, she had walked into her office, sat at her desk and proceeded to take a sip of coffee while simultaneously reading the name on the file. As soon as the name registered, she began to choke on her coffee, liquid gurgling down her chin and onto her blouse. Her next interview which would begin in ten minutes was with Ava.

Natalie headed towards a closet where she kept a change of clothes. She switched blouses and scurried back to her desk to review Ava's file.

Natalie's heart began to pound. Irrational thoughts and scenarios began to play in her head. Why was Ava coming to see her? Did she know of her? Had she discovered that she was Evan's married lover before their relationship? Would she attempt to extort her in exchange for her silence, knowing full well that the public's knowledge of a secret extramarital affair would tarnish Natalie's professional reputation? For the past year, Natalie had gained fame as a self-help expert. A secret affair would give her notoriety as a hypocrite, considering she encouraged people to remove all skeletons in one's closet—the premise being that one would fully be able to release his/her potential free from the strain of keeping damaging secrets. She often preached that self-disclosing one's darkest secret was a very powerful, motivational tool. One could control and navigate through such difficulties by taking ownership of their actions and accepting responsibility and consequences. There were two chapters dedicated to it in her first book and three in the second book!

Natalie took a deep breath when she heard the door outside her office open. She tended to expect the worst, stressing herself over things that were beyond her control. She had to take a page or two from her book and stop stressing over the unknown. She stood up, smoothed her skirt, took one last breath, and entered the adjacent room.

"Good morning, Ava. I'm Natalie Amini. I will be interviewing you today to see whether we can assist you in the treatment you seek, and if we aren't the right fit for you, I can refer you to someone who can do the job," Natalie said, deciding to play it cool.

When Ava reciprocated pleasantries, Natalie believed that she was in the clear. Ava was either a wonderful actress or oblivious to the relationship Natalie had with her husband.

"So, tell me, Ava, what brings you here?"

"I guess, I can best sum it up by saying that I feel like I'm not living the life intended for me…I mean, I have a wonderful life, and I'm grateful and all that stuff, but at the end of the day, I am not living the life that I wanted for myself."

"What elements have attributed to your belief that you are living a life contrary to the one you would perceive as ideal?" Natalie asked, gently trying to pry out information as effectively as she could.

"Well, I never really had a desire to become a mother. And two and a half years ago, I had triplets. I was not prepared for one child, let alone three. My husband—we weren't married at the time—really wanted kids and his attitude towards my pregnancy made me go along with it. About three weeks after the girls were born, a friend realized I was suffering from postpartum depression. We had hired a nanny, but with my condition, my husband hired two more nannies to help us out with round the clock care. The nanny situation is a double-edged sword, I don't want to do the hands-on work associated with childcare, it's just not in me, but I notice the girls form bonds with their nannies, and it makes me resentful; even though I realize I wouldn't be able to manage without them. 'Them' being the nannies. Rather than take care of the girls, I prefer to focus on growing my business. Thankfully, it has paid off, and I can justify being away from the girls. I also resent my husband because I feel like he convinced me to have children, but he never forced the decision on me. And I feel like our relationship is defined by my unexpected pregnancy, because we had just started seeing each other, and I almost immediately became pregnant. Who knows if we would even be together if I didn't get pregnant?"

"Did you seek care for your postpartum depression?"

"Yes, with a therapist that specializes in postpartum depression...for six months after the girls were born. I felt better after the girls were four months old, but I stayed on with my therapist for another two months," Ava replied.

"Are there any aspects in your role as a mother that you particularly enjoy?" Natalie inquired, assured now that Ava's visit was purely coincidental and not an opportunity for a confrontation.

"As long as it doesn't require feeding them, changing them or putting them to sleep, I enjoy them. I guess I like the fun side of motherhood—playing with them and dressing them up. When they start getting fussy, I can't deal with them."

Arlette Eshraghi

"How is your relationship with your husband?" Natalie persisted with her questions, trying to get a better understanding of the connection between the two.

"Again, as I said, I feel like our relationship has been defined by the girls. We got together, and I became pregnant so soon after, that we really didn't have much time to establish a bond between ourselves outside the context of our pregnancy. I can tell he is disappointed by my lack of interest in the children, but he never actually says anything about it, directly...he will make a passive-aggressive comment occasionally. It's not that I don't love my daughters, it's that I don't care to take on the traditional role of a caregiver. Who knows? Maybe I resent them a bit, too. If I didn't get pregnant, I might not have been with their father. Right before I got together with my husband, I had broken up with a man that I would describe as the ideal man."

"Why did you break up if he was your version of the ideal man?"

"He was older. We were in different stages of our lives. We wanted different things, and we couldn't compromise..." Ava summed up her break-up with Richard, concealing the real reason, "but sometimes, I wish I had never left him. Evan is a good catch and all, but I was still hung up on Richard when we got together. Sometimes, I think I still am."

"What makes Richard more appealing than Evan?"

"His status, and wealth. The lifestyle he was able to provide. Evan is successful and wealthy, but Richard's wealth is on a different level. Also, Evan always seems like he is holding back, or hiding something from me, emotionally. Who knows? He had an affair with a married woman before we got together," Natalie stiffened, and her cheeks became flushed. Was she being goaded? "He never told me who she was. Maybe he would rather be with her than me. Which supports my theory that we probably would have never gotten together if I hadn't gotten pregnant. I think part of my resentment towards motherhood stems from the fact that the girls keep me bonded to Evan. Maybe I would have gotten back with Richard if it didn't happen. I know it makes me sound materialistic and shallow, but sometimes, I feel like I downgraded."

Natalie's heart rate slowed down, certain now that Ava did not know that she was Evan's married ex-lover. Once again, she possessed a calm manner as she addressed Ava,

"You have a sense of self-awareness. That is a good thing. It's useful in therapy." Natalie responded graciously, but she wanted to tell her she was a self-absorbed twat, "but I want to stop you because based on what you have told me, I don't think my practice is necessarily the best fit for you. This practice focuses more on motivational therapy and self-help techniques. Your situation would be better suited for a family therapist. I can refer you to a therapist I believe would work well with you. She works with a lot of couples that have a hard time adjusting to becoming parents, and although I don't think you are suffering from postpartum depression anymore, she specializes in that, too. It won't hurt to talk to someone who has a deeper understanding of your past. It seems you have some underlying issues that you need to resolve. It's commendable that you are seeking help. Most people ignore these types of feelings hoping that they will resolve on their own. They usually don't." Natalie handed Ava a business card of the colleague that could help her.

After a few more minutes of answering Ava's questions and realizing their session was coming to an end, Natalie alerted Ava that their session had concluded.

"Thanks for your time, and I will be sure to contact…" she looked for a name on the card, "Rachel Bloom," Ava said as she shook Natalie's hand and left the office.

Natalie had tried to avoid thinking of Evan the past year. Her cyberstalking of Ava's Facebook page had dwindled, considerably. When she had visited her page, the pictures on her timeline reflected a portrait of a happy couple and family, but based on Ava's disclosure, it was clear that the two were far from happy. Occasionally, she wondered what Evan was up to, if fatherhood had changed him, or if he was happily married to Ava. This unforeseen meeting with Ava answered these questions. It was obvious that Evan was enamored by his daughters, but not so much by Ava. Natalie felt she had an accurate read on Ava. She could see why Evan would be charmed by her initially; she was beautiful and exotic. Having achieved professional success and maintaining a career, allowed her to carry herself with great confidence. However, as he would get to know her better, her allure would fade. Daily interactions would bring forth her narcissistic, shallow, and self-absorbed true self, resulting in Evan tiring of her—which seemed like the case already.

Being caught off-guard by their interaction, Natalie had forgotten to ask Ava who had referred her to her practice. She hoped that Evan wouldn't be so insensitive, as to send his wife to his ex-lover for therapy. What did he seek to gain from such a twisted move? Perhaps he was trying to send Natalie a message? Was that an invitation for Natalie to contact him? The Evan she knew would not stoop that low.

Though she had brought herself to thinking of him less frequently throughout the last year, Natalie couldn't help mulling about Evan for the rest of the day. She wondered if she would ever feel for someone as passionately as she did for Evan.

****

Over a year had passed since Ava had come to Natalie's practice. Still oblivious to how Ava had come to contact her for therapy, she had let the incident pass and had refrained from contacting Evan.

Natalie had taken up running in the morning. She would make her way to a trail near her home before she started her day. She loved the peacefulness at that time. The air was brisk and cool, and the morning light absent the brightness of the sun in the early hours, created a serene, picturesque backdrop to her morning fitness routine. A portion of the trail cut through a park. The park was restricted to residents of the gated community that Natalie resided in. It boasted a lake, bike paths, exercise equipment, sports courts, and a playground. Natalie's run ended when she reached the park. Because she ran earlier in the morning, the park was near desolate at the time of her runs, so she would sit at a bench that overlooked the lake and take ten minutes to meditate to clear her mind. Though she had been resistant to buying a home in a gated community, the guard gated entrance and enclosed perimeters gave her some peace of mind considering she lived alone half the month; but it was access to this marvelous park that cinched the deal and propelled her to make an offer over asking for her current home.

That morning, Ava sat at the bench and watched a few ducklings hesitant to follow what Natalie presumed to be the mother duck into the lake. The larger duck swam in the same circle, close to the edge, attempting to entice the smaller ducks into the water. So mesmerized was Natalie by the interactions of the ducklings, that she didn't notice when another runner came off the trail and made his way to the bench.

"Good morning," he said winded, "mind if I sit here for a few minutes. He sat before receiving an answer, leaning over his legs, as he tried to catch his breath.

The man, who was still crouched over trying to catch his breath caught her staring from his peripheral vision and looked up, "Beautiful morning for a…."

"Oh my god!" Natalie exclaimed, "What are you doing here?" Natalie was stunned to be sitting next to Evan.

"I didn't realize you owned the park," Evan replied facetiously.

"Don't be stupid; you know what I mean. Do you live here? You have to live in one of these communities to use the park, and the trails don't run through public access roads. They run through one of the four communities that surround this park."

"I moved here a year and a half ago, and you?" Evan asked.

"I moved here a few months ago," she replied.

"Which community are you in? I've never seen you here before. Do you come here all the time?" Evan inquired.

"I'm here every day. I run every morning. I haven't missed a day yet. I'm in Westfall, and you?"

"Oh, nice. I am in Birchwood."

"Oooh, swanky."

"Yeah, my wife thought our 3800 square foot home wasn't large enough for our family, so we moved into one that's almost double the size," he said in an apologetic tone embarrassed by his wife's extravagance. "So, tell me, Nat, how have you been?" He was obviously happy to be in her presence.

"I'm good, thanks. My career keeps me busy. I'm happy and proud to say that I've done well for myself. The boys are growing fast. They are fourteen and twelve."

"And Eric?" Evan asked shyly.

"Eric and I are divorced. I left him six or seven months after you dumped me," Natalie said snippily, "he has remarried since then, and his wife just had a baby."

"Are you seeing anyone?" Evan wasn't wasting any time trying to extract the pertinent information.

"Yes, and no…I mean, I date…a lot, but I haven't had a serious relationship. What's going on with you?"

"Well, business is good. I have three, beautiful, little girls. They are triplets and a handful at three-and-a-half-years-old, but I adore them. And my wife is a handful, but her…I don't adore so much," Evan responded.

"Yeah, I got wind of that when she came to see me last year. Did you send her to me?" Natalie asked with a hint of anger in her voice.

"No, no. I would never do that. She found your business card in one of my drawers and asked me if I had been to therapy. I told her I was seeing you for panic attacks a few years ago, for a brief time. She asked if you were any good, and I told her that my experience with you was very positive. A week later, she told me she had made an appointment with you. I couldn't make a big deal out of it, or she would be suspicious. And I couldn't bring myself to calling you to tell you about it either. I figured if you realized she was my wife, you would contact me if you had any questions. I didn't want to encroach on your space after the way things ended between us. I know I blindsided you, and you were hurt, but it wasn't my intention at all."

"Ok," Natalie said in an indifferent tone.

"Natalie, I understand now where you were coming from. I totally get it. I know what it feels like to be detached from your partner, but feel obligated to stay for the sake of the kids. This last year has been an eye-opener; it's helped me understand why you couldn't leave Eric. I get it now," Evan moved closer, turned towards Natalie on the bench and continued with his revelation, "I would hate to disrupt the lives of my children, and cause them pain. Even though I am no longer in love with their mother, it would devastate them if we broke up our family unit. I see the benefit of waiting until they are older to divorce. I am sorry for giving you a hard time about it. It was never my intention to compound your stress."

"To think, if you hadn't given me an ultimatum, we might have still been seeing each other every Tuesday," Natalie said gazing in the distance.

"Oh, no, I would have still left if you wouldn't commit. I just wouldn't have pestered you about it for so long. I would have put it out there for you to accept or reject, but I would have been more understanding and less combative, in hindsight," Evan retorted.

"Uh-huh…" Natalie muttered, at a loss for words.

"I love that I have gotten to experience fatherhood, but Ava and I are unhappily married for the last year and a half. And in all honesty, I still think of you, Natalie. I've come close to showing up at your office with hopes of rekindling our relationship…"

"That's awfully presumptuous of you, Evan. Why on Earth would you think that after four years I would want to rekindle anything with you? After I agreed to leave my husband, you just fucked me over!"

"See, I wish you could look at the situation from my perspective. I wanted to have a kid, and I seized the opportunity. Would I be happier if you were the mother of my children? Absolutely; but you didn't want that. So, I had to do what I had to do. Things happen for a reason, and I'm happy that I have my girls, but my life is lacking without you. I love you, Nat. I always have, and I always will. And I know you feel the same way about me. It's emotional, and it's physical. I can feel the magnetism between you and me. It's palpable. You can't deny it. Just give me a few years. Once the girls are a little older, I will be ready to leave Ava. Until then, please let's go back to the way we were before we broke up."

Natalie was taken aback by the evolution and the role reversal of her relationship with Evan. Years earlier, it had been Natalie who pleaded with Evan to continue their affair until Natalie was ready to leave Eric, mostly for the stability and well-being of her children. Now that Evan had experienced the unconditional love of parenthood, he was confronted by the exact dilemma Natalie had struggled with.

"While I agree that there is an inexplicable chemistry between us that has kept me emotionally tethered to you

345

over the years, I can't agree to see you…And it's not that I don't want to, it's that you are married."

"You were married," Evan challenged her.

"Yes, but when we had our affair, it was my marriage I was jeopardizing. I can't be held responsible for the demise of someone else's marriage. Even though you have checked out of your marriage, if our affair were discovered, the perception would be that I wrecked your home. If we do get together in the future, I don't want our relationship to be stigmatized by that."

"We will be careful," Evan protested.

"You can never be too careful. Remember, one of my friends had suspected we were having an affair?" Natalie reminded him. "You know, the last time we spoke you said something that stuck with me—and you were right. Timing has always been an issue with us."

"Yeah, but we keep making our way back to each other, Nat."

"Our lives…we exist on two different parallel planes. Occasionally, they converge and intersect, but these lines always manage to diverge and cause us to go our separate ways. That's how it's always been with us." Natalie said.

"Parallel lines don't intersect. It's impossible," Evan said.

"Well, it seems that us being together is impossible, too."

"I disagree, Natalie. I think we are meant to be together, discreetly for now, and publicly after I leave my wife."

"Evan, don't you find this role reversal ridiculously ironic? Both of us have experienced our relationship from various perspectives. Initially, I wanted a relationship, and you didn't until I started seeing Eric. Then throughout our affair, you wanted me to break up my family and be with you. Now, you are the one with the family, and I would like nothing better than you to leave your wife for me. Maybe this undying attraction towards each other is fueled by the fact that one of us is always unavailable to commit due to existing familial obligations. We always want what we can't have. Would we even know how to be with each other if both of us were unattached?"

"Natalie," Evan interrupted, as he scooted closer to her on the bench "why can't we just start seeing each other again? Ava and I are very detached from each other. I stay with her for the sake of the girls. I don't think she would oppose a divorce if I wanted one, but I don't want to disrupt my children's lives. You wanted me to continue to see you while you remained married to Eric until your kids were old enough that you were ready to leave. Why can't you do what you asked of me?"

Natalie's palms, flat on the cold concrete bench on either side, propped her as she slightly rocked her body back and forth. As her palms drew in the coldness of the slab, like an osmotic transfer, Natalie's demeanor changed, and she became more standoffish. Evan made a compelling argument to resume their relationship, but Natalie had not moved past his decision to leave her. Evan had dumped her right after she agreed to leave her husband.

"Evan, the day you dumped me after I almost left my husband, was the day I realized that I could not rely on you. You could have been a father to your daughters without being with Ava. You could have offered financial support, and still be their father without marrying her. It could have been like she was a surrogate. In fact, after meeting her, I think it's safe to assume that if you compensated her accordingly, she would be willing to relinquish her maternal rights."

"Natalie, she didn't want children. She wanted to have an abortion, and she probably would have, had I not gotten together with her. I admit what I did to you was fucked up, but you had been stringing me along for two years. When she told me she was pregnant, I thought I fell in love with her instantaneously. What I didn't realize was that I fell in love with the idea of being a father."

"Evan, I'm happy that you finally have kids of your own, but I can't see you, not while you are married. It was nice to see you, but I got to go. Take care." Natalie planted a kiss on his cheek, got up, and proceeded to jog back to the Westfall trail.

On the run back home, Natalie, still dumbfounded by what had just transpired was recounting her conversation with Evan. Though she was happy that Evan had gotten a chance to experience fatherhood, she was disappointed in the dilemma it posed in the advancement of their relationship. Yet, she understood why he couldn't leave Ava just yet, at least not until his daughters were older. Seeing Evan that morning set Natalie back emotionally. Being in his presence made her realize how much she missed and longed to be with him. She wished things could have ended differently for them, and that neither Ava nor his daughters were in the picture, but she couldn't alter reality, and she would not engage in an affair with a married man. Though it was clear that Evan and Ava's relationship was fractured, and the two wanted out, Natalie would not chance being scapegoated as the cause of the dissolution of their marriage.

Back at home, Natalie hastily made herself a smoothie and drank it as fast as possible without getting brain freeze. She still had to prepare for an important meeting later that day. It was pertinent that she kept herself from being distracted by her interaction with Evan.

Natalie was startled when the doorbell rang. The guard at the entrance gate had not notified her of a visitor, nor was Natalie expecting a guest. She glanced at the security keypad to view the front door camera and was surprised to see Evan standing in her porch. She figured he had Googled her name to find her address, and taken the trail leading to her community.

When she opened the door, Evan immediately spoke,

"Natalie, please, give me two years, and I promise I will leave Ava."

CHAPTER THIRTY-FOUR
Moving Forward (2019)

Forty minutes later, Natalie and Evan lay sweaty and breathless, with their heads partially hanging off the foot of Natalie's bed. Natalie had tried to resist Evan and uphold her stance of refusing to be involved with him as long as he was married, but she faltered the moment he showed up at her door. Though she had every intention of rejecting Evan's advances, she was unable to follow through.

Watching the ceiling fan blades rotate, she had an epiphany. She came to realize that their affair had come full circle since their initial romp six years ago. Like the years spent apart before the weekend in Palm Springs, their desire for another though subdued due to a lack of interaction, steeped and flourished when they allowed themselves to delve into the far reaches of their memories to reminisce about their shared past. When they unexpectedly ran into one another, that compounded lust brewed over and was the catalyst that ignited the explosive episode in Palm Springs.

Palm Springs was six years ago, of which they had been apart for four of those years. They now found themselves in the same predicament. Only this time, their roles were reversed, with Eric assuming the role of the married adulterer, and Natalie, his willing co-conspirator. Natalie despised that their bond was woven in sordid deceit. She wanted to be with Evan, in the open as a couple, but just as she had beseeched him for more time to leave Eric, so too was he imploring for more time to leave Ava.

Natalie was unsure if she could wait around for another two years, but then what was the alternative—to start seeing someone else with the possibility of being unavailable once he finally left his wife? Whatever, or whoever happened, the two were always drawn back to each other. The cycle of unavailability would repeat itself over and over until one of them conceded to wait around for the other.

Though Natalie had narcissistic tendencies, she also possessed a firm sense of self-awareness. She didn't know if she was capable of sharing Evan with Ava, even if their strained relationship was a ruse staged for the benefit of their children. It was possible that his inability to be completely committed to Natalie for the next two years would make her unhappy and have a negative impact on her life, but she couldn't be certain.

The chemistry between the two was always the constant, while their life circumstances were the variables. It was unlikely that Evan would struggle with his choice to commit adultery, as Natalie had. The apathy he felt for his wife shielded him from feelings of guilt. She didn't know if, or when he would leave his wife. She knew that for now there would be subsequent visits from Evan; she would welcome them, but she didn't know what the future held for them. She would stop trying to make sense of her inexplicable attachment to Evan after all these years and just live in the present.

"Ok," Natalie said, as she turned to her side, propping her head up with her hand.

"Ok, what?" Evan asked confused.

"We can resume our weekly relations. I can't promise you that I will be able to wait for two years, but I can promise you that I will try."

Evan, satisfied with Natalie's decision, drew her in his arms and kissed her.

Moving forward, Natalie was determined to stop being influenced by hypothetical external forces. She would have to relinquish her need to control every aspect of her relationship with Evan. She would have to learn to appreciate the moment and live in the present. She would expect the worst and hope for the best—hoping one day that circle would loop into their happy ending.